Somethi...
Dru's mind.

The castle's ... ...ns of its master had ... ...e had set on it. It ...

Dru was up ... ...e realized the stairs should not have been there. He had a momentary vision of teeth, blue-green fur, and the eyes of a lost enchantress before a massive paw struck him on the left side and sent him hurtling against a newly formed wall.

"Cabal could play with you for long time, little one! Tell what you have done with lady and it will be short!"

The breathless spellcaster tried to stall, hoping his mind would clear enough to defend himself. "How did you get... get in here?"

Cabal's endless array of sharp teeth filled Dru's eyes.

"Where *is* lady?"

Now! Dru thought. *I have to strike now while its mind has turned to her!*

Dru tried to concentrate, but Cabal instantly batted him with its paw. "*Mistake*, betrayer of lady. You do not answer, you must play with Cabal."

The wolf opened its maw wide...

A. KNAAK

Firedrake

Ice Dragon

Wolfhelm

RICHARD A. KNAAK

the SHROUDED REALM

ORIGIN OF DRAGONREALM

WARNER BOOKS

A Time Warner Company

WARNER BOOKS EDITION

Copyright © 1991 by Richard A. Knaak
All rights reserved.

Questar® is a registered trademark of Warner Books, Inc.

Cover illustration by Larry Elmore
Cover design by Don Puckey

Warner Books, Inc.
666 Fifth Avenue
New York, NY 10103

A Time Warner Company

Printed in the United States of America

First Printing: June, 1991

10 9 8 7 6 5 4 3 2 1

PROLOGUE

Toos the Regent, king of Penacles, stared down at the rolled missive the courier had just left in his hands. Undistinguished as it looked, the crimson-tressed ruler knew it for a thing of potentially great importance. It was the latest in a series of communications he had had with Cabe Bedlam, the warlock of the Dagora Forest. They were comrades of some fifteen years, and spellcasters both.

As he carefully broke the seals, both seen and unseen, he pictured in his mind the youthful visage of the warlock. Cabe's more regular features contrasted sharply to his own older, foxlike image, and it was hard to believe that so much knowledge and power rested within a man who was less than a third of the regent's own hundred-plus years. Of course, Cabe would probably look the same even when he was two hundred. There were benefits to having a talent for spells.

Alone in his study, Toos unfurled the parchment and started to read.

My greetings as ever to the regent, it began.

Toos chuckled. Cabe insisted on using the self-chosen title as much as possible. Each year, the people of Talak had presented the former mercenary with the crown and each year Toos had declined it. Someday, his lord and master, the Gryphon, would return and on that joyous occasion, he would return control of the city-state to him and quickly and quietly resume his position at the legendary monarch's side. No one had, so far, succeeded in eroding his determination, for the regent was the most stubborn of men.

Dismissing his thoughts, Toos continued reading, suspecting he already knew much of what the warlock's communication was going to reveal.

> *The death of Drayfitt of Talak still leaves a dark blot in what has been, for the past two years, a relatively peaceful time. His papers, of which there seem an endless tide, fill all corners of the room at the time of this writing. My wife and children claim I neglect them and I am apt to agree. Still, it was not my choice to begin this project, since the Gryphon, a scholar at heart, would have eagerly plunged into this mire, which I, instead, must battle through. Unfortunately for both of us, he is across the sea and there is no news as to when he and his brood may return. That leaves it to me, though I've not yet been able to figure out why. Since I am the chosen one, however, and it's you who read the fruits of my research, I will once more make no apologies for my rambling style and merely continue on.*
>
> *My admiration goes out to Drayfitt. I find it difficult to understand a fraction of what he'd gathered even with so much knowledge passed down directly to me from my grandfather, Nathan. One thing I have discovered is that my own pet project will go for naught. The information concerning the mysterious Vraad is, at best, a thin veneer of half-hinted legends and exaggerated rumors masking a gulf of ignorance as vast as the Void itself. The bulk of his work perished at the hands of Mal Quorin, advisor to King Melicard I of Talak and agent of evil for the late and truly unlamented Dragon King, Silver. King Melicard, whose capable queen, Erini, I trust to keep him honest, assured me that what I received was all that remained. Those writings by Drayfitt that I have succeeded in organizing will be sent to you by separate couriers, likely a drake-human pair, as I would*

prefer to keep the two races working together as much as possible.

These, then, are my conclusions concerning the Vraad, of whom poor mad Shade was the last—I hesitate to use the word "living"—representative.

Toos found suddenly that he was sweating despite the coolness of the evening.

Drayfitt used many words to describe them, but arrogant and frightening seem to sum them up best. If I read his notes correctly, at their peak they were able to tear the heavens and earth asunder... you recall what Shade, in his final moments, did to the army of the Silver Dragon. Not a trace left. That was nothing. I think when you read some of what I am sending you, you will see as I did how fortunate we were that it was only Shade who defeated death for so long. The greatest irony in all this is that they were also our ancestors. We have the Vraad to thank for being here instead of that place I mentioned in several of the earlier missives, that twisted world they called Nimth.

I've found even less on that dark, fearsome domain than I have on those who once dwelled there. The Vraad left it a ruined place, abandoning it like the gnawed core of a srevo. The succulent flesh of the fruit had been eaten; they had no use for what was left.

Something must have gone awry, for they came here and vanished as a distinct race almost overnight... leaving us lesser spellcasters as their only legacy.

I'm sorry that there isn't more. A pity the libraries beneath your kingdom have chosen to be especially vague concerning the Vraad, though somehow that doesn't surprise me as much as it should. Darkhorse, our great, eternal friend, refuses my inquiries when he makes one of his rare visits—he still cannot accept that Shade is truly dead—and says only that the Vraad are better left a fading memory. Once, though, when he said that, I caught a wistful tone in his stentorian voice. It makes me wonder.

Gwen gives her love, you old fox. The children are fine ... both human and drake.

Yours,
Cabe Bedlam

The regent allowed the parchment to roll closed, his mind sifting through what the warlock had and had not said. A world of *Shades!* A chilling thought. Standing up and walking over to the fire that kept his study warm, he threw the parchment into the greedy flames. It was difficult to say why he thought that necessary. There was nothing in the missive that was earth-shattering to him, not after the past notes. It was only that he found within himself, as Cabe had confessed he *also* had, a desire to forget anything concerning the arrogant, destructive Vraad ... and a crippled, murdered place once called Nimth.

I

In all of Nimth, there stood only one true city. It was a tall, jagged thing so diverse in design that the best way to describe it was that it was a reflection of its creators. There were spires, ziggurats, towers that leaned at horrific angles ... no one style dominated, unless *madness* could be called a style. Those selfsame beings who had built it with their sorcerous abilities even now gathered, as they did every few years, within its walls. It was the time of coming for the Vraad ... perhaps the last to ever be held here in Nimth.

In deference to its neutral nature, the city had no name. It was simply *the city* to one and all. The Tezerenee had taken to utilizing it for their own needs, and who was about to make feud with a clan as huge and deadly as theirs? The rest of the Vraad patently ignored the slap in their faces, pretending it was beneath spellcasters as mighty as themselves.

Despite the supposed neutrality of the city, sorcery was very much in evidence. Brilliant auras clashed with one another, and new and old arrivals paraded about with entourages consisting chiefly of their own creations ... beasts that moved as men, living stick figures, myriad sentient lights.

The Vraad themselves were no exceptions. Most of them were tall and beautiful, gods and goddesses come to life. Few of them wore the faces and bodies they had been given at birth. Long, flowing hair was popular now, as were bright chameleon tunics, flowing from one shape and design to another depending on the tastes of those who wore them. Not to be outdone, other Vraad wore suits of mist and light, seeking to both tantalize and distract.

The air crackled with so much pent-up magic. The sky, ever warring of late between shades of bloody crimson and a dark green touching on decay, stirred itself to greater fury this day because of all that power. Outside, the rumbling of yet another tremor to the west gave voice to the earth's protest at this latest coming of Nimth's masters. Once, the land had been a rolling field of green grass and the heavens a blue so brilliant even the otherwise indifferent race of sorcerers had often paused to admire it. No more.

"We have finally created a world *suitable* to our personalities."

So Dru Zeree felt as he looked from the assembled throng well below his perch to the bitter sky above.

"You think *that* spectacular, Sil?" someone in the crowd taunted, intensifying the loudness of his voice so that the one the words were intended for could not escape hearing them. "Your skills as well as your tastes have reached new lows!"

The second half of the exchange was lost in a thunderous explosion that was part of no natural phenomenon. Dru waited, but the aftermath he had expected did not occur.

"Not *yet*," he whispered to himself.

Nearly seven feet in height and somewhat narrower than his counterparts, Dru was markedly unique among the many spellcasters who strove for that very effect. His narrow face was handsome, true, but not in the beautiful way that most had chosen to sculpt their features. The somber mage had a hawklike appearance that was complemented by a thin, well-trimmed beard the same dark brown as the rest of his hair. It was, in contrast to the blues, greens, and multihued tresses of the others, his original hair color. A *real* novelty among the Vraad, save for the Tezerenee, who prided themselves on maintaining their original outward appearances as much as possible.

Dru was a Vraad in the end, however. For this coming, he had added to his hair a streak of silver directly down the center. Simple as it was, it had earned him his share of stares, as had the plain, unmarked gray robe he generally wore. Perhaps, he thought wryly, he would be responsible for starting a trend toward basics . . . a trend very *un*-Vraad-like, considering their tendency for excesses.

A black and gold beast fluttered onto his broad shoulder and hissed, "Dekkarrrr. Silestiii. Seeee."

The Vraad scratched his familiar on the fur beneath its predatory beak. The familiar opened its maw wide in pleasure, revealing an incongruous set of sharp teeth within that beak. Had someone taken a sleek wolf and combined its parts with that of a swift, huge eagle, they would have found themselves confronting something resembling Dru's familiar. The torso, tail, and upper legs were lupine. The head, though furred, was more avian, and the lower extremities ended in claws capable of tearing apart creatures far bigger and stronger-looking than their owner. The round, amethyst eyes that gazed into his had no pupils. Dru was, in Vraadish fashion, quite proud of his handiwork.

"Where are they exactly, Sirvak?"

"There. There." The beast pointed its head toward the eastern side of the great courtyard, where most of the newcomers entered.

He saw Dekkar first. Tall but exceedingly wide, a living wall of strength, both sorcerous and physical. Dekkar had a striking visage, though it was made less so by the fact that it was, in many ways, much too much like the faces of those around him. He was clean-shaven and his long, orange/blue hair fell back behind his head like vast tentacles. The expression on the other Vraad's face was typically arrogant. The sorcerer wore a tunic of rainbows that literally shifted with each breath . . . a masterful piece of work, it had to be admitted. Dekkar had put a vast amount of detail into the subtleties of its design.

It was a pity he could not put in as much effort in aiding the coming exodus of the Vraad.

"The epitome of predictability." Dru followed his counterpart's gaze, knowing he would find Silesti at the other end. "And there is his brother, *foolishness incarnate*." The other Vraad had evidently noticed his rival, for he stared back at Dekkar with a look that so matched the broader sorcerer that it was no wonder some took them to be kin. In point of fact, Silesti had always chosen to look very much like Dekkar, and Dru found himself wondering if there might have been a reason for that. No one could recall what had started their thousand-year feud, likely not even the combatants themselves. A thousand years was a long time, even for a race that was nigh immortal. Dru suspected that the two Vraad had continued on with their battle long after the original reason was lost strictly because it kept them from falling to the deep ennui that so many Vraad suffered.

That made them no less mad than the rest, Dru himself included.

"Seeee, masterrr! Seee!"

"I see, Sirvak. Hush now."

Silesti was wearing a brilliant black suit that clung to his form and covered all but his head. As his eyes narrowed on Dekkar, one gloved hand went to a pouch hanging from a belt around his waist. Many of the assembled Vraad watched the two with mild interest, though a good number ignored them completely. Feuds were just one more thing in the life of the sorcerous race. The only interest was in what sort of action the combatants might take.

Dekkar struck first, creating a miniature rainstorm above Silesti's head. Without pausing from his own task, the latter sorcerer created a shield that made the rain bounce off and slide down to the earth around him, leaving Silesti high and dry. Dekkar, however, seemed none too upset over that abrupt change. He stood quietly, openly challenging his adversary to do his worst.

The other Vraad was only too happy to do so. From his pouch, Silesti took out a tiny, wiggling form that Dru could not make out even when he amplified his vision. With careful precision, Silesti tossed it toward the expectant Dekkar.

True to form, Dekkar did not wait for the creature to reach him. With a wave of his hand, he stole from his own raging storm a single bolt of lightning. It struck the hapless servant of Silesti and sent the bits scattering. A wind rose up, blowing them toward their original target, but Dekkar was hardly in danger from ash.

On Dru's shoulder, the familiar shifted, raising one claw and then another as it tried to comprehend the apparently useless assaults by the two spellcasters . . . men capable of raising mountains, if need be.

"Masterrrr . . ."

Dru smiled grimly and shushed the beast. He understood what Sirvak could not. After so long a struggle, the feud had become ceremonial. What seemed like minor touches of Vraad power would soon lead to far more.

As if in response to his thoughts, the true assaults took place.

From around Silesti's feet, the torrent of rain rose upward *around* his shield, creating a cocoon of some silky substance whose binding force was the counterspell the ebony-clad sorcerer himself had cast. Dru knew, as Silesti now knew, that the trap also grew beneath the latter's feet, essentially sealing him in.

While Dekkar laughed and some of the spectating Vraad clapped their approval, Silesti's spell came to full fruition. The ash had settled on the broad Vraad's person, including his face and arms. Dekkar had, of course, ignored it, and it came as quite a surprise, then, when he found himself suddenly sprouting tiny, toothsome heads that rose on serpentine bodies and proceeded to viciously bite their host. More and more vermin sprouted from his clothing and his flesh, taking root wherever possible. There were even a few on the ground near his feet, but Dekkar stomped them to death.

Many of the Vraad thought that they were finally seeing the culmination of the millennium-old struggle. Dru doubted that it was so. Both adversaries had faced a vast array of traps in that time. It would take more than these to kill the two.

True enough, both assaults began to falter. From within the cocoon there rose a tremendous heat, one that even touched Dru despite the height and distance separating the balcony he stood on from the site of the duel. A simple spell of his own cooled the area around Dru, but Silesti's prison lacked any such protection. It sizzled and melted, evaporating to nothing by the time the residue reached the ground again. Even the cloud had dissipated.

Dekkar, meanwhile, did little but stand and wait. Once his initial surprise had passed, he stood smiling despite the bites he had suffered. It was soon easy to see why. The vermin began falling off, first a few, then in great numbers. Each one was dead, that is, each one that had *bitten* the sorcerer. Dru caught sight of one of the last, true to its mission, snapping at

Dekkar's unprotected hand. Once the creature drew blood, it instantly recoiled, as if ready to strike again. Instead, the monstrosity shook, spat the blood of its victim from its mouth . . . and fell to the earth, its grip and its life both things of the past.

"Masterrrr?"

"Poisoned, Sirvak. Dekkar's blood is poisoned. I wonder how he survives it? It would have to be a strong poison to kill one of those creatures, I suspect."

Like two bedraggled but triumphant bookends, Dekkar and Silesti faced one another, each ready for the second round.

"Masterrr!" Sirvak's talons bit deep into Dru Zeree's shoulder, a signal that the familiar was more than just apprehensive. A dark shadow blotted out all but the artificial illumination the Vraad themselves had created for the coming.

The sky was filled with dragons. Huge monsters, larger than the tallest horses and quite able to fell said animals with one blow of their massive forepaws. There was a rider on the back of each emerald horror, a sure enough sign, not that one had been needed, of who the newcomers were.

"Tezerenee . . ." Dru muttered to himself.

Below him, the crowd, whose interest in the duel had grown with each passing second, suddenly became silent save for a few hardy souls who dared to whisper what Zeree himself had just said.

Tezerenee.

There were more than forty and Dru knew that these were only a token representation of the clan. Vraad, by nature of their egos, were not a familial race. Dru and his daughter, Sharissa, were a rarity. Under the draconian rule of their patriarch, the Lord Barakas, they were a cohesive and masterful family of sorcerers. They were also skilled fighters, another aberration in a race that relied so heavily on their magical prowess.

Dragons began to land on the roofs and walls of the city.

From a distance, each rider seemed identical. Dark green armor covered them from head to toe, forged from the scales of the very beasts the Tezerenee rode. Ferocious dragon-crested helms all but obscured the savage faces of the Tezerenee. Two of them wore crimson capes, Lord Barakas and his eldest son,

Reegan. Nearly a third of the riders were sons of the patriarch, spread across the five thousand years of his life. (How many more there were and how many had died one way or another during those millennia was something no one spoke about within earshot of the Lord Tezerenee.)

Barakas Tezerenee had landed on the roof of a building that had flattened itself out at the moment of arrival. From his vantage point, the overwhelming figure overlooked all but Dru. Barakas stroked his heavy beard and stared long and hard at the two duelists.

"This is the final coming." His voice, augmented by his power, sent a tremor literally through the city. Oddly, despite his bearlike appearance, the Lord Tezerenee's voice was smooth and calculated. It was also the voice of one so used to commanding that even a simple "good day" would have seemed an order to be obeyed.

"This is the *final* coming, Masters Dekkar and Silesti. From here, the Vraad will be moving on to a better, less disreputable home." The warring sky rumbled, as if punctuating his statements.

The two feuding sorcerers glanced at each other with disquieting looks.

"See that these two finish their absurd duel once and for all." It was not evident at first to whom the patriarch was speaking, for he still studied Dekkar and Silesti. Then, two riders remounted their reptilian steeds and rose into the sky. The two rivals began to protest, but a sharp glance from Barakas froze them where they stood.

Dru blinked, leaned over the rail of the balcony, and studied Dekkar and Silesti closer. *Frozen, indeed.* Neither sorcerer was moving, save to look around futilely for someone who would free them from the Lord Tezerenee's spell. The dragons descended to points just above the heads of each hapless Vraad, raising dust storms that sent the throngs backing away, and, at a command from their riders, grasped Dekkar and Silesti in their forepaws.

The riders looked to their clan master for further orders. Barakas Tezerenee considered, then said, "Take them west. Do not come back until there is a victor... or until both of them are *dead*."

With a renewed flapping of their huge wings, the dragons

rose swiftly into the air. In seconds, they were mere dots in the sky to even the most skilled of observers. In less than a minute, they were out of sight.

Barakas scanned the remaining Vraad—who were still uncharacteristically silent—and finally said in the same tone of voice he had used to dispose of Silesti and Dekkar, "May the spirit of the coming be with you."

Without another word, he turned, visibly dismissing the throng from his interest, and eyed the waiting Dru.

Dru inclined his head briefly toward the patriarch. "I came as you directed."

In the next instant, the Lord Tezerenee was standing beside him. Sirvak, who had a distinct dislike for anything of draconian nature, let out a low hiss. Dru quieted him while Barakas looked on, a cold smile playing across his lips.

"It is only fitting that you should be here, Zeree. This is your doing as well as mine."

The intended compliment did nothing for Dru, though he pretended to be honored. "The credit goes to you, Barakas. To you and your sons, Rendel and Gerrod."

For the first time since he had arrived, the patriarch looked uncomfortable. Dru noted with particular interest his discomfort at the mention of those two sons. "Yes. Yes, they've done their parts. You laid the groundwork, though."

Below, the other Vraad had returned to their other interests, Dekkar, Silesti, and even the watchful Tezerenee forgotten for the most part. Barakas laughed harshly.

"Weak fools! Children! If not for us they'd still be bemoaning their fate!" He took Dru by the arm. "Come! The tests draw near, Zeree. I want *you* to be there when the time comes."

The world around them seemed to curl within itself.

When it had unfurled again, their surroundings had changed. They were now in a vast chamber in which nearly a dozen Tezerenee sat on the outline of a pentagram, one at each point and corner of the design. A single hooded figure sat quietly in the center, different from the rest by nature of the long cloak, scaled tunic, and high boots he wore. Wisps of ice-white hair dangled free of the encompassing hood, identifying him readily enough for Dru.

"Father." Another Tezerenee, clad identically to the one in

the center, knelt before the clan patriarch. Barakas deigned to put a hand on his son's hooded head.

"Gerrod. Explain what occurs here." Beneath the calm tones, there was an undercurrent of suspicion and the first traces of righteous fury.

Gerrod looked up. In contrast to most of the male members of the Tezerenee, he was handsome. Dark hair hung down slightly on an aristocratic visage that took greatly from his mother's side. He was slim compared to such as Barakas or Reegan and hardly the warrior type. He and the still figure at the heart of the pentagram might have been twins, so much did they resemble one another. Yet, there were more than a thousand years separating their births. Twins they were, but in the soul, not the body.

"Rendel couldn't wait, Father," Gerrod informed Barakas, speaking with much more calmness than Dru thought he himself would have been able to muster.

"Couldn't *wait?*" Suddenly it struck Dru what Gerrod was implying.

The younger Tezerenee inclined his head toward his father, shivering slightly as the patriarch's grip on his head tightened. Barakas could crush his son's skull like a piece of soft fruit if he so desired.

The Lord Tezerenee glanced imperiously at his companion. "Rendel, it seems, Zeree, has jumped the chasm. His ka is now over *there*—in the *Dragonrealm*."

II

"The *what?*"

Stirred by the tensing of its master's body, Sirvak opened its eyes and hissed. A small wyvern perched on a ledge returned the familiar's angry sibilation and stretched its wings in challenge. Dru silenced Sirvak with a few whispered words while a single glare from the Lord Tezerenee quieted the wyvern.

Lord Barakas smiled, a feeble attempt, if it *was* one, to reassure Dru. "Forgive me, Zeree. We have come to call the realm beyond the veil the Dragonrealm. Since no one else has put forward a name for it, we thought this one would do just as well."

We meaning *you*, Dru thought sourly. The patriarch of the Tezerenee, who had personally raised the dragon up as the symbol of his clan, knew he had the rest of the Vraad at a distinct and unique disadvantage. Each day, since the first discovery that another domain, unblighted, lay just beyond their own, Barakas Tezerenee had worked to ensure that it was he who commanded the situation. When the first mad attempts at crossing over physically had failed shamefully, Barakas had turned his talents to studying the works of his rivals. It was only because of Dru's own experiments that he now shared in the successes of the clan. He had devised what had become the Vraad's hope, the Vraad's *triumph*.

It galled the rest of the race and made Dru careful as to whom he spoke with. Vraad were nothing if not vindictive.

A disturbed Dru, in an attempt to keep from commenting on the Tezerenee's presumptions, studied the prone form of Rendel. The patriarch's son might have been dead, so limp was his body. It was quite possible, in fact, that Rendel *was* dead, his ka trapped in some endless limbo. What the Tezerenee proposed to do was lofty, even by Vraad standards.

Which left another question, one that Barakas had, as yet, left even his "partner" in the dark concerning.

Of what use was transferring the ka of oneself if there was no suitable vessel awaiting it at the other end of the journey?

The Lord Tezerenee had promised success to his rivals and counterparts. Even he knew better than to fail in those promises. Failure would erode not only his standing with those outside of the clan, but the rest of the Tezerenee themselves. He had trained them to be too much like himself and that, Dru Zeree had always thought, was the most dangerous mistake that Barakas had ever made.

As fearful as they were of their lord, enough Tezerenee

banding against him would send even the overwhelming Barakas to the dragon spirit he so revered.

"Rendel's . . . enthusiasm . . . is commendable." With great effort, Barakas removed his hand from Gerrod's head. Dru was certain he heard the younger Tezerenee exhale in relief, though that would have been considered a sign of weakness by Gerrod's parent. The patriarch's son rose and stepped quickly aside.

Walking at a measured pace, Barakas led Dru forward. The method of ka travel was his own idea, but one, in his mind, that he had always restricted to Nimth. After all, where else *had* there been to go besides the Vraad's own world?

The realm behind the veil—the *shrouded* realm, as Dru had first called it—had altered the lives of the near ageless Vraad as nothing else had. The ghostly domain had flaunted its rolling hills and lushly forested lands in their faces as far as they were concerned because, quite simply, it could not be *touched.*

Some had immediately scoffed, claiming the trees and mountains that superimposed themselves on Nimth's own battered and unstable landscape had been nothing more than a prankster's illusion. No one laid claim to the supposed trick, however, and it soon became obvious that this was no mirage after all. With that, the Vraad began to study the place in earnest . . . as a second home.

When was the last time the sky was blue? Sharissa had asked her father once. Dru could not recall then as he could not recall now. Not in her lifetime, short as that had been so far. Of that he was certain. Nimth had started dying long ago. Its death was a slow, lingering one that might go on for millennia . . . save that long before then it would be unsuitable even for the Vraad.

Gerrod shadowed them every step of the way. There was more beneath that hood than either Barakas or even Rendel knew, Dru suspected. Gerrod observed everything with a cunning eye. He was keenly interested in what the outsider his father had brought with him had to say about the spells cast here, of that much Zeree was certain. Interested in a way that puzzled Dru, for it was almost as if the younger Tezerenee hoped to find fault with what he himself had helped create under the very nose of his lord and progenitor.

"Here it is, Dru Zeree. The missing link in your work and our salvation."

Following the grand wave of the Lord Tezerenee's arm, Dru gazed upon a body. He knew what it was, having created such beings before, but the size and scope of it made any initial comment superfluous. Under the waiting gazes of his two companions, he dared to reach out and touch the nearer arm. It was warm and very much living to the touch. Dru wanted to shrink back from it, but knew that only he would suffer from such a cowardly act. The Tezerenee neither respected nor worked with those they considered lacking in nerve. At this point in the alliance, such an action might have been tantamount to suicide on his part.

"A golem made of flesh," Gerrod informed him needlessly.

Had it been standing rather than lying flat on a marble platform, it would have come to Dru's chest. *The same height as Sharissa*. Zeree had no idea why that should come to mind now, save that he had already been away from her longer than he had planned. It was also for her sake that he had accepted the patriarch's original offer. A solution, however insane, that saved her life was worth entering the domain of a horde of ravaging dragons like the Tezerenee. It was not a Vraadish notion, to be sure. Most elder Vraad would have gladly given up their offsprings' lives to save their *own* hides.

"You may be wondering about its . . . incomplete construction," Gerrod prodded in a more daring manner.

Dru grunted. *Incomplete, indeed!* A poor excuse of a golem, taken on face value . . . or rather on *faceless* value, seeing as how it lacked a visage of any sort. In fact, it was lacking in much more than merely features. There was no hair, no mark upon its person. Its hands and feet, he saw, were little more than stubs at the end of each appendage. The golem was neither male nor female, an asexual, living puppet.

As a Vraad over three thousand years old, Dru had seen far worse than this . . . yet the golem had some quality about it that made him want to shiver. Some difference beyond its visual deficiencies.

Then it struck him as to what it was he sensed.

"This was *grown*, not fashioned from bits and pieces."

Gerrod's eyes brightened. For the first time, Dru noted how crystalline they were. Barakas, meanwhile, smiled approvingly at the befuddled spellcaster. He indicated to Dru that he should continue with his guesswork.

The narrow Vraad did, forcing himself to touch the golem's bare torso again. The skin had a peculiar leathery feel to it, almost like . . .

"Not Vraad after all." He ran his finger along the arm, forgetting, in his dreaming, the dread he had been experiencing previously. What did he know that felt like this?

It came to him and the realization rekindled his dread of the gloom. "This has been spawned from a *dragon!*"

"You see, Gerrod, Master Zeree has a nimble mind. A mind worthy of a Tezerenee."

The hooded figure bowed, his reaction, if any, totally shrouded by the cloak. Dru wondered if Barakas simply pretended not to notice or was so caught up in his belief in his control of the Tezerenee that Gerrod's actions escaped him.

That was a question for another time. "This is to be the vessel for the ka."

"Yes." Barakas reached out and caressed the golem's shoulder as one might a lover. "The golem has no ka, being neither dragon nor Vraad. It is a shell, open to possession, that has no true essence, no life of its own. The only thing it carries is the inherent magic of the dragon. Only a carefully structured spell gives it the appearance of life. A Vraad ka, entering, will find no resistance to its presence and take it over completely. The golem is malleable; it will become what the Vraad wants it to become."

"A superior body for a new world," Gerrod added, speaking as if by rote. He had evidently heard his progenitor preach this often.

The Lord Tezerenee nodded approval to his son. "So it will be." His attention returned to his guest. "It will be a true combining of our soul with the magic of the dragon. Through that, the Vraad will be more than they could have ever *hoped*."

Dru kept his expression indifferent, but, inside, the disturbing feeling was growing. It was more than just the golem now. The Vraad had a new world awaiting them, but it was one that Barakas Tezerenee was mapping out to his own desires. The anxious sorcerer looked down at the still form lying next to them and could no longer repress the shudder.

"Is something wrong, Zeree?"

Before he could respond, Gerrod spoke. "Father, Rendel will need some watching for the next hour. Despite earlier expectations, he is not yet in the Dragonrealm. We have judged the cross-over to be a slower and more tedious process than originally calculated and his body must be kept well during that extra time. If I have your permission, I would like to discuss with Master Zeree what opinions he has concerning our progress here and the possible difficulties we may not have foreseen... unless, of course, you have need of him still...."

The Lord Tezerenee's gaze measured Dru. "I have no need of him now. What say you, Zeree?"

"I would be only too happy to add whatever I could to ensure the success of your spell."

"Very good." The patriarch reached up and took Sirvak's beaked countenance in his hand. Dru could feel the familiar's nervous breathing against his neck, but Sirvak, to its credit, did nothing otherwise during the span in which the large Vraad studied it. When Barakas finally released it, the creature carefully lowered its head and pretended to resume its napping.

"A splendid piece of workmanship. How would it fare, do you think, against a wyvern?"

"Sirvak has a certain skill in combat." Dru purposely smiled as he looked at the beast and scratched its throat. "As for wyverns... he killed both of them in under a minute."

The patriarch's face darkened, but he kept his voice composed. "A splendid piece of work, as I said." To his son, he commanded, "I am to be notified the moment something occurs. The *exact* moment."

"Father." Gerrod bowed, staying in the subservient position even after the Lord Tezerenee had vanished in a verdant cloud that threatened to spread throughout the chamber. Finally standing, the younger Tezerenee dispersed the greenish mist through an open window with a violent twist of his hand. He glanced at Dru. "He's quite mad, Master Zeree, even more than the rest of us." When there was no response, he added, "And we would have to be mad indeed to think of toppling him. Come take a look at this."

With that last peculiar twist, Gerrod had turned toward the pentagram and those who maintained the spell. Dru followed silently, thinking about how much truth there was in his guide's words.

"You have, of course, thought of the one difficulty with my father's plan, haven't you?" With his back turned to Dru, Gerrod looked like nothing more than a vast piece of cloth hung up to air out. His steps were surprisingly inaudible, a contrast to the heavy thuds that generally accompanied his armored relations.

Dru knew what the hooded figure was talking about. "Your golem is here; how will he get it to the Drag— How will he get it to the other side?"

"It was *my* idea . . . mine and Rendel's, that is. A matter of power, as Father would say. Power will always prevail if you have it in sufficient quantities." A low laugh escaped the all-encompassing hood. "Father is such a philosopher."

"And what *was* that idea?"

Gerrod turned and indicated the pentagram. At that moment, the smile on his face was all too much a copy of his father's. "What one Vraad cannot do, perhaps more, acting in concert, *can*. A group like this is out in the middle of the phantom forest, sitting among trees that are not quite there, stretching forth with the might of the Tezerenee, and creating for Rendel—and those who follow—vessels drawn from sources of the shrouded realm itself."

It made sense of a sort and would only work with such as the Tezerenee. Only they could gather enough Vraad willing to work together to have a chance at success, even if that success was no more than a ghostly hand invading a ghostly world. The Vraad could not travel physically to their new home, but their power would build them another path.

Dru blinked. "Are there *dragons* over there?"

"Of course. It was—let me see—a cousin or brother or maybe even a sister, I forget which, who saw it. You can imagine how *thrilled* Father was. Our destiny was clear then. Until we found the beast, Father had intended on using some of those damn elves."

Whispers of creatures inhabiting the shadow lands had slowly circulated through the network of spies and allies among the various Vraad. The elves were the most interesting, being a race long extinct on Nimth. They had been the first to suffer at

the hands of the early Vraad. As Serkadion Manee, a singular
sorcerer who had decided to chronicle the rise of his kind, had
written, the elves had been too peaceful and giving to coexist
with the new race. They had vanished virtually overnight.
Nimth had seemed to die a little then, if Manee's words were to
be believed.

Living elves meant only one thing to the Vraad. Slaves and
toys. It burned deep within Dru that his initial reaction had
almost been as terrible as that of the rest; he had thought of
what it would be like to study one, to take it apart and see how
it differed from his own kind.

Sharissa would have abandoned him there and then had she
only known.

He realized that Gerrod was staring at him, the younger
Vraad's eyes glistening.

"I want it to *fail*."

At first, Dru was uncertain that he had heard the other
correctly. When Gerrod's expression did not change, however,
he knew that the sons of the dragon were indeed all insane. In
the end, Dru could only ask a simple "Why?"

The hooded Vraad looked at him helplessly. He seemed
unconcerned that anyone might hear his traitorous words—
traitorous to both his clan and the Vraad race as a whole.

"I don't *know*! I feel it sometimes, as if my head were about
to split in two! That something very wrong awaits us, something that means death . . . and more . . . to the Vraad, *all* Vraad!"

Suddenly Gerrod stared up at the ceiling. His mouth drew
shut, a tight, thin line across his countenance. His head
snapped down a second later. The eyes that met Dru's were full
of both relief and despair.

"Rendel's made it. I can feel him. His ka now definitely
inhabits the realm beyond. Our success"—Gerrod hesitated,
visibly tasting the words and disliking their content—"is a
certainty now!"

For the second time in only a matter of minutes, Dru could
not hold back the shiver that coursed through him.

Though it had no mouth, it screamed.

Though it had no eyes, it turned its head toward the dark,
raging heavens, as if seeking some power to end its agony.

Its visage was blank. No mark, no hair, graced its head. There were no ears, though it seemed to listen. Naked, it stumbled to its feet, which had no toes, and grasped the tree it had fallen against with hands that were little more than stubs. It was a sexless being, devoid of any distinguishing feature over the expanse of its entire body. It could feel the elements warring around it, but could do little else.

It was a golem, the first to be grown and the first to be claimed by the Vraad.

A flock of wyverns, half as tall as the helpless creature staggering below but capable of tearing asunder predators thrice their size, huddled fearfully in the few trees dotting this area of the storm-drenched field. It was not the wind and the lightning that sent shivers through their reptilian forms. What they feared was the being feeling its way around the trunk of the tree on which many of them perched. It was not exactly the scent that stirred their anxiety, but a presence of power so foreign to their limited existences that it frightened them into immobility.

The faceless monstrosity guided a foot over the upturned root it had previously tripped over. As it did, bulbous growths sprouted from the end, twisting and shaping themselves into individual toes. The other foot was also whole now, though the change went unnoticed by the creature itself. It could only feel its pain.

The storm had swept across a clear evening sky mere moments before, but it was already at its height. As it vented itself, the thing paused, seeming to consider something.

It suddenly pulled back its fist and, for no apparent reason, harshly struck the trunk of the tree. The wyverns squawked in panic; the blow nearly cracked the trunk in half. Sorcery crackled in the air around the blind wanderer. As it pulled the hand back for a second try, blood dripping to the already-soaked earth, stubs emerged from the front, mad little points that stretched and wriggled, creating fingers and forming a true hand in the space of a single breath. The blow stopped in midflight, the hand's owner only now becoming aware of what was happening. If its empty visage could have indicated anything now, it would have been pleasure—the pleasure of a dead man who had been given a reprieve.

It wiggled the fingers on both hands, seeming to admire the

movement that it could not see. The storm was a thing forgotten. The creature put a hand to each side of its head, feeling for and finally locating the budding ears. Like a child, it became aware of yet other alterations in its form. Pale white hair sprouted with astonishing alacrity, lightly covering the body and richly overwhelming the top, back, and sides of the head. He was male, too, a fact that he had known always but could not have proven before this instant. The body itself grew until it was well over six feet in height and swelled as the rib cage expanded and muscles stretched into being.

As the torso transformed, so, too, did the blank countenance. A tiny protuberance rose near the center. Below it, a slit formed, first little more than a tear in the skin, but soon a gap that spread across the emerging visage. Above, two tiny folds twitched, the beginnings of eyes.

Through the thin-lipped mouth and the arrogantly curved nose, he breathed deeply, for the first time, the air of this land. A smile, with just a touch of self-congratulation imbued in it, curled into life. Teeth gleamed white.

The eyes opened, glittery, multihued orbs that saw everything and forgot nothing. For a time, they studied the eye of the storm, a black abyss that was no cloud but the remaining effect of his passage to this new world. Even as he watched, it began to recede, giving way to the heavens once more. He sighed in relief, pleased now where he had been in agony moments before.

Fully whole, Rendel gazed down at himself, assuring that all was in order. The smile broadened.

The chill wind, a last remnant of the storm he had helped cause, reminded him of his lack of protection. The smile died, replaced by a look of petulance with just a hint of confusion added. He gestured angrily at his form.

A dark suit of the finest scale, scale from the greater cousin to the hapless beasts above, wrapped him from neck to toe. A green cloak and hip-high boots completed the image of some majestic but frightful forest king. Rendel left the hood of the cloak back, enjoying the feel of the wind on his face. He laughed, his triumph, which he had begun to doubt more than once since his arrival, completely erasing the earlier pain and fear. That, of all things, pleased him most. To one who had suffered little in the areas of pain and fear before this day, such emotions were doubly strong.

The wind was dying down now. Rendel turned his gaze toward a distant chain of mountains. Among them, he spied a giant among giants, a peak that seemed to summon him.

Turning briefly to the field and the spot on which the golem had lain, the mage executed a low and somewhat sardonic bow. That done, he straightened and, without hesitation, walked off in the direction of the mountains. An arrogant smile dominated his features.

The wyverns watched him depart, now bunched together so tightly that they threatened the stability of their perches. Beyond them and hidden by the tall grass, something else watched the receding figure of the Vraad with deadly interest.

III

With Rendel's apparent success, Gerrod chose to speak no more concerning his conflicting desires. Dru knew better than to press him. There was enough to ponder and enough to worry about, and joining the other Vraad in the coming was proving a two-pronged decision. What Dru had learned so far only emphasized the need to continue his secret work, which even the Lord Tezerenee, with his multitude of prying eyes, had no knowledge of—he hoped. On the other hand, what Dru had learned also made that work seem superfluous, for what support would he get once Barakas announced to the others that *he* held the solution to their growing predicament?

Dru left the chamber by himself, Gerrod preferring to monitor the health of his brother's body rather than join in their father's encroaching triumph. The news would reach Barakas nonetheless; Gerrod evidently did not want to have to be the bearer, not after what he had confided earlier.

Walking was not a necessity in a city designed to supply its users with all comforts. Dru could have commanded the citadel to carry him along until he arrived at his destination or he could have teleported, but the tall Vraad cared for neither choice. A long, mind-calming trek through the myriad corridors and staircases of the structure was what he needed . . . that and his daughter.

He had wandered in a gradual upward direction, slowly making his way to where Barakas and the others were gathering, when a slim figure materialized around the corner of the stairway. There was no going around her and it was too late to turn back.

"Dru, sweet thing, I was wondering where you were!"

She had her arms around him and kissed him soundly before he could peel her clinging claws away. The struggle was made all the more difficult by the fact that part of him did not *want* to break away.

"Melenea . . . I didn't see you earlier."

"Didn't see or don't want to, sweet thing? Am I so bland and undesirable?"

In a world where beauty was commonplace, there was nothing common about the scarlet- and ebony-tressed sorceress. *Enchantress* was a word whose definition included Melenea. Her oval face was the color of pearl. Her lips, round and sensual—and *soft,* Dru recalled almost with shame—complemented her partly upturned nose and the narrow, tear-shaped eyes. Her brows were arched high, which tended to give her a calculating and commanding look. She had chosen to emphasize her cheekbones further than in the past and the effect was such that the memories it brought to life made Dru regret his not having departed instantly upon first sighting her. Her hair was short and tightly wrapped about her head, almost like a helm. Wisps of hair darted across her cheeks from each side, complementing her bone structure.

Where many of the female Vraad openly displayed their continually changing attributes, Melenea had, in contrast to the last time they had met, worn a form-fitting, glittering dress of deep green. The dress, by virtue of its clinging, displayed her full shape to far greater success than her counterparts. One reason Dru suspected he had not seen her earlier—and he had been watching just so he could have avoided this moment—was that she had likely been surrounded by admirers of both sexes vying for her favors.

Once, Dru had been one of the more ardent.

Melenea laughed lightly, pure music, and Dru's pulse quickened. He realized he had been staring.

"Sweet thing." She put a hand on his cheek and caressed it. Dru wanted to but did not move. "You're so much more fun than the rest." Her eyes twinkled, a trick she had mastered as no other had. The smile grew knowing. "You play the games with more feeling, more defiance."

That snapped the spell. He reached up and grabbed her tiny, firm hand, but not before she left bloody memories of her long, sharp nails in his cheek. With a careless twitch, he healed the wounds.

"I don't play your games. Not anymore."

The laugh, the *smile*, they both taunted and tempted him. He knew his face had grown crimson long ago, but that was one thing beyond his abilities to prevent.

"You will, dear sweet Dru. You'll come to me because I am the only way you can pass the centuries without thinking *too* deeply." She artfully turned his grip on her hand into an opportunity to let her lips brush against his knuckles. Dru released her hand instantly, pulling his own to his side.

She took a step toward him and watched with visible amusement as he forced himself to stand his ground. "How is darling Sharissa? It's been *so* long since I saw her. She must be a beautiful and desirable woman by now... and so *new*."

"Sharissa is well... and no longer any concern of yours." He would *not* give her this victory! He would not flee from her!

"She will always be my concern, if only because she's your concern." Melenea waved off the subject as if it no longer entertained her. "Barakas is making his silly speech and simply destroying the mood of the coming. A shame what he did to Dekkar and Silesti, isn't it? I understand neither of them will be coming back."

Dru gritted his teeth. There was no way to avoid some loss of face; he *had* to get away from her now!

"If Barakas is speaking, I should be up there. I trust you will be able to do without my company, Melenea"—he executed a mock bow—"as I have been more than able to do without yours."

Now it was her visage that shone scarlet, the smile faltering just a little and the eyes narrowing. Some of Dru's confidence returned. He started to walk past her, indicating to Melenea, he hoped, that her presence bothered him so little that he felt no need to instantly teleport far away.

Her voice snared him as he continued up the steps. "Lady Tezerenee is here, Dru sweet. I think she, too, would like to give her love to Sharissa. She seems to have been looking for both of you, in fact."

He stood on the steps, his face carefully kept from her sight . . . a futile gesture since his sudden immobility spoke volumes concerning the success of her barb. It was the one thing Dru had not expected because it was the one thing he thought Melenea could not understand.

With her low, knowing laughter cutting through his heart, Dru curled within himself and vanished from the stairway.

His new destination was far from the balcony on which Barakas Tezerenee, his eldest son Reegan, and a host of other Tezerenee stood, overlooking the expectant throngs. The patriarch was already into the thrust of his speech and his presence could be felt even from where Dru stood. Yet another shiver coursed through the tall sorcerer, but this time he could not say as to which reason was the cause.

"Masterrrr?"

Sirvak! In all that had happened, Dru had completely forgotten the familiar, despite it being perched on his shoulder and wrapped around the back of his neck. Despite its seemingly awkward size, the familiar could make itself virtually unnoticeable, an ability that Dru himself had personally added during Sirvak's creation.

"What is it, friend?"

The familiar gently licked its master's cheek with its long, narrow tongue. Being a part of Dru, it sometimes understood him better than he himself did. "Meleneaaaa."

"She caught me unawares, nothing more."

"Frightens, masterrrr. Lady frightensss."

"She's disturbing, Sirvak, but hardly frightening." The creature's fears, however, transmitted themselves to him. He knew Melenea's tastes—all *too* well—and knew her propensity for games that tended to leave others damaged or, at the very least, in disarray.

Dru shook his head. She had just been *toying* with him, nothing more. Petty cruelty was a streak common in the Vraad race and more so in the temptress. That was all it was.

And you make yourself such an open target, he scolded himself.

The sky flashed, the green and crimson clouds swirling violently as if in response to the explosion. Dru turned at the sound of thunder, wondering it if was going to rain for once. There had not been any rain for over three years now. If not for the powers of the Vraad, Nimth would have perished from thirst.

A second flash lit the heavens in the direction of his own domain.

A massive peak, clearly seen and as solid as any, stood in the distance, its white tip and vegetation-enshrouded base taunting him. Dru gaped.

It was—it *had* to be—a piece of the shrouded realm thrusting through the veil *into* his own world!

"There you are!"

Dru whirled around, but saw nothing. He glanced up and discovered the source of the voice directly above him. A Tezerenee riding a dragon. From where he stood, Dru could not make out the features of the rider. It could have been one of the patriarch's sons or a cousin. In fact, if he had not heard the voice, Dru would have been hard-pressed to identify the newcomer as male or female without augmenting his vision again.

The rider urged his mount lower. "The Lord Barakas Tezerenee has dispatched myself and several others to search for you! You were to be at his side by the time he began to speak before the crowds!"

"I found it necessary to be away. It seems my absence had little effect on his speech, anyway." Dru desperately wanted to leave the city, to explore the rift. If there was truly a physical way through . . .

The Tezerenee seemed horribly ignorant of the vast sight in the distance. He only had eyes for the object of his mission, a protesting outsider. "The clan master still desires your presence! You will return with me!"

Dru felt all the anger and frustration of the past hour battle against his slipping self-control. He eyed the rider and the beast. "I am not one of your toy-soldier brethren, Tezerenee! I come when I wish to! Matters have come up that demand my return to my own domain! You can convey my *regrets* to Lord Barakas, but not me!"

"You—"

"That is all I have to say to you, Tezerenee!" Raw power crackled like an aura around the narrow spellcaster, a sign of the fury within him straining to be released.

The dragon protested the difficulty of continuing to hover, but the rider ignored him. Dru matched stares with the airborne Vraad. At last, the Tezerenee signaled for the dragon to rise again.

"The clan master will be furious!"

"You may relay to him my apologies and my wishes for the best in the hours to come! I will contact him when it proves possible!"

In the end, it was likely the authoritative tone that backed the dragon rider away. From his time in the company of the patriarch, Dru had picked up on the voice that Barakas utilized to exercise his control. Trained from birth to obey that voice, the rider could not, in the end, match wills with Zeree. With a final muttered response that the wind, which had picked up despite protective spells surrounding the city, carried away, the Tezerenee rode off.

Dru sighed and smiled. Sirvak hissed in satisfaction. It was always nice to gain a victory, however small. The rider would probably wait until his master was finished speaking, rather than disrupt the patriarch's great moment. That gave Dru a little more time before Barakas began trying to contact him. Time enough, if he hurried, to see his daughter.

The claws of his familiar tightened on his shoulder. The creature had gone from pleased to dismayed in only seconds. Even before he turned, Dru suspected what he would see.

The peak was fading. Slowly, to be sure, but far too quickly for Dru's needs.

It was with a mixture of relief and anxiety that he vanished from the city only a breath later.

"*Sharissa!*"

A soft mist settled around Dru as he appeared in the central chamber of his gleaming citadel. The pearl luster of his home generally filled him with a feeling of peace, of sanctuary. Not so, now.

"Sharissa!"

His call echoed through the corridors. When he had created this castle centuries before, he had added a spell that would relay sounds from one room to the next. For the most part, it had protected him from several angry rivals over the years and kept his most important work secret from even the best of his counterparts. In the twenty years since his daughter's birth, Dru had essentially used it to locate her. Two people did little in the way of filling a void so large as this structure.

"Father?"

"Where are you?"

"In the theater."

"Stay there." Dru curled within himself and vanished again, almost losing Sirvak, who had carelessly assumed it was safe to climb off. The familiar let out an annoyed cry and dug its talons in deeper. This time, Dru winced.

The scene that he found himself in the midst of threw the sorcerer completely off balance. He was in a chamber filled with dancing couples. They twirled and twirled, completely ignorant of the towering figure caught in the center of the ball. To the side, a nonsensical group of animals that were also instruments played the music. A huge, furred thing, loosely related to Sirvak's lupine half, beat on a drum in its middle while a four-legged monstrosity with a pipe-stem mouth played a merry tune.

One of the male dancers came within arm's reach of Dru. The spellcaster's eyes narrowed; it was his own face, but as it might look if he had allowed it to age more. Lines crisscrossed his features and the visage as a whole had filled out. Dru quickly turned and studied another dancer. Again, it was his face, but clean-shaven and with a somewhat bulbous nose. This one was also shorter by half a foot.

A quick scan revealed that *all* of the male dancers were variations on his appearance. Tall, short, fat, thin, old, and young . . . he was astonished at how numerous the combinations were.

Then his attention fell on the women.

They were *Sharissa*.

It did not surprise him, not really, since she had no one but the two of them to really go by. Nonetheless, as he watched the couples sweep across the floor, Dru was struck by a feeling of dread. Looking at them, he could see her as other Vraad would see her . . . fully adult and ready, physically, at least, to make her mark among them.

To use and *be* used, as was the Vraad way.

With a furious gesture, he dismissed the dancers. They dwindled instantly into tiny whirlwinds of dust, puppet images drawn from the life of the world itself. Unlike golems, who had some solidity and could comprehend orders, the dancers were no more than intricate toys, an art form that occasionally amused Vraad. He had taught it to his daughter when she was only a few years old and had been pleased with her immediate skill with the not-so-simple spell.

Dru was not so pleased now. There were too many things to worry about to keep adding to the list, though this was really part of his first and foremost fear, he supposed.

''Sharissa!''

''Here, Father.''

She came to him as more of a mist than the child that he had expected. The billowing silver dress that clung to her proportions reminded him of what he had just tried to force from his mind, that, though only two decades old, his daughter was a woman. For someone three millennia old, two decades seemed hardly enough time to learn to walk.

Tall, though she only came to his chin, Sharissa was not willowy. She had grown to fit her frame, looking exactly as she should have looked if she were a foot shorter. Her hair was silver-blue—natural, as far as Dru knew—and flowed down her backside to a point just below her waist. Like many Vraad, she had crystalline eyes, aquamarine gemstones that shone brightly when she was pleased with something. Her lips were thin, but perpetually curled upward at the ends. Even when Sharissa was angry, it was all she could do to force those lips into a straight line much less a frown.

"What is it, Father? Did something happen at the coming? Was there a duel?"

He stirred. Caught up in *dreaming*, again! "No, no duel. One, actually, but the Lord Tezerenee put an end to it."

"That's no good! A duel should reach a dramatic conclusion on its own!"

Among Dru's earliest attempts to entertain his daughter had been tales of some of the more interesting duels he had witnessed . . . and occasionally been part of. Much to his regret, Sharissa had proven to have a Vraadish taste for such things. It was one of the chief reasons she had begged to go to the coming and one of the chief reasons Dru had not taken her. He was thankful that she had listened. By this stage of her powers, she could have easily ignored him and gone on her own.

"Never mind that now! I gave you some duties to perform while I was away." Those duties had been partly to keep her busy for a time, but *some* of them had had true purposes. "Did you take care of them?"

Sharissa looked down. "Some of them . . . I . . . I was bored with them. I thought I'd finish in a few minutes." Her eyes were wide with worry. "I only had the ball running for two or three minutes; that's all!"

Dru forced himself to breathe calmly. "The crystals. That's what I want to know about. Did you adjust their settings? Did you refocus the spell as I asked?"

"Oh, *yes!* I did that first because you made it sound the most important!"

"Serkadion Manee be praised!"

Hugging his daughter, Dru felt the first relief he had experienced since before his departure for the coming. If things were as they should be . . .

"What happened? What about the Lord Tezerenee's plan? Did something go wrong?"

"I'll tell you later. For the time being, we have work to do, you and I." Releasing his daughter, Dru twisted his head around so that he could look Sirvak more or less in the eye. "To your sentinel duties, my friend. Some young drake of the patriarch's might come looking for me. I want to know before he or they get here. I also want no one else prying into this!''

"Masterrrr.'' The familiar stretched, spread its magnificent wings, and flew off. Dru had complete faith in the creature's abilities; Sirvak was single-minded when it came to its duties. It would monitor and protect the castle better than either the sorcerer or his daughter.

"Come.'' He took Sharissa's hand. "This may literally prove to be a key to our predicament!''

As one, they folded inward and vanished from the theater— only to *reappear* at their exact starting point a second later.

Sharissa moaned, holding her head as if struck by some unseen assailant. Dru felt little better, finding even his legs unsteady.

"Father . . . the spell . . . like yesterday . . .''

"I know.'' Yesterday, Dru had found it necessary to adjust the design of the eastern tower so as to allow for the softening of the soil beneath. From a base of rock, the earth had turned to so much mud. Despite his best efforts, however, the Vraad could not alter the composition of the ground. Mud it had become and mud it was determined to stay. In the end, Dru had been forced to create a bridge and pylon system . . . and *that* had taken two attempts. For a time, his spells had either gone awry or failed completely.

"Why not just let the castle take us there?''

Dru considered the plan and dismissed it. "I would rather not be caught between floors if the castle magic began to fail.''

"We walk, then.''

"That we do.''

Fortunately, their trek was a brief one. Had he chosen to visit his sanctum for any other reason, it was probable that he would have walked in the first place. His excitement was leading to carelessness, something the spellcaster knew was far too dangerous at this juncture. The two of them had been fortunate that they had only returned to their starting point. Another time and they might have materialized in the midst of a wall or floor.

A gigantic, metallic figure blocked the doorway through which Dru and Sharissa wished to pass. Its features were roughly hewed and vaguely reminiscent of a hound. The leviathan stood on a pair of blocky legs and held in its two enormous hands a shield taller than its master. A stylized gryphon decorated the shield.

Sharissa mouthed a single world. Though her voice was nearly inaudible, the golem understood. It stepped aside and went down on one knee, a supplicant before its lord and lady.

"Did you teach it to do that?" Dru asked, eyeing the unliving servant with distaste.

A momentary look of guilt passed across his daughter's otherwise perfect visage. "Only this morning! I just thought it would be amusing to see such a horrible-looking creature act so civilly."

"It will do this no more." The other Vraad would have laughed at him. Kneeling was one of the least commands they would have given their own golems. Dru, though, had found it too ridiculous. There was nothing magnificent about commanding a chunk of metal that could walk and kill. The golem was still no more than a toy.

Another sign of how he had changed. Once, he, too, would have laughed.

The golem rose silently, Dru's words now law. The two Vraad continued on, the massive doors swinging open for them as they neared.

The sanctum of a Vraad was a far more individualistic thing than his or her outer appearance. Here, the subconscious played an active role in the design and maintenance. Here, a sorcerer's mind was free to act and create, with varying results. In the chambers of his counterparts, Dru knew, one could expect to find anything within the realms of the imagination . . . and often beyond.

Dru's own chambers, on the other hand, were bare—bare, that is, with the exception of countless crystals of all shapes and sizes orbiting or floating all about the room.

The spell, of which the gems were only the physical aspect, was the culmination of his work so far. Since the discovery of the realm beyond the veil, Dru had cleared out the paraphernalia from all past experiments—some of those items raising protest—and set aside everything for research into the nature of the wraith world. While others were pounding their magical might futilely against its phantom boundaries, he and a few of the more patient had sought out answers through careful study.

That study had brought about, as a side result, the rediscovery—
not *discovery*, as Barakas had put it—of the method of ka
travel. The early Vraad had known of it, but for vague reasons
no one could explain, they had forgotten soon after the founding
generation of the Vraad race had passed on. He had discovered
many other secrets as well, but all of them paled in the face of
the greatest challenge. Somehow, the stubborn spellcaster still
tried to believe, there was a way to travel physically to this
other place.

Perhaps now . . .

Dru and his daughter stared curiously at the patterns formed
by the floating crystals. The primary crystals, larger and generally fixed in one place, were, as he had hoped, arranged in the
pattern he had asked Sharissa to set them in. It was something
that had to be done by hand and his requested appearance at the
coming had made that impossible. Sharissa, while occasionally
prone to dreaming, was as excellent a helper as he could have
dared hope. Soon, she would be able to conduct her own series
of experiments and—

*And that would only happen if they found a solution before
Nimth began to pull the Vraad down with it in its death
struggles.*

The secondary crystals, which had been organized to catch
the natural emanations of any sighting and record them for his
later need, floated in a complex spiral cluster near the focus, a
foot-wide black sphere that kept surveillance on the nearby
regions surrounding his own domain. Principal study of late
had been on the very area where Dru had seen the rift.

Sightings, the sorcerer had noted early on, always occurred
near unstable regions. Whether one resulted from the other—it
was debatable which way *that* worked, too—he could not say.
They just seemed to be related, like opposite ends of a magical
beast.

His eyes took in the myriad pattern of colors and shapes in
the spiral, noting what changes had resulted from this latest
opportunity and wondering what they would reveal. The crystals were still absorbing information, so all he could do for the
moment was wait.

An irregularity caught his eye.

There were three crystals, two golden and one turquoise, that should *not* have been part of the spiral.

"Sharissa," he started quietly as he studied the possible ramifications of the error. "Did something happen to the spiral? Did the spell fail? Did you try re-creating it without my guidance?"

Knowing her father as she did, his daughter waited until he had exhausted all questions. When Dru grew silent, attention still focused on the crystals swirling about, she replied, "Nothing happened to the spiral, Father. I added those three on my own."

He turned, unable to believe his ears. "You did that of your own volition?"

"It makes sense, Father. See how they play off the amethyst and emerald ones below them."

"They cannot! To do that would mean—" Mouth still open, the gray-robed figure could only blink. The new additions were indeed playing off of the crystals Sharissa had mentioned and to far greater effect than he could have believed. But . . . "Impossible!"

"It works!"

"They should make the spiral unstable, cause it to explode!" Dru walked toward the spiral and dared to touch one of the golden gems. It pulsated in perfect harmony with the rest. "The combination has never held before!"

Sharissa held her ground. "I saw that it would work the moment I started adjusting the primaries. You've always taught me to use my initiative."

"Not like this." Still awed, Dru stepped back. They *were* functioning. Crystal work was very delicate, even for beings as powerful as the Vraad. Many of the sorcerous race could not even work that particular magic successfully. The ability to move mountains, while it tore asunder the natural laws of Nimth—what remained of them—was far and away more simple. That required only will and power. Crystal work required patience and finesse. Sharissa, to have seen what was needed, had developed a skill that would soon surpass her parent.

There was more to this, however, than met the physical eye. Dru turned his gaze to another plane of sight.

The world remained the same, but now he could see the

jagged patterns that bound Nimth. Spirals, once neatly formed and organized, had reconnected in haphazard fashion, the world's own natural attempt to make up for the damage the careless Vraad had done to it. Things were far beyond repair, however.

All seemed as it had been until Dru looked closer. Then he began to notice the intruding lines, forces that came from nowhere, but bound themselves to the fabric of Nimth.

But from where?

Where else? Dru followed the invaders as far back as he could and found that all of them dwindled at the same point. The region where he had noted the rift.

The Vraad had been trying with little success to break into the shrouded realm . . . and here it was, *encroaching* now upon their own!

IV

Gerrod stood on the plain where a group of Tezerenee, led by his cousin Ephraim, worked to provide the clan and those allied with it the bodies they would need in the days to come. The other Vraad as yet did not know that proving one's loyalty to the sons of the dragon would be a prerequisite for their survival.

He had come here to escape the wrath of his father, if only for a time, who had been livid from the moment it was discovered the outsider Zeree had left the city. Gerrod both admired and scorned the outsider. Admired him for both defying Barakas and providing the research that had been of such immeasurable value. Scorned him as an outsider and weak man when it came to certain necessities. Still, Dru Zeree had been the only man Gerrod felt safe admitting at least some of his feelings to for now. He had not told him everything, but it was safe to assume that a quick mind like Zeree's was capable of reading much from the tone of his voice.

The deeper truth was that unlike his multitude of obedient relations, the young Tezerenee had no desire to live in a world formed by his progenitor's continually growing religious fervor. As a matter of fact, he had no desire to live anywhere his father lived, dragon spirit or not.

Ephraim, his armor hanging oddly loose on his body, finally rose from the center of the pentagram etched in the earth. Gerrod frowned impatiently. He had stood here for nearly twenty minutes, far too long for a respectful wait. That was one of the problems. Among his own clan, he felt out of place, unnecessary except as an assistant to Rendel. This despite all the work that *he* had done.

"What is it you want?"

The voice was horribly dead of any emotion, something terribly alien in the violent Tezerenee. Gerrod studied his cousin before answering. Ephraim's face was pale and gaunt, hardly the heavy, weather-beaten figure who had come here only three days ago. There was also a faraway look in his eyes that chilled Gerrod.

"Did you feel it when Rendel took over the first golem?"

"Yes. It was painful for him." Ephraim's eyes would not meet his but insisted on staring beyond the hooded Tezerenee's shoulder.

"You've made changes, then?"

"We have."

"How soon can you begin on the others?"

"We have nearly a dozen completed." The pale face broke into a thin, satisfied smile.

"Already?" Gerrod was taken aback. Small wonder that his cousin was so pale, if they were already hard at work on the hosts for the Vraad ka.

"There seemed no reason to wait. It's quite . . . entertaining." The ghostly smile remained fixed, as if forgotten by its bearer.

This was news Gerrod knew he would have to take to his father personally. He could ill afford to hesitate with this, despite his lack of desire for the cross-over's success. Not just the jump on creation of the golems, but the effort being put in by the group. If Ephraim was any indication, the strain must be terrible. Barakas would have him punished if something went wrong and it could be proved that Gerrod had been at fault.

"You'll need help. Father will send others to replace those who cannot go on."

"*No!*" A white, cold hand reached out and snared one of Gerrod's wrists. "*We* will not falter! This is our calling!"

The eyes of his cousin blazed bright. Gerrod peeled his hand free. Ephraim's gaze finally met his own. It was not one the hooded Vraad cared to stare into for very long.

"As you wish, Ephraim. If you need anything, though, you must—"

The other interrupted in the same monotone voice he had utilized earlier. "Do you know that it should be possible to take a portion of a ka and keep it after the one to whom it belongs has died? We've discussed it, the others and I. No one would truly ever be dead, then. They could be called up, using golems for temporary form, and made to—"

"What are you talking about?"

Ephraim quieted. "Nothing. We have found that we only need a part of our selves now and so we talk. The strain lessens with each one. Perhaps we are adapting to the Dragonrealm."

Gerrod had heard more than enough. The strain might be lessening, but it had evidently already driven the group mad if its leader was any example. He doubted that his sire would send anyone to spell the group until they began dying. Why waste any more? If Ephraim and the others lived long enough to complete their task, that was all that his father would want.

He wrapped the shroudlike cloak about himself, once more becoming more of a shadow than a man. Ephraim took a step away. Gerrod hesitated, then said, "I will inform Father of your success and your confidence concerning your ability to continue."

"That would be good."

Perhaps they will die when no one is around to see, Gerrod thought. *If only there was another way than Father's, I would . . .* He curled within himself, feeling, as he had the last couple of times, a curious hesitation, as if the teleportation spell did not wish to work. It did, however, and he gratefully left his cousin and the others.

Ephraim, for his part, waited until Gerrod had left. Then, he silently returned to the center of the pentagram. The others looked up in unison, and had anybody watched them then, it would have seemed that they were one mind with eleven bodies . . . a mind that was no longer Tezerenee.

Dru looked over the information his crystals had gathered for him and compared them to those he had utilized in the past. There were definite signs of a potential breakthrough, yet there were aberrations that still made no sense.

Made no sense unless . . .

He recalled the change in the pattern that Sharissa had wrought. A pattern that should not have been stable. The intruding forces from the other realm were affecting the natural laws of his own world in much the same way as Vraad sorcery did, only without the damage. Could it be that what Dru thought made no sense merely did not because his mind refused to accept that the binding forces of Nimth had been altered by the intruding power?

"A change in the laws of power like none before," he muttered.

"What will you do now?"

"What will *we* do? Don't look at me like that. I'm beginning to think that you know more than I do . . . or *will*, before long. Besides, what I hope to do will take two people and I think I prefer to trust *you*."

Her eyes were wide with realization. "You think you can *cross!*"

Again, she had anticipated his next moves. Dru's smile masked mixed emotions. "It may be possible. What we have to do is go to the point where the forces from the other realm merge and fade away. *That* is the point of weakness, I hope." It was also quite possible that due to the combination of Nimth's power and that of the other, the location would actually be the point of greatest strength. If such were the case, Dru might find himself beating against a wall so incredibly hard that not all the Vraad in the world, even had they been able to cooperate, would have been able to bring it down.

"Will we have to walk there?"

He considered their options. "I do not care to try to teleport, especially not after what I've seen and what the crystals have verified." His eyebrow arched. "We can *ride* there."

Sharissa caught his meaning. "I'll saddle them up!"

Dru watched her hurry off, her childlike glee a direct contrast to her elegant face and form. If there was one thing that she had never outgrown, it was her fondness for the creatures of the stable, specifically the horses. They were rare and wonderful beasts taller than Dru, and fearsome to all save his daughter. She rode them expertly and without the aid of sorcery. They might not be as powerful or majestic as the gryphons, which she also enjoyed, but they were swifter and more companionable.

While Sharissa went about her task, Dru reached out with his mind and strengthened the link between himself and Sirvak. The familiar's mind opened, knowing that orders were about to be given. Dru informed it of his intentions to investigate and how long he thought they would be. To his surprise, instead of acknowledging all and returning to its duties, the beast protested.

Masterrr! Take Sirvak with! Will need!

Not for this, friend. I only go to research, as I have done in the past.

Do not leave Sirvakkkk! Sirvak will guard!

Your duties are here! Enough of this! What's gotten into you?

The creature sulked and would say no more. Still perturbed, Dru broke contact. As if he did not have enough difficulties! Now, even Sirvak was causing him worry!

"Father, the horses are ready." Along with Sharissa's words came the echoes of animal sounds, hooves clattering on hard earth and the snorts of the two mighty steeds.

"I'm on my way."

The walk to the stables was not as long as it sometimes was, especially when one was propelled, as the sorcerer was now, by a desire to be done with things. Sharissa waited at the mouth of the central stable, a horse on each side of her, their reins in her hands. Again, she had used no magic save her own charm and skill. It was not due in any part to the gentle nature of the horses, either. As one Vraad—sardonic Krystos, wasn't it? Dru remembered vaguely—had once discovered, these animals were particular as to whom they allowed close. Krystos had escaped with his fingers intact, at least. A few more arrogant visitors, invited and not, had discovered that the stables of Dru Zeree were no place to vent their arrogance. Like their master, the animals were willing to strike back . . . and were doubly protected by the spells that he had layered over their forms.

"Was Sirvak upset?"

"Yes, how did you know?"

"It just seemed that way. I could feel the poor thing all the way here. Why not take Sirvak with, Father? The castle will defend itself adequately."

Dru shrugged off her suggestion. "And Sirvak will defend it superbly. Never underestimate others, Sharissa. A Vraad always has rivals and those rivals always look for weaknesses in your defense. With Sirvak here, it will be as if they are fighting me . . . and you know what success they've had so far."

Sharissa's perpetual smile broadened. Despite his more peaceful way of life since her birth, her father was not one to be underestimated. After the Lord Tezerenee, Dru was one of the most respected of the Vraad. Even his most bitter rivals occasionally came to him for assistance and advice.

Taking the reins of the larger of the two animals, Dru mounted. In general shape and color, the two steeds were identical—proud, auburn-furred animals built for both speed and battle. Dru had chosen to forgo the use of sorcery when breeding them and had found, to his pleasure, that the results exceeded what he had originally wanted. As with many things over the past few years, he had discovered a diverse pleasure in not performing spells to accomplish his needs.

When both of them were ready, Dru urged his horse forward. Sharissa's steed followed close behind. With the cool wind in his face, the sorcerer slowly calmed. Things were moving in the proper direction for once, and if his theories held out, the Vraad would not have to bow to the will of the Lord Tezerenee. Barakas would be upset about that, to be sure, but Dru had no qualms about destroying his "partner's" dream. It was only because there had seemed no other way at the time that he had let the situation go on for as long as it had. Now, the cross-over would no longer be necessary.

The sky rumbled again, tearing him from his musings and making him look up. The dark, foreboding green was dominant for the first time in months. Dru frowned, recalling the violent changes in the land when that had last happened. The dominance of either color in the sky spoke ill for Nimth. Things were always best when the two were more or less even.

Change could have only come about from some extensive use of Vraad sorcery. Dru knew of only one cause . . . the spells of the Tezerenee tearing at the boundaries and beyond. The great cross-over was *hastening* the death of the world, if Dru read the signs right. Now, more than ever, the importance of his *own* plan became unmistakable. Unconsciously, he urged the horse to greater speed.

"Father!" Sharissa suddenly called out, her voice partly obscured by the continued rumbling.

He turned toward her, careful to make certain that the steed was following a safe path, and saw what had caught her attention.

A crack had opened in the earth far to the north of their present location. It was small now, little more than a scar, but it was widening with each passing moment. The walls of each side of the growing ravine crumbled, causing a rain of rock and dirt. The sight would not have disturbed Dru save for the fact that the path of the tear would cut through his own domain closer than any such vast instability had prior to this. In fact, the horses might not be able to clear it on the way back. He would be *forced* to use his sorcery . . . and so near to an untrustworthy region.

Complications and disaster; it seemed he was never to be free of them. Dru hoped that the point of intersection would at least prove peaceful, like the eye of a storm.

The horse stumbled, nearly causing him to lose the reins. The path was rocky and rose higher than he recalled. When he pulled on the reins in order to slow the animal, it gave him no argument. Sharissa's mount caught up to them, then slowed to a similar pace as the young woman copied her father's action.

The wind was picking up, much the way it had at the city. There seemed, however, no one direction to its movement, for it struck the tiny party from all sides, changing with each passing breath. Dru cursed his own impatience, for they had left their cloaks behind. With some trepidation, he stretched out his left arm and summoned one for each of them.

On his outstretched arm appeared two brown cloaks with hoods. Sharissa took hers and gratefully put it on, drawing the hood partly over her massive waves of hair. Dru donned his own, but left the hood down for the time being. He had simply wanted the garment as a precaution.

"How much farther?"

Dru pointed at a ridge. Though both of them could follow the lines of binding, the odd strings of power cut through the ridge and came out somewhere on the other side, completely hidden. "Over that ridge! This must be where the rift was birthed!"

"But that was elsewhere!"

"The power . . . the flow from the other realm . . . spreads as it enters Nimth! The rift was the weakest of spots, perhaps created by some surge! I don't know yet!"

Their conversation continued as they encouraged their mounts around the ridge. As they drew closer to their destination, the wind abruptly changed again, this time dying to next to nothing. It was so calm, in fact, that Dru felt as if he had ridden into a tomb. The only sounds were the clatter of hooves against loose rock and the breathing of the riders and steeds.

"Serkadion Manee!" Dru tugged tight on the reins as he spoke, for the horse had begun to shy at the disquieting sight before them.

"It's—" Sharissa struggled futilely for words and finally just let her silence speak for her.

Dru had seen the phantom lands three times before, but they never ceased to stun him. A part of his mind that still functioned understood what Sharissa, who had *never* seen such a sight, must be feeling.

The ridge that was truly a part of the Vraad's world was a sharp, twisted thing that rose high in the air and went on for some distance. A few scraggly trees stood here and there, along with some equally misshapen bushes. Of animal life, there was no trace. The ridge was more or less a great gray-brown mass of dirt and rock, hardly worth looking at by itself.

Not so, the *other* realm.

A forest of spectral trees, high and strong, seemed to stand guard at the base of the ridge. When Dru looked closer, he saw that the forest went *into* the ridge itself, much the same way the lines of force had on the other side. Transparent waves of grass, knee-high to the spellcaster, dipped back and forth, brushed gently by some breeze that existed *there*, but *not* in Nimth. A tiny form flitted beyond, an avian of some sort, though it looked like no more than a shadow. The curious mist hung over all, making both regions appear blurred.

"It's frightening . . . and *beautiful*," Sharissa finally managed to say.

"Yes." Dru stirred, knowing he was wasting valuable time. "Stay where you are. I want to go farther."

"Father! You can't do that! This isn't like the others, the intruding power—"

He was already dismounting. "I won't be able to find out what I want unless I walk through it." That was not quite true, but he could not resist. This was not the solid, absolutely real mountain peak he had spotted earlier, but it was the most complete image yet. More important still, the point of intersection was almost in sight. There, he would learn the most.

Dru started to hand the reins of his mount over to Sharissa, then decided it might be better to have the horse handy. He whispered a short spell to the animal, calming it in case the unnatural landscape made it too distraught.

"Be careful."

"I will. You watch. Let me know if you see anything out of the ordinary."

"Everything *here* is out of the ordinary."

He chuckled. "True."

He slowly walked into the chaotic region leading the horse. Even the ground, the watchful spellcaster noted, had its wraithlike counterpart. Twice, he stepped into depressions that he had assumed were not part of his reality and once he nearly tripped when what he thought was better footing proved to be a slightly more solid-looking bit of the other realm.

The translucent field of grass invited him to enter. After a moment of hesitation, he put a foot forward. Finding nothing but the hard soil of his own world, he grew more confident.

All around him, Dru began to feel a tingling. He was close to the invading lines of force. For reasons the sorcerer could not fathom, a great revulsion at the thought of using Vraad magic overwhelmed him. He had not had any desire to cast a spell, but the feeling was with him, regardless. Dru steadied himself and pushed the emotion to the back of his mind. It continued to nag him, but no more than if he had been experiencing a mild headache.

Halfway through the field, Dru paused. The forest was far more solid now and tinges of color pervaded it. The lines converged within the forest after all, but he could still not make out where.

"Father!"

Dru whirled back, but all he saw were Sharissa and the other horse. She did not appear fearful, only worried. He waited for her to say or do something.

Sharissa pointed at the treetops, which Dru had more or less ignored. It was hard to hear her; the shrouded realm seemed to deaden sound. All that he could make out from her shouts and gesturing was that she had seen some fairly large shape in the trees. The master mage turned and studied them for more than a minute, waiting for some sign of whatever it was his daughter had noticed. His own impatience, however, got hold of him and he finally turned back to her and shrugged. She still looked disturbed, but indicated her willingness for him to continue if he wished.

His steed was beginning to act up now, despite the spell. Dru held tight to the reins and talked to it. Slowly, he got the animal under control. When he was at last able to gaze upon the forest again, it had grown even more real. Now, he could almost imagine the sounds of wildlife.

Within a few yards of the first trees, Dru paused again. The true landscape of Nimth was no longer visible through the trunks; he might have very well been standing at the edge of an actual forest, though none such remained in his world. Leading the reluctant horse on, Dru moved to within arm's length of the nearest tree. Slowly, cautiously, he reached out.

His hand waded through something that had the consistency of mud. It was as if the tree was there, but not quite.

The horse reared, screaming as it did.

A man-sized shape with a wingspan greater than the length of the maddened steed fell upon the startled Vraad. Dru saw taloned hands and feet and a beak designed for tearing flesh come racing at him. So sudden was the attack that it was all he could do to raise his arms in a feeble effort to block the airborne monstrosity. There were spells that he wore upon his person that *should* protect him, but *should* and *would* were two different things. Whatever assaulted him was a creature of the other realm and there was no way of telling what powers it might have.

An odd twinge coursed through Dru's body. He stared in amazement as his adversary fell *through* him. In his surprise, the sorcerer had forgotten that any creature of the land beyond the veil would have the same consistency as its habitation.

It seemed that the winged horror would continue down, battering itself against the earth of its phantom plain. Then the creature somehow managed to flap hard enough to keep it above ground level. With great strain, it rose swiftly into the air and back toward the forest. Throughout most of the moment, Dru saw little more than wings, feathers, and limbs all tangled together. Not until the attacker was disappearing into the treetops did the spellcaster get a good look at it.

Avian it was, but also manlike. It could walk on its hind legs and grasp things in its hands, of that he was certain. Standing, it was probably nearly as tall as he was. From its ability to compensate for its mistakes and the nearly human form it wore, Dru knew that it was likely that it was intelligent as well. If such was the case, then the Lord Tezerenee's precious Dragonrealm might not prove so idyllic a place . . . although the sons of the dragon *might* actually look forward to fighting an actual foe for a change. Perhaps Barakas already *knew* what awaited the Vraad.

Barely audible, the worried voice of Sharissa finally broke into his reveries. "Father! Are you all right? Father?"

The disheveled spellcaster scanned the region for the horse. There was no sign. For some reason, that did not sit right with the Vraad. His horse *had* to be somewhere nearby. At the very least, Dru should have been able to sense the equine. As hard as he tried, however, there was no trace. It was as if the horse had vanished. . . .

"Father! Did it hurt you? I think that was what I saw!" Sharissa reined her mount to a stop and leaped off. She rushed over to Dru and wrapped her arms tightly around his torso. She buried her tear-tracked features in his chest. "I was certain you were dead! It was all over you and then I suddenly remembered that it had to be a wraith just like where it came from and—"

"Hush, daughter. Take a deep breath and calm yourself. I'm

fine. Like you said, it was only a wraith. Perfectly harmless.'' Though his words were for his daughter, Dru's attention was still focused on the missing horse. Was it possible, he wondered, that the animal was no longer in Nimth? Could it be . . .

''Sharissa.'' He stroked her silver-blue hair. ''Can you tell me what happened to my horse? Did you see where it ran off to?''

Her emotions slowly coming under control again, the young Vraad looked up at her father. ''Your horse? Can't *you* find it?''

''I find no trace.''

''That cannot be so!'' With the determination of youth, she utilized her own powers to seek out the errant steed. After a few moments, she frowned and said, ''You are right! I cannot feel its presence anywhere! I think I do recall seeing it . . .'' Sharissa hesitated, replaying the chaotic scene. ''I think it . . . oh, Father!'' Her eyes grew round. ''It ran *into* the forest!''

''As I thought.'' Dru separated the two of them and turned to study the forest. A thin mist still permeated it, but, for the moment, it looked more real than the landscape it had replaced.

''Is it one of those rifts you mentioned?''

''Possibly. I have to go see.''

Sharissa nodded. ''I guess you'll be safe if those things can't touch you, but be careful!''

''I will, even if it means using sorcery. I want you, though, to ride back to where I left you and stay there this time. Keep an eye on the lines . . . if they change, I want to know when I get back.''

''All right.'' With some reluctance, Sharissa obeyed his orders. Dru forced himself to wait until she was beyond the edge of the translucent field and then turned to face the dark woods.

As a Vraad, he should have had no fear, yet Dru felt his heart pound wildly and could hear his own rapid breathing as if someone had magnified the sound a thousandfold. Those two sensations were beginning to become normal with him it seemed, the spellcaster thought sourly. Nevertheless, curiosity held the edge. A cautious curiosity, to be sure, but one that would not, in the end, be denied.

Dru entered the forest.

Just past the first trees, he paused. Becoming lost would have been the culmination of all his troubles. Reaching into a pocket of his robe, the sorcerer pulled out a small, glittering cube. It was a beacon of sorts, one that he had shaped gradually over the past few years so as to give it great strength. He had meant to give it to his daughter, but had forgotten because of his excitement. Still, knowing where the edge of the forest was would do just as well. The horse might be beyond his other sight, but not so this device. It would allow him to backtrack to this spot without error. He placed it on the ground where he had previously walked and made certain that it was secure. Feeling a bit more confident now, Dru moved on, picking up his pace and anxiously waiting for the first sign that he had *finally* reached the point of intersection.

He was careful to note his path as he wandered among the tall trees. Though the cube would lead him back, it could not warn him of the obstacles that he might have to deal with, or of those things that might lurk in the forest itself. He had not mentioned it to Sharissa, but if the forest continued to grow more solid, it was more than likely that the denizens, including the avian monster that had attacked him, would follow suit. Dru had a spell handy, just to be on the safe side, but hoped he would not need it. In this place, it was possible that his spell might not even go off properly.

Now several yards into the woods, Dru could still feel no trace of the animal. More annoying, however, was a new obstacle to his success. Here in the forest, it seemed, the lines *curved*, moving off to the right and bisecting trees here and there. For some reason, he could still not see the intersection. A Vraadish temper Dru had once thought he had tamed completely rose for the second time this day, bathing him in a golden aura of his own sorcerous might. That action, however, caused disruptions in his sight, distorting his view of the lines he had been following. Breathing deeply, the Vraad fought back his anger. Not now. Not so close to his goal.

He had to be close, even with this latest twist. A few more steps and he would be there. Dru kept telling himself that, unconsciously turning it into a litany.

It was tempting to try to walk *through* the trees in order to take a more direct route, but Dru decided it would be safe not to aggravate things. The gray trunks were more solid than not and he might find himself trapped within one. Not a pretty way to die and certainly not a dignified one.

A horse neighed somewhere ahead of him. Oddly, he could still not feel its mind.

How far had he walked now, the sorcerer wondered suddenly. The second ridge, the one in which the forest actually continued on as if the massive formation were so much air and not stubborn rock, had to be nearby, yet Dru could not find it. The canopy formed by the treetops made seeing the heavens nearly impossible. The lack of illumination made it troublesome enough to see his path... though he was not tempted in the least to alter his vision to compensate for the darkness. He might turn himself blind instead.

One thought that he instantly dismissed was the possibility that he might have walked *into* the ridge. Dru was of Nimth, as was the ridge. If he needed proof of which reality he belonged to, he only had to look at the wavering, dull gray trees around him.

Wavering? Dull gray?

The forest was fading. Slowly, yes, but definitely fading. The Vraad cursed. He had wasted too much time with his thoughts!

Throwing caution to the wind, Dru ran on, following the lines of power as best he could. Trees constantly blocked his way, almost as if intentional, but Dru, even knowing that they were growing more and more insubstantial by the minute, insisted on going around them rather than through. Even still, the spellcaster could see that he was drawing closer. A few of the lines had already begun to merge. Why he could still not make out his goal nagged him. Only a step or two more. That was all. Only a step or two more.

In this one instance, his thoughts proved all too correct. Dru *did* find the point of intersection... or perhaps it could have been said just as easily that the point had found *him*.

It sprang to life before his very eyes, a huge, pulsating thing of light and darkness. As it swelled, it burned as bright as any sun. As it contracted, it turned as black as the deepest cavern. Dru, his foot raised for his next step, was caught unawares. He twisted in surprise and lost his footing. The ground—both of them—rose to meet his face as he tumbled forward.

Dru felt the padding of wild grass attempt to soften his fall, grass that had not existed in the landscape surrounding the Nimthian ridge.

"Serkadion Man—" The oath died as he looked up and caught sight of the vast mass of energy before him.

The darkness, a black far deeper than that of the forest, was growing faster than its opposite . . . and with each increase in size, the forest faded more.

He had no intention of finding out what would happen to him if he stayed so close. Curiosity was one thing, but in the end survival won out. As he rose, Dru cursed his Vraadish arrogance for leading him to this predicament. There were other ways he could have dealt with this situation, only he had refused to see them, preferring to face the mystery personally. Now, it was possible he would pay for that mistake.

His dignity a moot point, the sorcerer fled the way he had come. This time, he ignored the unsettling presence of the trees and charged through them, hoping deep inside that he would not find one that had, for his benefit, chosen to remain solid. That would end his flight very quickly and very painfully.

The mist was thickening even as the phantom landscape was fading. The trees were no more than shadows now, but the uninviting terrain of Nimth was just as murky. It was as if he were caught in between both of them, yet existed in *neither*. Full panic attempted a coup and was only barely beaten back. Dru stumbled to a halt. So far, he had not been thinking very much and that could prove more treacherous than the mists. Somewhere out there was the cube, his beacon back to reality. All he had to do was feel its presence.

That was *all* he had to do, yet he could not. Seeking out the cube proved no more simple than seeking out his steed. Nothing met his heightened senses no matter which direction he turned. The sorcerer might as well have been buried deep within the earth, so thoroughly was he cut off from everything. Dru could not even sense the lines of force. It was as if he were trapped in some sort of limbo.

He had only one choice. Though something within him warned that Vraad sorcery stood an equal chance of being either his salvation or his *death,* Dru had to make use of the one tool still remaining to him . . . *if* it still remained.

Curling within himself, Dru forced the teleportation spell through. Where once he could have performed it without conscious thought, now he had to complete the spell a bit at a time, urging each successive step on.

Slowly, the last bits of landscape—both Nimth and its wraithlike brother—dwindled to nothing, and only the mist and a peculiar whiteness that seemed like pure *nothing* remained. Dru, his body wracked with pain, did not relax, knowing that he was not safe until he stood on solid earth once more.

"Father..."

Sharissa's voice! Encouraged, the spellcaster pressed harder. In all his existence, he had never struggled so with a spell. The sweat covered his body and every muscle was taut with pain. Only a little more now. . . .

Where had he heard *that* before?

No! he screamed within his own mind. *I will succeed! I will!*

A rocky, wind-torn land abruptly greeted his eyes, almost jarring his senses with its sudden appearance. Never before had Dru thought he would be so happy to see the unfriendly domain of Nimth.

"Father! I'm coming! Hold on!"

Straightening, though every muscle shrieked during the process, Dru saw the tiny figure of his daughter running toward him. He stood, it appeared, in the center of where the field had been. Not his destination, not exactly, but close enough. Just so long as he was free of that other place.

With great relief, Dru put his hands to his face and wiped the sweat away. Blinking the moisture from his eyes, he happened to stare at his palms.

They were fading, already translucent enough that he could see Sharissa through them.

"No!" Something that would not be denied began pulling at him. He felt as if his body were being torn asunder. Nimth...and Sharissa...began to fade away once more.

"Father! Run to me! You're still too cl—"

Her words faded away along with the rest of the world. Dru's eyes flashed this way and that, seeking some object, however tiny, that he could fix on. There was nothing. Even the mist was gone. The only thing remaining was the white emptiness that he had noted briefly during his attempt at teleportation.

Dru now floated alone in that emptiness . . . with *no* idea as to where he was or *how* he could escape.

V

Gerrod kept his head down as he stood by his father, thankful that the bulky cloak he wore covered so much of his body. Barakas could not see—at least Gerrod thought—that his son was trembling.

Rendel would not have been treated with such scorn. That was true as far as it went. Rendel *would*, however, face much worse if he did not contact the clan before long. It was not due to any problem with the spell; Rendel had either left the region where he had crossed over or simply refused to respond.

That had only been the latest thrust. The outsider Zeree's departure—and his refusal to return—were eating at the patriarch as nothing else had. For the first few minutes Lord Barakas had ranted and raved. Then he had fallen into one of his deathly silent moods. Gerrod, who had been the object of his parent's anger more than once, would have preferred the ranting.

"I wonder what he plots?"

The question, the patriarch's first spoken words in over two hours, caught Gerrod and the others assembled by surprise simply because they had all been resigned to waiting in silence for the rest of the evening. That was how things normally went. A change in tradition now meant disaster for someone.

"The outsider?" Gerrod ventured.

"Zeree, yes, who *else*?"

Rendel. Perhaps Ephraim. Are you so blind, Father? The

young Tezerenee wanted to shout at the clan master, but knew what results that would bring.

"You said nothing more to him than what you told me?"

"Nothing of importance, Father." Nothing save his desperate words toward the end.

"Leave it alone, Barakas dear."

The throaty voice belonged to perhaps the only member of the Tezerenee who could dare to speak back to the patriarch. She strode elegantly into the chamber that the clan had usurped from the city as sort of a second throne room. Clad in green scale, a living warrior queen, she stood nearly as tall as Lord Barakas himself. Her face was more striking than actually beautiful, but the grace with which she moved—or even breathed—was such that it added an entire dimension to her that most female Vraad lacked. The newcomer was desirable, but where Melenea had been a temptress, this woman was a queen.

The patriarch moved to take her hand. "Alcia."

Around them, the rest of the Tezerenee, Gerrod foremost, knelt before her in obeisance. Most of the clan whispered, "Lady Alcia."

Gerrod and a few select others simply said, "Mother."

"The others are getting restless out there, Barakas. You might have another duel or dozen if you don't let them enjoy themselves."

"I gave them permission."

"You have dragon riders perched on every roof nearby. *They* don't draw the comfort from them that you do." She smiled through perfect lips, assuring him that she, unlike the Vraad outside, *did* share his appreciation.

"It will be done." Barakas pointed indifferently toward the nearest of his people and snapped his fingers. The appointed messenger rose, bowed to his lord and lady, and vanished. "Where have you been, Alcia? Were you looking for someone?"

"Hardly. I was accosted by that she-devil earlier, though, the one Reegan seems so *fond* of." She stared pointedly at their eldest. Not all of the patriarch's sons were hers, indiscretion a fact of life for beings with countless millennia on their hands, but the heir and Gerrod were. Rendel was also. It sometimes amazed Gerrod that he and Rendel were related to a creature like the burly Reegan.

The heir, titled so only because Barakas felt it necessary to appoint his eldest to such a role, looked sheepish. His lust for Melenea was an open secret with the Tezerenee, made more comical in some eyes by the fact that the temptress could, when she so desired, make him look like nothing more than a great pup. Alcia did not care for her people, especially her offspring, to be made fools of even if they themselves had had a part in the process.

"Have you been outside in the last hour?" Alcia asked her husband.

"No. There have been complications—minor ones—with the various aspects of the cross-over. I've been busy sorting them out."

The Lady Tezerenee tensed. "Rendel! Is something wrong? Has he—?"

"Rendel is fine," the patriarch lied. No one dared to contradict him, although Gerrod was sorely tempted. "He proceeds with his tasks. There's nothing to worry about. You had something you wished to convey to me, however."

"Yes. The city is being buffeted by powerful winds. The protective spells seem to be weakening."

"It's to be expected. *Nimth* is weakening. That's why smooth progression of our work is so important. Gerrod!"

The hooded Tezerenee leaped to his feet and straightened as his father whirled on him. "I await your command."

Barakas looked him over, as if seeking fault. Alcia, on the other hand, beamed proudly. Reegan and the rest might be her husband's, but Rendel and Gerrod were *her* favorites. Unlike most of the clan, she had been born an outsider, and in those two sons, the matriarch saw her identity passed on.

"You seem to get along with Master Zeree fairly well," the Lord Tezerenee commented. "I give you the task of visiting his domain and bringing him back here. It looks bad when one's partner seems...reluctant to be present at the culmination of his work."

"We don't need him, Father!" growled Reegan.

Gerrod smiled from within the shadowy confines of his hood. When Reegan spoke, it was generally to put his foot in his mouth.

"We don't need him!" the heir continued. "The outsider

gave us everything of use! Let him take his place in the courtyard with the rest! Better yet, see that he gets left behind!''

Barakas stood silent for several moments. Then he walked over to his eldest and slapped him across his furred visage. It was a gentle tap, Gerrod noted with some satisfaction. The heir struck the stone floor end first, causing a yard-long crack along the surface. Lady Alcia remained stone-faced throughout the incident.

''He was given the bond of the dragon—*my* bond of honor! Never speak that way again unless I permit you!'' Barakas focused on his younger son. ''Go, Gerrod! Leave now!'' The patriarch's voice was more of a dragon's roar. The young Tezerenee hastened to obey, folding within himself and vanishing from the room instantly, secretly gleeful to have any excuse to be far away from the mad rabble he was forced to call his family.

Emptiness.

What could one do with so much emptiness?

That was the question that pervaded Dru's thoughts as he continued to float helplessly in . . . in . . . this *void*, he finally decided. It was a shorter, more succinct name and, more importantly, had pushed back his boredom for at least a hundred or so breaths.

Breaths. There was no way of telling time here, if time was even a familiar concept in this nondimension. The number of breaths he took was the only way he could make any estimate. Even then, it was tricky, for Dru had discovered earlier that it was not *necessary* to breathe in the *Void*.

He was at a loss as to what to do. Several failed attempts had proven to him the uselessness of Vraad sorcery here. That had come as a shock. Even with all the chaos on Nimth, Dru had never conceived that there might be a time when he had *no* sorcery at his command. There had been times when he had abstained from the use of it, but he had always known the magic was ready should he need it.

In growing desperation, he had tried pushing himself along with his arms and legs, an awkward parody of swimming. There were problems with that, however, chief among them being that it was impossible to tell if he was making any progress. Everything looked the same and he could feel nothing on his face. He soon gave the attempt up. Where was there to go, even if he was moving? There was nothing to see from his position save for *more* nothing.

A part of him did marvel at this place, however. The realm beyond the veil had been amazing enough, but this was truly something the Vraad had never conceived of in all their years. What was the Void? he wondered. Just emptiness? If he had accidentally fallen into it, had others? If so, what had happened to *them?*

With nothing else to do, Dru chose to rest. He was only now feeling the exhaustion caused by his transition from Nimth to this place. Perhaps, the sorcerer hoped, when he was rested he would be able to conceive a feasible plan. Perhaps something in his surroundings would change by the time he woke.

No sooner had he closed his eyes than he opened them again with a start. Suddenly Dru felt refreshed, as if he had slept for hours. The Vraad frowned, puzzled at the change. What could have given him so much energy?

Then a tiny orb floated into his range of vision. It shocked him at first, being the one object other than himself that he had seen, but then he recognized it as one of his own possessions. As he retrieved it, he noted other objects from his pockets. They all floated in lazy fashion about his person. Two questions were answered then. He *was* moving, albeit at an incredibly slow rate, else his belongings would have been scattered farther apart. He had also *slept,* yet there had been no feeling of time passage. It dawned on Dru then that he might float here for the rest of . . . of *whatever* . . . with only sleep to entertain him.

It was a Vraadish version of hell.

One by one the sorcerer retrieved his errant possessions, studying each in turn in the hopes of finding something that would aid him in his escape from this horrible place. They were all useless trinkets now, even the ones that had once been his most powerful tools. Everything he had derived from Vraad sorcery . . . and he could not touch upon that here, it seemed.

In a fit of anger, he took a hand mirror, once used for scrying but now only sufficient for staring at his frustrated features, and threw it from him. To his horror, while the mirror went one way, *he* went the opposite. Not far at first, but far enough so that the remainder of his escaped items were now out of reach.

The horror was quickly exchanged with an almost childlike glee. He *could* travel. There might not be anything to find, but at least Dru now knew that he could explore. His exploring was limited, however. Waving his arms did little to keep him moving; throwing an object in the opposite direction—a *nebulous* term at best—was the only way to assure himself of momentum.

Reaching into one of his voluminous pockets, he pulled out the orb that had originally begun the present chain of events. It was no more than a piece of metal now, but one that should start him on his way. Using the other floating trinkets as his means of perspective, the sorcerer threw the orb. His momentum was not great, but he slowly returned to somewhere very near his earlier position. Utilizing the cloak he wore, Dru scooped up as many of the other pieces as he could. He might need them later.

The drifting spellcaster's present course took him nowhere in particular, which was the only place to go in the Void. Nonetheless, he now had purpose. As he floated, an act he more or less had to assume, he kept watch for something, anything, that might also exist here.

His euphoria passed into boredom again without one change in his surroundings. Dru could not say whether he had been floating for a very long time, but he knew that more than a thousand breaths had passed before he lost count. Still his eyes were greeted with nothing, great and endless quantities of nothing. There was nothing as far as the eye could see. Dru wondered if he would know when he finally turned completely mad at the sight . . . if one could call emptiness a sight.

Then, an object in the distance caught his eyes. It was only a speck, but, in so much emptiness, it stood out like a glittering crystal beacon. Dru discarded another of his items and altered his direction. Perspective was a problem, he realized. The object might be very close and very small or it might be far, far away and larger than his castle of pearl.

More than two hundred breaths passed before he was close enough to make out what it was. Deep disappointment vied with the simple pleasure of actually touching something else.

It was a rock. A jagged, brown rock that looked as if it had been torn from some hillside.

Through sheer luck, he had aimed himself near enough so that the rock would pass within arm's reach of him. As the two of them closed the gap, Dru stretched his left arm out, intending on taking hold of the object and using it to send him in another direction.

He caught the rock . . . and was sent *spinning* away madly, his arm *twisted* back and wracked with mind-piercing pain. The rock continued on its oblivious way.

Despite the agony, the calculating portion of Dru's mind knew what had happened. He had assumed, because it seemed to float so serenely, that the massive stone had been moving slowly. Not so. The Void had played him for a fool. Perhaps the rock had been falling when it entered this place; he could not be certain. Dru only knew that what he had tried to catch had been moving faster than the swiftest steed, so fast, in fact, that it had *broken* his arm.

It was an arm that would remain broken, too, for he had no sorcery with which to repair it.

With deliberate effort, he forced himself to put the broken limb back in place. It was a difficult enough task, what with the unceasing spin. Dru screamed readily, unashamed to do so since no one would hear him. Pain gripped him without pause. Once he had the arm back the way it should have been, he pulled off his cloak and turned it into a sling of sorts.

The pain still rocked him, but Dru knew he would have to live with that. His next quest was to cease his twirling before he grew too dizzy. The arm was draining his strength too much already.

How could he stop himself? Dru reached into his pocket, but the angle at which he was spinning made it an awkward movement that in turn put pressure on his broken limb. The Vraad screamed again and nearly passed out.

"It does! It makes sounds! Loud ones!"

The voice seemed to boom within his head. Through tear-drenched eyes, Dru hurriedly scanned his vicinity. More nothing, yet . . . he had heard a voice. *Felt* was perhaps just as good a description, but the point was that he was not alone.

So where was the other?

"Hello, little one! Do you talk? I am coming to you!"

"Where?" the sorcerer managed to choke out. His arm was on fire now; at least, that was how it felt.

"You *do* talk! Patience, patience! This one is not far!"

Dru screamed once more, but not because of pain. He screamed now because the emptiness to his right had suddenly burst into a huge, ever-shifting field of darkness. His first thought was that it was the point of intersection and he had somehow been drawn back to it. Then it shifted form, as if an inky liquid. It was no liquid, however; Dru, staring at it, felt himself seem to fall toward the thing, as if it were a bottomless pit and he had been thrown into it. Fear battled with pain.

The massive blot changed form again, solidifying a bit. The falling sensation passed.

"There! That is better!"

"What—what's better?" He could still see no sign of the newcomer. Was the blot his method of travel? Is that why Dru had felt he could fall into it? Hope for an escape from the Void stimulated him. "Where are you?"

"Here! Where else is there, little voice?"

"But..." The sorcerer's gaze narrowed on the inky darkness through which he had expected the other to enter. "Are you ... is that ..."

This time, he saw the darkness quiver. "You are a funny thing! I will not have you join with me yet!"

The blot was no path, save perhaps to *death*. It was, despite Dru's inner protest, a living *thing*. *It* was the voice he had heard in his head.

"What do you mean about 'joining with you'?"

The sensation of falling into the darkness overwhelmed him once more. It lasted only a moment, however. That was far and away more than enough for Dru. It was all he could do to keep from passing out.

"I have not taken from you, have I? You seem to be less than whole." The thing sounded annoyed, as if it had underestimated itself.

"My arm ... this"—he indicated the broken appendage—"I injured it badly."

"Injured?"

Did this monstrosity not comprehend pain? the sorcerer wondered. Perhaps not. How could one harm a blot?

"It does not work properly."

"Silly little voice! Take it in and make another!"

Now it was Dru who did not comprehend again. "Take it in?"

"As I." A crude limb formed, little more than a narrow bit of darkness. It stretched forth for nearly a yard, then slowly sank back into the primary mass of the blot. "How else?"

Dru shook his head, partly in response and partly because it kept him conscious. "I cannot do what you do and the way I heal does not work here."

"Too bad! Would you prefer I take you now? You will no longer know pain."

"*No!*"

"Your voice grows! I must *try* that!" The blot commenced with a variety of sounds, some higher and some lower than what so far had passed for its voice. Dru did not interrupt; if such entertainment took the creature's mind from the prospect of devouring him, then so much the better. As it was, the agony continually raking through his system was making it impossible to think of any other way to save himself.

The ever-shifting creature's interest in the noises it was making soon waned. "Not so much fun after all! Tell me, one of many voices, why you cannot do like I do?"

It took Dru a moment to realize his unnerving companion was speaking of the broken arm again. "I am a man. A Vraad. We can shift our forms, but not like you and not without sorcery."

"What is sorcery?"

This creature did not know what sorcery was? The Vraad was astonished. Based on what little he had already seen, Dru was certain that the entity was part inherent magic itself. How else to explain its existence and its method of travel?

If he could somehow get it to take him back to Nimth . . .

"It's . . ." Pain made him grimace. "It's an ability that allows one to change things about them."

"What is there to change? With the exception of curious little entertainments—like you—all is as it always is."

Dru shook his head. "Not where I come from. If I was

there, for instance, I could make this arm work properly again. I could make the hair on my head''—he indicated each part of his body that he spoke of in case the creature did not understand—''so long that it would go down to my knees.''

''Is *that* all? I know this 'sorcery'!''

''So I thought. Tell me—do you have a name?''

''Name?''

''I am Dru. Dru is my name. If we had a third voice with us and he wanted to speak to me but not you, he would say something like 'I will speak with Dru.' '' The explanation sounded weak to the sorcerer, but it was the best he could do. Unconsciousness was becoming more and more inviting and he did not dare let that happen until he was certain he would wake up again.

The mass of darkness grew and shrunk, twisted and reshaped itself. Several breaths passed before it finally replied. ''I am 'I' or 'Other.' ''

''No . . .'' Dru held his forehead as he tried to think. ''That's not what . . . not what . . .''

''Come! This is too interesting! Do not fade away!''

The Vraad shrieked as raw power filled his being. He felt both omnipotent and helpless. The world was at his beck and call, yet he was the lowest form of existence. Pain and rapture tossed him from one to another like a rag doll.

He was suddenly himself again and the initial sensation was like striking the earth after falling from the highest peak. When that had passed, Dru found himself feeling stronger and more alive than he had ever felt before. The amazed spellcaster undid the makeshift sling; his arm was whole again!

''You were saying I could not be called 'I'! Why is that?'' Dru flexed the arm. It was perfect. ''You did this?''

''You did not finish explaining this thing about names and I thought I would help if I gave to you a little of I!''

''Thank you.'' His mind as clear of fog as the Void was of everything but itself, Dru asked a question that had just occurred to him. ''How is it we can speak? Are you—?''

''We speak because I *wished* to speak! That is nothing! I want to know about names!'' The darkness shifted menacingly.

The entity had somehow picked at his surface thoughts, the sorcerer suspected, and learned the language of the Vraad instantly in that way. Yet, it did not understand many concepts, which either meant that it lacked the power to delve deeper or it had not wanted to damage him. Dru was willing to bet on the latter.

"Perhaps I shall take you now."

"Names!" Dru shouted with such vehemence that the living hole shifted away despite its obvious superiority. "What do you want to know?"

"Know? I *want* a name! Can I be *Dru* also?"

"That wouldn't do for you." A huge, living pit of darkness bearing *his* name! It might have been humorous if his predicament had not been so tense.

"What, then?"

What, indeed? If he could give the creature some name it found entertaining enough, it might reward him by helping to find a way out of here . . . providing there *was* one.

Descriptions! Descriptions were always a good starting point! "Let's draw a name from the way you look and act."

"I act like me!"

"But what are you? Powerful, ever-changing, dark, compassionate . . ." Dru trailed off, hoping his strange companion would pick up on the flattery while it pondered what it wished to be called. At this point, ingratiating himself in any way to the shifting horror seemed his only hope.

"I am all that and more, but 'Powerfuleverchangingdark' is too long a name for my tastes! I want something short, like you have!"

The sorcerer was willing to just fling names at the monster and let it pick one, but he suspected that such an act might just bore the entity into forgetting the entire thing. If that happened, the blot might decide it was time to absorb him.

The mass of darkness pulsated, evidently pondering its choices so far. Apparently unable to come to any decision, it flowed nearer to the hapless mage and said, "I see only me! I cannot describe me! Give me more to choose from!"

Dru took a deep breath. Much of what he would have liked to have said would probably stir the dark creature to anger. Still, it might pick up on *something*. . . . "I was not whole when you first came to me, so my thoughts were muddled . . . there was a burst . . . the darkness was suddenly there before me . . . where there had only been emptiness before.'' The nebulous form was still. ''I thought you were a hole yourself, an emptiness that led to . . . to a place far from where I float now. I—''

''I *like* that! That will be my name!''

''Your name?'' Already? What had he said?

''Not so short as yours, but I am more than you! It has good, strong sounds!''

After a brief moment of soul-searching, the Vraad dared ask, ''What *is* your name now?''

''I am the *Darkness!* Does it not ring with me?''

''Ring with . . .'' Dru could not help smiling. ''Darkness is truly a good name for you!''

Darkness shifted form again and again, openly gleeful about its new possession. ''A name! I have a name! It is a good thing!''

''No one can take it from you, either. No matter what they do it will always be yours.'' The sorcerer was reminded of Sharissa as a tiny child. The blot—*Darkness,* Dru corrected himself—was as much an infant as a godlike entity.

Sharissa. Thinking of her made Dru double his efforts now to gain his odd companion's aid.

''I've helped to give you that name, Darkness,'' he pointedly reminded the other. ''Will you give *me* something now?''

''You wish to be taken? Very well—''

''I do *not* wish to be taken! No, I want you to help me find my way home. You have the power, don't you?''

Swelling, Darkness responded, ''I can do anything . . . and if *I* cannot, then Other I can!''

Dru puzzled over the being's words. '' 'Other I'?''

''The one from which Darkness was formed, of course!''

''Of course.'' The sorcerer decided not to press, suspecting he would not care for the answer.

''So tell me . . . . Dru . . . what 'home' is.''

Another concept his companion did not understand. ''Home is where I came from, where I stay when I am not doing anything—hmmm—where I was *made*.'' He spread his arms wide. ''The Void is your home, though you were only made in one particular portion of it.''

An appendage rose from the creature's disturbing form. It came toward Dru, pausing only a foot or two from him. To his surprise, part of it folded away, revealing . . . an *eye*. It was an ice-blue eye with no pupil and a stare that made the Vraad turn away before he became lost in it. Darkness pulled the ghastly eye away, using it to scan their very meager surroundings.

"This is called the Void? I did not know that!"

Dru was beginning to have visions of floating for the rest of his existence, trying to fight his way through a convoluted conversation with something that half of the time viewed him as a meal. "Do you understand what I mean?"

Stentorian laughter nearly deafened the mage. He put his hands to his ears, but the effect that had was less than negligible. The laughter went on and on until Dru thought his ears would burst. Then, as quickly as it had begun, the raucous sounds died.

"That was entertaining!"

"What . . . was?"

"I got bored listening to this voice so I thought I would listen to your other one as well! It says such humorous things! Fright is a fun thing! Do I frighten you much?"

Piecing together the full situation from the mad comments of Darkness, Dru realized that the unnerving creature had chosen to spy upon his thoughts. It now knew of the sorcerer's fear and desperation. There was no saying how deep the probe had been, but it had been deep enough.

There was no sense lying . . . for now. As he worked to shield future thoughts, Dru answered, "Yes, you frighten me very much, Darkness! You remind me too much of what my kind are like, what I was once like! You could swallow me up with hardly a care! You've invaded my mind! Shouldn't I be frightened?"

To his surprise, the entity contracted until it was only half its original size. The eye stalk sank back into the depths from which it had come. "I did wrong, it seems. I understand that now. I understand more, having listened to your inner voice." Darkness *sighed*, a sound so human that Dru could only stare in astonishment. "I will help you however I can to take you home."

"Thank you."

Darkness grew jubilant again. "So, my little friend! Where is it?"

Dru had been so desperate to get this far that he had not even thought about what to do when the moment came. "It's . . ." He paused. How could he explain to Darkness what he himself did not understand. "I . . . wasn't prepared when I was thrown here."

The inky blot laughed again, albeit much quieter this time. The sorcerer silently thanked him for the sake of his ears. "You are such an entertaining little Dru! Are all Drus like you?" Before the Vraad could explain how names worked, Darkness continued, "Give me access to your inner voice again! Let me experience your arrival again!"

It made sense to let Darkness survey his memories of the incident, but Dru could not help feeling as if the creature might tear his mind apart seeking those particular memories. They were not surface thoughts; they were conscious and subconscious impressions that even under the best of circumstances the Vraad would have been hard-pressed to recall.

"Come, come! Are you afraid of *me?* I am *gentle!*"

Shuddering, Dru finally nodded. When there was no reaction from his amorphous companion, he realized that Darkness did not know what the nod meant and quickly added, "Go ahead. Do it."

He expected the worst. He waited for the blot's probing to wrack his mind. Dru waited for something, *anything,* but felt only his own heart as it beat anxiously.

"But this is *fascinating!* Unbelievable! I must see these things! So much . . . so much *filled* Void! How do you stand being so *cluttered?* How can you not feel squeezed together?" As Darkness spoke, his shape contracted farther until he was only a little larger than the floating spellcaster. There was awe in his thunderous tones, awe at the existence of so many things, so many *solid* things.

Dru feared that the blot had experienced too much, was no longer able to cope with the situation, but that was dispelled when Darkness suddenly expanded again, growing and growing and *growing* . . . until it seemed he—*he?*—would fill the entire Void with his ebony self.

"I *must* go there! I must go with you! The *forms!* The . . . the . . ." Darkness apparently had no words for many of the things he had experienced in Dru's head. The Vraad made a note of that; his nebulous friend was not perfect.

"Can you find a path out of here?"

"To be sure! Can you not feel the many ways? Can you not feel the paths that cross through here? There are endless choices, though some I will avoid since you are so fragile! I think I know the best way!"

Hope sprang to full life within the breast of the sorcerer. Freedom would soon be his! At the moment, it mattered not to him that his freedom would also mean letting the creature sorcerer loose upon Nimth. Darkness was no worse a threat to the world than the Vraad race had ever been, and with power once more his to command, he believed that he could hold his own against the black entity.

His thoughts were interrupted by yet another change in his unnerving companion. Darkness was contracting again, but now his form was also shifting. More and more, he resembled a crude black mouth, like the maw of some huge beast. The maw was disturbingly close to Dru and was getting closer with each passing breath.

"Darkness! Wait! What are you *doing?*"

Did the mouth actually smile? "Have no fear, little Dru! I am only making myself into a form that will be able to carry you! I will not, as you constantly fear, take from you! You have given me too much entertainment and I owe you! In fact, I owe you for an entire existence! To think of all that solidity together!"

Closing his eyes and gritting his teeth, Dru waited for the creature to envelop him. When he felt nothing, the sorcerer dared look.

"Serkadion Manee!" He floated in the center of a huge bubble in which there was no light save two pinpricks of an ice-blue color. There had been no feeling of transition, no sense of being swallowed whole. He breathed a sigh of relief, then nearly choked when the two blue dots swelled and became a very real pair of glittering eyes that lacked pupils.

"You are whole?"

"Yes . . . yes. Thank you."

"You will be cushioned in here. I will let you see how we travel. Perhaps you will be able to do it yourself . . . should you need to, that is." Darkness's understanding of the Vraad language was becoming stronger and stronger. Except for an excess of formality, he spoke as well as any Vraad.

The bubble began moving; Dru knew this only because Darkness *informed* him of the fact. The sorcerer tried to brace himself for anything, then realized the futility of the attempt. What could he do, lacking power as he did?

For a long time—several hundred breaths, by Dru's count—nothing happened. The Vraad watched as emptiness was replaced by more emptiness. His companion spoke little during that period, a sign that this was a tense situation even for the nearly omnipotent creature. Safe and secure within, Dru began to wonder more about the thing now calling itself by so apt a title as Darkness. Was it a demon of legend? Serkadion Manee's books had mentioned the summoning of such spirits, but no Vraad living now had ever succeeded in summoning them. It had long ago been assumed that demons were either the products of great imagination or golems of fanciful design. Yet, his companion certainly fit the descriptions of a demon.

Could it be, Dru pondered, that some being much like Darkness had been the truth behind the legends?

He was never able to answer his question, for in the next breath, Dru collapsed, his mind suddenly a chaotic cornucopia of intense sensations. Pain, happiness, fear, sadness, indifference, anger... he went through each emotion in the blink of an eye. Other feelings that he could not exactly identify intermingled with the rest. The Vraad crawled to his knees and put a hand to his head. Darkness said nothing, but the bubble that was his form trembled constantly. The sorcerer fell again, but struggled forward even still. His eyesight was blurred, giving him liquidy images of the same emptiness that he had become so sick of and—

And was there something out there now?

Still Darkness did not speak, but Dru knew that the "demon" did not have the effort to spare for such a minuscule thing as conversation. His unearthly companion had located what appeared to be the way out of the Void and the two of them were even now breaking through. The emptiness had finally been replaced, but by *what* was hard to say for certain.

It looked very much like a pale path of light... a path that, when Dru looked behind them, seemed to run on into infinity. Ahead of them was a different tale. The path continued on for some distance—as well as the Vraad could judge—but then faded away slowly until it became—Dru forced his eyes to focus—until it became a mist *very* much akin to that which had blanketed the wraithlike forest.

"Free!" the sorcerer hissed without realizing it.

His joy turned to panic as the path before them suddenly split into one and then countless identical paths that turned in all directions and faded away in the same manner as the first. Which one led to *his* world, the Vraad fretted silently, and *where* did the others go?

One path that Dru did not want Darkness taking was a single path that appeared to curl within itself like some perpetual double loop. It was exceedingly inviting, for reasons that Dru could not define, yet it also filled him with a sense of mortality, of the death that had nearly claimed him. He breathed a sigh of relief when his companion ignored it.

At some point, the overwhelming assault on his brain had ended. Dru hardly felt comforted by that fact, faced with what seemed the impossible task of choosing a path.

"So many..." he whispered. To Darkness, the hapless sorcerer quickly asked, "Do you know which one?"

The icy orbs stared at him in resolute silence. Whatever decision Darkness had come to, the Void dweller had chosen not to include the tiny, insignificant human in it. Perhaps that was for the best, but Dru could not help feeling a bit of Vraadish indignation at the exclusion.

They alighted onto one of the paths.

Around them, the others faded completely away.

Darkness had made his decision and there was no time to turn back. Already, the incredible creature was nearing the mist. Dru closed his eyes, hoping that a repeat of the onrush of sensations was not in the offing. Hoping, too, that they would not be destroyed or, worse yet, left again marooned in the midst of the hellish Void, this time with the knowledge that there *was* no escape.

Absorption by Darkness would be preferable to an eternity here.

They plunged into the mist . . . and a tear—a literal *rip* in the emptiness—opened wide before them. Dru waited for some horrific assault on his mind and body. It never came. A brilliant glow temporarily blinded him.

"Through!" Darkness laughed gleefully, a child who had

succeeded in some great task his parent had set for him. "I am Darkness! I am truly amazing!"

Dru made no attempt to argue with him. He only wanted to step onto the scarred surface of Nimth and take his daughter into his arms. At this point, he was even willing to take Barakas in his arms. Anything, so long as he was free again . . . and once more a mighty Vraad.

"Such a wonderful place! Are all these green things the trees that I learned of from your inner voice?"

Green things? Trees?

Dru frantically pressed himself against the clear body of his "demonic" savior and peered at the world to which he had been brought.

Trees, hundreds of trees, a vast forest, greeted his eyes. A mountain range stood proud in the background.

A resplendent blue sky completed an image of beauty and tranquility.

"So overwhelming! Nimth is truly a wonderful place!"

The Vraad could not respond. In his desperation to be free of the Void, he had forgotten of the two lands, the two worlds, buried in his memories. Darkness, as was his way, had dug only so far into those memories . . . and had pulled up the most recent, the most vivid.

The *wrong* ones.

Darkness had brought him to the other side of the veil . . . and to the shrouded realm.

VI

It had taken Rendel far longer than he had supposed it would to reach the outskirts of the immense mountain chain. His barely constrained impatience, however, had gradually been supplanted by an even more virulent emotion—anger.

None of his spells worked as they should. Oh, they did what he wanted them to do, but generally to a lesser degree. They also had a tendency to fail the first time, as if the something did not *want* the spells completed. His growing distrust had forced him to walk the entire trip and suffer the effects of an unbroken world. Rendel stared with arrogant distaste at the scenery around him. It was pretty, yes, but hardly interesting, especially after having seen so much of it. Someday soon, though, he and the others would subdue the Dragonrealm and make it as it *should* be.

By now, Rendel thought, choosing a rock upon which to sit for a moment, his father and the others knew he had abandoned the plan. Barakas had probably taken much of his anger out on Gerrod, but the pale-haired Vraad could do nothing about that. That was what his younger brother was for, taking the brunt of things. Rendel liked Gerrod as much as he liked *any* of his brothers, sisters, and cousins—which was not *that* much at all—but, in the end, it was his own concerns that mattered. And was that not what his father had always taught them?

Rendel had his own agenda, one only he was privy to. The Lord Tezerenee had always been bringing up the outsider, the fool Zeree, as the one most knowledgeable about the ka and the nature of the realm beyond the veil. Never had the patriarch really asked his son if he knew more than he said. Rendel knew *far* more, having studied greatly in secret. Each sighting had been personally visited, albeit surreptitiously. Each phantom land had been carefully mapped. Each had been scanned for anything out of the ordinary...or perhaps it was best to say anything out of the extraordinary, for even Rendel had to admit that as a whole the Dragonrealm was truly different from his Nimth. Trouble was, most of it had no place in his grand designs.

Eyeing the first intrusion of night in the early evening sky, the Vraad cursed the time differences between Nimth and the Dragonrealm. Three days of walking and now the setting sun reminded him again that he had to push on before the trek became too treacherous. Until he had a better grasp of the intricacies involved in utilizing his powers, he would keep their use to a minimum. That meant facing an even harder walk than the one he had just completed. Yet, if he persevered—and

Rendel had confidence in his ability to eventually turn every situation to his own advantage—then all his plotting would have been worth it.

In the mountains, he knew, there was a place he could rest, a place where he could attend to his needs, and begin to carve out a domain of his own, one that would equal, nay, *surpass* his father's and all the rest. One where Rendel could at last be *alone*.

Inspired, the Vraad rose from his resting place, ready to continue even if it meant wandering through the dark of night. Only a little farther and the cavern he had discovered, along with all its treasures, would be his.

His higher senses chose that moment to warn him of the closing presence of one or more creatures. Rendel whirled and studied the trees he was leaving behind. The damnable forest. All throughout his journey, he had felt the eyes upon him. Not merely the eyes of beasts, but ones belonging to other observers, observers who succeeded in staying beyond his reach. They had let him be so far, but he knew that was about to end. Rendel did not fear them. Even with his abilities hampered as they were, he was still a Tezerenee . . . and a Vraad, of course. There was nothing more potent than that combination. His kind had conquered and broken one world; the Dragonrealm would be no different.

The grandiose visions forming in his mind were shattered by the fluttering of massive wings all about him. Rendel summoned a fiery staff, then summoned it *again* when the first attempt gained him nothing but smoke. Simultaneous with his spell, the rock he had been sitting on *melted*. Rendel grinned at the feeble attempt on his life and took a step toward the trees. Large things flittered about the treetops, but always just out of sight. His watchers had finally chosen to come for him. He would make them regret that decision.

Raising the flaming staff high, the Vraad put both hands at the center and twirled his weapon around and around, building speed as he did. When the staff was little more than a blur, tiny balls of fire shot forth in every direction. Treetops became orange infernos in a matter of seconds. If his adversaries would hide from him, then he would just remove their cover.

As the seconds passed, he heard no shrieks and saw no

winged figures fleeing from the damage he had caused. The fire continued to spread, reaching other trees through intermingling branches. If left unchecked, it would likely spread throughout the entire forest. Rendel was unconcerned about that; all that mattered was mastering his unseen companions.

Then, as swiftly as the fire had grown, it began to die. The sorcerer glared at the treetops as, one by one, the flames were snuffed out by magical forces. Rendel swore. This was not how it should have gone. The staff had always been one of his favorite and most potent devices. The magical flames were stronger, more resistant to counterspells or even natural attacks, like wind and water. They should not have died out so easily. Rendel had underestimated his foes.

Dismissing his staff—which, as it happened, coincided with the withering of a pair of trees to his left—the Tezerenee folded his arms and gazed intently at the area where he had heard the rustling of wings. He stood motionless, forcing his will upon the world, taking from it what he needed for *this* assault.

A wind rose. It was a light breeze in its infancy, but Rendel pushed it beyond that. From breeze it became a prestorm wind, full of vibrant life and shaking even the stoutest of limbs as it coursed through the nearby forest. Still not satisfied, Rendel pushed harder, turning the wind upon itself, making it follow its own tail around and around. Leaves, dirt—anything loose and tiny enough—were swept into the funnel. It continued to grow, a tornado twice as tall as any of the brown and green leviathans it stood among.

Rendel was still not satisfied; he wanted a rampaging maelstrom that would tear the forest out by its roots . . . and with it his shadows.

The unseen watchers had not counterattacked, which to Rendel meant that they had used what they had and were even now cowering in the trees, holding on for dear life. He was slightly curious as to what they looked like, if only because they might prove useful slaves, but it would be just as satisfying if the elemental force he had unleashed tore their limbs from them and battered their bodies into pulp. Rendel had never fought a foe who was not one of his kin or at least one of the other Vraad. The golems and other constructs his clan used in mock combat did not count. His would-be attackers here had been a real, albeit minuscule, threat. The Tezerenee allowed the satisfied smile to spread farther across his face. He felt a growing pleasure at his handling of the brief affair. His had been the *first* conquering blow. His enemies had fallen before him like . . . like leaves in the wind, he decided, laughing.

The maelstrom he had created chose that moment to completely *dissipate*. A brief shower of refuse buffeted the treetops and then nothing was moving. No wind. No birds. No animals. Rendel stood frozen, suddenly uncertain as to *who* commanded the situation now.

The silence was broken at last by a sound already familiar to the stunned Vraad.

A great rustling of wings, as if a score of massive birds were taking to the sky, filled his ears, echoed in his head.

Shadows dotted the clearing around him. Rendel looked up.

Their wingspans were at least the length of his frame. They were vaguely Vraad-shaped, having arms and legs and a narrow torso. How the wings, as long as they were, succeeded in lifting all that perplexed the studious side of Rendel. Sorcery, perhaps. The creatures glided effortlessly to the ground, more than a dozen of them surrounding him. A part of Rendel demanded to know why he was standing here like a fool and not striking. Yet, the Vraad could not push himself to even the slightest of efforts. His only inclination was to gaze upon those who, in his misplaced arrogance, he had thought he could so easily better.

One of the avian beings walked up to him, contempt for Rendel in every movement, every breath. It came within reach and simply matched his gaze. The Tezerenee found he could not turn away from the visage before him. His counterpart opened its sharp, savage beak and squawked something at him. Rendel wanted to shake his head, tell the creature that he could not understand it, but even that seemed hardly worth the trouble. In the back of his head, the same part that had fruitlessly demanded action now informed him bitterly that he was under a spell. He, who had been so confident of his power, had been captured effortlessly by his shadows. Rendel had not even felt the spell.

The avian leader, for that was who he assumed the creature was, leaned closer, cocking its head to one side so as to better observe him. That one eye, inhuman as it was, reminded Rendel all too much of another eye. His father's. In his captors, the Vraad had found a race whose arrogance appeared to match that of his own kind.

Seeming to find nothing of worth in what stood before it, the leader started to turn away. It paused midway, however, and slowly turned back, visibly contemplating something.

A taloned hand shot out toward the startled and helpless Rendel's face. He would have screamed, picturing in his mind what those long, needle-sharp claws would do, but the world—the world he had thought *he* would conquer—suddenly turned into a welcome darkness that enveloped Rendel and took him away to a place where he could hide.

"Eat this, girl."

Sharissa shook her head, not wanting anything from the Tezerenee woman who stood above her. For three days, since the dark one called Gerrod had found her lying near where the rift had last been, she had been a "guest" of the clan of the dragon. For three days, she had been questioned, in order that they might *help* her, yet she had not spoken a word to them. The first two days, the patriarch, a man who made Sharissa shiver when he stared at her, had chalked it down to panic. Why not? Something had happened to her father, something unexpected. What they wanted to know—what the Lord Tezerenee in particular wanted to know—was exactly *what* had happened to him?

Gerrod, who unnerved her with his ghostly appearance, had explained how he had found her there, still sobbing and unable to say anything coherent. It seemed to her that the patriarch frightened his own son as much as he frightened her, for the half-seen Tezerenee continually shrank deeper into the protective folds of his cloak, becoming, by tale's end, little more than a walking piece of cloth.

Lord Barakas had been gruff and his lady had been sweet, caring almost, but Sharissa had said nothing. They did not push her after a certain point, likely because they still wanted, at the very least, the semblance of cooperation between the elder Zeree and the clan. A sudden break between the partners would raise the already strained suspicions of the rest of the Vraad. It pained her to remain silent, since if anyone was capable of aiding her in rescuing her father, it was the clan master. He had the most knowledge of the phantom realm.

The strain of three days of fighting her own fears had taken their toll. She was worn, thin, and unable to think. What was worse was that they would not let her alone, not allow her the needed privacy to work things out. Their "concern," as Lady Alcia had put it, forced them to watch her day and night.

An impatient sigh from her latest guardian stirred her. "Weakling! I'll leave it here. Maybe when you stop blubbering, you'll be able to swallow it...though anyone who can't conjure themselves up a meal on their own..."

Even as the voice faded off, Sharissa knew she was now alone. Like most Vraad, the Tezerenee had little patience for those unable to fend for themselves. Another one would be replacing the snide woman shortly, though, so Sharissa's privacy was temporary, at best.

They are right! Nothing but a weakling! Sharissa scolded herself bitterly. She raised herself to a sitting position and slowly dragged the food over to her. A delicious odor drifted past her nose. There was no denying that the patriarch *was* treating her well—on the surface. What could she do now, however? There was no possibility of leaving the city without a score or more of the Tezerenee, not to mention any exceptionally paranoid Vraad celebrating the coming down below, from noting her departure. Sharissa was uncertain of her father's true present status with the patriarch. Would he send dragon riders after her? Would he actually lay siege to the castle? Even Sirvak, skilled as the familiar was with its master's defenses, would be hard-pressed to keep them out.

"Sharissa Zeree."

A deathly cold wrapped itself about her spine and spread quickly throughout her person.

Gerrod's shrouded figure stood at the doorway. "Are you better?"

He had treated her with nothing but respect and could have been considered harmless in comparison to those others she had met, but Sharissa could not warm to him. Gerrod lived in two worlds, and had hid too many things from even his lord and progenitor. He was, Dru would have said, an outstanding example of Vraad duplicity. Sharissa could feel that even though they had actually spoken very little.

"What do you want?"

Gerrod folded his legs and sat down on empty air. He floated nearer to her, *much* too near for Sharissa's tastes. "This is foolish. Each moment that passes lessens the chances of Master Zeree's survival. *I* know where he must be; I've searched everywhere *else* for him." From the bitterness in his tones, Sharissa guessed that the bulk of the task had, indeed, been foisted upon her visitor. For the first time, she was able to sympathize with Gerrod. "I know he must be across the veil." The half-seen face moved closer. "How did he do it? Tell me."

"It doesn't matter," she finally replied, deciding that a partial truth might aid her. "The way through is no more. He can't come back and no one can go after him."

"Oh?" Gerrod straightened. His glittering eyes, temporarily visible, widened. "Then there *is* a way in which to—?"

Whatever his next words were to have been was something Sharissa would never discover, for one of the countless multitude of armored Tezerenee cousins or brothers materialized between them, anxiety evident in his agitated manner.

"Gerrod. Father wants you! Something—" The newcomer glanced at Sharissa, but appeared to find her of little importance. "Something is amiss! Go to him now!"

The hooded figure shifted, as if about to protest, then gradually sunk deeper within the protective layers of his cloak. "Where is he, Lochivan?"

"Ephraim." It was all the other brother had to say. One moment, both Tezerenee faced each other in uneasy silence, then Sharissa was alone again. The clan of the dragon were not known for their long farewells, she decided.

The patriarch's grand design was in jeopardy. That much was evident from Lochivan's distress and Gerrod's instant compliance at the mere mention of that other name. Sharissa had no proof that there was any connection between whatever the Tezerenee struggled with and the disappearance of her father save that both were tied to the land beyond the veil. Nonetheless, the feeling swept over her that the Vraad were facing something beyond their arrogant plans, beyond, perhaps, their varied and supposedly limitless abilities.

And here she sat, doing *nothing*.

Sharissa had spent most of her brief life secluded from the rest of her race. Dru Zeree, knowing the Vraad as he did—and remembering his own excesses—had wanted his sole child to have nothing to do with the others until he felt she was ready. The only question was, when was that to have been? As skilled as she had become with the use of sorcery, Sharissa was still an infant when it came to dealing with her kind. There had been a few scattered individuals throughout her life, but none who her father had wanted her to know intimately. Only a handful of names came to her from those passersby. One she remembered better than others, so alive had that particular Vraad been. Perhaps . . .

Mistressss?

Sirvak? It was only the second time the familiar had contacted her since the horrifying events at the ridge. The first time, Sirvak had witnessed with her the fading of the forest and her father's last desperate attempt to escape his fate. The familiar had broken contact with her moments after Gerrod had reached her, emphasizing that *it* would reestablish the link. Sirvak distrusted the Tezerenee—all Vraad, in fact—more than even Dru had.

Alone, mistressss?

Yes. Is Father—

The creature silenced her with a mental hiss. *No, mistressss. Masterrrr issss still away.* Sirvak apparently refused to accept the possibility that its master was dead. Sharissa wondered if there was an even stronger link between the magical beast and her father than the one of blood between Dru and herself. *Come home, mistressss.*

What is it?

Hesitation formed a silence that stretched Sharissa's nerves taut. When she could wait no longer, the young Vraad asked again, this time with more emphasis in case the familiar was forgetting *who* she was.

May be a way to find masterrr, mistressss.

She almost shouted out loud, so overjoyed did the startling announcement make her. Sirvak, however, was quick to dampen her spirits before she grew too happy.

May, mistressss! Not certain! Need your guidance!

I'll come instantly! There's no need to wait!

Must not! It was as if her father himself had scolded her. *Must take care. Never trust a Vraad, master always said.*

They're busy with their own problems, she retorted.

The familiar let loose with a mental sigh. *Do as you must then, mistresss. Take care, though.*

Sirvak broke the link.

Rising, Sharissa stepped over to the doorway and leaned outside. The hall was empty. The young Vraad stepped back inside and moved to the sole window of her chambers. Her view overlooked the courtyards where the Vraad still gathered, talking and attempting to outshine one another. The coming had spread to the surrounding lands—as her father had said it usually did, and she could see some of her more flamboyant counterparts showing off. There was now a mountain of glittering diamond beyond the northern walls and a vast lake of *water*— truly a difficult spell, she acknowledged silently—on the eastern edge of the mountain. Beyond, there were flashes and sounds, none of which Sharissa could identify with anything that she had learned.

Dru had spoken of the subdued manner of this, the last coming. Only those with long-standing grudges, like Silesti and Dekkar, were likely to stir things up. Such massive displays of sorcery, however, spoke for the confidence of the Vraad race in the Lord Tezerenee's plans. Everyone understood, at least somewhat, that the more sorcery unleashed, the worse Nimth grew. Already, the sickening green covered the murky sky. It saddened Sharissa to think of what her kind would be leaving behind and she hoped that the new land would not suffer the same.

That was if they ever succeeded in migrating over there.

No one would miss her for some time; Sharissa was certain of that now. Lord Barakas would have his entire clan working to solve whatever disaster had befallen his dreams. He would have no time for her or her father's disappearance. Other than Gerrod, they probably thought he was dead by now, not that *she* had not thought of that herself constantly. With great effort, Sharissa once again pushed the ugly vision from her mind. Sirvak's confidence bolstered her. It had to; it was the only thing she had to lean on.

Sharissa gazed down at the throngs one last time and her eyes caught on a lone figure seeming to watch the rest with barely constrained amusement. She leaned forward, not thinking to adjust her sight accordingly.

As if feeling the eyes upon her, the single Vraad looked up. Sharissa was greeted by a vibrant smile that washed away the terror and distress of the last few days. It was such a wonderful feeling that she could not help being caught up in it. She smiled in return.

In the next breath, Sharissa was no longer alone in the chamber. The other female was with her, reaching out to take her in her arms, ready to comfort the younger woman. Sharissa went to her gladly, knowing that she had found someone with whom she could share her problem.

"You look both distraught and beautiful, dear sweet Shari! What has that beast Barakas been doing to you? Why are you here instead of with your father?"

"Father's in terrible trouble!" Sharissa burst out. It had been so long since the two of them had seen each other, but the feeling of safety and assurance she felt now washed away the years of absence.

"Why don't you tell me all about it," her companion said, smoothing Sharissa's wild, tangled hair. "Then we can see about doing something." Sharissa started to speak, but was cut off. "No, on second thought, let us go elsewhere; too many Tezerenee here for my tastes."

"I was going to go home. Sirvak said I should. He said—"

"Hush! Let us depart for your father's wondrous castle of pearl, then, sweet Shari." The smile broadened, smothering any doubts Sharissa still had. "You'll have to do it, however. Your father lets no one in and I think Sirvak must be the same. So very distrustful."

"Sirvak has no say in what I do," the young Zeree commented defiantly. "If I want you with me, he'll obey."

Melenea stroked Sharissa's hair again. "That's exactly what I *thought*."

VII

"Come, come! I grow bored at this! How long will you dawdle there, little Dru?"

Dru did not answer him at first, still caught up in his thoughts. Day had given way to night—a night *filled* with stars and *two* moons!—and yet the sorcerer was only beginning to comprehend the patterns of the world around him. Unlike Barakas, he had never intended on charging into the phantom domain, uncaring of what obstacles might lay in the immigrants' path. Dru knew that even with the tremendous abilities of the creature who floated beside him, there might be dangers too great to combat. His own powers, while they *had* returned, were unpredictable, even more so than they had of late been back in Nimth.

Shifting form again, Darkness once more tried to berate his companion into movement. Behind the blustery tones were undercurrents of fear and excitement. "You can protest all you want, little Dru, but I *have* brought you home! Even if you cannot remember it, *I* can!"

That was the other thing that kept Dru from moving on, the shadowy blot's insistence that this *was* Nimth. Even after the sorcerer had given Darkness permission to search his memories again, the entity had argued that he had not made an error. Dru had decided not to push too hard; Darkness had an ego as great as his interior, the latter of which seemed to go on into infinity when the spellcaster stared long enough.

Somewhere along the way, Dru had chosen to think of the creature as male. Perhaps it was the deepness of the blot's voice or perhaps it was the overbearing arrogance. In some ways, his companion reminded him of Barakas. Knowing that Darkness could pick up the thought, Dru had buried it deep. He

suspected Darkness already knew how he felt about the patriarch of the dragon clan.

"I want to try something," Dru finally said. "When I'm
through, then we can move on for a short while."

"What is a 'while'?" Darkness pulsated. Despite the light of
the two moons and the stars, the lands around them were barely
visible. Darkness, however, was blacker than the night, so
much so that he almost stood out as a beacon.

Dru knew better than to try to explain time to a creature who
dwelled in a place that itself did not comprehend the concept.
Instead, he concentrated on a tree before him and muttered a
memory-jogging phrase.

The tree should have withered, should have dwindled to a
dry husk and crumbled before his eyes. It did nothing, but a
black death spread across the grass beneath the sorcerer's feet.
He leaped away, forgoing pride for safety.

"Good! Now we can depart!" Darkness rumbled, ignorant
of the failure of the Vraad's spell.

"Wait!"

"What is it *now?*"

Kneeling by the blackened, dead blades, Dru tried to inspect
the damage in the dim illumination. As he had spoken the
fanciful phrase, he had felt the familiar twinge as the essence of
Nimth bowed to his overpowering will, but it had been checked
by a fierce protesting force from the shrouded realm itself.
The sorcerer touched the grass, only to have it disintegrate
into a fine powder. Dru cleared his throat at the thought of
what might have happened if he had remained standing on the
spot.

This world will not bend to us so easily as the last, he
concluded nervously. This was not just spell failure; this was a
battle of wills, so to speak. He already knew that a second or
even a third attempt would gain him the results he had intended, but that was only a pitifully tiny victory. Like Nimth, which
had turned mad from the massive abuses of Vraad sorcery, the
stronger the spell the more this domain would battle back.

Suddenly, a world-heavy weariness swept over the frustrated
Dru. He slumped back, visions of a land swallowing up each
and every Vraad dancing about his tired mind.

The entity Darkness shifted closer to him, the two icy orbs

staring down at him in what the Vraad vaguely recognized as anxiety for the sorcerer's well-being.

"You are fading? You lack essence?"

"I'm tired."

"What *is* that?"

"It means that I must lay for a time in quiet. Probably until after the sun has returned." When that was, Dru had no idea. Time felt different somehow, almost as if the shrouded realm moved more swiftly.

The creature seemed annoyed that nothing else would be accomplished for now, but evidently understood that his tiny associate was lacking in many ways. "What shall I do while you lay down?"

"Remain nearby. I cannot protect myself as I thought I would be able to. I'll have to ask for your aid in case something tries to attack me."

"They would not *dare!* Not while *I* am here!"

Dru winced. "One more thing. *Please* make as little sound as possible while I sleep . . . lay down, that is. It will help me to recover my strength sooner."

"As you wish," Darkness replied in a rumble only slightly less deafening.

The sorcerer grimaced, but consoled himself in the fact that anything nearby would get as little sleep as he did. Still kneeling, he looked around for a more comfortable place to rest. At the moment, he was too tired to trust another spell, yet there was no area around him that looked inviting. Dru sighed and, pulling his cloak tight around him, simply lay down where he was. He wondered briefly at the sudden intensity of his exhaustion, then drifted off.

"Are you rested yet?"

Dru straightened with a start, turning his head this way and that. The sun was just over the horizon and the sounds of the day were already well into their second movement. Gradually, his eyes focused on the huge, ungodly thing next to him.

Darkness was a contrast to all around him, *un*life surrounded by life. Even the period in the Void, where the gigantic horror had been the only thing visible other than the helpless Vraad himself, could not compare to the scene now unfolding before

Dru. Yesterday, he had been so turned around that he had failed to notice it. Now, though, Darkness's disturbing form fairly shouted at him. This was the creature who had befriended him.

"Are we to do *nothing* again? You promised that once you were whole we could move on! I want to see all there is to see! All this solidity!"

The rest had aided in rebuilding Dru's reserves, but not completely. Nonetheless, the sorcerer himself was now eager to move on, if only to get a better idea of what he might have to face. He also wanted to find the way back, something he now knew still existed. At a vague point in his slumber, it had occurred to his unconscious mind that the fact that he could still draw upon his power in Nimth meant that there *was* a gap between the two realms. One of them had to be like the tear that he had fallen prey to. This time, though, he would not run. This time, Dru would make use of the rip in reality.

He stood up and looked the Void dweller straight in the two pupilless eyes. "Let us go."

"At last!" Like a child unleashed from his studies, Darkness bounded forward, a hole of black space frolicking among the trees. Dru heard the frightened cries of birds and watched as many flew into the sky at insane speeds. In the woods themselves, small animals departed with equal haste.

Both amused and dismayed by the entity's antics, the spellcaster followed close behind.

Dru had tried to map as carefully as he could the translucent sightings, but none that he had studied resembled this one; though, being in a forest, it was possible that he just did not recognize where he was yet. He supposed it did not really matter save that he was interested in locating Rendel and the Tezerenees' point of arrival. Dru imagined the countless dragon-borne golems, a sea of still, blank-visaged beings who contained no true life of their own, who were merely vessels for the migrating Vraad. The sorcerer shuddered. If—*no*—*when* he found the way back, the Tezerenee plan would be abandoned. Barakas might still desire to cross and seize control of a body, if only because of their draconian origins, but none of the others would.

"Something watches us."

"Where?" Dru could sense nothing, but he knew how faulty his senses might be.

"It is gone now." Had he shoulders, Darkness would have shrugged off the incident.

Dru would not allow that. "What was it? Where did it go?"

His nebulous companion seemed more interested in a stream that was just coming into sight ahead of them. Darkness had never seen water and was visibly attracted to its fluid nature. Dru was forced to repeat himself, this time in much more demanding tones.

"It was Dru-sized! How does this solid move as it does? It seems almost like me! Look how it races and shapes itself! It went away. It was there and then it was not there."

It took the Vraad a moment or two to understand that the latter portions of the creature's comments were in response to his question. "The watcher simply vanished?"

"Yes, yes!" Darkness moved closer to the water. A rough limb extended from its central mass. The limb dipped into the water. "What a truly fascinating sensation! This is the most fun yet! Come feel it, little Dru!"

Dru glanced around, wondering where the unknown watcher had vanished to after its discovery by Darkness. He wished he had asked the entity to alert him more cautiously about intruders. He wished he could trust his own senses better.

Water splashed all over the sorcerer. Darkness was tossing the clear liquid about, awed at how it allowed itself to be scattered all over the area and yet seeming to re-form in the steam. Dru was reminded once more of how childlike the astonishing creature actually was. No, he thought, it would never do to thrust Darkness among the other Vraad. His innocence would be his downfall.

Shaking his head and momentarily putting his present worries aside, Dru wandered over to the stream and kneeled down to drink. He cupped his hands and swallowed mouthful after sweet, cool mouthful, allowing it to dribble down his chin and onto his gray clothing. To his left, Darkness stopped playing, now interested in the novel entertainment his tiny companion was performing for him.

"You are *taking* it within you! I did not know you could do that! We are much alike!"

Dru paid him no mind. With the acknowledgment of his thirst, he was forced to acknowledge his great hunger as well.

It stunned him to think that he had not thought of either since arriving here, almost as if he had not, until his first drink, actually been a part of this realm. The spellcaster stood, eyeing the forest around him. It appeared much more real now; his higher senses now functioned more as they should have. He could even sense the passage that the unseen watcher had taken when it had departed. Darkness had been correct; it *had* vanished. What it was, however, remained a mystery.

Aside from hunger, other functions were now demanding their due. Dru spent more than an hour near the stream, the bulk of time involving the picking of berries from a lengthy expanse of bushes and fruit from a tree overshadowing the stream just south of his original location. Darkness took everything as part of his continual game of discovery, much to the Vraad's annoyance.

When he was at last ready to depart, Dru had a destination in mind. The intruder had been in the woods to the north and the stream originated from somewhere in the same direction. That meant that there might be civilization there. There was also a distant chain of mountains that Dru hoped *might* be the ones Barakas had mentioned once or twice. Rendel would be there, directing efforts on this side of the veil, so the tall Vraad assumed.

Their journey that day was uneventful, something Dru felt very grateful about. While he walked, the sorcerer continually investigated the binding structure of this world. With his higher senses, he surveyed the lines of force running gridlike throughout everything. It was a much more basic, more stable pattern than Nimth's spirals, stronger, too. This was indeed a world that would resist the coming of the Vraad.

A chill wind came up at that point, a wind in Dru's mind. The uncomfortable idea of a land consciously resisting outside invaders stirred. He shook his head, trying to rid himself of such a mad concept. The idea retreated, but did not leave. Dru threw himself back into the trek and his studies and was able to at least temporarily bury the unnerving theory.

Surprisingly, it was Darkness who called for a halt as the sun neared the evening horizon. The entity was unusually subdued. "I would have us stop here, Dru."

The sorcerer was all for stopping himself—the berries and fruit from the stream insufficient for an entire day's activity—

but he wondered at his huge companion's change of attitude. "Is there something wrong, Darkness?"

"I must..." The creature was at a loss for the proper words. "This form is not right for this world. I do not fit in. I am not part of the world."

It was the same feeling Dru had had earlier, but he had not thought Darkness would suffer from anything similar. "What do you plan to do?"

"I think...I think it will be as close to your sleep as I can come. I wish to make myself over into something acceptable."

"How long will it take?"

The blot pulsated. "I cannot say. I have never done anything like this...ah, how your land affects me! I never want to return to the foul emptiness again!"

That was the last Darkness spoke. As the Vraad watched, the huge, pulsating hole drew within itself, becoming more compact. The sorcerer had had enough trouble dealing with a hole that also had mass; he wondered what new miracle Darkness would present to him...and how long it would take. With the creature's notions of time, or lack thereof, it might be years before the transformation completed itself. Dru could hardly wait years, but his companion had not given him an opportunity to say so.

He had no choice, anyway, not now. Whatever Darkness had decided to do, he was doing it. Dru was left to fend for himself and hope that the wait would not be for the rest of his life.

It occurred to him then how much he had come to depend on his unusual ally, both for protection and *friendship*.

Food became his own priority. He wanted something solid, something that would give him the energy he needed. Throughout the day's travels, he had picked at berries that seemed safe enough. There was no denying the bounty of this land. It was merely a matter of the Vraad taking what he wanted, and that was surely an easy enough thought for one who had grown up on that very principle. It had only been his uncertainty that had prevented him from attempting sorcery. Now, however, Dru was willing to take risks, if only because his stomach now controlled his reactions.

His first thought was to merely conjure up a sumptuous feast, table and wine included, but a part of his mind fairly shrieked at such a wasteful display of power. It was a sensation that Dru had felt ever since his arrival here, but not to such a degree. He dropped the notion instantly, suspecting that it would not have worked out the way he wanted it to, regardless.

"Am I to starve, then?" he muttered. His mind turned to other methods. Perhaps it was the intensity of his sorcery that created the problem. If so, the safest use of his power might be a mere summoning spell, something that would allow him to bring a bird or small animal near enough so that he could capture and kill it. Dru could not cook, but he hoped that a second minor spell would prepare his feast for him. He grimaced at the image of himself physically preparing a bird for eating. No Vraad dirtied themselves with such menial tasks, but then, no Vraad had ever been in his position before. If it came down to it, he would do what he had to do; that was one Vraadish conceit Dru adhered to.

The first elements of the spell went smoothly. Dru worked slowly, hoping that by doing so he would ease his spell into completion. Then, the resistance began, first softly, then harder as the Vraad lost his patience and began to batter it. A wind rose, but Dru scarcely noticed it.

The summoning went out. The sorcerer felt as if he had been struck by a bolt of lightning, but at least the spell had held. There had to be another way, however. Continually fighting against the land each time he attempted to use his powers would drain him. He could not rely on Darkness for everything, especially now.

He heard the animal well before it came into sight. A large creature, far larger than he had wanted to call. If it was a predator, Dru had doubts about his survival. The renewed fear over his own mortality froze the Vraad for a moment, allowing the oncoming beast to step close enough to see.

It was a *horse*. *Dru's* horse, in fact.

The steed snorted and trotted closer, visibly pleased to have found its master. The sorcerer was at least as pleased and hugged the animal tight. It was a childish notion, but here was the only other creature from his home, the only link he really had to his citadel, Sharissa, and even Sirvak. More importantly, it was proof positive that had he remained where he was, he could have easily passed through to the shrouded realm. Surely, Dru pondered as he calmed the excited horse, the path worked both ways. He just had to keep going until he found one . . . that is, if Rendel and the Tezerenee monstrosities were not to be found.

"Good boy," the Vraad whispered. He stroked the steed's backside, smoothing out its coat. As his hand went across again, it froze midway back.

Where were the saddle and bridle?

Dru carefully inspected the horse's mouth. There were no bloody marks that indicated the animal had pulled itself loose. Nor were there signs that the saddle had been dragged off as the steed had moved through the woods. There was only one explanation that fit what the spellcaster saw before him; some-one had removed the saddle.

A quick scan of the darkening landscape brought no answers. He could not see a stranger simply removing the saddle and letting a horse as fine as this one run free. It now seemed too coincidental, too, that Dru's spell had summoned his very own animal.

His senses touched nothing out of the ordinary in the trees and bushes, yet Dru was almost certain that he was under the scrutiny of others.

The horse chose at that moment to pull away and trot back toward the direction it had originally come. Physically, the Vraad was no match for him. Used to controlling the steed by power alone, he fought fruitlessly to keep it from going any farther.

"Come back here, you misbegotten—" Sharissa had always had the way with animals. They tolerated, even liked Dru, but obeyed more because they had never had much choice.

He turned briefly to see if there was any change in Darkness, but the entity was still rolled up into some sort of obscene ball, pulsating all the while. Unwilling to lose the massive horse a second time, Dru reluctantly followed after it. He was not certain as to what he would do, but he had to do something.

It had never left his mind that this might be part of some trap. Yet, the value of the steed, for travel alone, pushed him on. If worse came to worst, he would unleash his sorcery and damn the agony it caused him afterward. A strong enough will would put down the protests of the land. He was, after all, a Vraad.

The horse continued to evade him, turning to the northeast as it somehow trotted through the wooded area without so much as a pause. Dru stumbled after it, hampered by both the clutching branches and the continual rise of the earth. He was near a hill or a ridge. The trees had obscured this fact. It could not be a high one since he had always had a fair view of the regions in the distant north, but it was high enough to tire him further than the day's trek already had. His determination did not waver; in fact, Dru actually began to look forward to any challenge before him. His growing anger would fuel his will. Anyone seeking to cross his path would be in for a terrible awakening.

At last, he came near the top of the formation. The horse vanished over the other side, which told Dru that it was a hill, for he could hear the steed's steps as it continued on its way. The Vraad reached the uppermost edge and took his first look at what lay on the other side.

What had been a fairly low hill on his side was a *vast* ridge on the other. Dru gazed down at a valley that had once likely been fertile, but had given way to dust over the centuries. That, however, was not nearly so interesting as what stood within perhaps half a mile from his present location.

A city! Not a leviathan stretching out to the horizon, but a large city nonetheless.

Dru squinted, correcting his first observation. The *ruins* of a city. Even from where he stood it was evident that the place was in disarray. Several towers had crumbled and the walls were little more than a jumbled mass of rock. Once, it had been a sprawling place covering a hill at least as great as the one he stood on. It was perhaps more of a vast citadel, for Dru could see that each and every building within was connected. Most were round, like spheres buried partly in the sand, but there were rectangular structures as well and even a courtyard barely visible.

Despite its ragged appearance, he knew it to have once been a place of power. The builders had been on a level equal to that of Vraad, which stirred up the question of what had happened to them. Why was this place now abandoned?

The horse had paused at the bottom of the incline, gazing up at its master with an almost impatient look. Despite the height, there was a path that allowed one fairly easy access to the valley. Dru knew he was supposed to follow the animal and knew also that whoever had sent it *wanted* him to know that the sorcerer was being purposely guided. That spoke of someone who wished to converse, not to kill.

"And shall we enter the dragon's maw?" Dru whispered nonsensically to himself.

He thought of Darkness, who might revive and find him missing. Separating was perhaps not the most prudent of choices in this land, but Dru's inquisitive, arrogant nature would not let him miss this opportunity. Even with his skills hampered, he felt more assured. Someone obviously wished to speak to him and his mind interpreted that as a need for his aid. Being Vraad, it appealed to him, eradicating all other possibilities, including a few which likely would have been seen to bear more merit, had Dru thought them through.

He started down the hill, his eyes focused more often on the decaying citadel than the path he took. Twice he almost tripped, which would have ended with him rolling the rest of the way, but luck was always with him.

At the bottom, he almost tripped again, but this time because the body in his path was so much the color of the earth it lay half-buried in, that he almost did not see it in time.

Dru's entire situation altered in the single breath it took the sorcerer to recognize the form for what it was. Near him, the horse waited silently. It no longer seemed impatient, but rather expectant.

The Vraad reached down and touched the corpse. It lay on its stomach, but he could tell it was manlike at least. Nearly as tall as the spellcaster, it had worn finely crafted cloth garments that crumbled when his fingers ran across them. To Dru's shock and wonder, the body, too, crumbled, collapsing within itself and blowing away with the breeze. Nothing remained after the first few seconds save a collection of fragments, mostly decor from the clothing.

How old? Dru wondered. *How old and in what way would one have to die to be preserved like this?*

The ravaged city no longer seemed such a wondrous place to visit. The sorcerer wiped dust from his eyes and glanced back up the way he had come. It would not be *too* terrible a climb. . . .

The sun was little more than a tired remnant of its once-glorious self. Climbing the hill might not be so terrible, but could he find his way back to his companion? Even granting that Darkness stood out even in the . . . the *true* darkness . . . he was still too far away for Dru to locate immediately. In the dark, the spellcaster might wander off in the wrong direction.

"Serkadion Manee!" Dru cursed his own stupidity. His powers and senses now functioned, at least somewhat. It would be a simple matter of focusing on—

Something snagged his left foot and threatened to topple him to the ground. Dru looked down to see the foot, up to and including the ankle, sink beneath the rocky surface. The grip that held him was tight enough to cut off circulation. His first attempt to free himself was to kick at the slowly encroaching ground. When his mind registered the idiocy of that act, the Vraad threw caution to the wind and summoned forth his powers as best he could. Whether they worked sufficiently or not, he would strike at the underground nemesis with everything within him.

The earth shook violently and the hillside threatened to collapse on the sorcerer. It was *not* the result Dru had intended and he wondered whether he had hastened his own death. Then whatever had hold of him lost its grip and the startled spellcaster fell back, arms akimbo as he sought uselessly to halt his descent. Dru stuck the ground hard.

A huge, monstrous shape rose out of the earth, filling Dru's vision. The Vraad looked into a visage of savagery, a long-snouted, red-orbed beast that seemed to glitter. The creature was covered with a natural body armor and stood on two bulky legs. It had clawed appendages large enough to grasp him by the neck and rip his head off, if it so decided.

The terror let loose with a maddened hooting noise that threatened to pierce Dru's eardrums. It raised a claw, obviously intending to rend the sprawled Vraad's midsection. The harried sorcerer desperately sought for control, hoping to make one last strike with his haphazard skills. The claws came down.

A black aura surrounded the attacking beast. It let out one frightened hoot, and toppled toward its intended victim.

Dru had, at the very least, enough sense to roll away from the collapsing figure. He had no idea what had happened, save that he had escaped death again—with help from someone or something. The sorcerer ended his rolling by returning to his feet, crouched low in case of a second assault. There was none.

Cautiously approaching his would-be killer, Dru frowned. The creature blended into the region around him with the exception of little spots of glitter buried in the folds of its armor. Suspicions already forming, Dru carefully prodded the huge corpse.

It collapsed the way the first had.

At the same time, the Vraad heard the flutter of wings. He looked up.

More than a dozen copies of the avian horror that had tried to kill him back in Nimth hovered overhead. The largest of them wore a medallion about its neck and cradled the artifact with one of its hands. Dru had no doubt that this was what had killed the armored creature.

It was now focused on *him*.

VIII

Among the celebrating Vraad, enmities began to spill over the mental dams in what could best be described as the first forerunners of one massive flood of hatred.

Gerrod noted it first in a Vraad called Lord Highcort, a pretty man bedecked in huge, glistening baubles. Highcort wore rings on each finger and was clad in a robe of majestic purple, giving him the appearance of some jaded monarch. The object of his wrath was a female who had once been his mate, or was it twice? She wore nothing but a multicolored streamer of light that occasionally revealed her charms for the briefest of times. Her hair hung low over her face, almost obscuring her eyes. She was presently taller than Highcort, though that could change depending on their moods. What her name was, Gerrod could not recall.

Highcort had evidently had no such trouble finding names for her. The last was the least in a long line that had initially alerted Gerrod to the argument down in the courtyard. "Minx! I grow annoyed at your toying! If you will not cease your diatribes, then I will have to remove the troublesome tongue that makes them!"

"You've been trying to remove that tongue for years, Highcort! What's the matter? Have I struck so close with the truth that you cannot take it anymore?"

The male gritted his teeth. A haze started to form around him, first simply a cloud, then a whirlwind that began circling around.

What the woman was doing, Gerrod had no idea, but he could sense her own powers at work.

Just as the two were about to strike, a pair of dragon riders materialized above them. Both Vraad turned their attention skyward, knowing where the more dangerous threat lay.

"What is it? What goes on?" His father's booming voice pulled the hooded Tezerenee from the window. Gerrod found he was disappointed that the combatants had not been allowed to continue. At least the others would have been thoroughly entertained and the mutterings would have ceased for a while.

"We can't mislead them for much longer, Father. The feuds are starting to brew anew."

The Lord Tezerenee was presently hunched over charts and notations that Gerrod and Rendel had made concerning the passage over to the Dragonrealm. Barakas absently stroked the head of the small wyvern perched on his armored shoulder as he digested both what lay revealed before him and his son's warning.

Reegan, ever a champion of the head-on charge, slammed a mailed fist onto the table and, ignoring the splintered remnants where his hand had gone through, said, "They should be brought under control, informed of who is in command here! If they knew their true standing, they would abase themselves before us and beg for a place in the new kingdom!"

Gerrod had had enough foolishness. The words escaped his mouth before he considered that he was turning attention away from his brother and back onto himself. "A kingdom we can no longer promise to deliver to them!"

His father jerked straight, causing the wyvern to flutter off in shrieking panic, but the Lady Tezerenee, standing to his left and just behind him, put a steady hand on his shoulder.

"Hush, darling. Gerrod is correct. The thing to do now is recoup our losses and see if we can salvage some sort of victory."

"I would rather recoup the *heads* of Ephraim and his band." Barakas took a deep breath, which threatened to exhaust the air supply in the room, and calmed himself. He turned away from Gerrod, who let out a silent sigh, and focused on one of the coven assigned to monitor Rendel's passage. They had given up trying to keep the body alive; it had passed away shortly after the initial news that the cross-over itself was in danger. "Esad! How many golems remain?"

The newcomer knelt instantly. "Father, there are some two hundred plus golems ready. That is the best we can say at this point."

"Acceptable." Barakas scratched his chin. "More than enough for us to cross over and still have some left for those we deem our allies. As for the rest"—he shrugged uncaringly—"they, being mighty Vraad, should be able to fend for themselves."

Which still did not answer the initial questions raised earlier, Gerrod thought bitterly. What had actually happened to Ephraim and those of the clan whose task it had been to create and shape the golems? Those shells were to act as the Vraads' receptacles when their kas passed across to their new domain. When it was reported that they had not responded to a summons, the Lord Tezerenee himself had gone out to find the reason why. All they had found were the pentagram etched in the dead soil and a few minor items that individuals in the band had carried with them. There had been no sign of a struggle and no misty apparition marking an intrusion by the other domain.

The patriarch was of the opinion that the band had somehow crossed, abandoning their bodies in some well-hidden cave so as to delay discovery of their deed. It was possible to create a lifeline of sorts that would enable the kas of each of them to cross to and including the last man. Such a task would require the first arrivals to remain linked mentally with those to follow. It was that part of the plan that Rendel had abandoned earlier.

"It is settled, then."

The gathered Tezerenee, mostly the combined sons and daughters of the lord and lady, grew silent, whispered conversations dying in midsentence. When no one else dared to ask, Gerrod took the burden onto his shoulders, as it always seemed he did, despite a continuing lack of gratitude on the parts of his siblings. "*What* is settled, Father?"

Lord Barakas glared at his son as if Gerrod had turned into an imbecile. "Pay attention! Our course is settled! We begin transferring over to the Dragonrealm before this day is over. I will summon those who will join our ranks. The announcement will go out that they will be but the first, overall order being done by lottery."

"They will never believe that."

The patriarch gave his son an imperious glare. "They *will* believe that because I will stake the bond of the dragon on it."

So it had come to that, the younger Tezerenee marveled with distaste. *The fine line of honor!*

In truth, his father could not be said to be lying, for lottery was to have been the original system, albeit with a few strings. The supposedly random pattern of who would depart first had been first suggested by Rendel. Gerrod's elder brother had reminded them that no Vraad felt they should come second to another. The lottery, with a promise that no influence would be made when the names were chosen, had subdued many arguments. What the other Vraad did *not* know, however, was that only certain names went into the first batch. Those were the ones Barakas knew could either be turned or bullied into submission. The rest would have eventually found themselves offering up their own wills in return for survival.

With the rampant displays of Vraad sorcery going on even now, Nimth would not last half as long as had once been supposed. The Vraad, certain of their continued existence, assumed that there was no reason to hold back and were celebrating accordingly.

Gerrod, his mind on such thoughts, abruptly found his air cut off and his body being dragged by some invisible force around his neck toward his father. The Lady Tezerenee gasped, but that was the only sound other than Gerrod's futile attempts for breath.

"You are proving yourself to be quite *inadequate*, my son," the patriarch said in the smooth voice that unnerved all, especially those for whom his words were intended. "I left you to organize the transfer. Its control escaped you. I left you to organize the creation of the golems, our hope for the future. Control of *that* escaped you as well. I placed the young Zeree female in your hands . . . and now she has run off to her father's citadel, no doubt." The spell holding Gerrod ceased, leaving the younger Tezerenee to gasp in precious air. "You constantly question my wisdom when you cannot trust your own." Barakas turned from him to his bride. "I have done all I can with our son. If he cannot redeem himself, there are others willing to take his place once the cross-over commences."

Lady Alcia started to protest, but noticed something in her husband's eye that warned her to remain quiet.

Barakas took her arm and started to lead her out. As the two departed, the patriarch calmly commanded to those behind him, "Begin the transfer. Reegan, you control it." The Lord Tezerenee gave Gerrod one last withering glance. "As for you . . . find out what the Zeree hatchling has in mind that she first holds back information and then sneaks off to the protection of her father's domain. If you manage to succeed, there will still be a place for you."

Gerrod nodded, keeping his visage composed since his father's sorcerous reprimand had knocked the hood back. Deep inside, however, he seethed. His progenitor was insane, highly so, though there were none here who would back up such a notion. Each of the "failures" mentioned had hardly been the fault of Gerrod, yet it was on him whom the iron hand of Barakas had fallen. Simply because he would not be one of the clan. How Rendel managed all this time, the young Tezerenee could not say, but he now understood that there might have been *many* reasons Rendel had chosen to abandon them.

When the lord and lady of the clan had departed, Reegan regained his nerve and began giving orders. Most of them were more apt for going into battle than organizing the cross-over, but he had been given control of the plan and there was nothing Gerrod could do about it. With his eldest brother in charge, though, he wondered whether *any* of them would make it across.

He began to wonder again if he really wanted to cross at all. It was a ridiculous thought. Here, he only faced death. In the realm beyond the veil, there was a chance for survival. Even despite his feeling that colonizing the so-called Dragonrealm would not prove so simple as his father had thought, it was better than remaining here and watching Nimth simply rot away over the centuries. He would not even survive long enough to see its end.

That in mind, Gerrod drew his cloak about him and departed from the domain of Dru Zeree.

In the selfsame castle that Gerrod sought to reach, Sharissa berated Sirvak. The familiar crouched before her, pitiful but still unremorseful about its actions.

"You disobeyed me, Sirvak! How many times do I have to tell you before you understand that?"

"Understand, mistressss! Only obeying master'sss ordersss! No one but you to enter here!"

"Father isn't here! I'm trying to save him and she can help!" Sharissa waved a hand in the direction of a bemused Melenea.

"Calm yourself, sweet thing," Melenea said soothingly. "I'm certain Sirvak meant well. You cannot expect it to so easily disobey an order given to it by Dru. After all," she added, smiling at the nervous familiar, "it has a limited imagination, a limited mind."

Sirvak dared a hiss at the intruder. Sharissa would have been dumbstruck if she knew all that the beast struggled with in that "limited mind." Powerful as it was, the familiar was next to nothing to Melenea now that she was inside. With the defenses of the citadel behind it, Sirvak could have matched her and more. Inside, however, the familiar faced her with only its own abilities. Sirvak feared for Sharissa's life if it dared reveal what it knew of the enchantress. From experience, the winged beast knew that Melenea would not hesitate to kill both of them. Sirvak could only wait and hope.

Dru was greatly to blame and even the familiar would have acknowledged that. Unwilling to reveal to his daughter any more than he had to about his past indiscretions, he had forbidden the familiar from speaking of those like the beautiful but dark sorceress. That command had now come back to haunt them. Sirvak hissed again, not so much at the enemy before it but at the unfortunate beast's own inability to protect its charge.

Sharissa, unmindful of the mass confusion in the beast's mind, stared it back into silence. "No more! You said you had something for me, something that might help us find Father! What is it?"

The creature looked from its mistress to the hated one and back again, frustration written across its odd visage.

"Sirvak, this is Father's *life* we're talking about!"

Reluctantly, the familiar told her. "The crystalsss. All information liesss in the crystalsss. Can predict when rip will open again, perhapsss."

It was obvious that the creature was uncertain and the idea did not sit well with Sharissa, either. Melenea watched them both, waiting, it seemed, for some explanation. Sharissa realized that her friend did not know about the spell her father had cast and explained it, going into careful detail as to how the crystals recorded images and sorcerous energy so that Dru could later study those memories at his leisure.

Melenea was fascinated. "Dear wonderful Dru! I always knew he was a brilliant thinker! So much potential in this! Do you realize the advantages this could give one over rivals?"

Sharissa had never considered that point but could understand how gaining knowledge of the magical patterns of both Nimth and what the Tezerenee called the Dragonrealm could teach a sorcerer ways of better utilizing the natural power. That was hardly a consideration now, however.

"What Sirvak says is true," Sharissa replied, forgetting Melenea's comment. "The crystals might lead us to another tear, another intense appearance by the shrouded realm. It might even show us a way to travel there with little danger."

The other Vraad's eyes glowed, a sight that Sharissa found both fascinating and disturbing. She had never seen such a sight before. There was so much that Melenea could teach her. . . .

"Shari darling, you may be correct! Wouldn't *that* turn

Barakas's beard around? He'd be livid if he found out, you know.''

It was a confirmation of everything the younger female had thought of already. She knew she could not allow the Tezerenee to know the truth, no matter how much aid they were capable of giving her. With Melenea to help guide her, Sharissa was certain they could do it on their own.

"Why don't you show me the crystals, sweet thing?" Melenea put a comforting arm around her shoulders. Sharissa took heart from the moral support.

Sirvak chose the moment to raise its head and cry out at something unseen. "Warning, mistresss! Someone stands without the bordersss of the master'sss domain!"

"Let me see." Melenea withdrew from Sharissa and, as the young woman watched, stared blankly into space for a short time. When the eyes focused again, Melenea smiled wryly. "It's your cloth-covered shadow. He's trying to find a way around Dru's defenses."

"Gerrod?" *They suspect,* Sharissa thought in panic. Then she realized that they could not. No, Gerrod was here for the simple reason that his father had likely thrown it upon him to drag her back. Again, she felt sympathy for his plight, but not enough to give herself up. "He can't get in. Father planned the defenses too carefully."

Melenea was thoughtful. "If this were that mountain Reegan, I might be inclined to believe you, but this Gerrod has a sharp mind . . . a treacherous one. He might be able to outthink a series of spells."

"Not if Sirvak is also monitoring things." Sharissa turned back to the familiar. "See to it that he does not gain entrance."

The magical creature looked upset, looked as if it wanted to say something else, but it finally bowed its head in obedience and simply replied, "As you say, mistresss."

"Go now! What are you waiting for?"

With much hesitation, the familiar rose slowly into the air and, looking briefly at Melenea with an unreadable expression, flew off.

"Where is it going?"

"There's a tower it uses for a roost. Sirvak prefers to observe from there."

"It has *preferences*? How odd to find so much personality in a familiar! I'd forgotten! Still, Dru did create it, so it shouldn't surprise me so much!"

Sharissa smiled at the compliment, then pointed at a hallway to her left. "This way. We bypass Father's iron golem."

"Then let us go. Let Gerrod hammer away until he exhausts himself." The other Vraad made as if to teleport. When nothing happened, she tried again. It was only then that the young Zeree recalled the earlier troubles she and her father had suffered.

"The rift was near here. It makes some spells more difficult. We finally found it easier to just walk. I think Father actually grew to like the physical activity."

"Did he?" Melenea sounded quite the contrary, but she finally shrugged. "I suppose it could be novel for a time. Very well, then. Lead on, Shari sweet."

Sharissa found herself talking incessantly. There was something about having another woman to talk to that allowed her to say things she would not have spoken of even with her father. Melenea seemed so interested, too. Adding a point here or there and listening very attentively when the younger Vraad spoke of her mother.

"Father says I look like she did when they first met. I don't know if that means anything; everyone keeps changing their appearances so. I don't remember her. She died in some duel. It seems like such a useless way to die." Sharissa looked at her companion. "I know I sound uncaring, but I'm not. It's just that it was so long ago and I hardly knew her in the first place."

An arm pulled her near the other woman. "I understand. The thing to do is harden yourself to the trials of life. To make everything, no matter how sad, into some sort of game. It is the only way to keep going after the initial four or five centuries. I have found life so much more fulfilling since I began looking at it that way."

"A game?" Sharissa had difficulty with imagining all that had happened in the past few days as part of a game, but Melenea had the centuries of experience backing up her claim. Perhaps when this was over—*if* it was ever over—Sharissa would try to take her advice.

They came upon Dru's inner sanctum. The two attempted to enter, but something refused to give them leave.

"I don't understand this!" The young Zeree stepped forward and put a hand out. She met with no resistance and kept walking until she was completely inside. Melenea also put a hand out, but hers was repelled. Annoyed, she put the hand to her hair and tugged on one of the locks tracing her cheekbones.

"One of Dru's safety precautions, lovely Shari," the enchantress commented. Her smile was a bit forced.

"I'm so sorry!" Reaching out with her mind, Dru's daughter disrupted the spell long enough for Melenea to walk through. "I grow so used to them that I sometimes forget, though I think this must have been a new one. It's keyed only to Father and me and follows the changes in Nimth that I discovered before . . . before Father went out and . . ."

Again, Melenea was there beside her, giving comfort when it was needed. Sharissa wondered why she had stopped coming years ago, but did not dare ask. It was almost like having a sister—or even a *mother*—and she did not want to break the bond they had been forming.

"Oh, darling Dru! This is fabulous!" The comforting arms pulled away without ceremony as Melenea moved quickly toward the far side of the chamber and the glorious spectacle of the magical crystals. She eyed each and every one separately, it seemed to Sharissa, mouthing silent comments about the patterns and colors. The elder woman knew much about the use of crystals, that was evident. Sharissa's hopes flamed higher; while she understood much of what her father had taught her, there were many things she suspected he had not thought she was ready for. Perhaps Melenea knew what to do.

After several long, agonizing minutes, the enchantress said, "The phantom lands . . . the shrouded realm as Dru called it; it affects the nature of Nimth, does it not? More so, I mean, than was assumed earlier."

She *did* understand! Sharissa nodded rapidly, adding, "It has intruded in some places so much that like the ridge, no one can predict how sorcery will work. That was why Father waited so long before he tried to teleport away."

Melenea nodded in turn. Sharissa had explained this to her earlier, had gone through each agonizing moment again and again. It had hurt her deeply to relive that time, but the other woman had insisted that she needed to know exactly what had happened.

"I wonder . . ."

"What?"

The enchantress shook her head. "Nothing. Idle thoughts, sweet one."

Sharissa came over and pointed at the additions she had made. "There's where I had to alter what Father had created."

"That pattern should not be *possible*," Melenea breathed in astonishment.

"Father said the same thing, but when he looked close, he saw that the other realm was intruding into our own. That was what sent us out to the ridge and . . ." She trailed off.

"Don't trouble yourself with that anymore." Circling the astonishing panorama once more, Melenea smiled. It was a smile unlike the others Sharissa had seen. This smile denoted satisfaction, great satisfaction. She wondered whether the enchantress had indeed discovered a way to recover her father.

"I think, pretty Shari, that you should add something here." A thin, elegant finger pointed toward the very center of the spiral. "And here." The finger now pointed toward a spot near the ceiling.

"Are you certain?" The locations that Melenea pointed to were certainly open to stable additions, but their purposes escaped the younger Vraad.

The brilliant smile banished her fears. "Oh, *yes*, Shari! We don't dare go on until you add crystals to those two points."

"All right." Sharissa walked over to a case on a worktable. The lock spell protecting it was one she knew, having opened it often in the past. The case itself was wooden, with intricate scrollwork. Dru Zeree's mark was upon it, emblazoned in the center. This was where he kept the crystals he used in his work.

"I—" She was about to tell Melenea that she knew neither the size nor the color of the proper crystals, but then another mind entered hers, interrupting her chain of thought.

It was Sirvak. *Mistressss, Tezerenee Gerrod departss.*

So soon? That did not sound like Gerrod. *Are you certain?*

There was a moment of hesitation, which Sharissa took as the familiar's attempt to confirm its own statement. *The Tezerenee is nowhere outside, mistressss. I have protected home asss best assss I deemed posssible.*

It was a peculiar way to put it, but she understood. *Keep vigilant, though, Sirvak. He may try to gain entry again. Do what you have to in order to protect the castle. Father's safety relies on you.*

I do what I mussst, mistresss. Mistresss, I cannot enter the master'ss sanctum.

If I need you, I'll let you in. It would be too time-consuming for now, Sirvak, and there's no need. Father's darkdwellers will assist with the work, if necessary. The darkdwellers were creatures of shadow that lived in the rafters above. They acted as extra hands for Dru when he experimented.

They are weak, mistresss, I—

That will be all, *Sirvak!*

I do what I must for the master and you, mistressss, Sirvak repeated again before breaking contact.

Sharissa briefly wondered at the last statement, not so much because of the words but the tone that Sirvak had used. The gold and black beast had sounded almost fatalistic.

"Shari, sweet thing?"

The crystals! "Sirvak linked with me, Melenea! Gerrod has departed, likely back to the Lord and Lady Tezerenee."

"Has he now?" Melenea smiled thinly. "Watch him, Shari. He is likely the most devious of them. You cannot trust his words or his actions at any time."

It fit with the way Sharissa had pictured the hooded Vraad. Gerrod was both a Vraad and a Tezerenee. What could be a *worse* combination?

"The *crystals*, Sharissa dear." The enchantress tugged at one of the locks of hair following the line of her cheekbones. She seemed to be holding back a building excitement within her. Sharissa took that as indication of their eventual success. It made the need for proper crystals even more urgent.

"Which ones do you need?"

"Any will do."

Sharissa's head jerked upward and she stared at the other Vraad. "But the size and color! You can't just put *anything* in there! You might destroy Father's work and then we'd never be able to find him!"

With swift strides, the magnificent sorceress devoured the distance between them and took hold of her younger counterpart by the shoulders. The grip was perhaps a bit stronger than Sharissa would have liked. "Shari, dear little one, I know the workings of the crystals. Don't you worry. Here." Melenea took out two of the larger ones, a blue and a clear. "You need not worry. These two will do *just* fine."

While Sharissa watched, still uneasy about the carefree choices, the enchantress returned to the brilliantly illuminated artifact and quite casually tossed the two new crystals into the center. Propelled by her power, the blue one immediately shot ceilingward. The clear crystal, meanwhile, struggled against the spiral pattern, which seemed to resist its addition with an almost living determination. Supported by Melenea's will, however, the clear gem soon overcame opposition and took its place within the structure of the one spiral.

Her own additions had made perfect sense to her father once he had inspected the final results, but the younger Zeree, even after several seconds of careful study, could not comprehend what purpose these new pieces served. She said as much to Melenea, who gave her a smile that warmed Sharissa so because of the care that she read in it.

"It will become obvious over time. I promise you that. Now, there's just one more thing. I'd like you to remove the crystals that would contain knowledge of the sighting where poor Dru vanished."

That was easy enough. Happy to be once more an active part in her father's rescue—and happy to understand what she was doing this time—Sharissa joined Melenea by the artifact. With deft skill, she summoned forth the magical gems in question, smiling as they broke away from their positions and fluttered to her waiting hand. While that went on, she brought forth replacements from the protective case. The newcomers fit into the places vacated by their predecessors with perfect ease.

Her skill earned her the praise of her friend. "How wonderfully deft you are, Shari sweet! Had I a daughter of my own, I could not be so proud as I am of you! Dru has raised you so well!"

Sharissa blushed deeply under the barrage of compliments from someone who was *not* her father.

"Now," Melenea added, holding out one smooth, pale hand. "Give me the crystals and we can be on our way."

"'On our way'?" Sharissa almost dropped the gems. "Where are we going?"

Taking the younger woman's hand in her own, the enchantress replied, "This is best done back in my own sanctum, dear love. I have methods I doubt Dru even knows . . . and I think you would be quite a bit safer there if blustery Barakas sends Gerrod back with a few more of his endless supply of relations. You see what I'm talking about?"

Sharissa did. No one really knew that Melenea was aiding her. The Tezerenee would hound her father's castle, wasting time in which the two women could study the crystals' findings. It made perfect sense to her and once more Sharissa was grateful for having the help of so good a friend as the caring enchantress.

"There are notes Father compiled that we'll need. He has them in his private chambers, but I'll be able to get them easily enough."

"That's fine. While you do that, I'd like the opportunity to inspect this chamber for anything else of importance to our goal." Melenea squeezed Sharissa tight for a brief time. "Soon, you'll see Dru again!"

Separating, Sharissa rushed from the room, the quicker to retrieve her father's work and return. Her mind had slipped from the present moment to her eventual reunion with her father. It was because of those dreams that she passed the shadow without noting how it differed from the rest.

"Sharissa."

She stumbled and fell back against one of the walls, disbelieving what she had heard. Her eyes scanned the corridor behind her, at last sighting the shadow that was no shadow.

It unfolded before her, revealing what she had known but had hoped was only her panicked imagination.

"Gerrod!"

"Zeree, listen to me! Sirvak tells me that—"

Sirvak! The familiar had betrayed her? How was that possible . . . unless Gerrod, cunning as Melenea had said, had somehow overwhelmed the beast's mind, making it a creature of his. "Stay away from me, Tezerenee!"

"Little fool! Your father protected you too well! You have no concept of what Vraad mentalities are like! If you only—"

Sharissa, taking advantage of his pontificating, rushed past him back in the direction of the chamber where she had left Melenea and safety. Not expecting such bold, nonmagical action from her, likely because he assumed her a weak, sobbing child, Gerrod was caught by surprise. His reflexes, a product of his upbringing, were exceptional, however, and he barely missed grabbing hold of her arm.

"Sharissa! No! Come back! Talk to Sirvak!"

She paid him no mind, knowing that the familiar would puppet the hooded Vraad's words. Her only hope, she decided, lay in Melenea and escape from the castle.

As she reached the doorway, through which Gerrod would *not* be able to touch her, she felt a tingling in the air around her. The Tezerenee was casting a spell. Without caring where she landed, Sharissa leaped into the room.

"Melenea, I—"

"Shari! Call these vermin *off* of me!"

The darkdwellers, little more than rags of darkness, flittered about the enchantress, moving in on one side to strike at her as she attempted to defend the other. A few marks on the floor spoke of those who had met their fate at Melenea's hands.

It made too much sense to Sharissa's distraught imagination. Through Sirvak, Gerrod must now control the darkdwellers, too. The citadel was no longer secure; even this room, where she thought to have a chance to think, was threatened by the Tezerenee.

"Sharissa!" Gerrod stood at the entranceway, pushing futilely at the barrier. How long that would last, she had no idea. Trying to ignore the threat behind her, she turned her attention to her friend. At her presence, the ebony creatures flew away, reluctant but obedient to her will. The younger sorceress did not question her luck, wishing only to see if her companion was injured or not.

Several scratches marred the ivory skin of Melenea, but the enchantress ignored them, choosing instead to grasp Sharissa's wrist painfully and pull her closer.

"We leave now! Hold on to me!"

"Zeree! You can't trust—"

The remainder of Gerrod's words were lost as the castle ceased to exist around them and Sharissa suddenly found herself in what could only be the domain of Melenea.

Failurefailurefailurefailure . . .

Gerrod struggled against the mad panic of Sirvak's mind. The beast had lost control the second its mistress had departed with Melenea. Even as he forced the familiar back to a state of sanity, he himself could not help fearing for the young Zeree. Gerrod was not fond of her, but no one deserved the ministrations of the enchantress . . . save perhaps Reegan, who would have likely reveled in them.

Sirvak! Listen to me!

He had succeeded in convincing the familiar that an alliance with him was the best hope. The familiar's fairly quick agreement had stemmed mostly from its knowledge of the Lady Melenea. It was a case of *the enemy of my enemy*. . . . Whatever the reason, they had hoped to catch Sharissa at a time when she would be willing to listen. Gerrod himself felt bitter about the failure, for that had been strictly his own fault. It called to mind what his father had said earlier and he now began to question the truth of that reprimand.

In the end, it likely did not matter. Gerrod had failed at his task and he could not go back empty-handed. Now, Dru Zeree's theoretical pathway to the shrouded realm was looking to be *his* only chance for survival. When the Lord Tezerenee hinted that he would leave a body behind, it was not a jest.

Failure. . . . The familiar was much more calm now, but it still was in no condition to aid in planning. That would fall to Gerrod again.

Though he could not enter the chamber, he *had* spied upon its occupants for a short time. Sharissa had mentioned Dru's earlier work involving the sightings and the binding forces of the two worlds. Perhaps there lay the key.

Sirvak! He treated the familiar as he would have treated one of the wyverns back in the clan's domain. The winged creation responded as if its own master had summoned it.

Listen to me closely, he began, *and we may yet save your master and mistress . . . not to mention myself.* He added the last slowly, knowing it was all too true. *This is what I think we must do. . . .*

IX

Dru woke to a new dawn not even knowing when he had blacked out. The last thing he recalled was the sudden descent of a number of the bird people, creating, in the process, a circle around him. He had tried to act, his mind screeching that he moved in slow motion, but was too late. The blackout occurred then.

His bonds held when he tested them. Attempts at spells left his head pounding at first and then filled with a buzzing that would not depart for several minutes. He gave up after two attempts, knowing that he was very much a helpless prisoner. With escape impossible for now, the sorcerer began to work on satisfying his ever-hungry curiosity. Studying his dusky brown captors in the early morning light, Dru supposed that they were nearly all male. None of them had any special characteristics that were visible, but four of the avians appeared adult even though they were shorter and slighter than their companions. Not knowing any better, he assumed these were the females. If so, the birdlike creatures were great believers in equality, for the four smaller ones worked as hard as the rest and were treated with equal respect.

The avians were little more familiar with this territory than Dru was; it was evident from their jerking movements, their constant vigilance. Territory had been secured, but they were surrounded by unknown lands. Likely, they were also more at home in trees, mountainsides, and, of course, the sky. His captors were in awe of the abandoned city and more than a little afraid of it as well, though they tried to hide both emotions under a mask of arrogance worthy of Barakas. Dru tried to speak to them, but all he received for his attempts were slaps across the face and unintelligible squawks. From their gestures during one of those sessions, he suspected that they had a way of communicating with him, but had debated whether it was necessary to do so. In the end, his captors chose to merely drag him along.

Dru wondered about the beast they had saved him from. Judging by the reaction of the bird creatures, its death was a cause for celebration. *Like the killing of a blood enemy,* he noted. It would not have surprised him if a war was going on between these two horrific races. From what little experience he had enjoyed so far, neither seemed any better than his own race and bloodshed was quite a favorite pastime of the Vraad.

That they had killed the other figure, the one that the sorcerer assumed must have been one of Barakas's elves, went without saying. What interested Dru most, despite the danger he was in, was why his captor and members of two other races would come to this place. What did it have that they all wanted so badly? Granted, most of his ideas were pure conjecture, but Dru was fairly certain he was on the right path.

As they grew nearer and nearer to the avians'—and his own, admittedly—goal, Dru wondered what had become of Darkness. A wild notion that his captors had instigated the entity's odd withdrawal passed quickly from his mind; certainly they would not have left such a threat at their backside. Neither had they been the ones responsible for his horse's odd actions. The avians had totally ignored the steed other than to initially note its presence. Horses were apparently common here and one wandering loose in the vicinity of the ancient city was beneath their concern. It had, in fact, wandered off at some point after his blackout. The trail it left steered to the north, but that was all Dru knew, unable to track it farther.

Up close, the ruins were even vaster. The outer walls had been more than five times the sorcerer's height; massive fragments of some still remained standing. The towers, those that had not collapsed, were much taller and easily comparable to anything the Vraad had created. Little remained of any writing or decoration; they had been worn away by the weather of millennia. The city was incredibly old. It had probably already been in ruins when the first of the Vraad race proclaimed themselves.

The party stood near what had been the city gates, the avians evidently preparing themselves mentally for entering the ruins. Only Dru noticed the tremors when they first began and, being so used to such in Nimth, he hardly paid attention.

The ground suddenly ripped open as huge, clawed hands tore at those above.

Dru, stumbling madly away from one claw, instantly recognized the creatures attacking them. The thing that had tried to kill him had not been alone, though the truth of that was only just sinking into the minds of the party. Dru swore at his captors while he tried to evade another grasping hand sprouting from the earth by his right foot. His captors *should* have searched more carefully; he had assumed they knew to do that much. Like some of his former rivals, however, the birds suffered from too much pride in themselves. They had been certain that they had contained the problem. Now, the problem threatened to contain them.

With a pain-filled shriek, one of the taller creatures was pulled swiftly into the earth regardless of the fact that the jagged crevice was too small for his winged form. Before Dru's disgusted and horrified gaze, the avian was reduced to a mass of mangled limbs and blood that, after all too long a time, completely sank into the soil. The Vraad renewed his efforts to evade the hands groping for him, wishing that, as his captors were belatedly doing, he could take to the sky.

Of the fourteen avians, all but the unfortunate who had just died made it into the air. Several reached for their medallions.

The air proved no more of a haven than the ground had been. From the earth rose one of the snouted monstrosities, a deep, challenging sound accompanying its appearance. It carried with it a needlelike spear as long as its body. The spear was hurtling toward the avians before the attacker was even completely free of the soil. Its accuracy was perfection itself; another of the bird people died, plummeting to the ground no farther than a yard from the hapless Vraad. The spear stood like a banner, one that had been planted so firmly into the victim's chest that it even came out the other side.

The avians finally struck back. Dru steadied himself, expecting the foul mummification spell he had witnessed earlier. Instead, a mist formed swiftly around the monster that had come to the surface. The sorcerer frowned. The intended victim hooted its contempt, waving one arm to dispel the light fog. It did not clear, despite the beast's attempts, but rather continued to thicken, so quickly, in fact, that the blinded earth-dweller was, after only a breath or two, no longer visible. A breath, perhaps two, passed, and then the wind, which itself had pounded fruitlessly at the fog, finally began to have an effect, slowly banishing the magical mist.

When it had at last cleared, there was no sign of the hulking creature it had enveloped. He might have never been, save that the earth was still marred by his initial eruption to the surface.

Another of the winged beings fell prey to a perfect strike, but that was where the newcomers' luck ended. Two more that rose to the surface suffered the same fate as the first; a fourth shriveled to a stomach-wrenching mass directly in front of Dru. After that, the assault ceased. Either the avians had killed all of their adversaries or the underground dwellers had retreated.

In pairs, the surviving creatures descended to deal with their dead. Two separated from the rest and took hold of the sorcerer, lifting him high into the air before he even had the breath to protest. Accompanied by a third, they made for the city, passing over the ruins of the gateway instead of trying to walk through.

Dru was brought unceremoniously to the ground in what had been a well-crafted street but was now a jumbled pile of smooth, broken stepping stones.

The Vraad had finally had enough. Bound and with death likely facing him, he turned on his captors, almost daring them to strike him down, and shouted, "Listen to me! I don't know what you search for, but tell me and I can help! At least have the courtesy to talk to me! I may know something you don't! I demand that you listen to me!"

He doubted that he knew much of value to his captors, but was not about to reveal that to the avians. The trio stared at him with identical one-eyed looks. Under the unblinking gazes, Dru shifted impatiently.

Without warning and with a speed that left Dru breathless, the two avians who had carried him suddenly stepped forward and took him by the arms. Uncertain as to what they planned, the Vraad could not help struggling, though he might as well have been a tiny child fighting a raging wolf, so powerful a grip the creatures had. The third one, once he saw that the sorcerer was held tight, slowly stepped up to his prisoner, halting within arm's reach and glaring haughtily at the human.

A clawed hand thrust out so swiftly that the spellcaster did not even have time to fear for his life. The leader's long hand covered the upper half of Dru's visage. The palm flattened against his forehead.

The world about him *altered*, shifting from a scene of long-lost glory to a dark and unsettling place. Somehow, his mind knew this to be a cavern in one of the mountains of a chain—*across a vast sea?* Yes, it was true. Darkness had brought his tiny companion to the realm beyond the veil, but apparently there was more than just one continent. He had been right in assuming that the bird people were unfamiliar with this land. They had traveled here after an arduous journey that had cut their numbers by a third before they even reached the shore of this place. All this Dru knew through feelings and images filling every niche of his mind.

Dru's view of the cavern widened until he realized that the central cavern housed a vast chamber that had, in the far past, been used as a throne room or a temple. A dim light illuminated the cavern, but its source was not readily noticeable. There were bizarre stone effigies, things that seemed alive in their own way. Some were human, some were not, but the amazing detail of each remained as testimony to the skill of some ancient master. The Vraad recognized something inherent in the tall statues, in the ancient chamber itself, that reminded him of the ruined city, as if both had been built by the same race despite the gulf of water separating them.

"That's it, isn't it?" he asked the avian leader, even though the latter was not visible to him for the moment. "You found the cavern and traced its origin to here."

A sensation that somehow indicated acknowledgment coursed through him. He did not try to comprehend how the sensations could possibly be translated into replies; that demanded much too much time of its own. Dru knew only that he had guessed correctly about the ruins and the winged creature had informed him so in its own way.

Dru watched as a figure he recognized as himself searched the city alongside the—Sheeka?—seeking something. The...there was the name again, the Sheeka, but somehow it did not work with him. The seekers...yes, the observing sorcerer decided, they were the *Seekers*. It was as apt a name as the one Darkness had chosen for himself and much more tolerable to the Vraad's ears and mouth.

The Seekers had found something—what it had been was carefully kept hidden from the sorcerer's mind—in the cavern, and that had led them to their journey to this other continent. Unfortunately, it had also led their bitter rivals, the ground diggers, to the same place. Dru tried to catch the term for the enemy, but the avian used only the most derogatory symbols for the huge monstrosities, none of which were at all suitable to the mage. He did gather, however, that the other race was more ancient than his captors' was and its power was waning...but not fast enough, as far as the avians were concerned. That might have been merely the arrogant opinion of the party's leader, but Dru took it at face value for the time being.

As abruptly as he had been thrust into the cavern, the Vraad was shifted to another scene, this time of vast rookeries, some natural, some created, and the glory that was the Seeker people. Their world, a combination of nature and design, began to fascinate Dru more than the reason for their being on this side of the world. The avians melded the forms of trees and hills with elaborate living quarters that might easily have been constructed by the mage's own race. It was evident that much of their society demanded that the Seekers be groundlocked at times and so it was no surprise that their buildings resembled those of the Vraad. Cities like these dotted most of the other continent, allowing the race to breed yet not destroying the nature.

Recalling his own world, Dru envied the skill of his captors.

The leader chose that moment to remove his hand from his prisoner's forehead. Dru had been correct in his assumption; the taller ones *were* the males.

Although it was guesswork at best in trying to read the more subtle expressions of the birdlike beings, the sorcerer caught what appeared to be a look of disgust and amazement on the leader's visage. It then occurred to him for the first time that the unique method of communication that the Seekers utilized worked *both* ways. Dru had unwittingly revealed to them his own origins, including the all-important fact that he was *not* of this world!

The Seekers evidently needed no physical contact to communicate with one another, for the look of revulsion spread to the two holding him still. He knew they were considering Nimth and its decaying state. He knew also what they must think of him, one of those responsible for spoiling a once-wondrous world.

He was not questioned further, which surprised him. Whatever the avians sought here, they considered it of far more importance than a lone representative of a decadent race from beyond. When the rest of what remained of the party materialized over the walls and landed around them, careful this time to observe the ground beneath their feet, the leader did not even take time to allow the others to digest what he had torn from Dru. Nonetheless, the Vraad was fairly certain that all of them knew what he had let slip, if only because of the difference in the disdainful glances they gave him at various times. Before, it had simply been arrogance at one who was not a member of their "superior" race. Now, it was that arrogance, but peppered with the look Dru's own race reserved for those Vraad with tastes even too perverse for their brethren to accept.

With Dru in their center, the two guards still holding him by the arms, the party journeyed deeper into the remnants of the city. Now and then, members would flutter off for several minutes, inspecting nearby structures and getting a cloud's view of the ruins themselves. Gradually, they began to steer toward the east. It was not the center of the city, but it was where the greatest of the rounded buildings lay. So great a building, in fact, that it could have easily housed the several thousand individuals who made up the Vraad race.

The sun was already nearing its zenith when they came upon the cracked and rubble-strewn clearing between themselves and the huge structure that his captors had chosen as their ultimate destination. Dru wondered briefly what, if anything, was happening to Darkness. He had hoped that the entity would revive before the Seekers located their prize and decided they needed their "guest" no longer.

One of the avians squawked and reached down to pluck something from the fragments covering most of the area before them. This had likely been a square, complete with statuary, but one of the towers nearby had completely collapsed and the remains were scattered all over, making even travel awkward. Several treacherous crevices crisscrossing the square bespoke of just a few of the possible dangers awaiting them.

It was not some shard from a crushed statue that the Seekers had noted. Things could not have been *that* simple. Rather, the object turned out to be a small pouch made of leather and decorated with symbols. Dru's own view was cursory at best, but he thought it looked akin to the style of the clothing the dead elf—if it *had* been an elf, that was still not clear—had worn. That was probably the case; the Seekers were certainly upset about it. Dru was caught between renewed hope and increased fear. This third party might be his salvation, providing he survived any pitched battle between his captors and them, but they also might prove no more hospitable than the avians had been. At this point, however, Dru was willing to take the chance.

The discovery of the pouch changed the attitude of the party. Already having lost three of their number—after having lost so many during the crossing of the seas—the Seekers evidently felt they could not spare any more of their kind. It was thus that Dru found himself walking before them, within easy enough range to be struck down if he attempted to escape, acting as unwilling first scout. Each Seekers had a hand on the medallion that they wore on their chests. Their vision identical to that of true birds, they kept one eye on their destination and the other on the ruins around them, waiting for any potential ambush.

Nothing happened. Dru reached the steps of the building and turned, uncertain as to whether the leader wanted him to continue on or not. The response he received indicated the latter, at least for the time being. The Seekers gathered at the steps, the sorcerer once more under the watchful gaze of two he suspected were the same ones who had acted as his jailers before. He still had trouble telling them apart, save for the leader, who somehow Dru could readily identify, now that they had linked minds.

After some silent discussion that the Vraad could only guess at, he was prodded up the steps. Though they had survived relatively intact, there were places that needed only slight encouragement to collapse, which they did several times for the bound spellcaster. It took more than twice as long to climb than it should have and Dru was out of breath by the time they reached the top.

Dru was tugged back from the doorway he had been about to walk through. He cursed the avian who had pulled him and who had nearly succeeded in sending him falling backward down the way he had come.

"What now?" he grumbled, more to himself than the avian who had manhandled him.

A Seeker, one of the females, moved in front of Dru and kicked at the rusted relics that had once been doors. They fell with a clatter that not only vibrated through Dru, but echoed again and again all through the building. A layer of dust rose up, creating a miniature storm. After allowing the dirt to settle again, the Seekers prodded their captive on. The female stood aside as he walked through the doorway, wondering what fate awaited him. A Vraad would have had a thousand lethal snares awaiting intruders, even if that Vraad had died a thousand years before. As old as the ruins seemed, they were in fairly remarkable condition. His fear of some lurking danger was soothed in no way by the actions of the avians, who obviously wanted him to act as a sacrificial lamb.

The builders of this edifice had not been raised on Vraadish ways, though, for nothing struck him down, no ancient spell tore the flesh from his skin, and no metal bolt pierced his chest. The structure, at least the front hall, was safe. Dru would have sighed in relief, but his companions shoved him forward again, eager to explore this place.

Draconian eyes met his own as he moved into the first chamber, a black place without windows. A maw, opened wide enough to swallow the entire party, beckoned. In the darkness of the windowless room, Dru believed he had finally come face-to-face with one of the Lord Tezerenee's dragons. Only when one of the Seekers summoned forth light did he realize that what he had seen was actually a huge stone representation. Dru froze where he was, but no one disciplined him for his actions; the avians were as overwhelmed as he was.

Unlike the dragons of his own world, big, lumbering beasts that acted as little more than pets and steeds for those like Barakas, this dragon was a monarch. The unknown artist had chosen to keep its vast wings folded—likely because of the difficulty it would have caused with the statue's balance—but it was still the largest, most majestic of its kind that the Vraad had ever seen. Here was a leviathan who ruled through both power and intelligence. There was no denying what the sculptor had intended; this was a master of all it surveyed, one who could outwit all but the craftiest of adversaries.

Unbidden returned the question of what had happened to the race that had ruled from here.

Excitement rose among the Seekers; they had recognized a row of items lying on a dais before the overwhelming statue. Dru only now noticed them, the eyes of the giant continually drawing his own despite his efforts.

The dais was more of a display, a platform on which tiny figurines that looked distinctly familiar to Dru stood even after all so much time. In this place, he did not question that. The city, for all its decaying state, was remarkably preserved for having been abandoned so long. The platform and its contents were the only items in the room, which was *not* to say it was bare. The walls, the floor, even the curved *ceiling*, were covered with somewhat surreal representations of worlds and races, most of whom the Vraad could not identify. He saw a tiny sphere that contained a Seeker and another that contained one of the avians' enemies. There was also what Dru assumed was an elf and another that reminded him too much of his own kind.

What is this place?

So many races were represented, but only he had eyes for them. The Seekers were far too interested in the figurines, squawking like excited children . . . like *Sharissa*.

Dru wondered if she was safe. In the citadel, she would have Sirvak to watch over her, but he knew that being his daughter, she would be seeking some clue as to his fate. That worried him, for it would be easy for her to gain the notice of one or more of his rivals and, especially, the Tezerenee. They *might* see Dru's accident as a new means of escape from Nimth, but it was not past the patriarch's madness to assume that Barakas *might* choose to destroy Dru's work. It *would*, after all, weaken the Lord Tezerenee's tightening grip on his fellow Vraad.

A crash made Dru turn back to see what was happening with his captors. Four, including the leader, had been inspecting the artifacts. The care with which they had studied each minute curve of each figurine spoke volumes of their interest. Now, however, something had occurred that infuriated them. The leader had taken one small statuette and flung it at the towering figure of the dragon lord, as Dru was coming to think of it. The relic had shattered, spreading fragments about the room, but the statue had been unmarred.

The sorcerer watched silently. Bitter avians abandoned the figurines, returning to the rest of the party. The leader, frustration and anger at the forefront, pointed at the entranceway, indicating that Dru was to lead them back out. He dared one last glance at the majestic dragon and again felt it return his gaze. The Seeker leader, however, had no patience left and swung a taloned hand at him. Dru fell back, the taste of blood on his tongue, and would have collapsed to the floor if not for his two bodyguards. They kept him on his feet until he had recovered his wits, then pushed him forward, always staying close behind.

In the same manner as they had inspected the first room, the party went through the next dozen. If anything, they were more disappointing than the first. More than one turned out to be nothing but a pile of mortar and rock, the ceilings having collapsed long ago. A few of those chambers that were still whole held nothing but generation upon generation of dust. If the occupants had died here, it had been so long ago that their corpses, even their skeletons, had faded away with time.

They found no trace of the other intruders, although, with the jagged and rocky surfaces they clambered over, it would have been near impossible to find any sort of tracks. Dru suffered over the worst of the treks, his bound arms making it impossible for him to protect his face when he slipped forward. Concerned with their own footing, his two guards often could do nothing for him. By the time they had explored the first floor, the Vraad's face and body were one mass of bruises and cuts. Given the opportunity, he could have easily repaired the damage, but his health was low on his captors' priorities. Dru wondered why they had bothered to even keep him alive, so unconcerned did they seem.

The sun moved ever closer to its daily death. The Seekers' leader grew more and more frustrated and his emotions were echoed by the others. Dru was beyond caring; the sorcerer only wanted to lie down, go to sleep, and wake up in his castle of pearl. He wanted to never have found the tear, the hole between this place and Nimth, even though that meant bowing to Barakas and his clan.

At what had once been the stairway leading to the upper floors but was now a jumble of rock, the Seekers finally lost their last reserves of patience. A look from the leader sent four of them leaping into the air. Dru stirred briefly from his worn musings to watch them fly through the hole where the upper portion of the steps had once led. Although it was a dangerous move, considering there still might be foes lurking somewhere nearby, the avians had chosen to split their numbers in order to facilitate their mad search.

Dragging the harried sorcerer with them, the seven remaining creatures continued their scouring of the main floor. They had come to such a point of desperation that they began to sift through the wreckage of each chamber the instant they entered. Under the watchful, one-eyed gaze of the leader, who held Dru while the search progressed, the avians picked at whatever seemed out of the ordinary among the chunks of ceiling and wall. A few items that they unearthed encouraged them and stirred Dru's curiosity. One or two artifacts that the birds seemed to puzzle over, he recognized but was careful to pretend otherwise. Slowly, some of the ancient race's prowess was revealed to the sorcerer. They knew much about crystal magic, that he could tell from the glittering fragments that the avians shoved rudely aside in their quest. What the Seekers sought, however, evidently had nothing to do with that; they seemed far more interested in objects that represented forms, such as dragons, animals, and things that might have been, in a vague way, referred to as human.

The leader, who still held him by the arm, suddenly cocked

his head to one side, as if listening to something outside. Dru strained, but heard nothing but the clatter of rubble as the avians tossed bits of ceiling away in order to burrow deeper into the wreckage. A breath later, the rest had paused in their work, also listening.

Dru heard nothing save the beat of his own heart . . . until he realized that the clap-clap pattern could hardly be coming from him if the others heard it. No, the sounds issued from an unknown location near the main hall, and were getting closer by the second.

Rising, the Seekers looked to their leader. He eyed Dru, then tugged the spellcaster around him and tossed him toward the doorway. Stumbling, Dru stepped out into the corridor. The unsettling clap-clap sounds continued to rise in volume, in some way as familiar to the sorcerer as the icons had been earlier. He tried to recall what made that sort of sound, but his attempt to harness his scattered thoughts into something functional was cut off by a harsh shove from the Seekers' leader. Lacking any choice in the matter—and that was becoming too common a way for one who had grown knowing there was little he could *not* have—Dru walked slowly down the corridor in the direction of the noise's source. The avians followed, spreading out as they moved. Two took to the air, hovering near the ceiling.

The sounds echoed continuously throughout the vast structure, almost to the point where it grew difficult for the hapless sorcerer to estimate where he had to turn. He turned back, and as if knowing his confusion, the leader pointed ahead.

"*Thank you,*" Dru whispered in bitter tones. There was no hope of avoiding a confrontation with whatever sought out the party. It did not sound like the massive creatures who burrowed beneath the earth—the Vraad would have expected their footfalls to be near silent, considering that blood enemies lurked somewhere within the edifice—and neither did he think it was the elves, whom he had still not seen. They, too, would have taken more caution.

What then lurked in the main hall and had the effrontery to move without care of detection into a place of possible danger?

He was so near now that the clap-clap sounds made it impossible to wonder further. The avian leader put a taloned hand around his neck, essentially turning the Vraad into a living shield. The two of them, with the others following as if all were puppets commanded by the same strings, stepped into the main hall and, all too soon, the confrontation.

Behind him, the avian started, almost losing his grip on the human. Dru could in no way blame him.

It was a *stallion* of the deepest ebony, an impossible and grand creature more massive than any the sorcerer had ever seen. As it slowed to a halt, the clap-clap noise, the sound of its hooves striking the hard surface of the floor, died. The steed stood taller than either the human or the avian. The animal shook its head, sending the wild mane fluttering. It looked at the two tiny figures before it as if they were specks of dust needing to be swept away and began pawing at the rock-hard floor.

Dru tried to step back, but the leader's stiff form prevented him from doing so. Before the eyes of the party, the stallion continued to paw at the floor with its hoof . . . and was quickly succeeding in gouging a *crevice* in it!

The steed lifted its head high and, instead of a loud neigh, *laughed* at their dismay.

X

Lochivan ceased screaming the moment he felt the hands upon him, knowing that he had already shamed himself before his clan. The raging wind and the stormy heavens could not take his mind from that fact.

"Have no fear concerning your reaction to the cross-over," he heard Esad, his brother, whisper. "Most of us screamed and the rest have all felt the pain. *No one* will speak of it when Father arrives."

The newly arrived Vraad gazed down at his naked form, at

last feeling the effects of the storm. "My clothing—" He looked up at Esad, who was clad in armor identical to that which they had been forced to abandon back in Nimth . . . along with their *old* bodies. The armor and the rest had been conjured, no doubt, but then why could Lochivan not emulate his brother's work? Why did the magic resist him?

"The first arrivals clothed me," the other Tezerenee said, reading Lochivan's mind. "It takes great effort and often more than one person to push the spell to completion." Even with the helm covering much of his features, it was obvious that Esad was under tremendous strain.

As Lochivan stood and shook his head, causing several locks of brown and gray hair to obscure his vision, he found himself clad once more in the comfortable feel of cloth and dragon scale. The Tezerenee nodded his gratitude to those of his kin who had aided him. "Have we all made it across so far?"

"Yes."

Something in Esad's tone encouraged his brother to survey the others assembled. There were ten, so far, including himself, and he could see that each and every one was there. Still, something was amiss. There was no mistaking the worry in Esad's voice, and Lochivan knew it was not for him. "Tell me what is wrong, brother?"

"A number of the golems are missing."

"*Missing?*" The Vraad whirled about until he caught sight of the still forms. Seeing them even now made his stomach turn, though he would not admit that to the others. That the body he wore had once been as these. . . .

It took him a moment to estimate their numbers and then he saw that what Esad said was true; there were perhaps a hundred of the flesh-and-blood golems remaining where Esad had reported two hundred or more. "The dragons!" Lochivan snarled, recalling the beasts that the golems had been formed from. "Ephraim will pay dearly for his betrayal! With he and his band of traitors gone, the dragons returned and devoured the—"

"No." It was not Esad who spoke, but one of their sisters, a tall, slender woman who favored their mother in form. *Tamara* was her name, if Lochivan recalled correctly. She had been born some eight or nine centuries prior to both of them. It was sometimes so difficult to keep track of those within the clan, much less the outsiders as well. "No," she repeated. "It was not dragons. There are no traces, no blood. The bodies vanished in too orderly a manner, as if those who had taken them had stood in line, one following after another."

"Logan will be crossing in one quarter hour," Esad reminded the two of them. "We should be preparing to guide him on this side of the veil. If we don't, there is always the chance his *ka* may become lost." The chances of such were slim as long as those back in Nimth still controlled matters; both Lochivan and Tamara knew that Esad was trying to steer them both away from a subject he found unnerving. Father would not be pleased and he would want someone physical to blame. For the moment, Ephraim was beyond his capacity to punish, but they were not.

Lochivan shook his head again. "Father must know before long. The greater our delay in informing him of this latest debacle, the worse it will be."

"We will still have to wait for Logan," Tamara reminded them. "We need at least eleven to reach through the veil and establish a *true* link of communications with the others. Any word we send now would likely be garbled, and I, for one, want everything perfectly clear when we report this to Father."

The storm, a side effect of the transfer, was rapidly dwindling to nil. Gazing up at the wondrous blue color replacing the dark gray clouds, the latest immigrant quietly cursed the misleading innocence that lay all about him. At any other time, the clear sky would have entranced Lochivan, who had never seen such a thing. Now, though, he thought of the problems the plan had suffered of late and how the Dragonrealm was not going to fall to Barakas's might so easily.

"Very well." Unconsciously, he stood in a pose that mimicked the patriarch almost exactly. If his relations paid no notice to it, it was only because they themselves were often guilty of the same mannerisms.

"We have a little over a quarter hour to decide *exactly* how we'll tell Father . . . and *how* we'll avoid his anger!"

Dru started to speak, but his mouth refused to answer his desperate summons. The laughter died away, though its echo would continue on for several seconds. Trotting closer, the huge ebony steed eyed the avian party with blue orbs that chilled any who stared in them. It chuckled, a low, spine-scraping sound that mocked those who would stand against it.

One of the Seekers held up a medallion and focused on the demon horse. Dru recognized the terrible mist. It started to form around its intended victim in the exact manner it had around the hapless earth dweller earlier. In the space of a breath, it was nearly impossible to see the stallion. The Vraad could feel the sense of triumph that flashed between his captors.

The ebony steed trotted forward, ignoring the mist as the sorcerer might ignore the very air he breathed.

"If that is the best you can do," the animal boomed, and its voice stunned Dru, for he recognized it instantly, "you should not have struck at all!"

Laughing, the entity calling itself Darkness winked at the captive spellcaster. "You should not run off, little Dru! I was most distressed when I found you missing! At least *I* waited while *you* slept!"

Two brown shapes dove down from behind the Void dweller, talons poised, while his attention was focused on the human.

"Look—" A backhand slap from the Seekers' leader silenced him before he could warn Darkness of the danger to him. Nonetheless, the massive stallion understood enough to twist his head around, though it was too late to avoid the attack.

The first avian struck, his clawed feet ready to rend the back of the impudent creature below. To his horror and that of the rest of the party, the diving attacker found *no* solid flesh beneath his talons. Instead, he kept diving, sinking into the darker than dark mass that was the phantom steed. The Seeker screeched once, then seemed to dwindle as he sank completely into Darkness. It was as if he had fallen into a bottomless crevice that sucked him ever deeper despite his efforts to the contrary. In mere moments, the would-be killer had vanished, taken completely in by Darkness.

A raucous noise rose among the Seekers as they voiced their dismay.

That was what he meant by taking me, Dru realized when thought was finally possible again. He swallowed hard, thankful for his escape from such a fate.

Unable to combat his own momentum, the second winged fury joined his brother, dwindling and vanishing even faster than the first had. It was almost anticlimactic after the first, though no less horrible, and in less than a minute, Darkness had destroyed—*devoured?*—two opponents without even striking.

"And *who* will be next? All you really need do is release my friend to me! What say you?" The shadowy steed indicated Dru with a nod of his head. Once, the thought of a talking horse would have been simply a matter of amusement to the Vraad; not so now. There was nothing humorous about the astonishing stallion that the Seekers faced.

The leader glanced at Dru, at his remaining fellows, and then back at Darkness. He released his grip on the spellcaster's neck, for which the Vraad was extremely grateful. The bonds vanished as quickly.

As one, the avians spread their wings and took to the air. With equally swift speed, they abandoned the hall—and, apparently, their goal—and flew out the same tall doorway through which the party had initially entered. All the while, Darkness kept a cold blue eye on them, openly daring them to face him down. As the last departed, he let loose with another earsplitting laugh, his final cut at the fleeing foe.

"This is too amusing! One adventure after another! I shall ever be in your debt, little Dru!"

The sorcerer did not answer, choosing to collapse to the floor, the first time he had been able to rest without the painful interference from his captors. Darkness trotted toward him, still chuckling. Dru shook his head at the incongruous sight, as yet unable to believe either the entity's new appearance or his own luck.

"It's fortunate that you left a trail for me to follow, friend Dru. Those *things* did not seem friendly sorts; I suspect they would have harmed you."

"They certainly seemed to be." The weary sorcerer knew that he should move on, but the opportunity to rest unhindered for once was too sweet to pass on.

"You have not commented on my form! Is it not exceptional? Truly, the sensations and movements are nearly overwhelming! I felt the urge to push to greater and greater speeds and never slow down again . . . it took some doing to not keep going once

I did reach this place.'' The shadow steed peered around at the ruins, his attention wandering as he finally got a good look at the ancient wonders around him.

''How did you . . . how did you come to take that form?''

Darkness snorted, recalling what he had been speaking of. ''This *magnificent* creature strode up to me as I unfolded, altered but still at a loss as to a final form. I thought of shaping myself into something akin to you, but the creature was so fascinating that I could not help but wonder what it would be like to move as it did, to live as it did.'' The ebony stallion laughed low. ''It was a most prepossessing being! Once it saw what I wanted, it allowed me to examine it. Then, when I was at last complete, it showed me the path you had taken. What do you call such a remarkable creature?''

The Vraad had grown colder with each passing word. ''A horse. My kind calls such a creature a horse.'' No horse was so knowing, however, at least none that Dru had ever raised. He was certain that the animal Darkness had met was the very same horse that he had once ridden. Yet, its actions had not been that of the true beast, but that of an intelligent mind. ''Where is it now?''

''Hmm?'' Darkness seemed distracted in his thoughts. He shook his head, sending his mane whipping back and forth. It took him another moment to answer. ''It departed! I do not know where. 'Horse'! I like it, but it lacks something!''

Dru puzzled over the last. ''What about it?''

The ghostly stallion gazed at his tiny companion as if he could not comprehend the latter's confusion. ''I have a brand-new *form*! I need a *new* name!''

This was hardly the time for such things and Dru tried to tell the entity so, but the shadow steed was already tossing words about, seeking a combination that would please himself. ''Mighty . . . black . . . amazing . . . majestic . . .''

''Dark—'' The tired spellcaster rose, trying again to cut into the creature's musings, but luck was not with him.

''Dark? Hmmm. Frightening . . . shadow . . . wondrous . . .'' The ice-blue eyes focused on the human. ''What say you to *Darkhorse*? I like the old name, but Darknesshorse runs too long.''

''It's . . . descriptive of your nature.'' Dru refused to even mention some of the meanings the name brought to mind. No one would jest about the appropriateness, not to such a being as this.

"Darkhorse it is, then!" The huge stallion shouted his name so that it echoed and echoed through the ruins. "Darkhorse! Darkhorse!"

Cursing, the sorcerer tried desperately to get his companion to quiet down but it was already too late. If there was anyone else in the city—and he knew that the Seekers, at least, would still be lurking about, waiting their chance—then they knew exactly where the twosome were.

Darkness—*Darkhorse*, the Vraad thought, correcting himself—seemed willing to listen now that he had found himself a new name. Hopefully, it would be more permanent than the last.

With the magic of the Seekers no longer dampening his own abilities and senses, Dru was becoming more and more aware of the aura surrounding—*overwhelming*—the ancient citadel. The building he stood in was especially awash in the sorceries of the long-dead race. It had the same feel as the natural forces of the shrouded realm itself, save that it was far more concentrated, as if the inhabitants of this place had filled their home with raw power drawn from the world. It would not have surprised him; the Vraad were capable of such, but not on the grand scale he suspected these ancients had.

"Those things that captured me—the Seekers—were looking for something in these ruins. Do you feel anything at all?"

Darkhorse sniffed the air, an act which put Dru off for a moment. Then the stallion replied, "There is a great concentration of power nearby, several such, actually. They tend to be moving, however."

"The power moves of its own accord?" Dru had never come across anything like that on Nimth. Wandering concentrations of sorcerous energy?

"That is how it appears. What is this place, little Dru? This is the most magnificent sight you have shown me so far! So much solidity, in some ways so random and some ways so orderly!" Coming from a place where matter was nearly as rare as a clear sky was in Nimth, Darkhorse did not know what ruins were.

The Vraad did his best to explain to him his theory about the ruins. Darkhorse became so interested that he interrupted only twice, curious both instances about the passage of time, a concept he was still having trouble comprehending. After the second interruption, he angrily dropped his queries and went back to the enjoyment of what, to him, was an exciting story.

When the tale was finished, Dru sighed. Even if Darkhorse only saw the theory as a great story, at least he understood most of what had been said.

"I have told you again and again, friend Dru, that this *is* your world! It may not be the location you desired, but this *is* where you asked to be taken!"

Dru gave in, knowing the futility of arguing. Perhaps later he would broach the subject again.

"And now," Darkhorse was continuing, "where do we find this 'goal' of theirs?"

"Find it?" The sorcerer had not had time to consider that. His mind was only now becoming organized enough to plan the future . . . and an important aspect of that future was finding a way back to Nimth, Darkhorse or no Darkhorse. Still, if the avians believed that what they sought was so important, then it might hold some key, for certainly, if anyone had ever known about the veil and Nimth, it would have been the builders of this edifice. Straightening, Dru smiled grimly. "Yes, let's find it. They thought it was in here, but I don't think that's the way to go about it."

The shadow steed had an eager gleam in his unsettling eyes. He was all ready for another game of discovery. "And how shall we go about it?"

"I can't sense the distinctive areas of power that you can and I doubt if the Seekers can, either. Tell me, are they in a pattern—a circle or something?"

Darkhorse shook his head after a moment. "They have no pattern. Their movements show judgment, but not a regular path."

The Vraad did not like the way his companion spoke of the power as something with intelligence. Darkhorse himself was difficult enough to accept. Dru was still getting used to the entity.

He considered further. "Is there any one area they tend to avoid or congregate near?"

When the wraithlike stallion answered, Dru's hopes rose

dramatically. "There is a place they move near and then away from. There is no place they seem to avoid completely. They . . ." The blue orbs dulled a touch.

"They *what*?"

"I do not know. It escapes me for now."

Curious but also cautious, Dru asked, "Have any of those . . . concentrations . . . shifted near us?"

"They have all crossed this place since I arrived. Some have even passed through this very chamber while we spoke."

"*What?*" The sorcerer's mouth fell open and remained that way until he was able to force his next question to the surface. "Why didn't you—?" Dru clamped his mouth shut and berated himself. Darkhorse was an innocent in many ways; the manner with which he had dispatched the two avians had made the human forget that. "Forget it. You didn't tell me because I didn't ask and you felt it was nothing dangerous, correct?"

"On the contrary! I only recalled when you asked me. For reasons I cannot fathom, my recollection of many things has become faulty. Is this what you termed 'exhaustion'?"

"Possibly." The worried spellcaster doubted such was actually the reason. From what he had seen, his companion from beyond did not suffer exhaustion as others did. Once again, the shrouded realm itself was acting against the outsiders.

"Shall we go to this place, then?"

"This—" Dru had forgotten about the location the black horse had mentioned, the one that the sorcerer suspected might house whatever it was the Seekers had wanted so desperately. "You know where it is?"

"Little Dru! I can find it easily! It has an aura of its own, one far different from that which surrounds this place."

"Does it?" That interested Dru. He started to move again, eager suddenly to be on the trail, but his body protested. "I need to rest a little. I don't think that I have the strength to go climbing over more wreckage just yet."

"There is no need for you to do so if it wearies you! Simply climb atop my back and I will carry you to our destination."

"Your *back*?" Memories of the two Seekers swallowed whole were enough to make Dru reject such a mad plan without further thought. "That would—"

Darkhorse laughed. "Poor, simple Dru! Of course my backside will be solid! You are too good of an entertainment for me to take you as I did those others! You are my *friend*!''

Mounting the shadow steed proved a bit difficult for the tired sorcerer, partly because Darkhorse had no bridle or saddle. There were those, like Sharissa, who could ride a horse bareback if the whim was upon them. Dru preferred his comforts. Once he was aboard, however, things changed. Darkhorse was not built exactly like the animal he had so boldly copied. Despite his muscular appearance, the ebony stallion's back was soft, almost padded. It was, in fact, better than a saddle. Dru wished all horses had been designed like his companion and decided that any he raised from now on would have a few minor magical alterations made.

He found it easy to accept Darkhorse as some fantastic steed. Thinking of him as such was easier than trying to cope with the concept of an intelligent black hole . . . not that Dru was going to truly forget what the entity was. It was just more comfortable thinking of Darkhorse as a physical being, especially now that he was riding the creature.

The fearsome stallion picked his way through the rubble to the doorway leading out of the ancient structure. Dru worried about some trap laid by the Seekers, but Darkhorse sensed nothing. The spellcaster wished his own senses were so infallible. He was lucky to even sense the aura of raw power that covered most of the city. Dru wondered if at one time a shield of such power had enveloped the entire citadel. The sorcerer who cast it could have literally made for himself a world of his own, for no one would be able to enter—or *exit*, if that was his desire—without his permission.

Useless conjecture, he reprimanded himself. Best to keep his eyes upon the ruins around him, just in case there was some threat that Darkhorse did *not* notice in time. What he would do if such happened was beyond him; Dru trusted his own abilities as much as he trusted the Seekers not to attempt one last ploy.

"How odd!" The shadow steed's booming words bounced again and again throughout the devastated city.

"What is it?" Dru peered around, looking for Seekers or elves or *anything* to justify his companion's cry.

"I saw a figure, but only as a vague form! It was built akin to you, but that was all I could tell."

An elf, perhaps. Yet, what was there about an elf that Darkhorse found so disquieting? "Why do you find that odd?"

"Because I could sense nothing from him. No presence. No . . . *existence*."

"An illusion?"

Darkhorse evidently knew the term now, for he shook his head with great vehemence. "Not an illusion. I think I would sense the . . . the sorcery . . . at least."

"Where was it?" The Vraad cursed whatever fickle trait made him miss everything that happened until it came crashing down on him.

"Directly ahead. It stood on our very path."

The sorcerer reached down to his belt, wishing he had a sword. While spells had always been a way of life, he, like many Vraad, dabbled in the physical, especially when it involved violence toward another. Dru was adept with many blades and had even killed one rival in a duel using nothing but a sword. "I was looking ahead. *I* didn't see anything up there."

"Beyond the tall structure leaning to one side."

The "tall structure" was a tower, far in the distance, that had partially fallen onto a smaller building on the other side of the street they were following. The only thing that it now revealed to the sorcerer was that they might have trouble getting around it unless they took a different path. Darkhorse's vision was evidently much more efficient than his own. The Vraad was not quite desperate enough to start experimenting with his eyes.

A low grumble from his stomach informed him of other matters he would also soon have to deal with if he hoped to continue on. The Seekers had fed him, but only small portions of some vile meat that tasted as if it had been stored in salt and left to age for a few years. All that could be said for it was that it had assuaged his hunger for a time.

Darkhorse continued on the route he had chosen, despite the mysterious appearance. The demon steed was confident in his ability to handle whatever threats confronted them and so was becoming more and more lost in his ongoing game of discovery. A statue that had somehow stood the test of time made him pause for a moment. It was unremarkable save that it was whole. Like the stone behemoth that the sorcerer had come across while a prisoner of the avians, this, too, was a dragon. In fact, it was identical to the other save in size. There were a few other statues and some had recognizable attributes, though they were, for the most part, cluttered together and broken. One was a wolf and another a human garbed in a robe. The rest were too broken up to identify readily, though Dru imagined he saw the gryphon and a cat in the pile.

They eventually reached a point where the Vraad saw that his fears about the fallen tower were true; the opening it left was too small for the sorcerer, much less the huge stallion.

Darkhorse was in the process of locating a new path free of blockage when they came across the elf.

She was young in appearance—though with elves that meant as much as it did with the Vraad—athletic in build, and had straight silver hair that would have reached her waist had she been standing. This elf would stand no more, however, for she was dead, a needle spear that had pierced her chest a certain sign as to who her murderers had been. Dru wondered how long ago she had died; the blood had congealed, but she still appeared too close to life to have perished very long ago.

"What is that?" Darkhorse asked innocently, curious as to this new form.

"An elf." The sorcerer recalled his one-time desire to capture an elf so that he could dissect it. That desire, that *Dru*, turned his stomach now. "There have been none in Nimth for thousands and thousands of years."

"Obviously there are. *She* is here."

Dru held back from commenting, having no desire at present to argue about whether this was Nimth or not. He dismounted and looked over the corpse for any clues, any bits of information that would better help him understand his situation. Unfortunately, the elf had nothing with her save her clothing and a tiny knife. The Vraad took the knife gratefully. As tiny as it was, it was still a physical weapon.

At last satisfied that he would find nothing more, Dru mounted up again, saying to Darkhorse, "The things that killed her have a habit of rising from the earth. It would be an excellent idea to keep an eye out . . . just in case."

"As you say, little Dru."

The sorcerer, about to suggest that they move on, shivered as something cold seemed to brush by him. He twisted back, scanning the area around him, but saw nothing. Dru was too experienced to think that he had imagined the sensation. "Darkhorse, was there something near us?"

"One of the concentrations of power passed *through* us. I think it wanted to know more."

"It wanted to *know*?"

"It exists, after a fashion. Much the way you think of me."

Dru gripped his companion's mane tight. "It thinks? Why didn't you say something *before*? I—"

"I did not know until it actually crossed me. Then I felt its thirst for knowledge—fascinating! Your world never ceases to amaze me! Shall we go forward again?"

"I don't—" Dru was unable to finish his sentence, for Darkhorse pushed ahead immediately after asking the question, despite whatever opinion his friend might have had. The sorcerer clamped his mouth shut and opened his senses as much as they allowed. Oddly, there was no resistance this time, possibly because he was now attempting to work *with* the land. In a vague way, the Vraad felt the massive concentrations of power around him and how they moved with purpose, though their patterns might have once appeared random. Dru knew he could not be far from the place that Darkhorse had spoken of. Whether he found anything there . . .

"You are so very quiet, friend Dru! Are you whole!"

A feeling of unease was gradually creeping over the weary spellcaster. It was as if every bit of rubble had eyes and ears and was following each move the duo made.

"I feel like a blind lamb about to enter the den of a pack of silent, starving wolves."

Wolves.

Dru gave a start. Darkhorse also tensed. "They are concentrating more and more in one location!"

The Vraad nodded, sensing an overwhelming level of raw power ahead of them. Though other structures still blocked their view, he knew that what he and the ebony stallion sought was very, very near . . . and it was there that the power concentrated.

Wolves.

There it was again! As if the wind itself had spoken!

"Something happens, friend Dru! Prepare yourself!"

Prepare himself? The sorcerer wanted to know *how*. His senses warned him that the danger lay everywhere, including above and below him. With his present distrust of his skills, how could he even consider fighting back against . . .

Against the ruins of the city.

It began with a tremor far worse in intensity than that which had signaled the rise of the underdwellers, the armored monstrosities from below. No, whatever caused the ground to quiver so, if it was not an actual earthquake, was far greater than them.

A building before them *exploded*, but the fragments, instead of raining down upon the two, flew high into the air above where the edifice had stood. Rubble from the streets flew up after them, joining together and forming great clusters. Nothing was spared; mortar, bits of marble from shattered statues, even vast pieces of the tower they had bypassed . . . all gathered together.

Beneath the Vraad, Darkhorse shied. There was a limit, evidently, to even his bravery. Had he turned and charged off madly, Dru would have urged him on. As it was, neither of them took up the option of flight. The form slowly taking on vague shape had them almost entranced. It stood taller than the great domed building where the demon steed had rescued his companion. There were four limbs, a tail, which was made at least partially from a column, and, if one stretched the imagination to the limit, a head.

Only when it opened its mockery of a mouth, revealing teeth formed from jagged, broken pieces of stone, did Dru identify it as any particular beast.

It was, as the wind had whispered to him, a wolf . . . more than forty feet *tall*.

XI

"Do you like my home, Shari darling?"

"It's so...*alive!*" the younger woman breathed. Melenea's citadel, what Sharissa could see of it, was awash with gay colors and glittering crystals. Silk was everywhere. Figurines of fantastical design capered and celebrated. A furry carpet that Dru's daughter was tempted to lose herself in covered the entire floor. Bright candles lit up the vast room they had materialized in, candles whose flames were of all sizes and more than a dozen different flickering colors. Panoramas of women and men competing in game after game covered one wall. The Vraadish symbol of gaming, used most often when announcing a forming duel, was the centerpiece of the wall across from the entrance-way of the chamber. It would be the first thing someone saw when they entered here. The symbol consisted of two masks, one crying and one laughing, with the former partly obscuring the latter. Sharissa knew that the masks represented the basic aspects of the Vraad mentality.

Her father had summed it up in his own special way. "When your enemy flaunts his weakness, look to your back. When your allies grow too friendly, trust in your enemies."

Sharissa was not certain she liked what she read into her father's definition, but she allowed that there was probably some truth to it.

"Have a seat, sweet thing! Rest yourself. I know how terrible things have been for you of late. There's so much I have to prepare, anyway."

"I really couldn't..." Despite her words, Sharissa wanted all too much to relax, to sleep. Her constant fears, the race against time, and the very dominant worry that it might all be for nothing, that her father might be dead, were taking their toll on her again.

"I insist." Melenea shoved her backward. As Sharissa fell, the thick, shaggy carpet swelled upward, catching her softly in what was, a second later, a comfortable couch. The soothing fur encouraged the young Zeree to rest. "I promise that I will not forget you, Shari. You may count on that."

It was too overpowering. Sharissa settled in and nodded, already half asleep.

"That's fine," the enchantress said, smiling at her guest. She raised a hand, palm upward, and formed a fist. When she opened it again, a small pouch lay within. Melenea took hold of the pouch and opened it. She reached in and pulled out a tiny, squirming figure.

Sharissa, though a part of her wondered what her companion attempted, could not rouse herself to do more than watch through half-closed eyes. Even when the tiny creature, now set loose on the floor, began to grow and grow, the novice sorceress simply stared. It was as if everything around her had taken on a dreamlike quality.

"Come, Cabal," she heard Melenea say to the creature, a blue-green wolf already as tall as its mistress. It had fangs that seemed as long as Sharissa's forearm, and though she was in no state to truly count them, she was certain that its teeth numbered more than a thousand.

When it was almost a foot taller than Melenea, the wolf ceased growing. Sharissa focused long enough to know that she was staring at the enchantress's familiar.

"I live to serve you, lady." The wolf's voice was little more than a deep growl.

"We have a guest with us, Cabal. Her name is Sharissa Zeree." Melenea turned and smiled at the younger Vraad. "This is Cabal, Shari sweet. It'll watch over you so that you can rest easy. Cabal will let nothing happen to you."

"Will I get to play with her, lady?" Cabal asked, eyeing Sharissa in a manner that seemed more suited for sizing up a snack as opposed to studying a potential playmate.

"Perhaps later. I have given you a duty to perform. You will watch Shari at all times, make certain she is secure."

"I obey knowing my life is yours."

"That's as it should be." Melenea stroked the head of the

massive wolf, then stepped closer to Sharissa, who tried in vain to concentrate enough to rise. The beautiful enchantress sat down beside her and stroked her hair. "No need to rise," she heard Melenea say, though the voice sounded as if it had passed through a long tunnel. "You sleep. Later, you'll have my undivided attention."

The kiss on her forehead tickled Sharissa, making her giggle rather giddily. Her last view of Melenea was of the sorceress rising and smiling to herself. The crystals she had gotten from Sharissa were in her hand. There was something not quite right about the image, for the smile had no warmth in it. Dru's daughter shifted uneasily, rest momentarily put off.

Melenea had vanished by the time she forced herself to look again, but the familiar, Cabal, lay watching her from no more than ten feet away. It had an eager expression on its lupine visage, as if looking forward to something. Its size further unsettled Sharissa. She rolled over so that if she opened her eyes again, they would not settle immediately on the massive wolf.

The masks stared back at her.

Frustrated, more awake than asleep now, the young Zeree squeezed her eyes closed. Of all places, this was the one in which she should have felt most at ease. Here, Sharissa should be able to get the rest that she *knew* she needed. It was only a matter of letting her exhaustion take over again. That was all.

Lying on the floor, with its gaze ever on its charge, the huge Cabal opened its mouth wide and yawned its boredom. Its eyes glittered in the candlelight, black, pupilless things that never blinked.

Outside, a storm was brewing. Such was not uncommon on magic-torn Nimth and, especially, near the domain of one such as Melenea, who cast spells almost wantonly. There would be no rain...there was never any rain. Sharissa enjoyed the sounds of a storm even though she knew that the storm itself was a product of Nimth's twisted nature. The thunder eased her troubled mind...and at last allowed her to sleep.

The stonework monster snapped its peculiar jaws closed, sending bits of mortar and marble flying. It was constantly losing pieces of itself, but new fragments continually replenished its form.

Go! Flee! The words sprang to life within Dru's head unbidden. He was sorely tempted to follow them, but some deep, arrogant pride kept him from doing so.

Below him, Darkhorse shook his head, as if trying to clear it of noise. The sorcerer suspected that his companion was hearing the same words, that those words had been planted by the chaotic creature before them.

Fear! Death!

On cue, the leviathan stretched forward, snapping its makeshift jaws at them. A shower of dust and fragments threatened to smother Dru. Fortunately, none of the fragments was large enough to injure him.

"They are all around us, friend Dru! One of them has taken on this form! I find it interesting, but also highly annoying! Must it shout within our minds so? Does it need us to fear it so much?"

That was the question that the sorcerer had been asking himself. For all its size and apparent strength, the behemoth was holding back. Why? If it meant to destroy them, it certainly had the opportunity.

Darkhorse had said that one of the unseen beings—they could no longer be simply thought of as concentrations of sorcerous power—had clothed itself in this form. The beings had known about them since at least the huge, circular edifice, yet had not confronted them sooner. That meant that they were guardians, yet as guardians, would they not be able to strike back?

Somehow, Dru suspected that they could or would not. The only question remained—if it was a case of the latter, was there a point that he might cross that would unleash their strength?

"Ride forward, Darkhorse."

"At our peculiar friend? Little Dru, you never cease to entertain me!" Laughing, the ebony steed pushed forward.

Wolves! Teeth that tear! Mangled bodies! Blood!

The words by themselves would not have bothered Dru, but each was accompanied by images of his corpse—what was left of it—scattered about on the rocky surface of the city. He saw the wolf grinding up his bones in its stony teeth. Despite his attempts, he could not help feeling more than a little uneasy as they drew nearer and nearer to the odd horror.

When they were within what the Vraad estimated was no more than twenty feet of the monster, it *collapsed*.

The ensuing storm of dust and rock caught Dru by surprise. He coughed for several seconds, trying to breathe in a cloud of dirt. Darkhorse froze where he was, evidently knowing that the sorcerer's grip was nonexistent and a wrong step would send him falling. The ebony stallion's grasp of human frailties was growing.

It took some time for the dust to settle, but when it had, Dru's view left him puzzled. There was nothing before him that seemed to warrant such protection. Yet, this close he could feel the consternation of the unseen beings, the questioning sensation, as if they did not know what to do about the twosome. In Darkhorse they must have sensed incredible ability. Dru pictured servants, much like his darkdwellers, whose ultimate purpose was something other than fighting. The darkdwellers would attack his enemies if there was no one else to protect his sanctum, but they would do so haphazardly, lacking as they did any real knowledge of combat. The guardians of this place, he decided, were much the same.

Wisdom, a voice, different from the first, whispered in his mind. *Understanding.*

Aberration, came another. *Not to be here.*

Darkhorse roared at the unseen speakers, shouting sentiments that matched Dru's quite closely. "Enough voices in my mind! Speak to us or be gone! Come! Are you so afraid of us?"

That was the truth of it, the sorcerer knew. The guardians *did* fear them. Not just because the two of them had come this far, either. It was because they knew the two to be different, to be outsiders.

Remove them! That was the first voice, the one that had taken the thought of wolves from the Vraad's mind and attempted to use it as a means of scaring them off. *Remove them!*

No, the one who had commented on wisdom said calmly. Each of the guardians seemed to have a separate personality or perhaps a separate characteristic. There were more than the three who had spoken, but Dru took these as the more dominant of the guardians.

No interference, the one who had called them aberrations said, almost as if reminding the others of something. *All must proceed.*

Darkhorse kicked at the rubble, frustrated that the beings would not speak directly to them. The sorcerer put a warning hand against the shadow steed's side. In his ear, Dru whispered, "Calm yourself. I think they may leave."

"Why should they leave?" Darkhorse asked much too loudly. The tired Vraad winced, knowing that the guardians must have heard his companion. For that matter, they probably knew what the sorcerer himself had said, so easily did they touch the mind.

No interference, a multitude of ghostly voices echoed suddenly in Dru's head. With that, the entities withdrew from both his mind and the vicinity. One breath they were there, the next they were gone. Dru could sense no trace of them.

"They have departed," Darkhorse announced needlessly. "Good! They were hardly entertaining company after the one dropped the fascinating form!"

Somehow, the ebony stallion's almost humorous attitude eased the tension that Dru was suffering. He leaned forward and stared at the visibly unprepossessing area they had been protecting. He could still see nothing of value and there seemed only the slightest touch of power.

"Do you know where they went?" he finally asked Darkhorse.

"I cannot feel them," the steed replied.

"What about the region before us? Do you sense anything there?"

"Only what I felt before."

The tall sorcerer straightened and rubbed his chin, which had developed stubble, he noted belatedly. "We may as well go and see what they thought was so worth protecting."

"Of course! Did you actually consider otherwise?" Still sounding amazed that his companion had even thought of turning away, Darkhorse worked his way across the rubble.

Dru turned his head this way and that as the phantom steed moved. He fully expected the guardians to return, this time with more than just bluffs as weapons. What sort of beings were they? Certainly not the builders of this city. If they were akin to familiars, as Dru thought they were, why did they remain so long after their masters had turned to memories?

The air shimmered before them, slowly peeling away. It took the sorcerer time to recognize what lay before them and Darkhorse, ever curious, had picked up his pace at first sign of this latest phenomenon.

"Darkhorse! No! Stop!"

The demon horse backstepped quickly, coming to a stop only a few feet from the shimmering gap, a tear in reality.

"What is the matter? I find nothing dangerous about this! Do you fear it?"

"It . . . it's like the thing I investigated just before I was cast adrift in the Void."

"Ah! Then perhaps this will get you to the home you keep complaining I have not brought you to! Shall we enter, then?"

Dru had not considered the idea that this might be exactly what he had been looking for. Whatever lay within the tear was not yet visible. Likely, they would have to literally be standing in it to see their destination. It was still a hope, however, and one that Dru was willing to cling to if it meant reuniting himself with Sharissa.

"Go in." He tightened his grip and prayed to some of his less repugnant ancestors that he was not making the final mistake of his existence.

Darkhorse stepped into the tear, which seemed to widen so as to admit him more easily.

At first, Dru was aware of nothing but bright illumination, as if he were staring into the sun of the shroud realm. Then, while his eyes were still recuperating, sound returned. The sorcerer had not even been aware of the fact that there had been no sounds until they had returned. With them also came touch and smell. Dru felt the cool breeze and smelled the flowers. He heard the small birds singing where there had been none in the abandoned city.

His eyes finally focused. Before Dru could speak, a voice from below him boomed, "Worlds within worlds! I shall never tire of your fantastic home, little Dru!"

The Vraad, on the other hand, was growing tired of being shocked all the time, though he was no less astonished this time than he had been when he had met his companion, been delivered to the shrouded realm, and discovered the city—was there nothing simple and straightforward in this domain? It was as if someone had designed everything as in a game or a vast experiment.

Where the two of them had once stood in the midst of an ancient, ruined citadel, they now stood at the bottom of a grassy hill on which was perched a beautiful and not at all ruined castle. Banners still fluttered in the wind, crisp and new, not tattered and torn. The castle consisted of spiral towers and a great wall, at least as far as Dru could see, with more buildings likely hidden. The grassy field that covered the rest of the hill was neat and orderly. Someone might have trimmed it only yesterday, so immaculate it was.

Dru did not even hesitate. Things had gone on too long for his strained nerves. He wanted answers, not to mention food, drink, and rest. "We go inside. Now."

The ebony stallion said nothing, but his laughter cut across the hillside as he reared and charged up toward the castle. They were at the gates before Dru even blinked. Regaining his breath, the startled mage wondered exactly how swift his companion was. If the time came, he would question Darkhorse thoroughly. Now, however, this *new* castle was priority.

The gate was open. Dru could sense nothing, but as usual did not trust himself. Darkhorse seemed disinclined to hold back. They were through the gate and into the courtyard in the next breath. As with the outside, the courtyard was in perfect condition. The inhabitants might have stepped out only this very morning. For all the sorcerer knew, they *had*.

Sculpted bushes and vast, colorful flower beds added to the feeling of walking into someone's home while they were away for a moment. Dru admired the marble benches and a tiny bit of his mind noted the style for later use when the Vraad settled in their new world... *if* they did.

"Hold up," he whispered to Darkhorse. The phantom steed came to a halt and Dru dismounted. For their purposes, he preferred to continue on foot.

"Worlds within worlds within worlds..." Darkhorse was saying. "What fun it would be if we entered and found a way to yet another! Just imagine if they went on forever!"

"I'd rather not! Nimth is the only world I want... *my* Nimth," he added quickly, noting his companion ready to argue the point *again*. Studying the buildings, Dru settled on the largest, the one whose towers they had seen from beyond the walls. "That's where I want to go."

Not waiting for Darkhorse, the sorcerer crossed the courtyard. He heard a chuckle from behind him. "And has impatience now become a *virtue*?"

Dru ignored him, fairly rushing through the open doorway. The main hall sparkled; he had not doubted it would by this point. From the doorway the sorcerer had just entered, Darkhorse stepped within, his hooves making the same clap-clap sound they had when he had followed Dru and the avians into the one rounded edifice. The sounds echoed throughout the building.

For reasons he could not explain, the Vraad felt ashamed of the harsh noise Darkhorse was making. The castle touched him in an unusual way; Dru felt as though the sounds violated a peace that had reigned here for thousands upon thousands of years. It was a different sensation than what he had felt in the ruined city. There, he had felt the ghosts of memory and the remnants of power. Here was tranquility, a rare thing to a Vraad. If he died, this was where Dru wanted to be laid to rest. Here, he could—

The sorcerer shivered. Beside him now, Darkhorse asked, "Is there something amiss with you?"

"No. Nothing." Merely, Dru thought, that he had been almost willing to lie down right here and now and wait for death to claim him.

More cautious now, he strode ahead. There were two massive iron doors at the end of the hall, each more than twice as tall as the Vraad. Somehow, he could feel their importance. Behind them were the answers to the endless questions filling his mind. Whether he understood those answers was yet another question, but one Dru was willing to live with for the time being.

Putting a hand out to where the doors came together, the sorcerer pushed gently. The hinges groaned, but access was still denied him. He pushed harder, leaning into the two doors, but was granted no greater success than in the initial attempt.

Putting his shoulder to the crack, Dru angrily threw his weight against the obstructions. For his trouble he received a sore shoulder. Even though there was nothing to indicate that the way was locked, the Vraad could not get the doors to swing back.

"Perhaps if I—" Darkhorse began.

"*No!*" This was one that the angered spellcaster wanted for himself. Worn beyond his limits, Dru could no longer check his Vraadish temper. It swept over him, a crimson curse that seized control of his body. Shouting words he would not recall later, Dru raised his left hand and brought it down on the massive metal door.

With a spark that seemed to course from his fist to the entire doorway, the Vraad opened the way. "Opened" was perhaps misleading. What actually happened, if Dru could still believe his eyes, was that the two doors flung back, going the full turn of their hinges and then tearing free of the walls themselves. While the two watched, Dru in dismay and the shadow steed in growing amusement, the doors, now free of all restriction, teetered for a breath . . . and then fell with a resounding clatter that shattered forever any remaining feeling of tranquility that the spellcaster might have retained.

"Nicely done," Darkhorse commented wryly. He had quickly developed a knack of sarcasm equal to any Vraad.

"It wasn't . . . I didn't . . ." Dru gazed at his fist, then at the battered doors.

"Would it be of interest to mention that the boundaries of this place seem to have suffered from your calm, collected solution?"

Dru turned and eyed the walls of the hallway. An intricate system of fine cracks ran along each wall. The ceiling and floor had suffered from a similar network of these skeletal branches, and Dru could see where bits of ceiling had fallen. "I did this?"

"It seemed a reaction to your power. I noted resistance, but you overwhelmed it."

His madness had defeated the shrouded realm's resistance . . . that is, if this was still the shrouded realm. He wondered how well it would work back in the ruined city. There was also the question of what these side effects had to do with it. They were too akin to what Nimth suffered each time the Vraad utilized their abilities. Was this how his world's death had begun? *Were* the Vraad going to destroy their new home as well?

Too many questions. Dru snarled and turned back to the chamber that his fury had finally allowed him entry to.

His eyes widened to saucers and his mouth grew dry. It

seemed the realm beyond the veil was not yet depleted of surprises.

Before him, obscured by robes that made them resemble lumpy sacks, knelt more than a hundred figures. They had their backs to the newcomers and all faced a clear crystal in the center of a pentagram that covered the entire floor. The crystal stood on a bronze, pyramid-shaped platform. As with all else, the ages had been unable to touch either the focus, for that was what the sorcerer knew the crystal to be, or the base upon which it stood.

Dru backed up a step. The figures remained motionless despite the noise and damage he had caused. They were, he noted quickly, lined along the points, corners, and sides of the pattern, creating, by themselves, a second pentagram atop the one etched in stone.

"Where did they come from?" he whispered to Darkhorse. The tall Vraad knew that they had *not* been there when the doors had fallen.

His companion did not reply and a glance at the creature's equine visage helped little. Darkhorse's eyes stared vaguely at the chamber, as if he had trouble seeing anything in there at all. A repeat of his question gave Dru an equally silent response.

Admittedly more secure now that he knew he could summon up tremendous power—despite the effect Dru knew it likely had on the land—the sorcerer stepped forward again. He made no attempt to walk silently, knowing that any folk who could ignore the earsplitting sound of two gigantic metal doors collapsing would hardly notice his footfalls.

Dru studied the area with his higher senses, noting how the lines crisscrossed exactly at the point where the focus stood. There were secondary lines as well, weaker links that followed the pattern of the pentagram . . . and piercing each cowled figure from back to chest.

He blinked, then squinted, returning his vision to the normal plane. There was something *wrong* with the meditators. Too much of what he saw already reminded him of something else, something back in Nimth.

"What do you do?" Darkhorse asked from behind him. A few hesitant steps informed him that his companion was following the sorcerer inside.

"I don't know," he muttered, running one hand through his hair as he pushed himself toward the nearest of the baggy forms. Was he mad to risk himself?

Stretching his left hand forward, calmly this time, Dru touched the figure.

Tried to touch it. His hand went through in much the same manner as it had in the wraithlike forest. Both emboldened and frustrated, he waved the hand back and forth, trying to draw *some* response.

"They don't exist," Dru finally told the shadow steed. "They're ghosts . . . no . . . they're *memories*."

"Memories?"

Nodding, the fascinated mage walked around the one he had tried to touch. Its visage was fairly covered by the hood, but he saw that the being before him had been human and male. The visage was disquieting in some ways, though. It was and it was not the features of a Vraad. Not quite elfin, either. The man's eyes were open and in them Dru noted an age far greater than the figure's appearance would appear. So great, in fact, that any Vraad would have been but a toddler in comparison. "You can still feel the vestiges of their power if you stand among them. It was so intense that even after all this time, the shadows of their faces and forms have been imposed upon reality . . . *burned* into it, you might say. I think my use of sorcery, even Vraad sorcery, was all they needed to grow substantial enough to see."

"All I know," the majestic stallion snorted, "was that they unnerve me. I could make no sense of their existence whatsoever." It was a deep admission, coming as it did from the amazing creature.

Dru continued to study the wraiths. There were men and women, all handsome in the same disturbing way, as if they were part of one tremendous clan, even more so than the Tezerenee. All stared at the focus and the image of so many sightless gazes chilled even the centuries-old spellcaster.

"These fantastical images that you call pictures . . . were they not also in the ruined city?"

Darkhorse's words broke the spell that had tied Dru to the lifelike images. He looked up, annoyed that he had been so engrossed in phantoms of the far past that he had not seen what might prove far more important to his immediate needs.

The ceiling was rounded, which gave it and the walls the appearance of being one. That in itself was nothing, but the pictures that covered the entire chamber stirred the sorcerer's memories of another place, a place where a dragon lord had gazed with stone eyes down at the avians and their mystified prisoner.

Again, Dru looked over countless little worlds, each with their own representative. The Seeker was there, as was the enemy. The elf, the Vraad-like human, a figure that looked like a walking salamander... there seemed to be more here than in the first building.

Directly above the focus was the only illustration lacking a living figure. It was also the largest, and in the place of a representative race, it had a city... one very familiar, despite the differences time had wrought on the actual one.

The Vraad's mind worked quickly. With growing suspicions, he looked down at the focus... or rather, the floor beneath it.

Another world was illustrated there, this one greater than the one above. In its center was the very castle they stood in.

"Let us go view something else! I grow bored in here!"

"Not yet." Dru studied the phantoms—who seemed just a bit translucent now—and then gazed at the worlds above and below him. There was no denying the similarity between what he saw here and what he had devised when researching ka travel. Yet, if the images around him—the races and the worlds they stood within—meant what he had concluded, then the ghostly inhabitants of this place had been to the Vraad as the Vraad were to a lowly insect or, worse yet, a simple grain of sand.

Dru had a great urge to be elsewhere—*anywhere*—as long as it was far away from these ancient masters of power.

"We're leaving. Now."

"As you like it." The shaken sorcerer quickly mounted and the black steed turned and trotted swiftly through the doorway. In less than a breath, they were already back in the courtyard. Another and they were out the citadel gates and heading back to where the tear had been.

There had probably been so much more that Dru knew he should have investigated, but what little he had seen with what little he had theorized was enough. There had to be another solution that would gain him Nimth. He wanted nothing to do with the memories within that place. Even the ruined city—*their* ruined city—was better than this.

A horrible notion crossed him mind. "Darkhorse! Can you see the way in which we entered here?"

"I cannot!" Despite the incredible speed at which the dweller from the Void raced, he sounded perfectly normal. Sometimes, it was difficult for Dru to recall that his companion did not have to breathe as he did. "But we are nearly at the spot, I think!"

"Then what will we do if it isn't—"

A gaping hole opened before them and, at the heartrending speed they were moving, swallowed them before the Vraad could finish.

"—there?" Dru stuttered.

They were back among the ruins, but, this time, they were not alone.

The Seekers had returned, apparently having followed the duo's trail, and among them, they now had a captive, who struggled vainly against their might.

An elf.

XII

Night, such as it was, had come to Nimth. With it came the beginning of the end, as far as Gerrod was concerned. He had returned briefly to the Tezerenee stronghold, a vicious-looking iron building that, if Gerrod had been asked his opinion, reflected his clan's personality perfectly. It was a toothy structure and cold to both the body and the soul. Wyverns and young dragons constantly flew among its dragon-head banners, while the elder beasts slept in their pens. Besides a nasty array of sorcerous defenses, more than a dozen riders generally patrolled the perimeter of the domain.

Not so now. The stronghold was abandoned forever, though it seemed at first glance that the inhabitants had every intention of coming back. Personal effects lay where their owners had last left them. Charts and books gathered dust. Some of the wyverns flew loose through parts of the edifice they would normally have shied away from. Food was left rotting. Even projects, such as those he and Rendel had been working on, were forever abandoned. The Tezerenee could take nothing with them.

It was Rendel's notes Gerrod wanted. Rendel knew more than he did about the shrouded realm. Not all of it had been shared with his closest brother, though Gerrod doubted they had been as close as *he* had once supposed. *You left me behind with the rest, brother dear.* He only hoped that Rendel had also left behind his work. It was quite possible that his elder sibling had destroyed everything so as to keep that much longer whatever advantages he had uncovered in his research.

Fortune was with him. Not only were the notes he sought easy to locate, but they had been so meticulously organized that Gerrod found the proper sections within seconds. Evidently, Rendel was unconcerned about what these notes contained. They verified what he had read in Dru Zeree's notes and added new information that the outsider had not known . . . or perhaps purposely ignored, dealing as they did with the region in which Melenea made her home. Gerrod allowed himself a quick, triumphant smile and closed the book. He knew that there were other notes, much more well hidden, but there was no time to search for those. What he had would suffice, anyway.

"So it *is* you."

"Mother!" Gerrod turned on her, wondering desperately how she had been able to sneak up on him and also wondering if there were others behind her whom he also could not sense.

"I came back to see our home once more. Silly sentimentalism, isn't it, my son?" The look on her face was unreadable, suggesting both mockery and truth.

"Some would not see it so," he responded in neutral tones, hoping she would draw her own conclusions.

"The plan falls apart, Gerrod."

He had suspected as much, but hearing it from the mouth of one of the few he trusted, the hooded Vraad shivered. "What happens *now*?"

Her smile held no humor in it, only bitter irony. "It would seem that the golems, not all of them but a great many, have vanished."

"How *many* are left, Mother?" The noose he had felt tightening around his neck since his last confrontation with his father began to choke him.

"Barely enough for the clan. To assuage suspicions, Barakas has selected a few outsiders already."

"And *me*?"

"For the moment, there is still a place for you. You know that much of the anger your father throws at you should rightfully be directed at Rendel?"

"I know." Gerrod smiled darkly. Rendel was his mother's favorite, but he saw no reason to hide his feelings of betrayal.

"You are your father's sons in the end, Gerrod."

"Speaking of dear Father—much as I'd like to avoid doing so—you may tell him that Melenea has the Zeree brat. It was not my fault; she must have been the one who instigated the girl's departure in the first place." Whether that was true or false, he could not say. What it *would* do, however, was steer some of the trouble from his shoulders to those of the enchantress. Perhaps even Reegan, Melenea's toy, would feel some sort of backlash.

"Leave her, Gerrod. There's no time to get her out. As it is, she probably would have been left behind, regardless." There was a trace of regret in his mother's face, but she was hardly willing to risk one of her offspring being left behind. Alcia despised Melenea as much as any being did, but there were higher priorities than the daughter of Dru. "I do not think Barakas will wait too much longer before he decides to finish the cross-over. Some of the outsiders have been raising a fuss. The coming has broken up."

Gerrod rubbed his chin. "How long left?"

"By dawn, your father wants everyone over. He will be the last to go."

"How brave."

She gave him a silent reprimand. "I cannot promise he will hold a place for you even that long."

"Then *damn* him, Mother!" He would have thrown the notebook, but recalled in time what vital information it held. "Perhaps I'm better off here!"

Lady Alcia wrapped her cloak about herself. In the flickering light, she looked as if she wore a shroud. "It may be so, my son."

Gerrod found himself alone. Snarling, he buried the notebook in the deep confines of his own cloak and also departed, leaving the keep of the Tezerenee and possibly his own future to the whims of crippled Nimth.

Where it had still been day in the tiny, hidden world Dru and his companion had discovered, it was now night. With the return to the ruined city, the sorcerer's weariness and hunger had increased a hundredfold, as if being in that other place had held back time for a space. Dru found concentration impossible, despite the threat before him. This time, the spellcaster knew that there would be no second or even third wind; his body had reached its limitations. He prayed that Darkhorse was still fit, else the two were lost.

The Seekers were late in noticing the newcomers, concentrating as they had on their captive. The elf was the first to become aware of the tall figure astride the demonic steed and it was her inability to hide her shock that alerted the avians to their danger. In the pale light of the one full moon, Dru knew that he and his companion must appear fearsome, but appearances and reality often had little in common. He clutched Darkhorse's mane tightly to keep from falling and whispered, "You have to deal with them! I . . . won't be much use!"

The shadow steed's laughter rang through the night, bouncing eerily throughout the skeleton of the once-mighty place. "They are hardly a matter of concern! Hold tight!"

"Don't hurt the elf!" Dru added, suddenly fearful that the Seekers' captive, possibly someone who *might* verify what the Vraad had guessed about the worlds within worlds, would perish in the course of the ebony stallion's rampage.

"Is *that* what you called an elf? Have no fear! It has not made itself worthy of my caring attention yet!"

Dru shivered. His companion, growing more and more comfortable in his form and role, was also growing more frightening.

The avians scattered, two carrying the prisoner into the sky while she fought them tooth and nail, crying out words that Dru, holding on for dear life, could not understand. One Seeker foolishly held her ground, locating but fumbling with her medallion. Darkhorse ran *through* her. The sorcerer, pressed against the entity's backside, caught a brief flash of a horrified visage . . . and then the female was no more.

"Ha! Let that—" The words never came. Dru heard a *swish!* and then he was being thrown into the air, his grip broken as easily as the sorcerer might have snapped a twig beneath his boots. He lacked the air to scream and so could only wait in silence for the ground to come up and shatter his body. His thoughts refused to go beyond his imminent destruction. The moons flashed by twice, a glimmering circle and a dim slash, one crimson and the other the pale of death, and their appearances remained fixed in his mind even as he noted that his descent was about to come to a very final finish.

No, said a voice within his head.

The earth was cheated of its prey. Dru felt everything freeze. Though his eyes were open, he could see nothing save the memories of the moons. It occurred to him that no sounds could be heard and he wondered what had become of the Seekers and Darkhorse.

No interference, came another familiar voice.

We are beyond that, added the third, almost eagerly.

We are, agreed the first. *They have all come to this place. To not interfere is to allow all else to fail.*

Dru could feel endless voices arguing for and against what the first being had said. Though the argument seemed to go on forever, the confused sorcerer knew that only seconds had likely passed when it drew to a conclusion. In the end, the first being's opinion was upheld, but only barely.

That was the last he knew. The world, *all worlds*, ceased to be of any import to him.

You are Vraad.

The defiant sorcerer nodded, not knowing where he was or

how he had come to this place from the chaos of the ancient city. Dru looked around, but could make out nothing save the chair he sat on and his own body. He felt refreshed, capable of doing combat with the strongest of adversaries, but knew better than to attempt any assault now.

He cannot be Vraad! They are rejected!

It was the second voice again. The tall sorcerer stared defiantly into the darkness and said, "I *am* Vraad! I am Dru Zeree!"

He has life! the third being mocked. Of the three who acted as speakers, this was the one who repelled Dru the most. It reminded him far too much of Melenea and her games, of how she looked at *everything* in life as some wicked game.

Games . . . I like that! We have played such a long, boring game . . . until now! the third commented playfully.

A cold sweat formed on Dru's brow. He shielded his thoughts better, though he supposed the effort was little more than futile. In these creatures Dru had found power that dwarfed even that of his companion.

What is the thing? asked the first.

When the sorcerer finally understood the question, he shook his head. Answering the question could do him no more harm than he was already due. "I don't know for certain. I met Darkhorse in an empty place I call the Void. He seems to come from there."

There was silence as he felt the beings mull over his words and his thoughts. They did not reprimand him when he spoke out loud and he wondered if they had their limitations as Darkhorse did or whether they merely knew he felt more comfortable hearing his own voice in this place where other noises did not exist.

How did he come to be here? the second voice asked. Of the three, it seemed the most indecisive.

You have seen it, the first reminded. They seemed indifferent to the fact that Dru listened into their conversation.

It was not made to be that way.

It was too long ago. You know that time drains, time turns all away from the purpose.

And we do nothing! *Always* nothing! the third interjected with disgust. *We who have the power to do anything!*

Such is not our purpose. The response came from several minds and reminded Dru of nothing so much as a litany repeated from generation to generation.

Our purpose is dead!

Perhaps, shot back the first. *Perhaps not. It may be these Vraad who provide what the masters sought.*

"What?" Dru blurted out. He cursed himself even as he spoke. The debate had already given him an insight far greater than he could have hoped and now he had brought himself back to their attention.

All of them must be returned to their places with their minds cleansed. This was a new voice.

The first voice, the one who seemed most commanding of the unseen beings, replied, *The Sheeka and the Quel cannot be cleansed of their knowledge so easily. Neither can we touch the elves here, who serve as we do, though they do not know why. Would you have us interfere more than we have already?*

There is no real choice! the sinister third voice said, cutting off any other response. *It is time we took control!*

No!

Dru screamed and clutched the sides of his head in vain as he sought release from the multitude of shouting voices vibrating through his mind. He collapsed against the chair he had been seated in.

Are you ill? Have we damaged you? It was the first voice again, concern weighing heavy in its tone.

The concern so startled Dru that he almost forgot his pain. "I'm . . . well . . . as well as can be expected."

We did not wish to cause pain. Despite the being's words, the Vraad thought he felt one bit of dissension among the ranks at this statement. He did not have to hazard a guess as to which one of his odd captors it was.

"Where am I?" Dru asked, deciding it was time to take control of the situation, if possible.

In one of the many pieces of the world that the masters cut free. It was never used so we thought it best to bring you here.

"And the—I find it hard to talk to nothing! Can you show yourself to me?" He pictured in his mind something akin to the rubble-grown wolf. "Not quite like that, please."

There was hesitation...underlined by worry, the anxious spellcaster noted. *Very well.*

Something glittered before him. Slowly, Dru made out two golden orbs and the faint outline of some great beast. The shape looked vaguely familiar, but he could not place where he had seen it.

It is the dragon lord you came across in the old ones' first city, where they lived when there were many. I took the form because you admired it. I will add scent if you like.

Dru recalled the smell of the Tezerenees' many wyverns and drakes. "The form will suffice."

The mock dragon dipped its half-seen head. *You wished to know of the others. They sleep.*

"Even..."

Even the enigma you call Darkhorse. He is not a creation of the old ones. He is from the rim areas between the Void, as you call it, and the true world. We did not recognize this until now.

"Why have you chosen me?"

The shadowy form moved, spreading wings that were and were not there. *You are closest to the masters. The Sheeka—you call them "Seekers"—have not become what they should have. Soon, they will join the Quel in the list of failures. Then there will be nothing left.*

Dru wanted to stand, but he was not certain there was actually a floor on which to do so. He squirmed uneasily on the chair. "The Seekers control this world?"

The greatest of the continents.

"You make it sound as if you put them there."

He could almost see the being shake its head. *The masters set such in operation. They made the tiny worlds so that when the turn came, each would open again unto this, the true world. They hoped that one would prove a successor to their own kind.*

The creature had informed him of everything in a simple, unattached manner, which was why its words did not penetrate immediately. Dru sat still as the impact of what his captor had said burrowed its way into his mind.

You understand correctly. The places from which the Sheeka, the Quel, and even you *originated are slices of* this *world.*

"Nimth...Nimth isn't...isn't real?" *Not possible!* the sorcerer wanted to shout. The birthplace of the Vraad a falsehood? A . . . *zoo?*

He could sense the sadness around him, a sadness that deepened his own horror at what he had come to realize. The mighty Vraad race had risen to supremacy of a cage, another race's toy!

Not so, the ghostly dragon emphasized. *Not a cage. More of a birthing place for the masters' successors. They were old; their race was tired. The masters wanted to leave behind a legacy, so they took from their own and worked to make them better. Then they set them in worlds of their own and let each grow. See it as it was.*

The dragon sank completely into the darkness and was replaced by a tiny image that expanded gradually, filling more and more of Dru's vision until he actually felt he was standing in another place, in another time. In some ways, it was like communicating with the Seekers, save that what Dru saw was not forced upon him. He could accept it or not.

He had no intention of refusing such an opportunity.

There were beings he could call human and many he would not have guessed could ever have been. The ancient race had chosen every conceivable variation they could think of, some of which even Dru, who had witnessed much over his gray life, found so revolting he was astonished that they even lived.

Many attempts did not. There were scores of empty little worlds, worlds created by slicing reality itself. Each had once housed a hope, but those hopes had died for one reason or another, sometimes in great wars that destroyed everything. More than a few were judged failures even if the race within survived; the elders had searched for certain traits among their children. Eventually, most of those failures destroyed themselves, only one had not . . . so far.

Dru knew without asking that Nimth was the one failure that had, up until now, not succeeded in destroying itself completely. The time was nearing, however.

"What about those that succeeded?"

There were those that matured to the second stage, the mock dragon responded. Images of various civilizations passed before Dru. He recognized only two. The Seekers and their enemy, the armadillolike beings called the Quel.

"But you said . . ."

They have failed. The Quel hang on, but nothing more. They will never rise to greatness again. The Seekers have begun their own descent. Their arrogance and communal thinking make them unwilling to face ultimate change. As for the elves . . . they will survive and aid us, but they lack the drive to become what they are capable of becoming. Because of that, they are lost to the plan as well.

"And we have also failed you."

Perhaps. Perhaps not. With time . . .

With time, they, too, will fade, the one who chilled Dru's spirit whispered.

Their death knell has begun already, added the fourth voice.

Dru shook his head, trying to clear away the confusing echoes within.

Not so! the mock dragon overwhelmed his counterparts. *There is still time.*

We have interfered enough, the fourth countered, but uncertainly now.

Give me leave to do what must be done. . . .

The sorcerer found himself in the midst of darkness again as the entities evidently discussed something *not* for his ears.

So many questions continued to clamor for answers, but Dru doubted he would ever learn everything. Still . . .

His musings were forgotten as the world returned.

The sun was in the sky, a brilliant, burning orb that the mage had never thought to see again.

The Seekers who came here have been taken care of. You will think of them no longer. It was the first voice, but there was no sign of the dragon form.

It will not be needed for this short time. You will listen, Dru Zeree of the Vraad. A wind picked up as the being spoke. *I have removed the one called Darkhorse from this place and returned it to its own domain. It should have never come here. It does not belong.*

"He did nothing to harm you!"

A strong gust blew a cloud of dirt into Dru's face, blinding him and causing him to choke for a few seconds.

It . . . he . . . has not been harmed. We have merely placed him where he should be. His presence was only one more catalyst for chaos in something we have been commanded to preserve.

"You interfere quite easily for something that isn't supposed to interfere!" the Vraad snapped. Darkhorse had aided him, had saved him several times. To be so carelessly removed was unfair to the ebony creature.

I leave you the elf, Vraad. That is all I can do for you. That your kind have breached their boundaries is a matter of importance. I must study what can be done to return things to what they were. If the Vraad are to succeed, they must follow the path set by the old ones.

Dru could not resist one more barb before his *benefactor* departed. "*Things as they were?* Complete collapse of your masters' hopes is all that remains if you steer things back that way. We're entering this world at this very moment. It's too late to turn things back!"

A mocking laugh made the embittered sorcerer start. He knew it was not the laugh of the servant he had been speaking to. He knew which of the entities now enjoyed his discomfort.

It will be easier than you think!

He was alone in his mind again. Around him, the wind died abruptly, a sign that the guardians had abandoned him.

A moan behind him reminded Dru that he had been promised someone who could guide him.

"You . . . you are not an elf or one of those monsters, are you?"

The Vraad turned to his new companion. "Obviously not, as you can see."

She was slighter than the dead female he had seen earlier, but identical in appearance otherwise. Her hair was bound back. Her eyes scoured his form, at last resting on his visage. Dru doubted that it was because she found him attractive.

"You are Vraad."

He looked at her with renewed interest. "How did you know that?"

The elf rose, doubling the distance between them as she did. Loathing coated her words. "We thought we had left you behind forever! Now all of our work is for nothing! There's nowhere left to hide! No hope of turning this insane sorcerer's experiment in our favor!"

A knife materialized from her left hand. She had moved so quickly, Dru would have almost sworn it was magic.

"I will still get the satisfaction of killing you, though!"

XIII

I've given up my future . . . and for what? The imbecilic child of an outsider!

Gerrod knelt behind a ridge on the outskirts of Melenea's domain. She could not possibly know he was so near, not if his calculations based on his brother's work were correct. This region would be in the midst of one of the greatest instabilities existing, nearly as great as the area where the fool Dru Zeree had vanished. Already, the hooded Tezerenee had caught glimpses of a ghostly elsewhere that he knew had to be the shrouded realm intruding into Nimth. Would that his father's so-called Dragonrealm would fully overwhelm the decaying world. Then, at least that problem would be solved.

It would still not solve the Vraad problem concerning colonizing a land that Gerrod felt wanted nothing to do with his kind . . . and *that* was likely why he had finally, in the hours since his last words with his mother, chosen to stay clear of the city. Missing the cross-over had likely cost him his life, yet he had not cared enough to abandon his plan to rescue Zeree's daughter.

There were more reasons than that. A matter of honor probably held as much sway as his insane fear of the land beyond the veil. His progenitor had questioned his abilities, and like any good Tezerenee, he had fallen into the trap of honor. He had gone out to redeem himself even if it meant his end.

Gerrod swore under his breath. He could go around and around with his reasons, some of which even *he* would have admitted were complete mysteries, but that would not remove Sharissa Zeree from the ministrations of the viperous Lady Melenea.

"Masterrr Gerrod!" Beside him, crouched low, was Sirvak. The familiar was in what seemed to the warlock a constant state of frenzied anxiousness. "She could be dead! She could be dead!"

"She's not, Sirvak. Now be quiet." He was, admittedly, a bit uncertain himself. Things had taken much longer than he would have liked. Day, such as it was, had returned to Nimth before he was confident enough of his own plan. All of it had depended on just how well the temptress's home was being affected by the instabilities.

"It must be as physical as possible," he reminded Sirvak. "Trust sorcery only when needed." Sirvak, out of necessity, had drawn first strike. It could fly. Gerrod would have to trust to small teleports and simple running.

"Understand, Masterrr Gerrod." Eagerness suddenly flooded the familiar's unsettling eyes. Its mistress was within the citadel. It had the help of a powerful ally, one it could trust as much as Vraad could be trusted. Gerrod could see that it would perform its task to perfection or die valiantly in the attempt.

Under former circumstances, the Tezerenee would not have feared for himself. Even Melenea had respected the clan of the dragon. With anarchy soon to erupt (if it had not *already*), she would have no qualms about killing both Gerrod and Sharissa. Worse yet, death might prove slow in coming. Gerrod respected Melenea's deceit. Her citadel might be one massive trap waiting to be sprung . . . if his theory proved inadequate.

The shrouded images of the other realm grew more distinct. "Go now!"

Sirvak leaped into the air and was gone from sight a moment later.

The wait tore at Gerrod's patience. His active imagination conceived of every flaw, every overlooked threat. His memories reminded him of Melenea's past *games*. He shivered.

When the time finally arrived for his part, he was thankful. His mind turned to the patriarch as he rose.

"Charging headlong into the enemy. I *am* your son in the end, just as Mother said."

He dared to teleport.

Sharissa woke, knowing she had slept for quite some time, but barely able to keep from falling once more into a deep slumber. She struggled against the urge, forcing herself to a sitting position.

A form shuffled near her. Through sleep-filled eyes, the young sorceress caught sight of the overwhelming form of Cabal, Melenea's familiar. The massive blue-green wolf yawned in her direction, once more revealing to her a multitude of savage teeth.

"Mistress says for you to lie down. To rest." Its rough voice assaulted her ears and made her head pound.

"I've rested long enough. It's day outside, isn't it?" She shifted closer to the edge of the furry bed. Doing so seemed to clear her mind more.

Cabal did not answer her. Unlike Sirvak, the wolf seemed more an extension of its mistress. What was it the creature had said to Melenea? The words were slow in coming, but Sharissa finally recalled them.

I obey knowing my life is yours or something to that effect. She frowned. Not at all a pleasant phrase. It almost indicated that Cabal expected death if it failed in its duty. Not like the Melenea that Sharissa knew.

With the wolf following every movement, she dared to stand. There was a brief instant when the sorceress thought the familiar was about to pounce on her, but it turned out Cabal was only resettling itself so that it could watch her better. Though it seemed foolish to believe anything would happen to her here, Sharissa could not help being cautious.

"Cabal? Where's Melenea?"

"The mistress rests also. She has worked hard. You should rest, too. Sleep until the mistress comes again."

"I'm not tired." It was true. Now that she was away from the soothing confines of the bed, Sharissa was wide awake. It was almost as if the bed encouraged slumber.

Cabal said nothing more, but it continued to play the role of sentinel.

Sharissa wandered about the room, admiring the statuary and other items that decorated it. During her arrival, she had only given the chamber a cursory scan. Now, however, the young Zeree was able to study detail. The capering figurines at first seemed comical until she leaned forward and looked again. Up close, the expressions on the tiny faces gained a cruel twist, as if the statuettes had no desire to play whatever game it was they played. She also read new actions in their movements. Instead of dancing, it seemed more likely that they were fleeing or, at least, trying to flee. Unsuccessfully, too.

Disturbed, Sharissa turned from her inspection of the figurines and walked toward one of the windows. This one faced the direction of her own home, and though she knew seeing the Zeree dominion from Melenea's citadel was impossible, Sharissa felt an undeniable urge to seek it nonetheless.

The heavens were one massive cloud of putrefying green that rolled and twisted within itself, seeming to gather strength in the process. A storm of gargantuan proportions was preparing to rage. The novice sorceress temporarily abandoned her initial desires and turned to better view the growing storm. Its center, she suspected, hung over the Vraad communal city. She wondered what could draw together such a force. Only an epic unleashing of sorcery could create such a magic storm. Her father's research had taught her enough to realize that. The cross-over might be enough, but she doubted that. No, something else was happening in the city.

A tiny figure cutting valiantly through the rising winds caught her attention briefly before vanishing into the clouds. Sharissa blinked and looked again. Nimth still had wildlife, as twisted as much as the world itself, but this figure had looked familiar. Likely, she assumed after a minute or two of useless searching, it had been her own desires that had made her believe she had seen Sirvak. The familiar was lost to her. Sirvak was now a puppet of the unsettling Gerrod. The hooded Tezerenee had no doubt taken the small beast and every bit of lore her father had collected and brought them back to the patriarch as an offering. At this late stage, there was no reason for him to come searching for her; the Tezerenee hardly needed her for their cross-over.

Behind her, Cabal began to growl.

"What is it?" she asked, turning at the same time.

The familiar stood, its imposing form nearly making the sorceress gasp. Like all else she had seen after her arrival here, she had forgotten exactly how huge the beast was. It towered over her. One paw the size of her head scratched at the floor. Cabal sniffed the air and continued to growl, curling its lip back as it did. Though the familiar looked at its charge as it snarled, Sharissa knew it was not her the beast challenged.

A swift black and gold figure burst through the window, shrieking a challenge as it soared toward the sinister lupine familiar.

"Sirvak!"

A gloved hand covered her mouth. "We are here to *save* you from yourself, Zeree! Don't let your pet die for the sake of your innocence and ignorance!"

Gerrod! Sharissa fought wildly, locating and kicking the Tezerenee's shin. Startled by her viciousness, Gerrod almost released her. He cursed loudly and said something else she could not catch.

Savage cries alerted her to the battle taking place. Sharissa stared in horror as Sirvak took on Cabal. The tinier familiar looked pathetic in comparison to Melenea's behemoth and she was filled with fear that Sirvak would be torn apart as easily as Cabal might have torn apart one of the drapes. Somehow, though, the winged creature easily dodged the wolf's initial attack and, in fact, struck the huge beast a powerful blow to the head. Jagged scars now decorated Cabal's left side. It roared at the insignificant little annoyance buzzing about its head.

"Don't fight me, Zeree!" Gerrod hissed. "Think for a change!"

Sharissa ignored him and continued to struggle. With great effort, she twisted her right hand free and unleashed the quickest, simplest spell that might serve her against her would-be attacker.

The Tezerenee lost control as a brilliant flash blinded him. Sharissa pulled away immediately. She had to find Melenea. The enchantress would be more of a match for the hooded kidnapper. Sharissa knew that her odds against Gerrod could only worsen if she continued to battle him alone.

Leaving, however, proved far more difficult than she had

hoped. Cabal's huge frame blocked the doorway, and in its combat with Sirvak, it was not unlikely that the beast would accidentally crush her.

"The dragon take you, you stupid—" Gerrod's hood had fallen back and the anger Sharissa read on his patrician visage urged her to take her chances with the doorway.

"Mistresss! No! Listen to Sirvak!"

The imploring tone made her pause and she looked up at her father's familiar . . . only to watch in horror as the winged creature, evidently caught up in its concern for her, forgot its own safety.

Cabal's mighty jaws caught the smaller familiar's right foreleg. The blue-green wolf bit hard. Sirvak shrieked in agony and quickly pulled away.

The tattered remnants of Sirvak's leg hung uselessly. Cabal laughed and swallowed the limb.

"Good meat," it rumbled. "Come and let me taste more."

"You will taste your own blood!" Sirvak howled back. The wounded animal started to shimmer, a sign that it was about to make use of its own sorcery.

"Sirvak! No!" Gerrod ceased his assault on Sharissa, though she made no use of the advantage, also caught up in the struggle of the two familiars.

Cabal, meanwhile, was preparing its own magical attack. The lupine form wavered, as if not quite real. Two forces stretched out and met between the beasts. Being constructs, the familiars used the most basic sorceries in attack. Basic, but very, very dangerous. Sharissa knew that Sirvak was capable of destroying a good portion of Melenea's home and assumed that Cabal was of at least equal ability. Despite her belief that her father's creation now obeyed a new master, she could not help fearing for it. Wounded, Sirvak might not be a match for Melenea's creature.

Her hesitation cost Sharissa her freedom. Gerrod caught her again, this time in a grip she knew would be unbreakable. He pulled her head back so that she was forced to look him in the eye. "Despite yourself, Zeree, we are going to save you from that witch you think is your friend! Did your father never tell you about why he demanded she never see either of you again?"

"I neither know nor care what you're talking about!" Sharissa tried to spit in the Tezerenee's face, but he turned her head away in time.

"You *will* . . . someday!"

"What have we here? Cabal! How did they get inside so easily?"

"Melenea!" Gerrod snarled under his breath, disgust emphasized in each syllable of the beautiful enchantress's name.

At its mistress's appearance, the huge familiar backed away. Its breath came in harsh gasps, as if its sorcerous battle had taken a toll not noticeable until now. Sirvak, too, looked fatigued, Sharissa noted, but that might have been from the wound that, while sealed by the winged familiar's own powers, still must have pained it dearly.

"I'll thank you to release my guest, Tezerenee."

"And leave her to *you*? I think not. Even a naive fool like this deserves better than *your* tender care!"

The stunning sorceress laughed, a melodious sound that, had he not known her reputation so well, might have lessened Gerrod's guard. "And she should trust *your* care? I think Sharissa knows who her friends are." Clad in a glistening silk robe that did nothing to hide her body, Melenea strode toward Cabal, placing an arm around the blue-green wolf's neck. "I've only done my best for her. I'm probably the only one who can save her father."

"Did you find something?" Even with Gerrod's arm around her, Sharissa forgot her predicament as visions of her father's rescue blossomed in her mind.

"I most certainly did, Shari sweet."

"Don't listen to her!" the hooded figure whispered in frantic tones. "The only thing she has waiting for you is a slow and painful death after she's done toying with you! Ask Sirvak what she's like!"

"Ask away! Shari knows that you control the poor beast." Melenea's visage expressed her deep pity for Sirvak's fate. "I'm afraid you can probably never trust the familiar again. It will have to be destroyed, I imagine."

Sirvak squawked. "No, mistresss! Sirvak is good! Sirvak wants only to protect you!"

With a speed worthy of Sharissa's swiftest steed, Melenea

reached out and pointed at the flying familiar. Sirvak shrieked in agony and started to glow blue. Sharissa gasped and struggled with renewed urgency.

"I'll regret this; I know I will!" she heard Gerrod mutter. Suddenly she was being pushed aside by the warlock, who pointed at the writhing black and gold familiar and mouthed something. Sharissa fell against the couch she had been sleeping on and stared in amazement as Gerrod actually worked to save Sirvak's existence. There was no reason why he should do so. Whatever knowledge her father's creation carried could have easily been supplied by his notes, which the Tezerenee surely had access to.

"Cabal!"

At the mention of its name by its mistress, the hulking figure charged directly toward the shrouded Vraad. Caught off guard, Gerrod tried to shield himself. Sharissa, for reasons not entirely clear to her, struck even as the monstrous familiar leaped into the air, jaws wide open.

As if caught by a net that was not there, Cabal stopped in midair, struggled futilely with the nothingness surrounding it, and finally fell to the floor with a howl of frustration and pain.

The citadel shook.

"I *knew* it!" Gerrod stumbled toward her, trying to reach out. Sharissa remained where she was, her thoughts in turmoil. She still trusted Melenea, but the young Tezerenee's nearly suicidal rescue of Sirvak, who could serve him no useful purpose, touched her. If there was a grain of truth in anything he had told her...

"What have you done, Tezerenee?" demanded Melenea. She fell against Cabal. The familiar somehow succeeded in regaining and then maintaining its balance, unlike Sharissa, who rolled helplessly on the carpet as the building trembled again and again.

"I only added to an overfilled pot, witch!" He groped for Sharissa, but she succeeded in steering herself away.

Though Melenea failed to understand, Sharissa did. She realized that this stronghold sat near an area that had grown unstable. Her companion had continually utilized her sorcery as if nothing had changed, as if the Vraad were still in full command of Nimth. Gerrod must have known what an effect such a concentration of power would have and how this battle would only serve to aggravate things. It was unlikely that he could have predicted the tremors so precisely, but the clever Tezerenee had probably researched her father's work enough to know that the potential for *some* disaster was high.

Above her, Sirvak hovered. The beaked familiar's wings beat slowly, barely enough to keep the creature aloft. Sirvak appeared not to notice, evidently still more concerned with its mistress and her safety than its own magical existence. "Mistressss! Are you injured?"

"No, Sirvak, I'm not!" Its concern was so genuine she could no longer believe the familiar was a puppet of Gerrod. Either Sirvak had broken free of whatever spell the shadowy Vraad had cast upon it, or it had never been under a spell at all. If the latter was the case, then much of what Melenea had said became questionable.

"Sirvak! Does Gerrod speak the truth?"

"Shari darling, you cannot—"

"He speaks *truth*!" the flying beast shrieked, purposely drowning out the enchantress. "She is evil! She only loves pain, mistresss! *Others'* pain! That is the nature of her gamesss!"

A portion of the ceiling gave way, crashing down very near Sharissa. Reacting instinctively, she rolled away. Her maneuver brought her nearer Melenea.

"Cabal!" the enchantress shouted.

The deadly familiar suddenly stood over Sharissa, its hot, stinking breath bathing her face. She grimaced and tried to drag herself away from the stench.

The wolf laughed. "Play with Cabal!"

"No, Cabal!" Melenea commanded. "Gently!"

Twisting its visage into an expression of annoyance, the massive beast bent its head low and caught Sharissa by the arm. The jaws clamped tight, not enough to cause great pain, but enough to keep the young Zeree from daring to pull free.

"Mistresss!" Sirvak came down low, but the winged familiar dared not attack. Cabal had bitten off its foreleg with the least of efforts; it would not take much more for the huge wolf to snap Sharissa's arm apart. Any assault by Sirvak would endanger her further.

A burst of thunder deafened the novice sorceress. As she

pulled without success, she saw some of the statuettes leap off their pedestals and run off, scampering through doorways and windows before the startled Vraad. The pedestals themselves were melting.

"Bring her, Cabal!"

The familiar tried, but the floor beneath its feet had begun to grow soft, and though it did not yet impair Sharissa's own progress, the tremendous mass of the monster was enough to make its paws sink. It growled, all the while maintaining its hold on its unwilling companion, and tried to lift one of the paws out. Sharissa ran her free hand across the floor; it felt more like soft butter than marble. Her father had warned her that this sort of thing would happen. Random waves of wild magic, the culmination of centuries of misuse. It would pass eventually, but other waves would come as the days progressed, until there came a time when the area would be forever beyond the control of anyone and nothing would be safe from change.

"Nimth's blood!" Melenea was wiping at her arm, where the sleeve of her gown now moved of its own volition. It appeared to be attempting to envelop her hand, almost like a mouth. As Sharissa watched, the enchantress, modesty the least of her interests at this point, tore off the crawling garment and threw it to the floor, where it attempted to return to her. Melenea pointed at the gown, fury marring her perfect features. The gown froze, but the new spell only increased the general havoc being caused. The chamber began to tilt to the side.

Sharissa heard a painful *crunch!* and found herself falling to the floor, her arm freed from Cabal's toothy grip. Her elbow sank into the floor, but she pulled it free, not suffering from the problems of mass that the familiar did.

Cabal was whining and growling, too maddened to see that its anger and pain were making it sink deeper. Gerrod stood just out of range of its claws and teeth, the shattered pieces of a stool in his hands and a satisfied smile on his half-seen face. While Cabal had been occupied with the task of releasing its limbs, the hooded Vraad had evidently come around the monster's blind side and, timing his attack perfectly, smashed the wolf's nose with the stool. It was probably the only attack that would have succeeded in releasing Sharissa without the loss of her arm.

"Mistresss!" Sirvak alighted on the edge of the couch, or what was left of it. The magically formed piece of furniture had sunk halfway into the carpet again, making it more of a lump. Sirvak carefully balanced itself on what remained, the lack of the one forelimb making it more difficult than normal. "Come, mistressss! Trusssst Sirvak!"

Sharissa did . . . now. The beautiful gold and black beast was probably the only one she trusted. Gerrod had succeeded in raising doubts as to Melenea's interests, but his own were just as debatable. One thing she felt certain of, however, was that Sirvak, even if the familiar *had* worked with the Tezerenee, was still loyal to her and her father.

"Plaything! You are being naughty!" Cabal had managed to lift one paw out of the soupy floor and was trying to reach her. Of Gerrod there was no trace, and for the first time, she feared for him. He *had* freed her from the horrible creature before her.

As the massive paw neared her, Sirvak flew from the couch and, paying no heed to its own safety again, attacked the limb with great relish. Cabal took an unsteady swing at the winged attacker, but the horror's lack of full movement made it impossible for the creature to twist far enough to make contact. Sirvak backed away from the paw until it was obvious that the blue-green wolf had overextended its reach, then moved in close enough to snap at the struggling adversary.

Cabal roared in pain. The toothsome beak of Dru's creation tore into the limb just above the paw. Sirvak ripped a chunk of flesh from its counterpart and quickly abandoned the attack before the huge monstrosity recovered. It had not been a total payback for the smaller familiar's loss, but Sirvak's triumphant cry spoke nearly as much about the extent of the damage inflicted as Cabal's howl did.

Sharissa felt the floor stiffening. Things were returning to normal, such as that was. She would have to make a decision now. Either she stayed and trusted Melenea or she left and trusted Gerrod the way Sirvak seemed to. It was not a choice that filled her with anticipation. She wished her father was here to make the decision for her.

He may be dead! she berated herself. It was up to her to decide her own fate. When her father had vanished, she had let Gerrod lead her to the Tezerenee. Her first attempts at independence had consisted of refusing to share what she knew with the overbearing patriarch, Barakas. Unfortunately, just as she had been deciding to lead her own life, the young Zeree had found Melenea, someone from her childhood. She had allowed the enchantress to lead her as if Sharissa were still a small child. No more.

The crystals. I have to find the crystals! I can't leave without them! Only Melenea knew where they were, however. Only Melenea could give her access to the crystals that might lead her to her father. They somehow held the key to passing from Nimth to the realm beyond the veil. Sharissa knew she could not leave this place without them, regardless of the danger that the enchantress possibly represented to her if Gerrod had been telling the truth.

"Damn you! Not again!"

She only barely recognized the Tezerenee's furious voice before something struck her from behind and sent her facedown into the carpet. Sirvak called out her name.

Someone bundled her up. "We're leaving! Now!"

Before she could protest, Gerrod had brought his cloak around the two of them and started a teleportation spell. Sharissa knew she should warn him about something, but the pain at the back of her head made it impossible to recall exactly what it was that the hooded figure had to beware of. By then, it was already too late. She felt the chamber shift around them, melt away, and become another place.

"Dragon's blood! This isn't where I wanted to go!"

"You're . . . you're lucky to have made it at all," she managed to gasp out. "We might have ended up in the shrouded realm . . . or some place even farther away!"

Gerrod's laugh was bitter. "That might have been better for both of us! Look about you!"

"I can't . . . wait . . . my eyes are clearing." The blow, obviously her unwanted companion's doing, had blurred her vision. The teleport spell had not helped matters. Fortunately, as the pain eased, her eyesight returned to normal. "Where have we . . . Serkadion Manee!"

"I think Father's betrayal has angered the rest of the Vraad." The sardonic tone in Gerrod's voice was unmistakable.

They stood in what had once been the courtyard of the Vraad

communal city, a place where only days before the race had first started to gather for the coming. It was a city now ravaged by those who had created it and who, Sharissa suspected, would likely greet a Tezerenee and the daughter of the patriarch's supposed ally with even *deadlier* fury.

XIV

Barakas, lord and patriarch of the Tezerenee, the clan of the dragon, gazed at what would be the beginning of his new empire. Gone were the ways of old Nimth, when he had been forced to share the world with so many arrogant and maddening outsiders. Now, only a handful of outsiders remained, all manageable. Most of those were female, too, for the patriarch knew that to start any new civilization required new blood. He had kept his clan to certain numbers because of the restrictions of space in Nimth. That was no longer necessary.

"Those mountains over there." He gestured at the same peaks Rendel, days ago, had set out for. "I want them explored."

Reegan looked abashed. "We have no flying drakes and our powers work haphazardly, sire."

"Do not state the obvious with me, Reegan. I have trained you to do what you must to obey my commands. See to it that what I say is done." Though Barakas almost looked peaceful, his eldest son, reading into the patriarch's eyes, bowed quickly and rushed off to see what suggestions some of his brethren might have.

Lady Alcia, stepping away from a conversation with someone who was either a daughter or a niece—Barakas felt it unnecessary to try to keep track of *all* of his people as long as they did what they were told—joined her husband as he surveyed the fields and forest around them.

"You seem flushed with excitement," she murmured.

"I have a world to conquer. I have my people to obey me. What more could one ask for?"

"Your son?"

Barakas looked at her in distaste. "Which one, my bride? Rendel, who betrayed us once he was on this side of the veil, or Gerrod, who failed to do anything I asked of him?"

"I can't say anything concerning Rendel, but Gerrod did as he was commanded. You never paid attention to that fact, however. It may interest you to know that I ran across Gerrod before I returned from our old keep. Even though time was running out, he was determined to find Dru Zeree's daughter, as you commanded, despite the fact that he believed she was a 'guest' of Melenea."

"I waited as long as possible, Alcia. You saw how they were acting. Any longer and *we* might not have crossed in time." The patriarch's attention wandered to where Lochivan was trying to look busy. He still feared his father's wrath, though there was nothing he or the others could have done to prevent the disappearance of the golems. That had been Rendel's province. "Lochivan!"

"Father!" Despite the fear, the Lord Tezerenee's son rushed to his side and knelt. "You have a task for me?"

"This will be our initial camp. Begin expanding our perimeter. We need drakes, too. If you—"

Both Lochivan and the Lady Alcia looked at the patriarch, curious as to why he had stopped speaking.

"There!" Barakas pointed a finger at one of the nearby treetops. A horrible, agonized shriek filled the ears and souls of the assembled Tezerenee, all of whom turned to stare in the direction of the cry as if mesmerized by the strident sound.

A winged figure, now only a corpse, plummeted to the earth. It landed with a dull thud, a crumpled and twisted rag doll. Even from where he stood, the Lord Tezerenee could see that while it was avian, it was also humanoid. It had most certainly been spying on them, so he knew it was also intelligent. He wondered how long it—and likely others—had watched his people, all the while undetected. Though Barakas had appeared to know where the spy was, it had actually been a fluke; he had spotted a movement as he had surveyed that part of his new kingdom. No one would need to know that, however.

Pain abruptly wracked the hand from which he had directed his deadly spell. Barakas swore and rubbed at the sore spot. He felt as if part of his assault had backfired, though there was no method by which that could have happened so far as he knew.

"Lochivan!" His pain was assuaged a bit by the speed with which his son came once more to attention. "This is a hostile region! We have an enemy to confront! I want the immediate area cleared of any other spying eyes."

"We dare not trust our power, Father. Already, three who attempted spells have been injured. There is something amiss with the magic of this world."

Barakas released his injured hand as if nothing had happened to it. "I felt nothing. The spell worked as it should have." That was not true; it had been his intention to *capture* whatever had lurked in the tree for interrogation or, if it had proven to be merely an animal, examination as a potential food or sport source. For some unfathomable reason, he had unleashed a spell more powerful by at least a hundredfold. "I have commanded; your duty is to *obey*."

"Father." Lochivan bowed and backed away. It was evident in his movements that he would have preferred the patriarch's reprimand to such an impossible task. Yet, being Tezerenee, he would work to fulfill Barakas's command, no matter what the cost.

The Lord Tezerenee gestured to two clan members who stood nearby, still stunned by what their master had done. With their helms on, he could not judge whether they were his children or merely relations. It did not matter as long as they performed their duties. "Bring that carcass to me. I want to know what our enemy is capable of."

The Lady Alcia tried to bring the conversation back to Gerrod. "If you could only—"

She was cut off with an imperialistic wave of one gauntleted hand. "Gerrod is dead. Everyone back in Nimth is dead . . . or as *good* as dead. I will hear no more about them." Anticipation tinged his next words. "We must prepare for our first battle. It will be *glorious!*"

As she watched her husband stalk off to oversee the disposal of the monstrous corpse, the matriarch frowned. Barakas had found new playmates, actual adversaries. There would be no turning him from the task he had set for himself now. The role of conqueror was at last his to claim. Gerrod was no more than a soon-to-be-forgotten memory, as far as the lord of the dragon clan was concerned.

Glancing at the limp bundle of flesh being dragged to the waiting patriarch and thinking of what other potential dangers the new world might yet offer, the Lady Tezerenee wondered if the clan itself would be such a memory before long.

"Perhaps it would be for the best," she murmured, then strode off herself to help organize her people for the coming threat.

Dru and the elf faced each other, eyes locked. Considering the speed with which she moved, Dru questioned his chances of unleashing a spell before the knife struck home. He also wondered what sort of sorcery she might have to back up her assault, for the stories had always hinted that to some extent the elfin race had had its share of potent spellcasters. Somehow, he could not see the knife as her only weapon; his Vraadish mind-set could not comprehend a foe who would take on a mage with only a small hand weapon. No one was that insane.

Another thing occurred to him as he readied himself for the worst. He knew time had passed, for the sun was bright in the sky. Yet Dru could not recall either sleeping or eating. He was, however, fully rested and not the least bit hungry. The sorcerer thanked the guardians for small favors; maybe they had wanted him to be at his best when he died.

"What did they tell you in there?" she suddenly asked, the blade still poised for immediate use.

He almost laughed. Questions at a time like this? He would have expected such from himself had his mind not still been at least partly back with the very creatures she asked about. "They told me about this place . . . and about Nimth."

"It is all falling apart, is it not? Nimth, that is."

His gaze shifted briefly from her green, almond-shaped eyes to the knife and then back again. "Yes, it is."

"You destroyed Nimth. You destroyed it the way you destroyed everything else on it other than yourselves."

"Yes."

Confusion spread onto her face, lessening the anger a bit.

"You admit it? You are very cooperative. Why is that? What are you planning?"

"I have no quarrel with you, elf. If I have a quarrel with anyone, it is our former hosts."

"Do you think I am a fool because I use a knife against a Vraad? I know how chancy your spells are, but I also know how devious you are said to be. We went through the same difficulty with our own magic, for a short time, when we first came here. I can easily kill you before you take another breath."

Dru believed her. The grace with which she moved, even seemed to breathe, spoke of skill surpassing his. Still, if it came to a battle, he had a few tricks she could not know about. "The guardians put us together to survive."

"Or *kill* one another and save them the problem of dealing with two more who know about this place."

The sorcerer had considered that but had chosen not to mention it. He had not even dared to ask what had actually been done with the Seekers. The elf was no one's fool. "Do we do it, then? Would you like to kill me?"

She hesitated. "A trick?"

"Hardly. I would rather form an alliance than fight." A gust of wind blew his hair in her eyes. He pushed it aside, wondering if this breeze meant that some of the guardians remained, shielded from his senses. That might have been the true reason they had ejected Darkhorse from their world; he represented a potential threat to their security—to their *legacy*.

"You are Vraad." Was there just a hint of uncertainty in her tone? Dru wondered.

"A chance of birth."

She smiled at her poor attempt at humor, an effect that nearly dazzled him. So used to the unreal and exceedingly arrogant beauty of his kind, he was unprepared for the beauty that nature itself could offer. Dru forgot himself and simply stared. Only Sharissa could claim similar beauty.

Sharissa and her mother...

The knife was suddenly at his *throat*. "I could have killed you now. You didn't even bother to move."

He had been too engrossed in admiring her... something that *had* to be the work of this land and not his own doing. Dru had not survived all these centuries by letting his mind wander to pleasant things in times of crisis. No, it *had* to be the land playing with his thoughts. Yet, Dru realized that his adversary *did* remind him of his wife and daughter, too, so perhaps . . .

When her enemy continued to pay no heed to the death tickling his neck, the elf withdrew her blade and, after what must have been a tremendous debate with herself, sheathed it. "If you would desire an alliance, I can see no reason to turn you down. Not for the time being. You can call me Xiri. Not my birth name."

"Xiri." The Vraad did not ask what she meant by it not being her birth name. Elfin ways were mystery to his kind, who could only go by what little had been passed down over the millennia. Even Serkadion Manee, who seemed to want to chronicle everything, had been sparse in his details of the one other significant race in Nimth history. "Call me Dru, Xiri. My *birth* name, if you are interested. How did you know I was a Vraad?"

"It is *not* because I am *so* old that I remember your arrogant race," she bit back, though again with a touch of humor. "Those who passed to this place made certain we would remember the forms of our foes." She sized him up. "You do not seem exceptionally sinister. Merely tall and a touch too confident in yourself."

"You'll find enough of my kind that fit your darkest fears. Overall, we are probably everything your ancestors claimed we were, which is why we ourselves have been trying to escape Nimth." It was peculiar, he thought, how easy it was to talk to her even though she had come close to slitting his throat only a breath or two earlier.

"How terrible is it?"

Gazing around at the remnants of a civilization far older than his own, Dru pictured Nimth in a few thousand years. "These ruins will look picturesque in comparison to what we have left as a legacy."

"And now you've come here to spread your poison." The hostility had returned to Xiri's voice, but it was not meant for Dru personally. "The land will not permit it."

The sorcerer shivered as she said the last. "Why do you say that?"

Xiri began walking, if only, it seemed, to burn off nervous

energy. Without thinking, Dru moved beside her, keeping pace. He was taller than she by nearly two feet and his stride was nearly double her own, but the Vraad was still forced to walk faster to keep up with his new companion.

"You mean you cannot feel it? You cannot feel the presence that is the land itself?"

He had. More than once. He also believed it was the same force that had guided him into this world and then used his horse to lead him here. If what he supposed had truth in it, then there was a purpose for his being in the shrouded realm. Dru was not certain whether he should be pleased or worried.

"I see you have." Xiri had used Dru's musings as an opportunity to study his face, reading there the answer he had not given to her in words.

"Do the . . . the guardians know of it?"

She shrugged. "I am as much of a newcomer to this continent as you. Maybe. It could be that what we feel is like them, though you would know that better than I. Another 'guardian,' as you called them." Xiri mulled over his term. "Guardians. I suppose that describes them better than anything else."

They were taking a path that would more or less lead them back to where Dru, as a prisoner of the avians, had entered the city. The sorcerer did not ask if there was a reason for this particular direction; he was learning too much to be concerned with anything else. He found he also enjoyed Xiri's company, she being a more pleasant, straightforward companion than most Vraad . . . when she was not trying to kill him, that is.

"How long have the elves been here?"

"Thousands of years. We really do not keep track of time as precisely as you do."

He took a breath before asking his next question. They were on fair terms at the moment, but he knew that there were areas that she might not wish to talk about. Her skill with the blade had been impressed upon him quite sufficiently. Still, he had a question that had to be asked. *"How did you escape Nimth?"*

To his amazement and relief, she appeared undisturbed by what he had asked. "There is debate as to that. Some claim we found a hole in the fabric of Nimth that led us to here. Some claim the hole was opened *for* us.

"I think they made a mistake, whoever created all this. I think we were not supposed to be in the same place as your kind, but it took them time to correct that mistake."

That was likely close to the truth, the overwhelmed spellcaster thought. "How much did the guardians tell *you*? They'd indicated that they chose to speak to me because I resembled their ancient masters. I thought that I was the only one they spoke with because of that."

"Enough." Xiri, her eyes closing to little more than slits, related a tale much like that which Dru had suffered through, but less informative. She knew about the old race and how, for reasons she found insulting, her kind had been judged lacking and left to live out their existence in a place where others were to rule, such as the Seekers and, before them, the Quel. The guardians had said no more, not even telling her that they were leaving her with a Vraad. That the Vraad had been left to face eventual destruction at their own hands had long satisfied the elves. To find herself with Dru had come as a great shock to her. His presence meant that the elves had not left the evil behind them as they had hoped.

When she was finished, Dru told her his own story, including events leading up to the city itself. For reasons he felt were justified, the mage made no mention of the final world, the one in which he had found all that remained of the elder race. He wanted to forget that place. Where the citadel with the ghostly memories had once soothed him, it now filled the Vraad with dread. There were too many parallels to the cross-over and its potential results.

"I am alone, Dru," Xiri commented without warning.

"The others..."

"Dead. Some during the crossing—the seas between this continent and ours are extremely violent—the rest at the claws of either the birds or the shellbacks."

"How do you intend to return?"

She turned and faced him. In the midst of so much devastation, the two of them seemed so tiny to the sorcerer. He wanted to go somewhere and hide, a very un-Vraad-like reaction. Of course, Dru had not felt like a Vraad for the past twenty years, especially the last few days.

"I really do not know."

He laughed despite his efforts not to and when she asked what he found so humorous, her hand straying to the blade at her side, Dru pointed out his own predicament. They were two strangers in a land that did not want them with no idea how to get back to where they had come from. A teleport across a distance as vast as the seas that Xiri described would have been nearly impossible even at his peak of power. He did not know the other continent well enough, having seen it only as a ghostly image, and blind teleports, especially so lengthy, generally proved treacherous. It was easy to end up in the wrong place, such as the bottom of the sea.

Xiri sat down. She did not care that the ground was covered with broken marble. The elf sat as if it were the most important thing she could do. One hand toyed with a pouch akin to the one the Seekers had found. On it was a symbol that resembled the sun. Dru was uncertain as to whether it was decorative or representative of some belief and decided not to ask.

"What do we do, then?" she asked in a monotone voice.

If she was an example of the elfin race, Dru could understand how they might be found lacking by the guardians. Xiri was mercurial in nature, ready to kill him one moment and walking along with him the next. Her abrupt pause now was a surprise, but not great when Dru contemplated it in comparison to how she had acted in the few minutes he had known her. She was a confusing woman . . . more so than any whose path he had crossed in his long life.

"Where were we walking to?" he finally asked. Dru assumed the elf had a destination in mind.

"I do not know. I merely walked to put distance between myself and the guardians." A touch of bitterness underscored her next words. "I did not want to *offend* them any longer with my less-than-perfect presence, I suppose." Xiri clutched the pouch tighter. "All our work for naught."

"The Seekers and the . . . the Quel . . . didn't find whatever it was they sought. That should be something." The sorcerer knew it gave *him* some satisfaction.

Xiri looked up at the spellcaster, who felt uncomfortable at what he read in her expression. "They wanted to seize control of the power that made all of this. They found caverns left behind by the builders of this city, caverns that whispered some of the truth about this world and promised many things for those willing to look for the source."

That was what the figurines in the chamber of the dragon lord had reminded him of. They were akin to some of the talismans the Seeker leader had revealed to him through the avians' peculiar method of communication. "So they found a chamber carved out by the former lords of . . . is there no name for this world?"

"None that I know of. We did not feel it was our right to give it another."

It may yet be called the Dragonrealm, then, for lack of a better title, Dru thought sourly. He refrained from telling Xiri, not wanting to arouse her anger. "What purpose did the chamber serve?"

"I do not know. The Seekers control that region. The Quel . . . no one knows *how* the Quel learn what they learn. They just seem to know." The elf rose, stretching her slender legs, much to Dru's discomfort. He had stayed clear of the female of the species since the idiotic duel that his wife had died fighting. Again, he noted how Xiri reminded him of . . . of . . .

He had tried so hard to forget her death, to forget the pain *he* had suffered . . . that Dru had forgotten her *name*.

"Is something amiss?"

"Nothing," he snapped back. The shamed sorcerer knew his face was crimson. "My memory has failed me. That's all it was."

"I see." She did, in a sense. He could see that. Xiri knew that whatever had disturbed the Vraad had been very personal. It was a comfort that, unlike Melenea, the elf did not probe the open wound merely for her own amusement. Instead, Xiri glanced up at the blue sky and said, "The day will be gone and we will still be here wondering what to do."

Dru hesitated. Their key to escape might lie within the empty square where the rift was. Despite his desire to never return there—and the possible threat of the guardians, who might decide that eliminating an elf and a Vraad was worth breaking their own rules—the rift was probably the only hope they had. Even if Sharissa crossed over with the rest, there was no way she would be able to locate him. Not here.

They had to go back.

"I know a way." When she waited, a slight, patient smile enhancing her smooth, pale features, he forced himself to go on. "Do you remember when I rode into sight?"

"I remember. Your steed frightened me. I had never seen such an animal. Are all your horses like that?"

The thought of a stable filled with Darkhorses eased the tension in his mind and almost made him smile. "Hardly. What I ask is if you remember *how* I appeared?"

"I did not see that. I assumed you came from behind some building."

He had forgotten that no one had noticed the two of them until he and Darkhorse were already riding toward them. Dru shook his head. "No, we didn't. What you and the avians missed was the rift in reality through which we emerged. *A hole*, if that brings to mind what I'm trying to explain."

"A hole?" She rose, ever lithe in her movements. "You found a hole such as the one my people are supposed to have used?"

"Not just any. It leads to where the originators of this . . . experiment . . . last lived. It may hold the key to controlling everything."

Xiri gazed back in the direction of the clearing where she had first seen Dru. "The Sheeka never knew how close they were." Turning to the tall Vraad, she asked suspiciously, "Why did you 'forget' to tell me this before?"

There had been a time when nothing would have shamed the master sorcerer. Now, it felt as if his face burned all the time. "I was frightened. I . . . didn't want to . . . return to the central chamber."

"What was in there?" Her suspicion had turned to sympathy. From all she had likely been told about his kind, shame was not something Xiri would have expected from him.

Now it was his turn to gaze back in the direction of that terrible place. "The memories of the last of that race. The truth about Nimth. A feeling that the Vraad are too much like them and will fade away even as they have."

"All races fade with time. The Quel, the Sheeka, and their predecessors are all examples of that. Even the elves will pass on." Xiri gave the ruined city a look of contempt as she added,

"For all our 'failure' to live up to their expectations, we elves have lasted longer than most."

"I don't believe we have to fall. Not until all reality itself fades away." Dru clenched his fists. "I can find it fairly easy. I could never forget now."

"What about the guardians?"

He met her eyes, found no fear in them, only honest worry. "You're the one who reminded me we have no choice. I'd hoped you had a way out of here, a way to travel to where my . . . to where your people are."

Xiri put a hand on his arm. "I know the Vraad have come. You could not exactly hide it, Dru. We will deal with them when we return home."

She had not said "if," which strengthened the sorcerer's resolve a bit, though he was certain Xiri had used the word for her own sake. Neither of them wanted to think what would happen if the guardians, especially one of them, did, indeed, decide the Vraad and the elf *could* be removed despite the rules laid down by the long-gone lords.

"You are not so bad, for an ancient and terrible enemy," she commented without warning. "You might be elfin if not for your height and your odd visage."

"And you," he replied, starting back to the inner city as he spoke, "are not so mystically withdrawn as I thought elves were supposed to be."

"There are always those caught up in the wonder of themselves. Most of us have learned to relax. We find we get along much better now. There was a point where we were nearly at war with ourselves, because of our strict, pompous ways."

"What happened?"

She had moved ahead of him, again building a pace he had to work hard to match. "Our elders reminded us of the Vraad and how we were acting too much like them."

Dru could only see the back of her head, but he was of the suspicion that his companion was smiling.

Throughout the return, they sensed no presence other than their own. Xiri pointed out that it was hardly proof that the two of them were alone and Dru readily agreed. He kept waiting for the end to come, for the magical beings to take them up like rag dolls and drop them wherever they had disposed of the avians.

What *had* they done to the Seekers?

Xiri froze. "Wait."

"What is it?" He peered ahead, but saw nothing.

"I thought I saw a shape, elf or Vraad, but when I blinked, it was not there anymore."

Darkhorse had said something similar . . . in the same region, Dru noticed. Who else was here? "Not a Seeker or a Quel?"

"Neither. I would recognize a Shee—Seeker, if you prefer, quite easily. No, it looked manlike, but *incomplete.*" She shrugged. "I cannot explain the last."

Dru moved with more caution, expecting trouble at any moment. As for Xiri, the Vraad was unsettled by her almost casual manner. It was clear that she felt that at this point they had nothing to gain by stealth. A quick, direct march to their destination was what she obviously had in mind and Dru, understanding her more and more, knew the senselessness of trying to stop the elf now that she had decided on her course of action.

Before he was ready to be there, they had arrived at the square where the rift waited.

"I do not see anything."

"Did you see anything before I burst into sight?"

"No," she admitted. "It just seems wrong to not see something."

"If it had been so visible, the Seekers would have found it before either of us."

"But would the guardians have let them?" she countered.

It was one of many questions he could not answer. The sorcerous creatures had likely interfered because of the number of intruders, not the mere fact that there *had* been intruders in the first place. They had not disturbed Dru and Darkhorse after their initial attempt to frighten the duo away. In what was a somewhat naive manner of thought, they had probably hoped the two would leave without disturbing too much. The mage was astonished at how rule-bound such godlike beings were, even considering the fact that they had been as familiars to their ancient masters. To remain at their tasks this long, with the cracks in their ranks only beginning to form, was astounding.

Yet, if the one sinister guardian was a sign of what was to come, Dru worried that the future held even greater danger than the refugees from Nimth had ever imagined could confront them.

"No one has stopped us so far. We might as well go on." Though Xiri made it sound like a suggestion, Dru understood that it was more of a gentle nudge. Without realizing it, he had already stepped back a foot or so, as if his deep fear were stealing control of his body.

"It was this way." The reluctant sorcerer urged his legs into motion, leading his elfin companion to where he estimated the rift would be.

They saw nothing save more ruins. Dru began to worry that he had lost the gap, that they would wander this area for hours and find nothing but more rubble. Xiri would think him a fool. . . .

"There!" the elf shouted, her voice almost gleeful.

He saw it now, a tiny tear just below eye level. In that tear was a glimpse of another place, a wondrous place.

I said so! I said they would return! They must be removed! The savage voice in their minds made both explorers fall to their knees. Dru needed no help in identifying the creature that ravaged his brain merely by speaking.

Should not! came the voice that the Vraad had deemed the fourth. It sounded reluctant, as if it, too, no longer believed that noninterference was possible.

They had their chance! They betrayed our good faith! roared the attacker. Dru held his head, trying to keep it from bursting. *They—*

Dru's mind cleared.

Beside him, Xiri rose, her body trembling. "What happened? Where did they go?"

The sorcerer shook his head, then regretted the action as the world swam. Of the mental intrusion by the guardians, there was no trace. It was as if they had been cut off . . . or *fled*.

"Something frightened them." His head cleared.

Dru and his companion heard the scuffling sound at the same time. Xiri was the swifter of the two, so she was first to turn and see what stumbled toward them. It did her little good; the sorcerer could read the confusion on her visage even as he himself was turning to see what new twist the once-supposedly peaceful world had for him.

The newcomer shambled toward them, clad in a simple robe and cowl that covered its body all the way to the earth. It stumbled again, walking as if it did not really know where it was going. Not surprising, as far as Dru was concerned, considering it had no eyes. It also had no ears, nose, mouth, or hair . . . in fact, no markings whatsoever.

One of Barakas's golems, larger than before, but instantly recognizable as such.

How had it gotten here, when the cross-over had been set to occur on the other continent?

Dru forgot that question, forgot *all* thoughts, as the faceless golem was joined by a second and then a third.

Then they began swarming out of the ruins from all sides, the Vraad, the elf, and the rift their obvious destination.

XV

A taloned hand thrust itself into his scarred face, making new trails of blood.

Rendel did not scream. He had stopped screaming after the first day. That did not mean that the pain was any less, however.

Images swarmed into his tortured mind. Humans in dark dragon-scale armor, at least a hundred. The death of a flock member, who had watched and relayed the information. The realization that these were as Rendel was.

"So . . . what do . . . you need me for?" They obviously knew everything. Why then would his captors turn to him? Did they not know, too, that he had betrayed his kind, seeking, in typical Vraadish fashion, to rise above the rest by deceit? He shivered slightly, both from his anticipation of the torture he was certain was coming and the simple fact that they had stripped him of his clothing, allowing the damp, cool air to play havoc with his unprotected body.

The aerie overlord pulled away his hand and stepped back while two females brought water and some sort of meat to the prisoner. Rendel had a blurry view of his surroundings, not that he needed it. The Tezerenee already knew what the aerie looked like, a natural set of caverns within and beneath the mountain he had dubbed Kivan Grath. It was the chief aerie of the bird people since their setbacks in a war with what looked like two-legged armadillos, if the images Rendel had been shown were correct. The avians still controlled most of the continent, but their adversaries had a nasty habit of springing suicide raids from underneath the earth that had caused the collapse of more than one of the lesser dwellings of the race. The purpose had not been the death of the warriors; it was the next generation of avians that had suffered. The young, not yet able to fly, had suffered heavy casualties. Aeries could be rebuilt; the future was much more difficult to replace.

Rendel could care less for his captors' war. All he wanted was what the leader had taunted him with since his arrival. Just beyond the circle of bird people watching over his questioning were the towering and seductive effigies he had discovered in his research. How ironic that they should stand as silent monitors of the Vraad's torture. There was power in this cavern, power more ancient than that of the birds. They understood that, somewhat, and he knew that they had been attempting to both utilize what they had found and also locate the original home of those who had created this edifice within the mountain. It lay across a vast expanse of water, however, and so they had no way of knowing how their explorers were doing. He already knew that the overlord was growing impatient. The avian leader had already taken out his frustration on the prisoner twice.

When they were finished with feeding and watering him, he repeated his question. "What do you need *me* for?"

One of the other avians, an elder by the looks of his balding form, cocked his head so that one eye was focused on the leader and squawked at him for several seconds. The overlord's reply was short and succinct. It was also unnerving. The others instantly knelt, spreading their wings, smoothing their feathers, and cocking one eye earthward, essentially showing their trust in the leader by making themselves blind to his presence. He could have struck any of them down. It was a sign of submission, of course. Submission to whatever plan he had . . . *hatched*, Rendel though wryly. A plan that the sorcerer was evidently an integral part of.

He had an inkling of what it was even before the overlord reestablished contact. Unlike most times, Rendel now welcomed communication. It might be his only path to freedom.

Images of his clan, especially a bird's view of the most dangerous, a huge monster that Rendel knew could only be his father. The imprisoned spellcaster relayed an image of his own. His father as a leader. His father as a sorcerer of great strength. His father as an adversary who would crush the avians' bodies beneath his boots and plant the dragon banner in their blood-smeared chests.

From the earsplitting shrieks that filled the cavern and echoed until Rendel thought he would go deaf, he gathered that the entire aerie knew what he had told the leader.

A new image was directed back at him with such force that Rendel nearly passed out. It showed the Tezerenee scattered about the landscape, their bloody corpses all that remained of the once-proud clan. The dragon banner still stood, but this time it protruded from a gaping hole in the throat of the patriarch himself.

"A pretty picture," Rendel choked, "but not so easily accomplished."

Now it was his own image that appeared in his thoughts. He stood a free man, one working beside those of the aerie, unlocking the mysteries of the ancient lords. The avians' discoveries were his to share. He saw himself seated in a vast citadel of his own, a massive manor partly built, partly grown from the soil. It already existed, a ruined artifact from an even older race than theirs that the bird people had rebuilt to greater glory. It only lacked a master.

They wanted him to betray his clan again, to lead the Tezerenee into a trap in which they would perish to the man. In return, Rendel would receive his heart's desire . . . his own domain and the secrets he had sought for upon crossing to this world.

Not for one moment did the captive sorcerer believe he would ever live to see the day of reward. They *might* let him live long enough to aid them in their attempts to understand the talismans of the long-dead race, but Rendel would never see the domain they had promised him.

Nonetheless, he nodded his head in agreement, hoping they understood the movement. Apparently they did, for there was a sense of approval from the leader, who removed his hand from the Vraad's face and signaled once more to the two females who had fed the prisoner. Another avian, a tall male, undid the bonds that held him to the wall and caught him as he collapsed. The females took him by the arms, surprisingly strong for being so much smaller, and carried him from the council. He assumed that was what he had faced.

They brought him to a mat and assisted him as he slowly lay down on it. It was soft, so very soft. Every bone in the Vraad's body screamed as he moved. He would, he thought, be very stiff when he awoke . . . if he ever did.

When he had settled, the two females left. They were replaced immediately by four others, one carrying a bowl. Despite his sparse meal, Rendel was not hungry; he wanted only to sleep for the rest of eternity.

Two avians stood on each side of him now. The one with the bowl held it out to the others, who reached in and scooped out a thick soup substance that dripped all over his prone figure.

"Dragon's blood! Watch where you're dripping that muck!" What were they going to do?

When all four had a handful of the substance, they poured it on his naked form and began rubbing. Weakened as he was, the sorcerer struggled in vain against their combined might. The avians were quite capable of going about their task with one hand while holding him down with the other. With this method, they massaged his body from top to bottom.

There was no feeling of arousal, not when a talon reminded him now and then what his half-closed eyes could only vaguely still make out . . . that his companions were not human, but a vicious race of bird people. What they did, he realized as consciousness began to slip away, was necessary if the spellcaster wanted to be able to move when he woke. The massage and the substance, combined together, had already eased some of the pain. It made sense; his captors hardly had the time to wait for his recovery, not if he knew his father. The patriarch, once alerted to the presence of enemies, would not rest until they were beaten. The birds, meanwhile, hoped for a quick and treacherous victory, with their willing prisoner as the key.

Rendel's last conscious thoughts, concerning what *he* would do when the time came, left a smile on his face long after he fell asleep.

The golems continued to stagger toward them, like unliving horrors from a nightmare. Xiri had her knife out and was muttering something under her breath.

What were the golems doing here? How had they crossed the violent seas?

"These . . ." the elf finally managed. "These are what I saw! What are they?"

"Golems." He watched one fall, then right itself. After a moment, Dru realized that they did not walk as the blind in an unfamiliar place, but rather as children did who were not quite used to walking. The Vraad recalled his own daughter's first steps and how similar these were. The uneven ground certainly did not help.

There was something else, though. No matter what direction that golems came from, they all stared toward the same location, as if drawn by a great treasure.

"Xiri! Take my hand!"

He was pleased when she did not question his action. Cautiously, the sorcerer walked toward an area where there was somewhat of a gap between the faceless horde. "Be ready for anything!"

Dru allowed the golems to continue on unhindered, only making certain that he and the elf were not directly in the path of any of them. As he had surmised, they steered, not toward the two intruders but rather in the direction of the rift.

Xiri choked back a gasp as one of the robed creatures brushed her backside on its trek toward the tear. "They do not want us at all!"

"No. They want what lies beyond the tear."

"You called them golems. You recognized them."

The last of the unnerving figures had stumbled past them.

The first were nearly at the rift. The fascinated sorcerer released the elf's hand and took a step toward the line of steadily moving figures. "We made them. The Tezerenee, that is. I worked with them, though. These were supposed to be our new bodies when our ka shifted to this world. We could touch the land here—the shrouded realm, as I called it—but not physically cross."

"Then, these are your people." She shifted the blade, debating whether to throw it or not. Her skin was even paler than before.

Dru shook his head and started back toward the tear. Now that he knew the golems did not want him, he was curious as to what they sought. "No, those aren't Vraad. They would look like me, if they were."

"Then what *are* they?"

"I think we should follow and see." Whatever his feelings toward the citadel on the hill, they were secondary now.

"You know," she said, lowering but not sheathing the knife, "that they must be what the guardians feared."

"I know." Dru had a theory, but was afraid to tell it to the elf. He could scarcely believe it himself.

The first of the golems, walking a little more confidently now, stepped through the rift and vanished. The others began lining up and marching through two at a time. The sorcerer likened the image before him to a parade of macabre mario-nettes. In swift fashion, the golems entered the tear, never hesitating. The last crossed into the ancient realm of the creators, leaving only the elf and the Vraad in the ruined square.

"Do we wait?" Xiri asked.

Dru realized he had been hesitating again. This time it was more from awe than fear. Nevertheless, he knew that the longer they waited, the more chance that something might pass that they would miss.

"Follow me."

She took his hand in her free one. When he looked at her, Xiri smiled uncertainly and said, "I would rather not end up alone in a place I have never been to before."

He could have assured her that such would not be the place, that they would find themselve near one another in the gardenlike field at the bottom of the hill. He could have told her, but he did not. "Time to cross, then."

The sensation was akin to what he had felt earlier, a blinding brilliance and the late realization that all sound had ceased during the transfer.

"Rheena!" Xiri froze the moment they entered the world of the citadel. She looked at the birds flying merrily above and the trimmed, grassy field in which they were now standing. "It is so beautiful! As if someone had sculpted it!"

Not far from the truth, as far as Dru was concerned. Seeing it again, with Xiri, made him appreciate it that much more. Had it not been for the presence of the determined golems, he might have lost his fear of this place. They served, however, to remind him of what he might expect.

Unmindful of the beauty around them, the faceless figures strode upward, no longer awkward in their movements despite the climb. The closer they got to the castle, the more confident the creatures moved. It was clear they had some true purpose in mind.

"They know this place." Xiri was the first to utter what they both had known for some time. "They move as if they are returning home."

"I think they are." He recalled the ghostly watchers hunched about the crystal and the pentagram. How many had there been? How many more had existed besides these? He had hardly taken the time to inspect the rest of the massive structure.

"Guardians?" From the tone of her voice, it seemed that the elf wanted him to agree, even though neither of them believed that.

Dru shrugged, trying hard to keep the golems from getting too far ahead. Xiri was now leading *him*. "I doubt it, though I won't rule it out. I think the guardians in the ruined city gave evidence to what those things truly are. The exodus to this place only confirms it, as far as I see."

They were nearly at the top of the hill. The cowled figures were already vanishing through the open gate. Both the Vraad and the elf could see that the golems were spreading out as they entered the edifice. The newcomers appeared quite at home.

"I think that says it all," Dru whispered. He took a breath

before finishing. "I think the masters of the house have finally *returned*."

Indeed, there seemed no arguing with the statement. Following the last of the figures into the courtyard, the sorcerer and his companion watched in silent regard as Barakas's usurped creations entered buildings, climbed stairways, or simply studied their surroundings with eyes that were not there. None of them appeared to care about the two intruders.

Finally regaining control of himself, Dru leaned over and whispered, "The chamber we want is through there." He pointed in the direction of the building he and Darkhorse had entered on his previous visitation. A number of the featureless beings had already entered.

"There?" Xiri did not sound so certain, still overwhelmed and understandably anxious around the strange figures wandering about. Dru, knowing the forms from his time with the Tezerenee, was, if not comfortable with the golems, at least used to their appearances . . . or lack thereof.

"It's where I saw the crystal. In the room of worlds."

"All right." She had the knife in her free hand. Dru had thought she had sheathed it at some point, but could no longer recall. He pushed the hand down by the wrist.

"I doubt that will do you much good. It might even be detrimental for *us*." He gave her a smile that likely did not reassure her any more than it did him. "I thought *I* came from the bloodthirsty race, not you."

"As I said, we have changed since escaping Nimth." Xiri nonetheless did sheathe the blade. "You have a point about the knife, though, Vraad."

They moved slowly across the courtyard, partly due to caution and partly due to Xiri's fascination with the lifelike images sculpted from the shrubbery. "This reminds me of something back in my village," she whispered, smiling all the while. "There are those among us who can persuade the trees and bushes to take on new and fantastic forms."

"Is that what the Seekers do?" He recalled the unique aeries of the race, places both constructed and grown. The ones his captor had revealed to him had been stupendous works of art.

"In a sense. Like the Vraad, however, they *demand* more than request cooperation." The flat line formed by her mouth was sign enough that she would speak no more on that particular subject.

No one barred their way when they reached the open entrance and so the two entered the long hall. The female elf was awed by the grandness of the inner hallway. She glanced around as if expecting it all to vanish. It was not that the corridor was so richly decorated, but rather that it carried about it a feeling of majesty, a reflection, perhaps, of the builder's skill.

Dru, only slightly less awed even though he had seen the corridor before, led her farther inside. It was then that the sorcerer noticed a smaller room to the left that he would have been willing to swear had not existed the first time he had entered the castle.

A slave to his curiosity, he stepped closer to the entranceway of the new chamber . . . and nearly bumped into one of the silent figures as it departed that very room. Dru and Xiri kept a careful eye on the faceless wanderer until it departed through the front doorway. Dru cautiously peered into the chamber . . . and gasped.

"What is it?" Xiri circled around him so that she could see.

The room was immaculate and glowed with a brilliant illumination. Down to and including the overwhelming figure poised before them, it was identical to the chamber of the dragon lord that he had been nearly tossed into by the Seekers back in the devastated city. Yet, that first chamber was a pale memory in comparison to this one. Here was the dragon lord in all his glory, looking ready to leap into the air. If the other had seemed almost living, Dru was nearly certain this one was. Despite its wary eyes, he could have believed it was merely pausing to consider its next action. Even its muscles, carved taut by that long-dead master sculptor, emphasized the readiness with which the dragon lord waited.

The same statuettes were also there, and better able to view them this time, he realized that they also resembled the figures from the mind message relayed to him by the Seeker leader. One of the tiny artifacts reminded the sorcerer of the figurine that the avian had thrown and broken in anger. Emboldened by their luck so far, Dru stepped inside in order to learn more. Xiri, also very curious as to the purpose of this place, not only followed the Vraad in, but twisted around her companion and walked swiftly to the tiny effigies, her hands out before her as if she intended to pick one up.

"Wait!" He rushed toward her, fully expecting every golem in the citadel to come storming into the chamber, ready to strike the impudent twosome down for their transgressions. If, as he believed, they *were* the ancient race that had built all of this, they might take *special* measures for the disturbance of their most precious artifacts. The figurines themselves might be protected by a hundred different spells, all deadly, though it hardly seemed there had been enough time for the faceless ones to have affixed so many magical traps. Dru knew that he might be placing Vraadish paranoia before common sense, but the sorcerer also understood that he and Xiri knew next to nothing about the originators and their power, save that it made the Vraad race look childlike in comparison.

Xiri had stopped at his shout. She realized instantly what he feared and frowned in annoyance. "I know better than to touch something that I have not observed closely first."

Embarrassed by his own fears, a reddened Dru joined her. He pointed out the similarity of the carvings to both what his captors had discovered and what they themselves had revealed to him. The sorcerer also mentioned the shattered statuette and pointed to one that vaguely resembled the one he believed had been destroyed. Xiri was upset about the latter; anything created by the founding race should have been treated with the utmost respect as far as she was concerned.

"They feel almost alive when you stand this close to them." She had put her hands near the artifacts, but was careful to leave enough empty space in case of an accident. Neither of them cared for the thought of stumbling into the figurines.

"I don't recall the others feeling so." Though he had not been allowed to study them, Dru was certain he would have felt the aura surrounding the objects from where the avians had deposited him. "I wonder . . ." He took a closer look. The detail was so precise that he almost believed the gryphon he stared at would snap at him if his fingers came too near. "I wonder what they *do*?"

A scuffling sound alerted them to the entrance of three figures. The featureless golems might have been copied from one original, so identical were they down to their very movements. Somehow, they communicated, that much was evident. Dru supposed that they communicated in a fashion akin to the method utilized by the Seekers. That still did not make it any less unnerving. It was the silence that unsettled the sorcerer the most.

The three figures walked purposely toward the area where Xiri and the Vraad stood.

"I think they want to do something with the figurines," Dru suggested, whispering despite himself. "Now, maybe we'll find out what the purpose of this chamber is."

Since the two explorers stood in the way, they separated, each moving to one side of the platform where the figurines stood. As long as the duo did not interfere, Dru felt confident that the newcomers would ignore them as they had before.

Two of the oncoming creatures turned toward the tall mage. The other shifted to intercept Xiri.

Though initially stunned, the elf recovered instantly and reached for her blade. To her horror, the golem moved even *more* swiftly, trapping her wrist even before she could begin to unsheathe the weapon. Xiri struck her attacker with her free hand, but the blow, which would have stunned most adversaries, did not even slow the faceless construct.

The spellcaster had troubles of his own. His mind was a maelstrom of resurging doubts. He was caught between defending himself against a power incredibly old and the possible repercussions of unleashing his own strength in a place where it might do him more harm than help.

His hesitation cost him. The golems secured his arms and one of them put a hand to his temple. Dru felt as if his head swelled to twice its normal size. He tried to concentrate on a spell, but his mind wandered during the attempt. A second and third try yielded the same results. They had effectively blocked his abilities. Each time he tried to defend himself, his attention would turn to some triviality. He was barely able to concentrate on the mere fact that he was a prisoner, let alone how the two of them could escape.

Xiri was brought to his side and they were led from the dragon lord's chamber. The faceless beings were not harsh; they used only what force they needed to control their prisoners. Dru noted the direction they were going and smiled grimly. "They're taking us to the very place we wanted to go. The room of worlds."

"What do you think they will do?" The elf shut her eyes and the irritated expression on her otherwise perfect face told the sorcerer that she, too, had been prevented from using any magical abilities. "Why did they suddenly notice us? We touched nothing. We *did* nothing."

Dru had no answer this time. The faceless ones were complete enigmas to him. Everything about them had a question mark attached to it. Why return after all this time and why in such a manner? More to the point, what frightened the guardians so much? If these were their masters come home, should not the servants have been delighted? Their loyalty, with one or two exceptions, had seemed quite firm even after millennia of abandonment by those very same lords.

As they were marched toward the massive doors of the room of worlds—doors that the Vraad remembered demolishing during the peak of his earlier anger, but which now stood new and shining and *very* open—Dru noticed alterations in the corridor itself. It seemed higher and there were doors that like the first he could not recall seeing his first time through. *Redecorating?* he wondered in momentary amusement. Why not? It *had* been a few years.

His amusement was not long in lasting. At the doorway, two more of the faceless creatures met them. The ones that held Dru and Xiri released their grips, but did not move away. Not for a moment did either the Vraad or the elf think to fight or run. Both knew how little a chance they stood.

One of the newcomers pointed at the sorcerer and gestured that he should follow. The other turned to Xiri and mimicked its counterpart's actions.

Dru glanced at his companion, who met his gaze with a look of uncertainty that mirrored his own expression. Before either could speak, the two who had met the party at the doorway turned and walked into the chamber, moving in opposite directions once inside. No one pushed them forward, but their former guards pointed at the receding figures. The two prisoners hurried to catch up to their respective guides.

"Rheena!"

Xiri's words, the only sound other than the heavy falls of Dru's boots, reverberated throughout the room. She stumbled into the one leading her, her attention focused on the walls and the ceiling, and instantly sprang back, fearing a reprisal. The golem did not even appear to notice once it had rebalanced itself. It continued to walk to the opposite side of the room, always succeeding in matching the pace and movements of Dru's own guide.

When they stood across from one another, bisecting the chamber, the cowled figures halted. The sorcerer and the elf stared at one another from beside each. Dru managed a shrug in response to Xiri's anxious visage.

Other than the two who had led them inside and the three who still stood by the doorway, there were only four other golems in the room. Even the spectral impressions of the ancients were no longer visible. It was as if they were no longer needed now that the originals, albeit changed, had returned to claim their castle.

The four in the center of the room knelt before the crystal, as if inspecting it. One touched the top, which caused the focus to glow like a dim fire. It seemed to satisfy the creatures, for they rose and took a step back from the crystal as if expecting something.

Neither they nor the two prisoners were disappointed.

Dru leaned forward, careful to avoid the attention of his guide. The entire focus wavered as if it were composed of smoke rather than crystal and metal. The four near the center stepped back again, but it was due more to some ritual, the sorcerer believed, than any fear on their part.

The focus was no longer visible as such; it now swirled, a tiny, gray whirlwind. No, not a whirlwind, for it had shape of some sort, almost a crude rectangle. What had caused him to see it as a whirlwind were tiny shapes that ran madly across its surface in an eternal chase. It was going through a metamorphosis, becoming some other artifact. Dru wondered if it would have done the same for him or whether he would have ended up killing himself.

Xiri caught his eye. She frowned and indicated the odd form growing in the center of the room. It was hardly what she had expected. The Vraad was equally confused.

Again the four who had been the catalyst for the change stepped away, this time giving the object—or perhaps it *was* a familiar or demon of some sort—a far greater space into which to spread. That proved a wise move, for in seconds the rectangular shape had risen to a height nearly half again as tall as those who had summoned it. As it had grown, so too had the shapes scurrying about its frame. They were black and might have been reptilian in nature, though they moved with such speed that they were generally little more than blurs. Staring at them for more than the blink of an eye stirred an uneasy feeling in the disconcerted spellcaster's stomach. He had no desire to study them closely.

Returning his attention to the structure as a whole, he finally recognized what stood before them. Xiri had mentioned that her ancestors had discovered a hole . . . or a hole had *discovered* them, for as with so much that this ancient race had created, it had a life of sorts. A life in a similar sense to the way Darkhorse had a life. Certainly, it did not live as she or Dru did.

It was a *gate*. No, not merely a gate. That was hardly suitable for the pulsating, magical doorway standing before them. Rather, it was the *Gate*. A name more than a description since it lived. Dru dared to take a few steps to one side. No matter what direction he looked at it, it always seemed to face him. He knew that Xiri would see it the same way.

Glancing at the worlds painted on the walls and ceiling, he understood now how the founders might have crossed from here to any of their creations.

Nimth.

He caught sight of the image, stared at the figure of a Vraad, then felt an uncontrollable urge to face the Gate once more.

"Serkadion Manee!"

Within the frame of the Gate, there now stood the entrance to another world. Dru did not have to ask to know it was his own.

His guide left his side and stepped toward the waiting artifact. The shapes on its frame seemed to slow, though they were still not quite in focus.

Less than an arm's length from the passageway to Dru's world, the golem halted. It raised one hand, then lowered it in one harsh swing.

Nimth vanished, to be replaced by . . . nothing. More than nothing. The sorcerer knew what doorway had now been opened. His recognition of the Void was accompanied by a sense of growing dread.

The faceless being who had stood beside him turned then and, indicating the vast emptiness within the Gate, gestured for Dru to step forward.

XVI

There were still angry Vraad moving about what remained of the communal city, but most had departed. Ever distrusting of their brethren, the majority had returned to the safety of their private domains, there to brood and pout at the trick that had been played on them. They would be so engrossed in their self-pity and their eternal plots for vengeance that they would probably never get around to devising their own ways of escaping . . . something the Tezerenee had proved quite able to do.

It was those few who still remained, still seeking to find some stray ally of the dragon clan or merely desiring to unleash their frustration, who worried Gerrod. Having had one attempt at teleportation misdirected, he was not looking forward to a second try at any point in the near future. Sharissa shared his fear in that respect, which was why the two of them still remained in hiding, despite the occasional passing of a blood-thirsty sorcerer. The room they presently called safety was a tiny storage chamber in a flat, black building on the opposite side of the city from the building where the Lord Barakas had made many of his fine speeches of cooperation, including the one in which he had seemed to promise that *all* Vraad would indeed be crossing into the new world.

Oddly, it was Dru's daughter who had finally had enough.

She stalked over to her hooded companion and leaned over him, arms crossed. "The great and powerful Tezerenee! To think that I was afraid of you! What have you brought us to? How could you abandon Sirvak?"

Gerrod had no answer for the first question and he had already answered the second one more than a dozen times in the past few minutes alone. That, by no means, prevented Sharissa from asking it again. With her father gone, Sirvak was all she had. She no longer trusted Melenea, which, as far as the young Tezerenee was concerned, was the only good that had come of the whole incident.

"I told you, child! Sirvak flew out one of the windows the moment I snared you! It is likely back in your domain, awaiting us!" He looked up at her, more than matching her glare. "Try and remember that for at least a second or two, will you? I need to think!"

"Maybe one of those grateful folk outside would be willing to help you think! You've done nothing but brood since we found this place!"

He started to snap back at her, then saw that she spoke the truth. He was acting much like those he had always despised. The Zeree whelp had not helped his situation, however. He spread his hands wide and replied, "I would welcome whatever masterful plan you have conceived during all the time you've been berating me."

Sharissa clamped her mouth shut and gave him a stare that should have, by rights, burned a hole through his head.

"I thought as much." Stimulated by both her words and his growing shame, Gerrod pushed himself harder.

"Have you noticed something?" she asked, disturbing the peace he had *finally* gained.

"Besides the inability on your part to remain silent for more than a breath?"

She ignored his remark. "For all the damage they did to the city, it should have been far worse."

"I think they're doing an admirable job."

"I mean that they're in the same predicament as we are! They can't trust their spells!"

Gerrod straightened, feeling very stupid. He had understood that when dealing with Melenea, understood it because he knew she lived near an unstable region. The warlock had not considered it in respect to Nimth as a whole. *Sleep. I need sleep!* That was why he could not think straight. When was the last time he had slept? "And so? What else does that suggest to you?"

"I don't know." Sharissa looked crestfallen.

The Tezerenee slumped again. "Waste of *time*!"

"At least we could accomplish something if we were back home! I haven't given up on Father! I know he's alive somewhere!"

The eternal optimism of the child, Gerrod thought bitterly. It *did* gall him, however, to sit here, virtually helpless. He was used to acting—not without thought, of course—but what could he do? The business with Melenea was not finished; he knew her too well to think she would simply lie down and wait for the end of Nimth. No, to her thinking, he had made a master move. Now, it was her turn . . . and, perhaps, that was the fear that kept him sitting in this hole rather than doing his best to find a way to cross. As much as he despised the company of his clan, the shrouded realm did represent continued life and that was the hooded Vraad's primary goal now that he had the Zeree child.

He had hoped she knew more than she had let on, but such was not the case. The information was there, but . . .

Fool! His laughter, full and vibrant, brought a panicked look from Sharissa, who could not understand what he found so amusing. She would not have understood how the laughter was both a sign of his relief and his way of mocking himself for being so blind. He stood up and, in his merriment, took Sharissa and hugged her tight. Even after he finally released her, she stood there, stunned into immobility.

It was not his fault entirely. Tunnel vision was a trait that his race could claim as one of their most dominant features. A Vraad who deeply believed in or desperately wanted something would concentrate on that one thing with an obsession that would make them ignore a hundred more reasonable solutions or beliefs. It was what had kept many a feud going for centuries. It was why few Vraad mixed with one another for more than a few years, it that long. It was a stubbornness of sorts, one that made a solution to the eventual death of Nimth and its inhabitants impossible, for that meant putting aside their arrogant belief in themselves and working in cooperation with one another.

"We're leaving! Somehow, we're leaving! Even if we have to walk back to your domain!"

"Why? What do you have in mind?" Sharissa was smiling, caught up in his enthusiasm and the dream of returning to the citadel of pearl.

"We've both been wrong. You wanted to find a way to bring your father back here. So did I. Why?"

"I . . . he's my father!"

Gerrod sighed. "And you worry about him. Fine. Let me rephrase it then? What was *he* hoping to accomplish?"

"He hoped to find a different way to cross over to the realm beyond the—oh!"

"He *found* one! He has to be over there! Why bring him here, something we don't know how to do, when we can follow him there! If it worked for Master Zeree, then it should work just as easily for us!"

The fear had returned to mar her delicate features. She was not unattractive, he knew, but she had a way of grating on him that the young Tezerenee could not explain even to himself. "What is it now?"

Sharissa described her father's departure, including his struggle to escape.

Gerrod saw the problem instantly. "Then we shall be careful not to teleport during the change. That leaves us with only two more problems."

Emboldened once more—and evidently more willing to trust him now that he had made concrete suggestions in regard to her father—Sharissa responded, "One is the timing. It fluctuates. We don't know how long we might have to wait . . . if it will happen at all."

"Oh, it *will*." Having had both Dru Zeree's notes and those of his brother's to add to his own knowledge, he probably now knew more about the unstable regions of Nimth than anyone did, especially concerning the rapid rate of growth they had achieved. Nimth did not have half as long as his father had once believed. Of course, the Vraad would still all be dead before then, the wild magic of the world and their own stupidity a combination they could not possibly survive. "I doubt we'll have to wait for very long."

He started walking to the door, deciding that things were not yet desperate enough for sorcery, but she stopped him with a question. "What was the other problem?"

Gerrod looked at her in surprise. "Surviving long enough to get there."

Dru shook his head at the creature who stood near the Gate. If it came down to it, he would fight them with his fists and his teeth. A spell might be beyond him, but he would not go passively back into the Void.

The golem gestured again . . . and the Vraad's *body* obeyed even while the mind began to struggle against it.

Something flashed in the light of the chamber, a metallic missile that flew toward the pointing golem with remarkable accuracy. It would have struck the being squarely in the side of the throat . . . had it reached its target.

Less than a foot from the open flesh, the blade Xiri had thrown in a futile attempt to save him ceased moving and fell straight down. It did not even make a clatter when it struck the floor. The assembled golems, even the one who had stood beside her, failed to even look her way. They remained intent on the portal and the Vraad, who was nearly at the base of the huge artifact.

Only two or three steps from an eternity of endless nothing, Dru's body stopped. In the short walk, he had sweated profusely. Somewhere out in the Void, Darkhorse wandered, possibly looking for a way back, unless the guardians had broken yet another of their rules and removed that knowledge from his mind. It was a slim hope, but if they did send him through, the shadowy steed might find him again.

If not, Dru would float forever.

He readied himself, waiting the final push that would send him falling into the Void. When it did not come, he tried to observe the one who had forced him to this point. It was impossible; though the Vraad's eyes could move, his head would not. He was transfixed before the Gate.

When his body became his once more, the sorcerer was so startled he nearly condemned himself to the very fate he had thought the faceless ones had planned for him. A hand caught the back of his robe and pulled him to a position farther from the menacing portal. The Gate closed off the pathway to the Void. Its sleek companions increased their pace once again, ever chasing one another over and over the artifact's surface.

"Dru!" Xiri had her arms around him in a grip worthy of a Seeker. None of their "hosts" moved to separate the two and so they held one another tight in relief. Finally, the elf whispered, "I thought they would walk you straight into that . . . that . . ."

"It's the Void."

Her eyes widened. "Why do you suppose they put you through that torture?"

He shrugged. He had no intention of second-guessing the masters of this place if he could avoid it. Their ways were as different as those of the Seekers, perhaps even more so.

Hands reached out and finally pulled the two free of one another. A pair of the golems, possibly the same two who had led them into the chamber, took the intruders by the arm and indicated the doorway. Puzzled but relieved to be away from the Gate and its deadly potential, the Vraad and the elf accompanied them without protest.

Their guides walked them swiftly out of the room of worlds and back down the magnificent hallway. It was evident within seconds that they intended to deliver their charges back to the chamber of the dragon lord. Dru and his companion exchanged bewildered expressions even as they were ushered inside.

Nothing had changed within, which was almost a disappointment to the sorcerer. He had nearly expected the huge figure of the dragon lord to suddenly squat down, stare them in the eye, and speak. It *did* stare at him, but only as its counterpart in the ruined city had. Any life the statue contained was strictly a figment of Dru's nerve-wracked imagination.

A second pair of the faceless beings entered the chamber and moved past the foursome. It began to irk the Vraad that he could not tell any of them apart. Had he not followed them through the rift and into the castle, ever mindful of the numbers, Dru might have wondered if there were only a handful who ran back and forth merely to fool their two prisoners into believing they were many. The sorcerer knew it was a foolish thought, but his predicament was tearing at his sanity. There might actually come a point, he feared, when he might prefer the Void to remaining among the faceless ones any longer.

The newcomers stepped up to the figurines and passed their hands over each. A few of the statuettes were removed and hidden from sight, somehow, in the robes of the two. With what was evident satisfaction, they backed away and indicated the remaining artifacts. Dru and Xiri were led forward.

"They want us to choose," the elf whispered.

She was correct. One of their unsettling companions indicated each of the fantastic figurines, then pointed at the two reluctant outsiders.

Dru studied the carvings. Choose a figurine, but for what reason and what result? Would the wrong choices kill them?

Most of the figures were of creatures magical in nature. There was the gryphon, the dragon, a unicorn, a dwarf, an elf—he glanced sideways at Xiri at that point—and others whose names escaped him. Included also were beasts and a few human figures.

"Let me choose first." Xiri did not wait for his answer. She reached out and took hold of the elf. A reasonable, safe choice. Both waited for some grand reaction, but still nothing happened. One of the golems eventually took the figurine from her hands and replaced it among the others.

The sorcerer held his breath as he tried to choose. There seemed no particular purpose to what he was being asked to do. It was tempting to reach out and seize the statuette that most resembled a Vraad, but for various reasons he chose not to. He glanced at the gryphon again, thinking of how much it resembled Sirvak, and nearly picked it up. Then his eyes focused on the dragon, almost a miniature version of the overshadowing form before him, and he almost chose that one instead.

While he debated his choices, the faceless ones waited patiently. Dru knew, however, that he would have to make a decision soon. His hand wavered by the dragon, then by the gryphon.

Abruptly, the Vraad withdrew from the artifacts. He met the eyeless gaze of one of their disturbing hosts and said, "I make no choice at all. I want nothing from here."

An interesting choice.

The chamber had vanished. Dru, Xiri, and their silent companions stood within a place of darkness. The sorcerer did not have to ask to know where he was, especially when two gleaming eyes formed and the vague outline of a huge dragon emerged partway from the black depths.

The voice that had filled his head was the only one that would have given him hope at this late point. "You've returned."

From the glance Xiri gave him, it was evident that she, too, was included in the conversation.

Yes, both choices affect the outcome, the guardian whom Dru had labeled first among the commanding voices added with mild satisfaction. *They are pleased with your choice, though it also confuses them.*

As if in response to the mock dragon's words, the blank-visaged figures withdrew to arm's length of the Vraad and the elf.

"Are they your masters? Was I correct in my assumptions?"

The hesitation that followed chipped away at the confidence that had only just been returning to the spellcaster. After a time, however, the half-seen entity replied, *Yes and no.*

"Yes and no?" This from Xiri. "How can they be your masters and yet not be your masters?"

To explain that, I would need to explain their final leaving...a cross-over of a different yet similar sort than what the Vraad have undertaken.

The guardian's words were both confusing and enlightening. "If they will permit you, please do."

I am not exactly certain if they permit me or do not care. What inhabits your golems are a shadow of our lords. We communicate with them almost as little as you do. The others struggle to understand, to know their places. Some have even argued that this is proof we are now our own masters.

Dru grimaced. As before, he knew which one of his fellows the dragon spoke of.

I digress. Was there an undercurrent of annoyance with itself? Anxiety? Dru could not be certain, but there *was* something. However confident the guardian acted, the truth was otherwise.

They were few when it finally became obvious that they would not live to see the culmination—or failure—of their dream. They had us to do their work, but we were limited in what we could do.

The sorcerer found it hard to believe that such as this could be wanting in power. The guardian *was* power, even more so than Darkhorse.

We are . . . aspects . . . of their minds. Bits of personality traits. Your choice of the term "familiar" is as close as we can come. They formed us as such so that, together, we would preserve all that they were, should the worst befall them.

What part did the rebellious guardian represent, the Vraad wondered, and *how* dominant a trait was it?

There came a point, the ghostly figure went on, when the race had two options. They could use the Gate and seek out something, anything, that would revitalize their life force, give them the strength to continue on. It was an option steered toward failure and possibly even a quicker end to their kind. The second choice was the one that promised the most hope for their legacy, but like the first would mean a finish to all they had raised up over the millennia.

They chose the second. With it, though they would no longer exist as they were, they might still direct the course and final outcome of their grand plan. The true world might still one day greet the successors to the elder race.

Dru interrupted at that point, despite the uncomfortable feeling that the faceless ones were eyeing him with particular interest now. "Did they have no name? You say 'they' and 'them' but you give no name."

He could almost feel the other's embarrassment. *It has been so long, manling, that we have forgotten it. Even we are not immortal, though it might seem that way. With the passage of century after century, we have become a little less than we once were. There will come a time when we will fade as a dying wind.*

"Don't *they* know their name?" Xiri asked, her eyes ever keeping track of the movements of the blank-visaged beings.

In what they allow me to still tell you lies the answer to that . . . and perhaps other things. You, Vraad, have talked of the ka and how one can travel with it to places the body cannot reach. So it was with the elders. You saw the pentagram in the place you call the room of worlds. An apt name that, for with the Gate they could observe or travel to any of their creations. This last time, however, they chose to do something different.

The dying race numbered no more than a thousand or so by the time they came to their final decision, a thousand where there had once been millions. The guardian's tone was wistful, recalling the glory of those earlier days. In groups numbering close to one hundred apiece, they stepped into the room of worlds and never came out. Not until the last group was ready to enter did the founders deign to reveal what they were doing to their servants, their familiars.

We feared for them, but we were only the servants and so we obeyed when they commanded us to return to our duties and not interfere. We have never been allowed to interfere, save when they gave such orders. Still, their plan gave us fright, for it would place them beyond our limits, leave us with no one to guide us. You see, as with your kind, Vraad, their kas, their spirits, were liberated from their physical forms. The image of a hundred departing specters made both Dru and the elf uneasy, but they remained silent. *Your people created for themselves new bodies so that they could continue as they had always been. The founders did not. They had chosen instead a receptacle that would contain their collective consciousness, but it was more than a body, much, much more. It was intended that in some way, they would always watch over the world that had spawned them. They would be their world as much as the trees, the fields, and the animal life were.*

Dru blurted it out before the tale could go any further. "The *land*! The land itself! When I felt as if this realm would protect itself, it was more than my imagination, then."

The land. You, elf. When you spoke of the land being alive, you spoke truer than you thought. It is. It has a mind, albeit different from what you might consider one. It knows what those who live upon it do and moves to affect things in its favor. Yet I think that such a change affected those who created us, for the land is different. It is and is not our masters. Until your interference, we had thought the land dead once more, the founders having passed on despite their determination. Fools we were to be so presumptuous. Subtlety is not our forte. We could not see what the land was doing . . . even when it sought to bring you here, Vraad.

"Me?"

The dragon shape moved, as if uncertain itself about what it said next. *You or your kind. They have chosen to give the Vraad race a second chance.*

"It wasn't our own doing that weakened the barriers between Nimth and here?"

Hardly. The guardian paused again. When it spoke, it was already fading away. *I have said as much as they desire me to say for now.*

"What about our choices? What did they represent?"

A laugh, self-mocking, echoed through Dru's head. *I do not know. If you find out, I would be interested.*

The chamber of the dragon lord rematerialized around them.

A golem put its hand on the dumbfounded spellcaster's shoulder. Dru turned and fairly snarled at the creature before him. "*What?* What else do you want to amaze and confuse us with? Do you even understand what you're doing? Are you so little a shadow of what you once were that you perform movements without truly thinking? Why did you even return?"

He knew the answer to the last question, at least, or hoped he did. The guardian had said that the Vraad had been given an opportunity to redeem themselves. If they failed, the experiment failed and the ancients' dreams would die. The stolen golems gave the land hands to work with if it came down to the physical. Perhaps some elements of the presence had also simply yearned once more for solid flesh.

Dru got no further in his thoughts, for the faceless ones, for lack of a better name, indicated they wanted the twosome to follow them yet again. With little true choice in the matter, the sorcerer and the elf followed wordlessly. Xiri did shift over so that the two of them touched, but they did not so much as glance at one another during the duration of the walk.

Once more, they were returning to the room of worlds.

At the doorway, Dru and his companion finally exchanged looks of frustration. Were they to be shuttled back and forth from the two chambers until they collapsed?

The answer stood before them, its glimmering interior more reminiscent of a predator's maw than a portal to other worlds.

This time, Dru could sense that there would be no last-minute reprieve. Whatever world the cowled figures had chosen was to be their new home.

Xiri had apparently realized this at the same time, for she tried to push her guide away and break a path to freedom for Dru and herself. As with her earlier attempt, when she had thrown the knife at one of their captors, the golem was barely affected. The elf, despite her speed and obvious battle skill, bounced off the side of the robed creature and into the unprepared sorcerer. It was all Dru could do to keep both of them from falling to the floor. As they regained their footing, their guides reached out and took each by one arm. Both prisoners discovered that struggling from that point on was impossible. Having attempted violence, they had been stripped of control over their very bodies. Helplessly moving in time to their guides' steps, they walked to the center of the chamber and the patiently waiting Gate.

The spellcaster wished the guardian had not abandoned them back in the other chamber, but he knew that the mock dragon had really had little say. The guardians were used to obeying their masters blindly, and even though they *had* come to the point of questioning that blind obedience, it was not yet enough to save the two outsiders.

Vraad! the voice of the dragon guardian hurriedly called. *They have faith in you.*

That was all. One of the blank visages looked to the side, as if seeing something. Dru felt the guardian retreat in something akin to fright.

They have faith in me? What did that mean?

The Gate shimmered again, causing renewed agitation among its dark denizens. They scurried, if it was possible, even more frantically than earlier.

Nimth greeted the sorcerer's eyes. He took a deep breath, waiting for it to change to the Void or some other place, but Nimth still beckoned after nearly a minute had passed.

He was to go to Nimth . . . and they had *faith* in him. Faith to do what?

"Is that . . . is that Nimth?"

"Yes." Dru looked at Xiri. "They want me to go there. I think they want me to bring the Vraad to this world."

The concept still did not sit well with the elf, though both knew she no longer hated Dru. He, however, was only one Vraad. Dru himself had told her how terrible his kind could be.

"They'll change when they've been here for a time. They have to. The land won't accept them any other way."

"What about me?"

He had not thought of that. "They can probably send you to your own people. You can prepare them for our coming." The Vraad smiled in a cynical way. "Providing they aren't as bloodthirsty as you, we should be able to live together."

"I am not going back to my people, not yet." Xiri looked up into his eyes with a determination worthy of any of his own race. "I think it would be better if I came with you back to Nimth."

"You don't want to do that. Not when there must be so many bitter Vraad. Not now."

"Yes." She took hold of his hand. He could not have peeled her hand from his even if he had wanted to do so. "Now. With you. I want to see this through to the end."

Dru looked up and met the sightless gaze of one of the ancients. Even without eyes of any sort, he could feel the creature absorbing every movement, every facial expression. The golems saw more than many who had perfect vision.

"We're stepping through now," he told it.

To his surprise, the blank visage dipped in what might have been a nod. The way before them cleared. The Gate waited expectantly, pulsating, it seemed, to the sorcerer's rapid heartbeat.

Tightening his own grip on Xiri's hand, he led her into the portal and onto the soil of treacherous Nimth.

XVII

The Tezerenee had planned to strike first, attacking their foes while they slept. Those sent by Barakas to explore the mountains had returned prematurely, bearing a tale of discovery. An aerie existed, a vast cavern from which they had seen the bird people enter and depart.

Lord Barakas had slowly formed a fist when all was said and done, saying, "We will crush them while they still prepare! I want the drakes ready for flight!"

The clan of the dragon had only six representatives of their totem, not counting the eight small wyverns they had come across by sheer accident. The wyverns made good hunting creatures and pets—the first one mindbroken by the trainers had been given to the patriarch as a symbol of luck—but they were ineffective fighters for a foe such as this. Of the six drakes, only four were mindbroken and one of those had struggled too much during the spell, addling its brain. Mindbreaking, the method by which the Tezerenee could quickly and efficiently control and train their beasts, was more of an all or nothing method here in the Dragonrealm. Precision was impossible, and after the damage caused on the one dragon, the trainers had ceased their work, hoping to find a better way.

It was not a well-armed armada that would have flown off to do battle, but they were Tezerenee and that was all that had mattered.

Barakas knew, from examination of the corpse, that the avians were diurnal like his own people. Most would be caught napping. Time after time, the Tezerenee had played their games of war, preparing, through mock combat, for daring strikes such as this. Even though there were probably at least twice as many of the birds as there were the drangonhelmed warriors, the advantage would be on the side of the clan.

"We are might. We are power. The name Tezerenee *is* power!" Barakas had said. It was a ritual saying, one the clan had heard often in the past, but spoken with the fervor that only the patriarch could summon, it was *truth*.

It was unfortunate, then, after all that had been planned, that the avians attacked while the Tezerenee were still organizing themselves.

The new keep was little more than a dark, morbid box around which a pathetic, half-grown wall stood. As with the drakes, it was all the clan sorcery could provide under present circumstances. There was only one room, a communal hall.

Most of the Tezerenee were presently occupied with matters outside. Esad, chosen for the dubious honor of being one of the three dragon riders, was working with his mount, letting the large green beast familiarize itself with his scent. He and the other riders had the task of taking out whatever sentries the avians had posted. They were also supposed to prevent too many of the birds from gaining a flying advantage. Esad had his doubts about his ability to perform his task, but his fear of his father prevented him from doing anything about it.

He looked up and barely saw the winged silhouette in the thin sliver of the pale moon.

''Dragon's blood!'' The Tezerenee abandoned his mount and went rushing to the keep. He kept silent, hoping that he could spread the word through contact and give the clan some slight advantage of surprise yet. Esad knew that if he died *before* he was able to alert someone, the blame for the deaths that followed would fall to him.

An armored figure, female, nearly collided with him. He grabbed her by the shoulders and whispered, ''The birds attack any moment! Spread the word, but do it quietly!''

She nodded her understanding and started to move away.

A bolt of blue lightning caught her in midstep . . . and left only a thin trail of smoke to mark her passing.

The time for silence, Esad realized in horror, was over.

''Defend yourselves! We are attacked from above!''

The air was swarming with black shapes that fluttered into and out of the dim light of the two moons.

They had let him watch. Watch as they began what would, it seemed, be the end of the Vraad race. He was treated well, since it was his knowledge of the tactics of the Tezerenee that the avians had used and might still need, yet he was still a prisoner, not the ally they pretended he was. Bereft of his powers and watched over by fierce companions, it was a wonder the avians even made the pretense of *calling* him an ally.

Despite all that, Rendel was quite satisfied, though he knew better than to show it. It was not the destruction of his kind that pleased the sorcerer, but rather that his *own* plans still moved on unimpeded. The cavern was virtually empty of its inhabit-

ants, Rendel's practiced words—*images?*—impressing upon
the aerie's overlord that nearly every able fighter was needed. It
was a lie not *that* far from truth. Even with the advantages of
first strike and dominance in the night sky, the birds would take
hard losses. The Tezerenee would not die without a fight . . . and
would not even die, if things went as planned.

After all, he preferred human subjects to feathered monsters
like his captors.

The young who had been deemed too untrained to fight and
those responsible for their care had retreated to lower caverns on
the off chance that some danger might threaten the aerie. That
fear had been planted, albeit surreptitiously, by the Vraad
during his communications with what he still liked to term the
council of elders for lack of a more defined description. To the
avians, it seemed a reasonable precaution. As with now, he had
barely been unable to suppress his pleasure. Rendel had succeeded
in assuring that he would be left with only a few guards to
watch over him.

In fact, there were three. A few others were scattered about
the mountain and the mouth of the cavern, but the arrogant
creatures actually believed that *they* had tricked their captive.
Glancing at those standing around him, Rendel marveled that
this race had become the dominant one in the Dragonrealm.
Two were tall, muscular warriors, one of whom the Tezerenee
believed was the leader of the patrol that had taken him
prisoner. His remaining watchdog was the balding elder who
had spoken out during the offer of alliance. The overlord was
not here, having chosen to lead the attack, something that
would have earned Barakas's respect, but received only silent
amusement from Rendel. It had never made sense to him to
dangle such a prize as a leader before an enemy. Let the lessers
take the damage. There were always more of them.

The male he believed was his original captor squawked
something. Rendel turned completely from the glittering crystal
that acted as his eyes in the attack and allowed the avian to
touch him, establishing the link between the two of them.

The vision of two birds falling prey to a dragon rider's
mount was followed by a wave of anger. Rendel surmised that
the image he had been shown was only one example of how the
clan was fighting back. His erstwhile allies could evidently see

in the dark better than he could, either that or the mind link was even stronger than he supposed, for the Vraad could not recall any such image in the viewing crystal. That did not matter; he believed the avian when it spoke of the dragons and their deadly strength. Much larger than either a Vraad or bird man, the three flying drakes were wreaking havoc. The invaders, Rendel was informed, were refraining from using their medallions for fear of striking down their own. Drakes were swift and agile despite their girth. It would require a practiced aim and great daring to bring down the beasts without adding a few feathered misfits, too.

Rendel shot back the image of his people as warriors, leaving an unformed question concerning the avians' abilities in the same role. As he had expected, it made the huge figure furious. He removed his hand from Rendel's forehead and pulled the hapless sorcerer forward so that the razorlike beak was within snapping range of the spellcaster's pale visage. The Tezerenee stumbled at the last moment, falling against his irate captor. The creature pushed the cloaked figure back. With its great strength, Rendel fairly flew, landing several paces from where he had stood. To his surprise, the two warriors dismissed him from their attention, refocusing on the scene in the crystal. They apparently felt they had no more use for his knowledge, something he was not ready to dissuade them concerning. Only the elder still eyed him.

Rising to his feet, the sorcerer pretended to brush himself off. The damnable, half-plucked bird was still staring at him when he finally gave up the effort. Rendel put one hand to his mouth and coughed, starting back to the trio at the same time.

The elder's attention strayed back to the images of the battle before it evidently occurred to him that their prisoner was a thing not to be trusted despite the dampening of his sorcery. A watery but wary eye looked Rendel's way.

It was a decision made a breath too late. The unsupervised moment was all the Tezerenee needed. The one thing Barakas had taught him that Rendel had come to appreciate was to use anything possible as a means to an end. He had planned something similar to the provoked attack by his one guard, but a bit later. Circumstances had, however, worked to his benefit.

He had the medallion focused on the trio even as the ancient one became aware of the threat the Vraad intended.

Rendel had palmed the medallion knowing only that it had been designed to kill. He neither knew nor cared what sort of deadly force had been trapped inside by its maker, only that it would suffice as a means of removing the three tensed figures before him. The avians had assumed he did not know how to utilize it, but the spellcaster had used every glance to study the artifacts, noting how the markings were fingered and how it had to be focused. Now, his studies had rewarded him. He concentrated, willing the spell of the medallion to come forth and looking forward to the pathetic cries of those who had dared to make him their slave.

Nothing happened.

The amusement in the eyes of the one he had stolen the magical item from told the story. Rendel's prize was an empty vessel, a useless ornament. They had allowed him to betray himself, to pick the time of his own demise. As his face reddened in anger—anger at himself for being so easy a pawn—Rendel thought how like the clan of the dragon these creatures were. How often had Barakas employed similar methods?

The patrol leader strode toward him, needle-sharp claws waiting to rend, beak open in the closest the avian could come to a cold smile. A low, reverberating sound issued forth, laughter of a sort.

Rendel did the only thing left to him—he ran. The entrance to the caverns themselves was blocked by his executioner. That left only one path. He would have to hope he could escape to the lower tunnels and lose himself.

A malevolent form swooped down before him. The avian had flown over his head and blocked his way. Rendel swore and ducked among the stone leviathans, wishing he knew how to tap into the power he felt within them. Yet the birds had tried countless times and they had not succeeded. It was why they had sent explorers overseas. There likely lay the key to understanding and utilizing the elemental forces sleeping deep inside each figure.

Claws struck stone just inches from his throat. Rendel let out a yelp and scurried to a different effigy, this one a muscular, horned beast that looked as if the artist had caught it in the midst of contemplating its own mortality. The figure wobbled when the Tezerenee fell against it, the ground beneath broken from some past tremor.

It was not fair, he thought in bitter fear. At his best, the Vraad would have taken his attacker apart with the simplest of spells. The avians had refused to release him from the enchantment that dulled his abilities, their reason being that he had to prove himself first. Rendel had thought he had planned for even that hurdle, but once more he had overplayed a bad hand. Now, it would be he who was torn asunder, ripped to bloody gobbets by a freak of the heavens.

He screamed as a pair of taloned feet scored his backside, tearing apart the cloak and shirt in the process. They had disposed of his dragon-scale clothing and given him simple cloth ones for the time being. He now knew why. Talons alone would have been inefficient weapons against the likes of dragon scale and a long, torturous death was evidently what they had chosen for him.

As the avian rose for what was certainly the final assault, Rendel threw himself once more against the stone figure, trying in desperation to push through or climb over it . . . he could not say *what* it was he wanted to do, not now.

The ancient carving teetered, then started to collapse on its side.

It was debatable as to who was more horrified, Rendel or his captors. Impending death could not take from the frantic sorcerer's mind the fact that he was destroying the very things he had risked himself for. Rendel grasped the nearest edges of the statue in a foolish attempt to right a massive stone artifact with only his own physical strength.

"No!" The Tezerenee was thrown forward as the effigy came crashing down on its neighbor, shattering *that* figure as well. A horrible sensation of pain and loss flowed like a wave over the central chamber. The avians fluttered back, acting as if they had been physically buffeted by the death throes of the dwellers within. Rendel pictured a terrible domino effect in which more than half of the artifacts were reduced to rubble and his mind was ravaged by an undeniable flood of agony that he would be forced to share as one after another of the elemental spirits, if that was truly what they were, died.

He was fortunate. The second statue collapsed in a dust-enshrouded pile without so much as nicking the one next to it. The Vraad fought for breath and heard harsh, choking sounds from somewhere above him. He peered through the cloud that had risen and saw the other two birds rushing his direction in rather unsteady movements. The time for games was over. Despite the loss he had brought about, Rendel knew he could at least die with the satisfaction that these three would be made to pay for the damage he had caused in his desperate attempt to escape. The laws by which the avians lived were simple and harsh.

Dust continued to fill his lungs. Why was the cloud not settling? Rendel stood, hoping to evade his executioners for at least a little longer, when the rubble began to *move*. It was not merely a tremor, though. The broken statues were moving of their *own* accord, not merely being jostled by the quaking earth . . . and what tremor localized itself so precisely?

Hope and fear vied for Rendel, neither emotion able to gain the upper hand. His first thought was that the things within had survived and were coming to the aid of the one who had released them. That was impossible. Rendel had felt the deaths and knew that what now stirred was not the same. The battered Tezerenee stumbled back as the mound began to rise higher and higher.

An elemental force permeated the huge chamber, living and not living. It was and was not dissimilar to those he had accidentally destroyed, but it was certainly far more, too. Rendel found he did not really care what it was; he only knew that here surely must be what he had sought.

"Mine! You're mine!" the weary yet triumphant spellcaster shouted. The pain that coursed through his system was forgotten. "Come to me! Fill me with the power that is mine!" He had summoned it, accidentally the sorcerer supposed, but that *must* make it *his* to control. . . .

Despite his demands, the force appeared disinclined to obey. Earth and fragments of the statues flew upward, nearly striking the top of the cavern and bringing light that frightened off numerous tiny forms. The avians, who had frozen at the sight of it, began to stir. Rendel was ignored. They, too, had sought whatever treasure the ancients had left here. Whichever one of them mastered it would become the new overlord, not merely of this region but of the entire land.

Is there no end to the chaos your kinds bring? A vague, animallike shape formed. Molten earth burbled from the inner depths of the world, joining the dirt and stone in creating the image of life. Despite so much flying about, not one particle of dust or one drop of melted earth so much as touched the Tezerenee. Even the statues, so close to the center, remained unaffected.

Is there truly hope for such as you?

Though no one looked in his direction, unless those *were* eyes in the midst of the jumbled pile, Rendel knew it was he who had been asked the question.

"Cease your prattle! I am the one who commands! I am the one who judges!" Rendel's doubt added a quiver to his voice.

Fiery wings spread, composed almost entirely of burning earth. What had once been the mouth of the horned beast was now the mouth of an entirely different monster, but one growing all too familiar in shape with each passing breath.

You have daring . . . and nothing more. My obedience is not yours to demand. Nor theirs, either.

It spoke of the avians. Rendel started, wondering how he could have forgotten the onrushing creatures. He looked around, but the three had vanished.

They have been redirected elsewhere until something can be done with them. It is you who I have come for, Vraad, at the command of those who rule *here.*

"You can't take me from this! Not now! It's why I worked so hard to make the cross-over work! It's why I risked all, coming here alone though I knew there was the threat of danger!" Rendel knew he was babbling, but it was buying him time. His mind raced, seeking some solution to his predicament. He had been rescued from death for . . . for *what* he did not know, save that it would separate him from what was his by right.

Manling, I found much to admire in one of your kind, but I see little of those traits within you. Do not stir me to measures that I will be forced to regret . . . later. I have already interfered

*more than I am supposed to. Your destruction of this place, of
those who preceded my kind in the aid of our masters—elementals,
you might call them—was accidental, but your desire to abuse
their purpose was not.*

Rendel no longer had any thoughts concerning the glory that
was to have been his. Instead, he wondered whether he was
going to leave this place alive.

The mock dragon dipped its macabre head, the burning earth
giving it the appearance of a fire-breathing beast. It filled the
Tezerenee's entire field of vision.

You have no more need to wonder, manling.

The false jaws opened.

Rendel shut his eyes and screamed.

XVIII

"Is this what it all comes to? Does nothing but ruin follow the
Vraad?"

Dru could not respond to Xiri's question, not at first. The
portal, through either the whims of its creators or, as he
personally believed, *its* own, had returned them to Nimth near
the Vraad communal city. Though it was night, a dim glow
from above left the land in the equivalent of sunset, enabling
them to see. Even from the slope on which they had materialized, it was evident that some catastrophe had struck. From
what he could see, Dru knew already that the catastrophe had
not been natural. The destruction was too well organized.
Someone had *wanted* to destroy the only thing that had ever
linked the individuals of his race together. The Vraad swore
quietly, both saddened and ashamed.

"I've never seen such a *green* before," the elf whispered. "I
feel as if it eats the soul of Nimth." She was gazing skyward,
watching the maelstrom above. A massive storm was forming,

one that looked to cover *everything*, for it stretched as far as the sky itself. Dru did not want to be caught outside when it broke; what rained down upon Nimth would not be so simple and harmless as water.

"Take my hand again."

She did, squeezing it tight. The sorcerer drew some comfort from having another person to touch during this period of chaos.

"Do you plan to teleport?"

He nodded. "At least try, anyway. I have to chance it. Time is short. Nimth won't die today, but *we* might."

Xiri looked up again. "The sky?"

"This glow from the clouds is a new phenomenon . . . very new, I think. There is also a storm brewing. It won't be a normal rain like you might expect. We've not had a rainstorm for years. If it strikes, it will be magical."

"Which means it could produce *anything*. Will it necessarily be bad?"

He swept his arm across what lay before them. "Look around you. Do you see anything good coming from what the Vraad have done so far?"

His point was obvious, but something seemed to disturb her. "Will not your spell aggravate conditions? Is there not a chance it will act as a catalyst?"

"It might, but our choices are few. I either use my sorcery or we walk."

Her hand slipped from his as she visibly struggled with herself. "There is one other way."

"What might that be?"

Elfin eyes lowered. "I could try my own powers. Like you, mine have been returned to me."

In the suddenness of their release by the founders, Dru had forgotten that his companion also worked magic of some kind. "Do you need anything?"

Xiri smiled. "Luck?"

He stepped back as she concentrated. The natural, if they could still be called such, forces of Nimth stirred as they were summoned. Her way felt different from that of his kind, however. It was more gentle, asking instead of taking. A glimmer of light materialized before the elf. Dru rubbed his chin, trying to understand the nuances of her spell. Was this the course in which Vraad sorcery *should* have developed?

He heard a gasp then, and saw Xiri starting to crumple. Instead of following her desires, it almost appeared as if Nimth sought to use *her*. Not only had power answered her summons, but it was trying to pervert her spell, almost as if it consciously desired to do so. With the swiftness born of centuries of careful practice, Dru seized control of her spell. The power fought back, not as a living thing but in the way that a raging river might fight against a dam that had broken partly away. Yet he did not turn the spell to the way it would have been had he been the originator. Instead, the spellcaster strained to make a hybrid of the two sorceries, at least long enough to perform the spell. Dru doubted the two could really be joined without a cataclysm resulting.

The strain was horrible, but in the end a shining, circular portal stood open before them. His concentration still monitoring the strength of the spell, Dru reached down and helped Xiri to regain her footing.

"That should never have happened!"

Dru knew better. "You tried to use the binding forces of Nimth as you would those of your own world. Nimth no longer follows the same laws of nature, if it ever actually did. We Vraad have made it too much like ourselves. Vicious and hungry. Still," he added as encouragement, "I think what you accomplished was likely more effective than the results I would have obtained."

"We have not crossed through yet. Save your congratulations for then."

Stepping through the portal was only slightly less unnerving than entering the founders' living gateway. Dru had a brief vision of a path, one that reminded him greatly of those Darkhorse had utilized to escape the Void, before he and his companion stood once more on the surface of his home world.

They stood in the courtyard that Dru had stared down at only...only...the Vraad gave up trying to count the days since his unexpected departure. After all, those who had ripped the massive structure apart had probably only needed hours, not days. He could not help glancing away from his companion, however. Seen up close, the devastation that had overcome the city was even worse than he had imagined.

"The city of the elders fell to time," Dru whispered, again shamed of his kind. "Before a fraction of the same time has passed, this place will be a foul blot in comparison."

"A ruin is a ruin," Xiri said, more to mollify him than because she believed in the simple statement. "What do you hope to find here?"

"Nothing. I hoped that there might be someone. They can't have all crossed over. Not so many and not so quickly. This was done by those left behind . . . the ones I'm supposed to help."

"What do we do now?" Xiri clearly did not want one of their choices to be to remain in this dark and ugly place. Dru was not so fond of the idea himself. He had hoped part of the city still lived, that some of the magic that enabled it to serve the Vraad still functioned. From what his higher senses told him, nothing had been left undamaged. There would be no food, no water.

It seems I am destined to never eat a normal meal again! The guardians and their masters had removed his hunger and thirst more than once, but they were not available. Dru glanced at his companion. Could Xiri's sorcery provide them with the sustenance they would be needing before long? "Can you conjure food and drink?"

She mulled it over. "After what happened, I think I might be able to, but there could be a better way."

"Such as?"

"If we work the spell together, as we did more or less before, then it should be possible."

It made as much sense to Dru as anything else had in a long time. "Let's try it, then. We shouldn't go on without dealing with the problem. I'd hate to think what would happen if we needed food or water in some desperate moment and found we couldn't do a thing about it."

He began first this time, determined to keep the forces of Nimth under control from the start. The slow work annoyed him; it was like learning the use of his sorcery all over again. After a moment's consideration, the spellcaster decided that this was what he *was* doing.

"I have it," he told her.

Nodding, Xiri reached out and coaxed the power to work with her. The firm hold that Dru's consciousness had on it prevented a magical assault akin to that taking place during the teleportation attempt. He felt the elf turn the land's binding force to the task she had wished completed.

The sorcerer blinked. The abrupt completion of the spell left him dizzy. Xiri, too, was trying to reorient herself. Dru looked down at the broken courtyard floor.

A loaf of bread, some fruit, a bit of meat, and a jug of some liquid made an incongruous image when surrounded by so much destruction.

"Better than I could have hoped," he said, smiling.

They split every item into equal portions, save the contents of the jug since neither of them had thought to conjure cups. Dru was surprised when Xiri sank her teeth into the meat. He had supposed that being an elf she would abhor the thought of eating the flesh of some wild creature, even if what they ate now was actually magical in origin.

"Eating meat does not decrease my spiritual nature," she said, swallowing a piece. "*Wasting* meat would. A diet of plants is lacking in a few necessities. There are a few I know who believe it is the only way we can become more than we are now, but I notice they are usually the ones lacking in strength and mind as time progresses." With her fingers, Xiri tore off another piece. "I *do* give thanks to the creature that provided me with sustenance, though it might be impossible in this case since the beast never existed."

The jug proved to contain wine that tasted vaguely familiar to Dru. It took him several swallows to recall that it was one of his own creations. He wondered if the spell had somehow tapped into his own mind, then decided that it was a matter for a more peaceful time.

It took only minutes to satisfy themselves. Dru noticed that the food and drink had materialized in quantities exactly matching their present needs. Again, it was a thought for another day, but he did want to ask Xiri if she had planned it so or somehow the spell itself had known. He rose and stared in the direction of his own domain. A part of him wanted to fly directly there to see if Sharissa was there. She *should* have crossed over, but the signs and what the one guardian had said hinted that more than a few Vraad had been abandoned by Barakas. Unless they had dragged her to the pentagram themselves, the Tezerenee had likely just forgotten her. Dru could not say why, but he felt that left to her own devices, his daughter would still be here.

"Dru! There is another nearby!"

The sorcerer sensed it, too. It was almost as if the newcomer had literally *popped* into the city... and why not if he or she were a Vraad?

Someone laughed. It was loud and lacking somewhat in sanity. Male, that was all the duo could tell other than the fact that they were mere seconds away. It was as if he had been searching for them.

"What should we do?" Xiri asked, deferring to Dru since this was his world, *his* madness. She knew little about the Vraad and looked as if she would have liked to keep it so.

"We find out who it is." A dangerous decision, the sorcerer knew, but it might also be their best way to find out the state of things. Between the two of them, he felt they had a definite edge over the newcomer. It was even possible that they would find the intruder friendly. Not likely, of course, but still a possibility to consider.

The real reason, though Dru would have denied it after all he had been through, was that he was simply curious. His unexpected exodus had only temporarily cooled his inquisitiveness.

With the care only experience can bring, Dru and the elf made their way through the rubble of the courtyard and toward the sound of laughter. Neither was too concerned with silence. The newcomer's laugh continually rose so high in volume that they doubted he could have heard them even if they had stood behind him and shouted.

Xiri was the first to see him as she peeked around the corner of a roofless building that had been, as far as Dru's memory served, the place where he had first discussed his theories of ka travel with the patriarch. "He just sits there and *laughs*!"

Dru, looking over her, held his breath. "Rendel?"

It was indeed Rendel. The Tezerenee, clad in torn garments and looking as if he had risen from a harsh burial, sat on a battered bench. He was silent for the moment save for the gasping sounds he made as he gulped in air. *Readying himself for another round of madness,* Dru decided. What was Rendel doing here and where had he been?

"You know him?"

The tall Vraad nodded, unmindful of the fact that the elf had her back to him. "I'm going out there."

"You should not!"

Her words went unheeded. Dru stepped out and walked toward Rendel, trying, all the while, to maintain an image of confidence he knew to be false. When he saw that the Tezerenee intended to laugh once more, Dru called out.

"Rendel! It's me! Dru Zeree!"

The other Vraad leaped to his feet and shook his head. He was silent, though his mouth kept forming words.

"Rendel. I'm real. Where have you been? What happened to you?"

"What happened to me?" Rendel almost began laughing, but found the strength to resist. "What has not happened to me? You should ask *that*!"

Dru forced his own voice steady. "All right. What did happen?"

"It took everything away from me." The tattered Tezerenee's eyes revealed his close battle between sanity and madness. "Took it all away! I had worked so hard, given so much up!"

"Who did? Who took it from you?" Rendel's lost prize did not concern Dru so much as what power had returned him from the realm beyond the veil to dark Nimth.

"A dragon. It rose from the depths of the earth . . . only it was *not* a dragon! It was the *earth*!"

A dragon formed from the earth itself? One of the guardians. One with a fondness, it seemed, for the form of that particular leviathan. "The guardian brought you here?"

If Rendel noted the familiarity with which Dru spoke of the ancient familiar the latter had befriended, then he made no sign. "Sent me here. Said it had already interfered more than it had been allowed. Assumed that if I made it back to . . . to where I was . . . from Nimth, then I was meant to be there." His eyes snared Dru's. "But there is *no* way to cross! We are trapped here, Master Dru!"

The brown- and silver-tressed spellcaster hesitated, wondering whether his response would weaken or strengthen Rendel's sanity. He also wondered if he really *wanted* to tell the Tezerenee his belief.

Rendel, the remnants of his cloak wrapped around him, started to sit again. It was not clear whether he desired to continue with his pointless laughter, but Dru knew that listening to *that* much longer would drive *him* insane.

"There may be a way back ... if you'll listen to me."

"There *is* no way back!"

Dru stepped closer. "I crossed to the shrouded realm and back again. It's possible."

For the first time, hope crossed the Tezerenee's scarred visage. Dru wondered what he had gone through over in the other domain.

"Possible?"

"It is."

Drawing himself straight, Rendel managed a shadow of his old, arrogant self. "Then we can still win."

Rendel's widening eyes told Dru that the Tezerenee had finally noticed Xiri, who had joined them. A strange look crossed the battered figure's face for the merest of moments. "Who is that?"

"Xiri. My friend and companion." The description sounded inane and inefficient to Dru, but he was not about to attempt to define his growing relationship with Xiri at this time, not when he himself was not certain in what manner it had grown. "She's an elf. We met on the other side, when both our lives were in danger."

"An *elf*." Rendel looked her over as one might look over a prize pet. "I had forgotten there were elves."

"We have not forgotten the Vraad," she returned, her voice chilling.

"So I see." With each passing second, Rendel was becoming more and more his old self. Dru wondered if he *had* made a mistake.

His worries lessened a bit when the pale-haired Vraad turned back to him and asked, "What about this way across? How did you find it? Can we get there easily?"

"It found me." Dru described his involuntary crossing and went into vagaries about how he had returned. Rendel's eyes lit up at talk of the founders and the news that the golems' purpose had been usurped made him smile.

"Father must have been furious."

"I suppose." Dru tried to remain unsuspicious. "I would have thought you'd have come across Barakas and the rest."

"Circumstances separated me from where they were to arrive." Rendel would say nothing more about the subject. Taken with what the Tezerenee had said during his less lucid moments, however, a specter of the truth began to form. It was not a truth Dru appreciated.

"Well." The other Vraad crossed his arms. He still wore his tattered outfit, but no longer looked like one of the walking dead. His bearing was that of a man fully in control of his life. "What now?"

"We have to find whoever is left here. We all have to cross. I have this feeling that Nimth will be cut off at some point soon and left to rot. I don't want to be left here to rot with it."

"No, neither do I." Rendel growled. His anger, it seemed, was for someone else, likely the guardian who had delivered him back to the dying world. "I have a suggestion, however."

"What might *that* be?" Xiri asked, moving close to Dru, as if to show Rendel that the two of them were a united force. Neither Dru nor his companion wanted the Tezerenee to become the dominant partner. Their trust hardly ran that deep.

"Instead of seeking them out, let *them* come to us."

"Why should they come to us?" Dru rubbed his chin. "They came here once, expecting to begin a new life, and were betrayed. Why should they come here again?"

Rendel uncrossed his arms and indicated himself. A wry smile spread across his face. "Tell them that you have a Tezerenee, myself in particular, and they will come with the speed that only the hunger for revenge can give them."

He was offering himself as bait, in a ploy that could end in his slow, nighmarish death. Dru had to admire his daring, if nothing else.

"They will blame everything on you," the elf remarked needlessly.

"Concerned, little one? Let them, if it pleases them. They will forget when we show them there is a true path, one which would ensure they were never in debt to my father."

"Only to us. Only to you," Dru added.

"They *might* feel some debt to you, outsider, but not to an elf—whom you had better protect—or from me. From me it will only be a balancing of scales."

"He is correct, Dru."

"I know." He did not trust Rendel, knowing there was too much that the Tezerenee had not told them. Yet, the plan had merit. Further argument would only waste time they might not have.

"The only question remains," the other Vraad interjected, "is how to contact the rest. It will be a long task, I think. My own power works haphazardly, as yours likely does."

Dru looked down at Xiri, who returned his gaze with a smile, too. "We have a way around that."

Rendel glanced from one to the other, openly puzzled. "Do you really?"

It would have been impossible to perform the spell and keep their new companion from discovering the truth. Any attempt to hide their secret from Rendel would have only further weakened the bond they had forged. Dru wanted no trouble from the Tezerenee and admitted to himself that, of all other Vraad, it was Rendel who had the most knowledge concerning the shrouded realm, knowledge they might still need before all this was over.

"Step back." The curious Tezerenee obeyed without question. Dru and Xiri sat, the better to concentrate fully on their new task. Alone or with another Vraad, Dru doubted the summoning could have been performed with so much chance for success. Even Rendel's clan would have found themselves hard-pressed at this point. Oh, their summoning might have gone out, but not so clearly or so far. Besides, would anyone believe Dru if they knew that his supposed prisoner was *aiding* him in the spell?

Though much more complex due to the area that they were forced to cover, the spell proved far more willing than the last. What was sent out was not so much actual words, but images and sensations that repeated and repeated. Dru had intended on sending out an actual message, but it was Xiri who had performed that part of the spell and she had followed elfin ways. It really mattered little so long as what they desired was clear, but the end results reminded the sorcerer too much of the method by which the Seekers had communicated with him.

A glance at Rendel's suddenly chalky features made him wonder how well the Tezerenee knew the avians.

Dru had hoped that Sharissa would be the first to respond, but as the minutes passed, his daughter made no attempt to contact him, though she had to have noted the message. Instead, when the first response *did* come, it was as if the maelstrom that he had been eyeing anxiously had finally let loose with a rage intended to tear Nimth apart.

What was left of the tallest tower shook as if coming to life. Several fragments broke loose and struck the battered courtyard. A blue fire spread across the northwest edge of the city, burning solid rock as if it were dry kindling. A ferocious wind threatened to topple one of the smaller, outer towers. Cracks formed in the earth. Rendel had a grim smile on his face, well aware that whoever was coming wanted his head. Dru kept his eyes focused in the direction of the source of the attack, waiting for the Vraad to reveal his or her identity.

It was not *one* Vraad who finally materialized before them nor was it two. Dru almost wanted to laugh. If there was one other motive than survival that could band life enemies together, it was vengeance.

A full score and more faced them down. Dru was certain he counted at least three dozen, most of them the strongest among the Vraad, and leading them was one with a special hatred for the Tezerenee, a Vraad who should have been *dead*.

"*Silesti*," Rendel hissed. "Where is Dekkar, do you suppose?"

Dru stirred, realizing that the Tezerenee did not know about the patriarch's command that both Dekkar and Silesti finish their feud. He was certain that both of them had died, but if the black-garbed figure was truly who he appeared to be, then Rendel faced an added danger. Silesti was one of the deadliest sorcerers, his millenium-old feud having honed his skills. Nimth's situation had apparently not caused him much difficulty, if his entrance was anything to go by. It was evident that *he* had brought the others with him.

"Dru Zeree." Silesti dipped his head in formal greeting. "I had thought the reptiles had done away with you." His eyes were wide and bright. He wore the same darkly elegant bodysuit that he had been clad in the moment when Barakas had condemned the two rivals. There had been only one change, a small rainbow crest on the shoulder that Dru recollected had once been the symbol of his eternal adversary, Dekkar. It was a homage to a worthy foe.

"It was by my own doing that I was lost."

The leader of the unlikely band shrugged. "We have until Nimth takes us to talk of that. What concerns me, concerns *all* of us, is *that* one."

It was to Rendel's credit that he merely acknowledged the remark and made no sudden attempt to flee. Dru knew that in the Tezerenee's place he would have been considering any option that would have gained him freedom.

"Before you attempt anything, Silesti, I have a proposition."

"You want him first? By all means! You deserve it, only see that you keep him living!" He indicated those with him, a sea of nearly identical images with the *exact* same expression. Had looks actually been able to kill someone, there would have remained only a scorched mark where Rendel now stood.

"That's not what I meant." This would be delicate. If what Dru said failed to placate the bitter spellcasters, then he and Xiri would probably share Rendel's fate. He took a long breath and then, before the restless muttering grew any louder, presented them with the carrot on the stick. "I have a path of escape for us . . . all of us."

Several faces grew hopeful, but more than a few darkened. They had been betrayed once, and because they were Vraad, it was easy for them to imagine someone pulling the same ploy. Silesti's expression was unreadable, but his skin had turned a deep crimson.

"You . . . intrigue us. Tell us more."

There was a protest from within the group, but it quickly subsided after a single glance from their chosen spokesman.

Wishing he had the oratory skills of the patriarch, Dru detailed his mishap and what had become of him. The faces before him kept changing as emotions rose and fell. He said as little as possible about the guardians and their masters, deciding it was not yet time to tell as arrogant a people as his that they had been a failed experiment, but emphasized how there were those who shared their desire to survive. When he had finished, Silesti and the others conferred with one another.

Dru squeezed Xiri's hand and met Rendel's wary gaze. Neither could guess whether the vengeful band believed them. Dru was ready to defend both himself and Xiri with whatever it cost and Rendel would do no less for himself.

It was Silesti, as was expected, who announced the decision. His eyes kept switching from Dru to Rendel as he spoke. "If you were *this* one"—he indicated the Tezerenee with a savage jerk of his head—"we would already be taking our pleasure with your agonized screams. Because it is you, however, I, at least, am inclined to risk trusting you. That reptile . . . is there reason to spare him?"

"If you want my aid. Rendel is as trapped as we are. He knows more about the realm beyond than even I do." That was a matter of debate, but he was not going to tell them so. "We'll also need him when we confront Barakas . . . or would you care to begin your first moments after the cross-over fighting the Tezerenee?"

As angered as they were, Silesti's people were no fools. "Others might not agree with what you say."

"Between us, I think they'll force themselves to listen. Isn't life more important at this point? Do any of *you* want to remain in this hellhole *we* created?"

That was the point that none of them could deny. Even Silesti looked weary, now that the desire for vengeance was forced to subside. It was raw emotion that had kept these Vraad going. How were those with less strength surviving?

They were all looking at him in expectation, waiting to be told what to do. Why was *he* forced to lead them? All he wanted was to find his daughter and leave this place. When had he developed such a care for the survival of his undeserving race?

"I need help. From you, if possible. Many of the others will probably make their way here as the hours pass, and I don't think I can control them all. We might even have to fetch some of those still drowning in self-pity and convince them that I speak the truth. That's assuming *you* believe me. This is a sick jest. If I lie, you know I have nowhere to run from you. I swear I speak the truth. My life is my—" He stopped. His pledge would have sounded much too like the ones given by Barakas. Dru did not want to remind his counterparts of what had happened last time they had believed a pledge of honor. "I won't fail you," he finished up, wishing that he could have thought of something better to say.

"We've already given our assent, Zeree," Silesti commented. "You should have guessed that by the fact that the Tezerenee had not been flayed already."

Dru nodded in relieved gratitude. He knew what he had to say next. "I ask you to help coordinate steps, Silesti."

The mob leader's chest swelled. He acquiesced with a slight tip of his head. His eyes were gleaming.

The choice was the best one. Silesti's control of the band proved he had the presence and might necessary. It also gave the plan a look of cooperation. Making others an integral part of the plan would build up their faith in Dru. Unobserved for once, Dru tried to relax. It was a fruitless attempt. There was too much to do and he still worried over the fact that Sharissa had not shown up yet. Dru had expected her to be one of the first. More worries. *Would* it ever end?

"My father could not have handled it better." Rendel had come up behind him, but Dru had been too overwrought to notice. Xiri made it a point of switching sides so that she would be farther away from the Tezerenee. "You left out quite a bit, didn't you?"

"What if I did? Some of it probably would have resulted in your demise . . . and perhaps ours, too."

Rendel shrugged. "I meant nothing by it." He smiled in gracious fashion. "You have only my admiration."

There was a way that the Tezerenee had about him that demanded questioning by Dru. "You seem very pleased, more so than I would have thought."

"Why not?" With visible effort, Rendel created an emerald dragon-scale suit with a glittering cloak that moved even when there was no wind. He was greatly satisfied with his results and smiled again. "Despite that thing you call a guardian, I *will* cross again. I *will* have what is rightfully mine."

Dru wished he shared the pale-haired spellcaster's confidence. Rendel's words had stirred a nameless fear within him, a fear that the journey to the shrouded realm would be far from simple.

A fear that Nimth itself would not let them leave.

XIX

The night passed, though it was nearly impossible to believe that since the sky remained unchanged. The storm still grew, yet did not unleash its fury. Illumination from the green mass above still kept Nimth bathed in a parody of sunset. Xiri forced Dru to rest and he perhaps succeeded in sleeping an hour, but overall it was no use. Too much preyed on his torn mind. Vraad gathered in greater and greater numbers and still there was no Sharissa. Unable to rest any longer, Dru wandered among his people and asked several of those he knew if they had seen her. Several could not be bothered to remember. In some ways he could not blame them. They wanted to leave Nimth and be done with it. To most Vraad, the only reason to ask the whereabouts of a child of theirs was so that said offspring would not be able to mount a surprise assault on their domain.

Only when he realized that Melenea was also among those still missing did the tall sorcerer have an inkling of why his daughter might not have been able to reach him.

"I have to leave," he whispered to Xiri. "We have to leave. There is an enchantress called Melenea." Dru could not recall at the moment whether he had told the elf of his former lover, but that did not matter. Even if he had said something, he needed to say it *now*. "She's a Vraad of the worst extremes. Her entire life is built around what she likes to call games, but which others have often called insanity."

The Tezerenee returned. His eyes burned with anger and not a little fear. The more Vraad who arrived, the less comfortable he felt. Only Dru's presence and word of honor kept the growing mass from trying to take him.

"Going somewhere? I think not," Rendel warned, keeping

his voice low so that the rest of the Vraad could not hear him. He had remained close by, drawing protection from Dru's mere presence. An unwelcome, eavesdropping shadow that Dru was regretting. "Not, at least, until I'm across!"

The two faced off. "It's a fallacy that the Tezerenee understand what caring for a son or daughter means, but that doesn't give you the right to command me, Rendel!"

"Would you like me to tell *them* that you plan to abandon them? I doubt whether I'd have to worry much about my hide if I did! It would be you they were after, outsider! You and your sweet pet here!"

Xiri had already proven her bravery time and again, but the covetous look Rendel gave her turned her face pale. Her eyes were daggers as she tried to pretend his implications meant nothing to her.

"They'd still take you, don't think otherwise! I won't be bullied, dragon! You don't want me as your enemy!"

Rendel tried a new tactic. "You were given a purpose when the guardians sent you back here."

It could not be denied. Dru took a deep breath. "Rendel, I don't even know what I'm supposed to do except probably bring you all to the one rift that I know of, the one in the far reaches of *my* lands."

"Is *that* it?" The Tezerenee laughed out loud, causing more than one head to turn. "I'll take them there! Go on and find your get! I'll make certain they cross safely."

Dru could read some of what Rendel planned by the minute but visible changes in his expression. Somehow, Rendel would try to make certain it was he to whom the other Vraad owed a debt. He wondered just how much of a fool Rendel was. Most of the Vraad would still want his hide even after the crossing, preferably in many screaming pieces. He was a part of something they hated and this was their opportunity to strike back.

"If anyone leads them, it should be the one called Silesti," Xiri suggested. Her dislike for the Vraad race was still strong, but if there were any who could be trusted other than Dru, it was the somber Silesti. Dru agreed. Silesti's contribution to the new plan was growing with each addition to the ranks. He appeared to have been born for this moment. Everyone looked to him as the symbol of defiance, defiance against the draconian Tezerenee clan. Barakas had tried to kill him, so the rumors now went, and had failed.

Silesti had already proved his ability as a leader, something that came as a bit of a shock to Dru and possibly the somber warlock himself. Dru wondered if it was his way of filling the void left by the abrupt end of his lifelong duel with Dekkar. Thinking of the duel, he wondered again how Silesti had survived. The other Vraad had not offered a reason and no one had the audacity to ask. For now, it did not really matter. What mattered to him was that he and Silesti both trusted and *respected* one another now. Had he dared to consider the black-suited Vraad's last conversation with him, a simple talk over questions raised by some of the newcomers, Dru might have even gone so far as to say the two of them *liked* one another... at least a tiny bit.

"It will be Silesti."

Rendel's mask of calm nearly slipped away. Rage spread like wildfire and it was all he could do to keep from screaming. "As you like it! We will speak again in the Dragonrealm."

He turned and caught sight of Silesti and several others, all of whom had an avid interest in the conversation between Dru and the Tezerenee. It was clear that they were hoping for some kind of break between the two so that Rendel would no longer be protected from their wrath.

The Tezerenee paused, measuring their emotions, and stepped back until he was next to Dru. Without meeting Dru's eyes, he whispered in a cold tone, "I will be waiting for you, Zeree. Waiting for all of you to bow to me, not my father."

The pale-haired warlock pushed past Dru and strode off into the deserted sectors of the city.

"Perhaps someone will find him alone and unprotected among the ruins," Xiri suggested, watching the receding figure with disgust. "What did he mean by that last?"

Several Vraad had stirred the moment Rendel had walked away. Silesti rushed over to Dru and Xiri.

"What happened? Where did that reptile go? Is he coming back?"

It had only become clear to Dru now what the Tezerenee had meant. A search of the city would reveal nothing of him. "He's gone. He won't be with us."

"Will he escape to the Dragonrealm?" The ebony-garbed figure spouted. Not having another name for it, the Vraad as a whole had unconsciously adopted the one coined by Barakas.

First victory to you, patriarch! Dru thought in sour humor. "He may. Rendel knows where I planned to go and he knows much concerning the shrouded realm and its intrusions here. Still . . ." An idea dawned, one that he did not care for. "I could be wrong about the location. The place I fell through might not be our way out. Rendel might be following a dead trail!"

"If he gets left behind . . ." Silesti smiled at the image. "What a perfect fate! Better than any torture! Nimth will kill him far more slowly than we would!"

"Yet he may escape to the other side if the rift *does* prove open," Xiri pointed out.

Silesti still had a bit of trouble dealing with an elf. Because she was Dru's close companion, he had succeeded so far in treating her with at least some respect. "Then we will track him down at our leisure once *we* have finally reached our new home!"

That was Dru's opening. What Rendel did could be dealt with once they were all safe and secure, but Sharissa was a subject that could wait no longer. "I think it might be best to see if there is another path through. I know what to look for now. If the way I know of is closed or if it only opens periodically, then I should find that out before we dare lead the others there. Are there those you can trust to act in concert with you? Those who can keep our people trusting for a time longer? It might take into the morning to do what I must."

The other Vraad frowned. "That sounds as if you will be leaving us."

"I won't be here for a time, that's all. There's still more I have to do. I want the cross-over to work."

"You underestimate me." Silesti's visage grew troubled. "Or perhaps you do not trust me. That you care for your daughter is a mystery to many of us. Now she is missing and you want to find her; that is what you are really thinking about. You asked where Melenea was and I know that she's also among the missing. I, for one, would draw the same conclusion as you have, that Melenea has your Sharissa. She has always

been a vindictive and deadly bitch and this smells like one of
her mad games! Only she would play when the world is
crumbling about her!''

As opposed to the rest of the Vraad, Dru thought with what
he considered justified criticism. Left abandoned by Lord
Barakas, had they attempted their *own* plan of escape? Hardly.
He did not, of course, reveal any of this to Silesti. It would
have been unfair, anyway. Dru was just as guilty as the rest.
Only the past two decades had he attempted to redeem himself.
''I meant what I said about the cross-over, Silesti. I *do* want to
check my work before we try. We know what will happen if the
others feel they've been betrayed again.''

''And I would join you as one of those facing their combined
wrath.'' Silesti gave him a brief smile that would have looked
more appropriate on an animal being led to slaughter. ''I really
have no choice, do I? Get your little hellion and make certain
that you have a destination for us, that's all I care.'' The other
sorcerer's voice grew fatalistic. ''If you don't return by a
reasonable time, I'll do my best to see that *I* lead the mob that
comes for you.''

Though Xiri was taken aback by the threat, Dru accepted it
as normal. With time ever passing too quickly, he outlined the
basics of what he had in mind concerning the second cross-
over, only vaguely making references to the guardian who had
aided him. Dru hoped he himself understood what he was
doing. The guardian had said that he was to lead them to the
shrouded realm, but had never actually said that the rift the
sorcerer had fallen through was the correct path or that there
might be some other way altogether. The magical creature had
inferred a few things, but...

With an effort born of anger, Dru ousted the worries and the
second thoughts from his mind. He would defeat himself
without aid from either Melenea or Rendel if he fell prey to
his own fears.

Silesti nodded his understanding when Dru concluded. ''I
have it. Remarkable!'' he added, his dark mood fading as he
once more fell victim to the wonder of it all. ''To think escape
stood there waiting for us and we thought it was merely an
aberration, a part of Nimth's long dying! Why is it these others
sought us out in the first place?''

"That's something that must wait until we've crossed."

"Not going to tell me. As you wish. You can count on me, Zeree, if only so that I can be around to see the dragon lord's sickened face."

Dru's jaw nearly dropped until it occurred to him that Silesti was speaking of Barakas, not the statue whose likeness the guardian had taken on.

"What are you waiting for?" Silesti asked. "You of all people should know how quickly time is running out."

Dru's growing guilt made him offer the other Vraad one last chance to back down, though he prayed Silesti would not take it. "There will be several thousand, Silesti. We're talking about *all* of our people, you know. We can't leave anyone behind."

"I have some concept of the numbers. They will be here. Anyone foolish enough to want to remain behind deserves their fate, but we will try to convince them otherwise." A pause. "In fact, it will keep them busy and give them a reason why we have to delay! Perfect!" More confident now, he waved Dru and the elf away. "That settles everything. Now go! I want you here when the time comes . . . or I cannot promise what will happen afterward!"

Both men locked gazes for a time, the truth of Silesti's words a grim reminder of the fickleness and pettiness of their kind. Neither could claim to be above such things, either.

It was the other mage who broke contact first, physically turning away from the two. "Find the bitch and get your daughter back! I just hope your youngster doesn't pay you back with typical kindness when she finally *does* leave you!"

Dru watched him walk back toward the expanding crowd, then led Xiri away from the sight of the milling Vraad. When they were alone, she turned to him with a questioning expression. The elf wanted an explanation for the other sorcerer's last statement.

"It's good that Vraad live so long," he said in a hushed voice. "Most offspring die trying to murder at least one of their parents."

The horrified look he received made him burn with bitterness. "Yes, the founders and the guardians are very desperate if they think we are their last chance for a future! I thought you knew that already.''

"You are not like that! You could not have..." Though it was a denial, there was a hint of question in it.

His lack of reply was response enough.

They found a building that still retained enough roof to give them shelter for the brief time while they worked the spell that would send them to Melenea's realm. Facing Xiri but avoiding her, Dru took her hands. He was becoming tired, so very tired, but it was not yet the time to sleep. Xiri squeezed tightly, not from disgust but rather from understanding. Dru felt like a corpse given a second life. He dared to kiss the top of her head just before they teleported.

To enter the heart of a raging storm would have seemed a pleasant task in comparison to what Dru and Xiri found themselves in the midst of when they appeared. The duo was thrown to the ground as a quake rocked everything. Dru was certain he felt the earth *ripple* like a wave. A frog with tiny human legs rushed past his dust-covered face. Something he was thankful he could not see slithered over his backside. Beside him, Xiri coughed hard in an attempt to empty her lungs of dirt that she had swallowed.

"What in the name of Rheena?" she finally managed.

Turning over, Dru found that his vision had gone mad. That was the first and most sensible explanation for what he saw. The spellcaster almost wished the dim glow in the sky would fade, if only so that he would not have to see what was happening around him.

They were only a short distance from their intended destination, but that minute gap had probably saved them from disaster. Melenea's stronghold was only a chaotic memory of what he recalled. Its walls and cloud-capped towers twisted and swayed, snakes of marble and ivory. The entire edifice wriggled, a thing pretending at life. Things crawled all around it, nonsense creatures that existed only in the Vraad subconscious ...until now. It was magic gone wild, a region madly unstable. He should have known that her domain would be one of the first to be lost. Melenea had always been free with her spells, more so than even the Tezerenee. Worse yet, what they had seen so far was only the first stage. Anything would eventually be possible in an area like this and there was no way to turn it back once the instability had established itself so. Even as Dru stared, dumbfounded, one of the walls grew a score of mouths, each of which began babbling words of no meaning. The land itself turned and shaped itself like soft clay, hills rising and sinking at random moments. Now and then, some new aberration would go running by them. Plants, as twisted as any Nimth now produced, sprouted, grew, tried to reach them, then withered and died . . . all in the time it took to blink.

There could be no one in the citadel itself. Melenea would have no desire for a place that was no longer hers to mold as she willed. Thankfully, it also meant that Sharissa could not be there. If she *was* a captive of the deadly enchantress, Melenea would hardly waste her. This was one of her games and Sharissa was her prize piece. Her bait. The game he had unwittingly joined when he had taken her as a lover had never truly ended, not for Melenea. Dru had defied her in ways that none of the others had. It would not be over until he succumbed to her will.

Or when I kill *you.* That would end her games once and for all. The grim choice made, Dru rose and helped Xiri to her feet. "They have to be back in my lands. Melenea will be waiting for us there, ready to play a final hand."

"She must be mad!"

"No more than any other Vraad! Longevity has its price. Perhaps that's why the young try to kill their progenitors . . . to either unconsciously save their elders from further madness or prevent themselves from ever having to suffer it. Reaching adulthood is insanity enough!"

One of the sky-scraping towers twisted toward the duo, sighting upon them like a great serpent. Melenea had always been proud of her achievement. There were none stretched so high, not even in the communal city. Seen acting as some living creature, they were even more astounding.

"Time to leave," Dru whispered. "Serkadion Manee! I pray I'm right!"

"What if Sharissa is not there?"

His skin was white and he knew his present appearance chilled the elf. At the moment, Dru did not care.

"Then Melenea will learn—"

Blue-green fur swarmed over them.

Xiri was tossed aside, only to land like a wet cloth on the ever-shifting earth. The monstrous form ignored her. Dru stared into a maw filled with teeth.

"Lady said that someone would come, sorcerer! Said that I could play with you if you came!" The massive wolf loomed over the battered spellcaster. "You are Dru Zeree. Delicious! She would never let me play with you before, but she is gone now! Lady said I could have *anyone* who came, anyone at all!"

Dru had forgotten Cabal, though he found it amazing that he could have ever erased the memory of this monstrosity. Cabal was Melenea as she should have been. Her alter ego. Yet... yet now painfully reminded of its existence, he also recalled something else about the wolf. Melenea had destroyed the familiar in a fit of anger when it had tried to take Dru while he slept. Destroyed it with hardly a care for the loyalty it had always given her. That was why he had forgotten Cabal; it had not existed anymore.

This was hardly an illusion that stood over him. Dru could feel and smell its hot, nauseating breath.

Seeming to understand the changing emotion in its victim's expression, Cabal laughed again. "A long time, yes. You remember. A good trick she played, not telling you about me. Lady has punished me often, but there are always *other* Cabals!"

"I am legion!" laughed an identical voice.

A *second* Cabal emerged from hiding and joined the first, eyeing the limp elf with interest before turning a hungry gaze at the Vraad.

It should not have surprised Dru that there were more than one; it was typical Melenea. How many *did* she have? Dru envisioned an endless array of huge, blue-green wolves, all of them extensions of her twisted personality.

For all their strength, however, the familiars also suffered from her weaknesses. It was his only hope. With Xiri unconscious, Dru could not leave... even supposing his spell did work the first time.

Behind them, several of the towers had twisted their way,

rippling pseudo-snakes drawn by the movements. Dru developed a wild, desperate plan.

"Who plays with me first, then?" he asked, trying to seem interested rather than anxious. Their response would indicate just how much like their mistress they were.

"I caught you! I am first!" growled the one who had knocked the Vraad and the elf over.

The other snarled. "I saw them! I let you have first strike, but I play first with him!"

"Play with the elf!"

"No!" The second Cabal narrowed its eyes, studying the hapless spellcaster as it might a favorite treat. "I want *him*! He is mine!"

"After I am done!"

"I don't think I'll be much fun to play with after the first of you," Dru interjected when he saw the second reconsidering its position.

"I want him first!" it finally responded.

The twin behemoths turned and bared their multitude of sharp teeth at one another. As he had suspected, they were as possessive as Melenea. It was a common failing with familiars. Other than a few exceptions such as Sirvak, whom Dru had worked to make as separate an individual mind as possible, most were nearly perfect reflections of their masters and mistresses. Cabal was even more extreme than most.

"I will have him!"

"*I* will have him!"

The first one snapped at its doppleganger. That led to a snap from the second. Both were working to make the other back down, a futile ploy considering they were equally stubborn. Melenea would have never backed down and Dru hoped her pets would follow suit.

"Mine!" The two beasts shouted in simultaneous fashion. They leaped as one, coming together in the air, jaws biting and claws tearing. Dru crawled backward as fast as he could to avoid being crushed by their falling bodies.

Both Cabals landed on their feet, still locked together in combat. Identical scars decorated their shoulders and blood dripped from their jaws as each tried to tear out the other's throat. *There is no worse enemy than one's self*, Dru thought as he watched in horrified fascination. He still dared not take Xiri and attempt to flee. The moment the Vraad moved to escape, the twin familiars would forget their feud and turn on him. Of that he was certain.

The battling beasts stepped back from each other, blood spattering their faces. Magical though they were, in order to be useful to a Vraad, a familiar had to be flesh and bone. The wary combatants circled one another, baring their fangs and again seeking to frighten off one another.

Xiri stirred at that point, both cheering Dru with the fact that she was still alive and adding to the sorcerer's fear by moving so near the creatures. If she caught their attention, they might break off the battle long enough to make certain she did not try to escape.

Once again, the Cabals joined. So evenly matched, they might fight for days without pause, neither ever gaining an upper hand. Dru could hardly wait out all that time. Had this been the Nimth of long ago or even a few months past, Cabal would have been nothing to him. Yet, in a place where his sorcery was suspect, Melenea's familiar, doubly strong now, could easily be his equal or even his superior.

He glanced briefly at the wriggling towers, his thin hope there fading away. The citadel still acted like a living creature. Two smaller towers even sparred with one another, a reflection of the battle between the familiars. A portion of the edifice now seemed to be flowing down and away, not molten, for the walls and buildings still held some semblance of their function. As with so many things of late, it was a phenomenon that he would have dearly loved to study, but not during his present predicament.

It was now impossible to tell which of the wolves was which, not that it really mattered. They rolled in a jumble of fur, blood, and dust, their snarls loud enough to hurt Dru's ears. The two leviathans crashed into a low overhang and the rubble that fell to the ground sprouted arms and legs. A hundred or more magic-spawned gargoyles scattered to escape further fragmentation.

Even if the familiars never ceased their fight, how long would it be before the wild power affected Dru and his companion? He had no idea how much resistance elves had to such chaos.

Some of the living towers had returned their attention to the movements of the familiars. Dru studied the back and forth swaying of the snakelike bodies and tried to make himself as still as possible. The two Cabals had broken from one another again. Both turned one wary eye toward the Vraad, as if to warn that he had better not try to escape. Dru tried to look panic-stricken, which proved to be easy since he was not, in truth, far from that point already.

Satisfied, the twin wolves backed away. They had not abandoned their fight. Instead, each sought to find better ground from which to attack. It was their only venue left. An advantage of position would break the deadlock created by their identical abilities.

"Dru." It was a whisper, one barely heard among so much noise.

He blinked, trying not to show his shock. "Xiri?"

"What do we do? They won't fight forever."

That was debatable, based on what he knew of Melenea's nature, but it was still important that they escape before too long. Not merely for their sakes, but for Sharissa's.

"Can we outrun them?"

Dru shook his head, and whispered back, "They could catch us even if each of them had two broken legs and half their bodies ripped apart. Melenea knows her sorcery well. What they lack in personality and intelligence, they make up for in ability. They have reflexes a thousand times greater than the animal they resemble."

"What do we do?" Xiri's voice cracked for the first time that he could recall. He wanted to go to her and hold her, for *both* of their well-beings.

Dru looked up once more at the nearly hypnotic swaying of the towers. "We hope that it won't take much more."

Before she could question his statement, the familiars charged at one another. One Cabal had taken to a hill that kept crumbling. The second had opted for lower but more stable ground for its starting point. Each evidently hoped the earth itself would prove the deciding point. If the one above stumbled, it might lose its footing and fall, leaving it open to its counterpart's attack. If it maintained its balance, it would have the opportunity to leap onto its twin, crushing the other beneath it and enabling it to reach the neck.

As the two monsters closed, Dru caught a twitch of movement from the living citadel.

With a swiftness even the wolves would have had trouble matching, the largest of the towers, so very much serpentine in movement, *struck* at the charging combatants. It had no mouth, though it might have thought it did, but its girth and the pointed tip were sufficient. The living tower caught both wolves, coming down upon them with a mass so great that it continued on even after meeting the ground. It withdrew almost instantly, leaving behind a deep crater.

The wolves had never even noted its coming.

Dru was already moving, hoping that the actions of the one spire would hold the others back for a moment. Xiri was on her feet even as he reached her and the two ran with all the speed they could muster. Neither dared to look back, even when they heard movement.

A powerful shock wave sent them flying forward. As Dru tumbled, he saw another of the towers retreat, its strike having fallen short by only a few yards.

There was one benefit of the second assault. Dru and Xiri had been tossed out of reach of the murderous spires. The two of them lay where they had fallen until their hearts had slowed to something approaching normal. Beyond them, the towers of the citadel started to collapse like wax candles tossed into a fire. Even still, the tallest made one token attempt to reach them. It fell far short. A moment later, the entire tower fell for a final time, its base no longer solid enough to support it. It continued to flop around for a few seconds more, a horror suffering its death throes.

"That . . . was . . ." Xiri took another breath and tried again. "That was . . . I cannot find a word that satisfies me!"

"Astonishing, amazing, horrible, terrible, insane, unbelievable, impossible . . ." Dru's smile was wan. "Use all of them and more. It's the only way you might ever describe it in sufficient fashion."

She squinted, trying to locate something. "Do you think that those creatures are dead?"

"Cabal? I doubt there's much left that could do anything to us. For a time, I was afraid it wouldn't happen."

Her eyes became dishes. "You *knew* the citadel would attack them?"

"It was watching like a snake, striking at movement. I hoped that it would attack them before they decided to make peace."

"What if they had?"

He stood up and stared grimly back at the gaping crater that was all that remained of the wolves. "I'd rather not think about it. Let's hope there are no more of them."

"We should leave here," the elf said. She did not want to have to face more of those obscene creatures if they could avoid it. "But where should we go?"

Dru was still pondering the familiars and whether Melenea had truly wanted them to kill him. He would have thought her too possessive to let others, even bits of her own personality, do it for her. That was verification enough that she was not here.

"She could only be in my lands . . . as I said earlier. Where best to humiliate me and take from me everything I care for than my own home?"

"She must have loved you deeply at one time," Xiri whispered in a hesitant manner.

He was stunned. How could she think that? "Melenea loves no one. I thought that was obvious."

"Then why has she such a marked interest in you? I gather many have known her over the centuries."

"We're wasting time!" Dru barked, taking Xiri's hands a little more tightly than he had planned. She remained passive, knowing his anger would fade . . . and knowing it was aimed at himself, not her.

Behind them, Melenea's stronghold started its final collapse within itself. Melting yet not melting, it looked like a water-soaked drawing rather than an actual castle. That such power was now unchecked . . .

If it was a sign, neither of them wanted to know. They closed their eyes and were, a heartbeat later, at their destination.

XX

The disconcerting image of one land imposed upon another was possibly the most refreshing vision that Dru had experienced in some time. The shrouded realm was a victim of paradox; its presence was one of the few *stable* things that the sorcerer could still recall. Where everything else was suffering chaotic change in one manner or another, the region where he had made his accidental pilgrimage to the Void and beyond was nearly the same as it had been at that time.

"This is . . . beautiful." Xiri brushed a hand through several blades of ghostly grass. "Like seeing the spirit of the forest and the field."

"But not enough." The realm beyond the veil was too vague an image, too much like so many others he had investigated early on. Even from where he stood, he could see that the rift area was only a vague shadow of its once-mighty self. He could not say whether the spectral land would fade to nothing or strengthen until it was more real than the piece of Nimth it was displacing. Whichever, it was evident that for at least the time being, they would find no accessible path to the founders' world. Perhaps later, but not now.

Dru imagined several thousand vengeful faces and shuddered at what sort of reward Vraad imagination would create for him if his promises proved as transparent as the woods in the distance.

"I do not see him."

He did not have to ask who it was she meant. Rendel would have known after a few moments that there was no escape using this place. Dru had not expected to find him here, though he had scanned the region with care, just in case. The Tezerenee was none of his concern, however. Rendel had chosen to go his own way.

The sorcerer shifted, anxious to be gone from here. He had fulfilled his duties to the other Vraad; it now was necessary, not just for his own sake but theirs as well, that he return to his domicile. That his concern presently centered more on Sharissa than the fate of his race did not disturb him.

He sent his mind out, seeking the link.

Sirvak?

Xiri watched, both interested and anxious. He had explained earlier about Sirvak and how the familiar, like Cabal, protected the pearl edifice from outsiders.

Dru frowned. Sirvak rarely took so long to respond. The link between them was strong . . . or had been until now. Concentrating harder, he discovered only the barest thread keeping his mind in tune with the creature. Sirvak's end was a complete mystery. There was a fuzziness, as if the familiar was not quite there. Dru grew more uneasy. He called to the familiar again, this time pressing to the limits of his will.

After another long, nerve-twisting silence, a distant, tentative voice filled his head. *Masterrr?*

He knew that Xiri was aware of his success by the look of relief she flashed at him. Likely the same expression was plastered over his own. *Sirvak! What happened to you? Why didn't you respond? Is Sharissa all right?*

Masterrr. There are troublesss! You must come here!

"What about Sharissa?" Dru realized he had shouted, so frustrated had he become in the few seconds since contacting his creation. Why was Sirvak acting so upset? Why would the familiar not answer a question concerning Sharissa? *I'm coming! You will wait for me by the entrance to my work chamber!*

Masterrr, no! Danger! Let Sirvak guide you in! Will explain when you are safe!

Very well! Just do it! Dru broke the link, confused and very angry. He reached out to his right and took Xiri's hand. "My familiar will teleport us into my home. It seems quite agitated."

"Something to do with your daughter?"

"It must be. Sirvak wouldn't say a thing concerning her, but kept speaking of trouble. I—"

Nimth was no more. Dru suffered a brief period of total chaos where he floated in a dark limbo. He had lost his grip on

Xiri, somehow and realized that he had never brought her up to Sirvak. Had the familiar left her outside?

His feet touched the cold, hard surface of one of the castle's floors.

"Sirvak? Xiri?" His eyes refused to focus. "Sirvak? What kind of spell *was* that? What happened? Xiri?"

After a moment, a delicate hand touched his. "Hush, Dru. I'm right here."

He blinked, slowly making out vague shapes. The shapes tightened until they were actual forms . . . walls, doorways, torches, and, to his left, his elfin companion.

"How are you feeling?" she asked in concern. Her eyes were bright, as if she had actually enjoyed the transfer.

"Better than I did when I first arrived. Didn't you feel the disorientation? A sensation of being held in place for a moment or two?"

"A little. Perhaps it didn't affect me as much since I'm an elf." Xiri said the last with a touch of amusement in her voice.

Dru was unable to see the humor. He turned around and looked for the gold and black form of his winged familiar. Sirvak was nowhere in sight.

Sirvak?

Masterrr?

Where are you? Dru let his rising anger wash over the disobedient creature.

I come. The great reluctance with which the familiar responded caught the spellcaster by surprise. He would have questioned Sirvak then, but Xiri chose that moment to desire his attention.

"What is that in there, Dru?" She had drawn closer to him, nearly clinging to his arm. To his surprise, he felt uneasy rather than pleased with her nearness. Stirring himself, he followed her finger, which pointed at the doorway to his work chamber.

"That's our destination. That's where the key to crossing the ghost lands into the realm beyond waits. It should—" He broke off and stretched a hand out toward the unimpressive-looking doorway. "It's *open!*"

"Of course it is."

"That's not what I mean! Sirvak!"

There was no response from the familiar. With a new fear stirring in the pit of his stomach, Dru raced through the unprotected entrance. He had improved on the magical barricade surrounding this, one of the most important of his chambers, and left it active prior to his last departure from the castle. By rights, only he and Sharissa could have entered and neither of them would have removed the spell, even with all the other defenses implanted throughout Dru's domicile. Did this have anything to do with the dangers that Sirvak had mentioned in his ravings? Where *was* the familiar? Where was *Sharissa*, the only other person who had access?

When Dru saw the crumpled figure buried beneath the long cloak, he thought his worst fears had finally caught up to him. Then the sorcerer stared more closely and saw that it was a male body sprawled before them.

Rendel.

From the awkward angle that his body lay in, it was quite impossible that the Tezerenee had survived. Dru stepped closer, cautious because he still did not know what had killed the other Vraad. He also wanted to know how Rendel had gained entrance in the first place.

He touched the body. It was still warm, which was not too surprising since Rendel had only departed the communal city a short time before Dru and Xiri had. The dead Vraad's expression was that of puzzlement, as if even then he could not believe that something had, in absolute fashion, ensured that he would *not* return to the shrouded realm. He felt no remorse for the arrogant Tezerenee. As intelligent as Rendel had been, his ego had made him blind to common sense. He could not see the abrupt end his ways would bring him. Nothing had been beyond him, as far as Rendel was concerned.

Dru wondered what it was that the Tezerenee had desired so much that he would grow so careless. If it did lie in the realm beyond the veil, then someone else would someday claim it. Dru hoped he would not be around when that happened. Anything that so obsessed a Tezerenee could only be a danger to all others.

Stepping back from the corpse, he saw the cracked blue crystal, no more than the size of a nut, that lay nestled in the crook of Rendel's arm. Dru forgot about the body at his feet.

"Serkadion Manee!" He had slim hope that he was wrong, but a simple turn of the head was enough to show him the worst.

His experiment, the spiral patterns and the orbiting crystals, the work that was to have given him the answers he needed, was in disarray. A few stones still circled, but in mad curves that no longer had meaning. Several had fallen to the floor. The spiral patterns still existed, but they had deteriorated beyond repair. Rendel had destroyed not only the culmination of his research but the patterns that had been needed to find the nearest opening.

The master mage frowned. Viewing things, he saw it was not so much Rendel who had destroyed the artifact but rather the artifact that had killed the Tezerenee. But how? As he had created it, the experiment should have been harmless. This one had unleashed enough magic to make an end of the intruder.

"Sirvak!" Dru shouted, more out of anger than because he thought that it would have any more success in summoning the familiar than the mind link had.

"Masterrr."

The gold and black beast was a pitiful sight as it fluttered into the room. It gave Xiri a wide berth, glancing at her with pain-wracked eyes as it passed, and settled down on a table nearby. Dru studied the animal, taken aback by its disheveled appearance. Its fur and feathers were matted heavily with dirt and blood and it was even missing most of one of its forelegs. The spellcaster's anger deflated as he imagined the cause of the beast's injuries.

Sirvak stretched its ravaged wings, the effort visibly painful. "Masterrr."

Xiri moved to join Dru, taking his arm and watching the familiar from his side. Sirvak hissed in her direction, but shrank into itself when the sorcerer gave it a withering look. A slight smile spread across the elf's face.

"What happened here, Sirvak?" he finally asked. "Where is Sharissa? How did Rendel get in here and what killed him? Tell me."

The familiar opened its toothy beak and squawked in frustration. It could not take its eyes from Xiri, though it was evident that Sirvak could not abide her being here. Dru knew that not trusting outsiders was part of the creature's training, but it should have been able to make the distinction between those like Melenea and one who was so obviously the master's companion.

"I'm still waiting."

"Answer your master, familiar," the elf urged, still wearing the smile.

"The Mistresssss Sharissa, masterrr. It was by her doing that this one"—it indicated Rendel—"gained entrance here."

"What killed him? Was it my experiment?"

Sirvak's eyes were narrow slits that followed each movement Xiri made. "Yessss. It was the experiment."

Dru had been afraid of that. He had no doubt that the trap had been set for him, which meant that Melenea had been here at least once before. Had Sharissa let her inside? He recalled his own commands to the familiar, the ones that had made it virtually impossible for the winged creature to tell his daughter anything about Dru's time with the enchantress. Once again, the fault was his. Sirvak had only done the best it could under the circumstances.

"Where is Sharissa?"

"Sirvak does not know."

"Not know?" He quieted as the injured creature shut its eyes in shame. "I'm sorry, Sirvak. When was the last time you saw her?"

The familiar opened its brilliant eyes wide. "Mistress was with Tezerenee! Hood-faced one. Like this one."

Dru gave Rendel's body a glimpse and asked, "Gerrod? Do you mean she's with Gerrod?"

"Gerrod, yesss."

"This Gerrod is like his brother?" Xiri asked.

"Like Rendel, yes, but I didn't think he was quite so bad." He studied Sirvak's wounds. The familiar had fought wyverns before, but none had caused such damage. A larger beast, like Cabal, would have been more of a threat. Something did not sit right. "You've no idea what happened to them."

"No, masterrr." Sirvak was upset with itself. It kept staring at its lord's companion with loathing. Dru stroked the creature's head, trying to soothe it.

"It's been terribly damaged," the elf said, looking over the ruined limb and the scars. "Perhaps it might be better if you destroyed it and made a new one."

Dru said nothing, but rather stared into Sirvak's eyes. When the gold and black animal closed its eyes again, its body shivering, he leaned close to it and, in a quiet, companionable tone, asked, "Sirvak, will you do something for me?"

"Master?" It looked at him, weariness and pain giving its voice an unsteady pitch.

"I want you to go outside and search. Find Sharissa."

"Masterrr—"

"Do as I say."

Sirvak hesitated. It eyed the elf, then Dru again. Something changed in its manner. It spread its wings and shifted. "I will obey."

"You always know what I want, Sirvak. I trust you do now."

The familiar dipped its head. "Sirvak will not fail you."

Both Dru and Xiri stepped back as the once-magnificent creature flapped its wings and rose with awkward movements into the air.

"Are you certain it can handle this task? It looks nearly dead."

"Things are not always what they appear," was his reply. "Sirvak will do what it must, regardless of the handicaps it now suffers."

"And what do we do in the meantime?" Again, her arm was around his. "What do we do with him?"

She spoke of Rendel. Dru did not bother with the still shape. "The castle will take care of his remains. It, like Sirvak, owes its ultimate loyalty to me."

The downward corners of her mouth revealed her uncertainty concerning the phrasing of his response, but the elf did not say anything more, allowing Dru to bring her along as he suddenly started for the doorway.

"Have I raised any doubts in your mind?" he asked when they were out in the hallway.

"What?" She stumbled as she blurted out the question.

"Have I raised any doubts? Do you still want to remain with a Vraad? One of the unholy race?"

"You're not so evil." Xiri caressed his cheek.

Dru watched the hall ahead of them. "No, there are far worse."

"Melenea."

"And Barakas, for one, though he's been rather tame. I wonder if he has his empire yet or if the Seekers have left his bones to the scavengers. Have you ever seen one of their cities? What is it like?''

They moved through one hallway to another. Ahead of them, Dru knew, lay the theater where Sharissa had created and manipulated her fanciful dancers.

The woman at his side shrugged. "I'd rather not say too much. I didn't care for them."

"Ugly places of iron and stone sprouting out of the earth like sores, if I remember what you said before."

She smiled, not wanting the subject to go on any further. "You see why I don't like to talk about them. Horrible places."

"Yes."

"Where are we going, Dru?"

He sighed and squeezed her hand. "I want to show you another side of me. I want to show you the theater I built for my daughter . . . and my bride."

"Is it much farther?" She let the comment about Dru's mate pass, but he could see that it had touched her in some way.

"Not far. As a matter of fact, here it is *already!*" The theater *had* actually been farther away, but he had decided to risk using sorcery and have the castle realign itself. The sooner this was over, the better.

Dru had desired the chamber to appear to them in its simplest form . . . a soft dirt floor and blank curved walls. In some respects, it resembled a miniature version of the room of worlds minus the images covering the walls and ceiling.

"Is there more to it?"

"Much more." He waved his free hand and a marble floor of alternating black and white squares formed. "I can't say why we need a separate chamber to do what could be done anywhere, but Sharissa and I have preferred it this way."

He gestured to the left and the right. A slight tremor shook the room, but his spell still worked. Several figures, some human, some creatures of varying sorts, stood in what appeared to be random placement on the squares.

"Do your people have chess?" He briefly outlined the game.

She nodded, but her eyes were not on him. Rather, the figures themselves fascinated her more. "We have it, but not like this." Xiri started to walk toward one of the closest pieces on the giant board, a wide, armored figure holding a scepter and sporting a sadistic smile. "These playing pieces . . . is there something—"

Dru blinked and the board was now normal size. It rested on a glass table that was accompanied by two soft couches, one for each player.

"Why did you do that?" Xiri snapped. She immediately remembered herself and gave him an apologetic smile.

"You wouldn't like what you saw there. Shall we play a game?"

"A game? Now? When we still have to find Sharissa?"

Joining her, he reached out to run one of his hands in her long hair. "I thought you liked games."

Her face was stone. "You *know*!"

He tightened his grip on her hair. "You forget, Melenea, as much as you claim to understand me, I also understand you."

She laughed. Her form changed without warning and Dru found his hand holding nothing more than illusion. With daring quickness, Melenea took hold of him and kissed him long and hard. Dru finally succeeded in prying her away, his face deepening to a color akin to her hair.

"No, Melenea, not again. I won't be a part of your world. That's behind me."

"If you say so, sweet. Was it that question about those Seekers that told you? I wondered about that when you asked, though I thought you were suspicious before you mentioned them."

"They only verified that you weren't Xiri. You played a poor game. Tiny things that you knew that she couldn't. Rendel and Gerrod being brothers. The worst move yet, you couldn't even control your own personality. I gave you every chance. Sirvak wanted to tell me that it was under your sway. I guessed as much once I knew that you had gained entrance to the castle earlier, but Sirvak was unable to point you out as an imposter."

Dru turned from her, nearly daring Melenea to do something, and walked over to the chess set. He fingered one of the pieces, the one that she had tried to study up close. "I sent it away knowing you, wherever you were, wouldn't stop me. Sirvak has suffered too much already and I know you're to blame."

"You know, Dru darling, you were always long-winded." She ran her hands along the contour of her clothing. "There is so much more we could be doing." Her hands stretched out toward him. "So many games to play." Melenea blew him a kiss.

A force like a maddened stallion struck Dru, throwing him over the table and spilling the chess set.

Dru rose and smiled. Melenea took a step back.

"Yes, I know that was supposed to be more than an ill wind. The difference between us, Melenea, is that I can talk while I cast protective spells. You merely talk." He picked up one of the chess pieces that had fallen to the floor. "I'll ask this only once. Do you have Sharissa?"

"Of course!" She folded her arms and looked at him in triumph. He would do nothing to her if it meant Sharissa's life.

Dru shook his head. "That was the wrong answer. I said I know you as well as you know me. If you had my daughter, you'd be more eloquent about it. You'd give me some of the fine points of what you'd planned for her."

Masterrrr!

Yes, Sirvak?

Sirvak is yours again! She is Melenea! Beware!

I know that, my friend.

She took Mistress Sharissa to her home! Master Gerrod helped Sirvak to free her, though she fought us, but Sirvak could not get away! Mistress did, though!

Both pleasure and cold hatred colored the spellcaster's next words. *Thank you, Sirvak. Thank you for telling me all of that.*

Sirvak is forgiven? The beast feared that it would be punished for allowing itself to be taken over by the enchantress.

Of course. One more thing. Where is the one who came with me? The el—the female.

She wanders at the edge of home, seeking entrance. Masterrrr, her sorcery is strange.

Let her pass through, Sirvak. Guide her to me. I want her safe.

As you command, masterrr. The winged creature broke the link, its task clear to it.

He favored Melenea with a pleasant smile, satisfied to watch her react the way he had the day on the steps in the Vraad city. His silent conversation with the familiar had lasted all of a breath, perhaps two, at most. "You have nothing left to tempt me with, nothing left to threaten me with. Can you give me one reason why I should tolerate your presence here any longer, Melenea?''

His change had daunted her, but he knew that she was far from beaten. Melenea always had one more ploy, one more move.

She did not disappoint him. ''Perhaps these?''

In her hand she held two gleaming crystals.

''Where did you get those?''

The enchantress had regained the upper hand and knew it. Dru had not expected to see the crystals he sought. They had, he supposed, been destroyed when Rendel had sprung her trap. ''Dear Shari *gave* them to me, just before the trusting child left me by my lonesome. That was when I left my surprise and also made certain I could reenter your citadel . . . of course, that little mongrel creation of yours helped to a point. I should have known it would be unreliable in the end, however.''

''Sirvak is very reliable. Your mistake was not realizing how independent its mind is . . . not like your other self, Cabal.''

She allowed the crystals to balance precariously on the tips of her fingers. ''Whatever. Well, darling? Have I met with your expectations? Do you want these little baubles? Should I let them fall?''

Her hand twitched and both stones tottered. At the last moment, she curled her fingers inward, restoring balance.

''You know, Dru, the trap was never meant for you. I was certain that faceless whelp, Gerrod, would gain entrance somehow, as tenacious as he is. I thought it would be a delicious trick on him. He's very much like you, you know. Were you ever intimate with the glorious Lady Alcia? It would certainly explain the differences between Gerrod and Reegan.''

Dru did not dignify her with a response.

She tilted her head to one side. ''No denial? No agreement? No thought at all?''

''Give me those crystals, Melenea.'' He kept his voice neutral. She would not play him like an emotional puppet.

''Certainly. Here.'' Melenea turned her hand palm down.

Reflex betrayed him. Hoping he did not have to fight Nimth as well as the enchantress, Dru snared the crystals with a minor spell. The action lowered his guard. It was a minuscule opening, to be sure, but the sorceress knew him as few others did. When she struck, it was more subtle, more emotional. Where an attack on his body would have likely been repulsed with little effort and most of those against the mind turned with even less, her spell touched on the least-defended part of Dru Zeree.

His memories.

"Cordalene!" he whispered. Her name had been *Cordalene*. Though his conscious mind had forgotten his bride's name, the subconscious could not. She had been, to his surprise, so very interested in the same things. What had begun as a casual joining no different from any other had become a drawn affair and then a sealing of bonds. Permanent mates were a scarce commodity among the Vraad, though there had been a few now and then. She was tall, slender, and with deep blue hair that tumbled to the ground, though dust never tarnished its beauty. They were both as other Vraad, still arrogant, still vindictive. Dru had beaten off two challenges by those interested in Cordalene. She had turned them down, but typically, neither had believed she meant what she said.

Cordalene stood before him, waiting for Dru to embrace her. He tried.

She collapsed into dust. Caught in the throes of the spell, he had summoned up a likeness of her, much the way Sharissa had called up the dancers.

Somewhere, Melenea was laughing at his stumbling, laughing at his futile attempt to recapture a cherished memory. Rage burned through the struggling sorcerer and his vision briefly cleared, revealing the mocking form of the enchantress. He tried to reach her.

Dru became lost in a second memory. Sharissa as an infant. The shock of discovering that their continued care for one another now extended toward the child. Most Vraad left the care of their offspring in the hands of their magical servant, golems and such. It might be that was why the hatred between young and old developed.

Sharissa cried and Dru took the infant in his arms. She dissipated into air. Another creation of the theater that his mind vaguely recalled existed in Nimth.

"This is *so* perfect!" Melenea purred from beyond his

vision. "A wonderful place to end the game! I thought I would only be able to enjoy the torment on your face, but now I can watch you lose everything all over again!"

His hands almost found her throat. She backed quickly away, and before he could try again, the day of the duel confronted him.

"Serkadion Manee! No, please don't!" He could not stop it. Cordalene met with some nameless female counterpart, a Vraad who was also dead, the loser in another duel only three days after this one.

The combat itself was a swift blur; Dru had not been there to witness it. Despite his struggles, the inevitable conclusion confronted him. What remained of Cordalene was a curled ball unrecognizable as anything human. She had been turned in on herself. Dru remembered how he had secluded himself and Sharissa for months before he went seeking out his wife's killer. His need for vengeance was left unsated.

Then he had turned to Melenea.

"Melenea," he muttered.

She had brought back the memories and made him suffer them anew. The fog, the images—both those in his mind and the ones he had created with his sorcery—were swept away until only one figure remained. One that did not realize its mortality.

"Melenea . . ." His eyes impaled her.

The enchantress finally realized that her victim was no longer trapped in his delusions, but it was too late. There was no longer any means of escape. With his first coherent thought, Dru had sealed this room for the time.

"Melenea," he began for the third time. "You twisted me during a time when I was empty. You never knew me before Cordalene. You never really thought of how much of a Vraad I truly am, no matter how I might deny it now."

Her smile had died. Dru felt her mind tug at forces of Nimth, trying to create a path of freedom.

"You should have never made me relive all of that so realistically. You've reminded me of the danger you'll always be to Sharissa." He shook his head in true sadness, wishing she had not released the Vraad within him. "I can't allow that."

Unable to escape, she struck with another spell. It was less stylish, but very deadly.

Dru deflected it easily, the cold anger that Melenea herself had created fueling his will. He understood, however, that delay would eventually take its toll on him. This had to be finished before that happened.

She struck again and again, her spells taking on all forms and intensities that would have long destroyed any other foe who did not know her so well. When she had exhausted herself to a certain point, he took her and left her without the ability to move or even breathe. She would not die; the spell prevented that. He only wanted her to know exactly how helpless she would be.

"You like games, Melenea? I do, but more subtle, more ingenious ones. Chess, for example. I have just the place for you, a place where you can join some of my past adversaries, some of those who threatened what was mine and discovered that I am not so peaceful when it comes to defending my home."

He retrieved the chess piece again, tossing it to her as she stood frozen. At the last moment, he released her. Through sheer luck, the enchantress caught the object. She looked at it, not understanding, and then gazed once more at Dru, still defiant. She had always been able to play her way out of any circumstance. There had always been some weakness she had been able to exploit.

"Not this time," Dru whispered to her. He indicated the piece she held. "You thought you recognized the other. How about this one?"

An arrogant smile playing on her lips, Melenea held it up and stared at the tiny, detailed visage. Her eyes widened and the smile became a circle as she gasped. The chessman fell from her hand and bounced on the floor.

"You do recognize him? Some of them I allow to have the same form, though others often get a shape more representative of their personalities. They'll live on long after I'm gone, always pawns where they were once players, much like yourself."

"Dru . . . you . . ." She was no longer desirable. Melenea had become a frightened creature.

He felt Sirvak's nearing presence. Xiri was with the familiar.

Sirvak tried to make contact with him, but Dru refused. Not until he had finished.

"I should think this would thrill you, Melenea, my *sweet*. Haven't you always insisted that life is a game?"

Xiri could not be allowed to see him like this. Dru gestured quickly and the chess set re-formed on the glass table, the pieces all lined up in their starting positions. For the first time, it became obvious that the game was lacking one more figure. Dru smiled at that. He had not known he had been so close to completing the set.

Only a moment more. That was all he needed. A moment more of complete control of his powers. He faced Melenea, lover and nemesis, and pointed at the empty square.

"Your choice," he said slowly, drawing out her agony as she had drawn out his moments before. "What would you like to be?"

When Sirvak and Xiri joined him, he had just finished admiring the board and was now putting it away. The chess set was one of the few things he had decided to bring with him to the other world. It would serve better than anything else to remind him of what he was leaving behind.

"Dru!" The elf held him tight, her body shaking. He stood frozen for the first few seconds, then clutched her with equal need.

"Do elves take on permanent mates?" he whispered after he had kissed the top of her head.

"They do." She pulled his head down so that he could kiss something other than her hair. When at last they broke, she looked around. "Sirvak spoke of danger, of this Melenea! What happened to her? Did you—?"

"I've introduced her to a new game. It will keep her attention for quite a long time." He carefully ignored her questioning expression and looked up at Sirvak, who eyed him with an understanding that no other, not even Xiri and Sharissa, could ever match.

"Masterrrr," the familiar finally dared. "The mistressss is nearrr. Master Gerrod is with herrr."

Master Gerrod?

Low, rolling thunder shook the walls of the pearl edifice.

"The storm is finally breaking." Deadly news for the Vraad race. They would have to risk the storm if they wanted to leave here. Still holding Xiri, Dru opened his hand and studied the crystals he had retrieved from the floor. They were, he knew, useless now. Melenea had apparently drained them of their contents. She was beyond asking questions and so whatever knowledge his former lover had possessed was now beyond them. Rendel might have aided them, what with his vast knowledge of the two realms, but his haste had made an end of him, unless...

He separated himself from Xiri. "Sirvak! Show me where Sharissa and Gerrod are."

An image of the two on the outskirts of his domain flashed before him. Still caught up in the aftermath of his fury, it would have been a minor task to bring them to him. Yet, knowing how much worse he and Melenea had probably made the situation already, he turned to Xiri.

"Guide me." The urge to demand more from Nimth was hard to suppress. "I want to bring them here."

His emotion and her care brought swift results. Gerrod, open-mouthed, stared at the sorcerer and his companions. His eyes were shrouded by his hood, but it was very likely that they were almost as wide as his mouth. As for Sharissa, she took one moment to drink in her surroundings, focused on her father, and then ran to him, enveloping him in her arms.

"Father! I thought that you were dead! Melenea! Did you know that she—"

He covered her mouth with one hand. "Hush, Sharissa. We'll have time later. I'm sorry, but right now I need to speak to your friend."

"Me?" Gerrod's mouth, the only part of his face clear enough to judge, twisted in a guilty curve, though Dru had not accused him of anything and had never even intended on doing so. He made a mental note to ask the Tezerenee what there was to feel guilty for, but after they had dealt with the present crisis.

"You, Gerrod." He walked over to the motionless figure and put a companionable arm around the younger Vraad's shoulder. "We have to talk about things...like your brother, the shrouded realm, and why you are still here. Most important, we have to talk about getting out of here."

"Out of here? You mean—"

"Yes, I think you have information, or know where to get it, that I . . . that *all* of us are in need of." Dru paused and turned back to the others. "Sharissa. Xiri. Forgive my brusqueness. I think you can both understand. Talk to one another. I want you to know one another as much as possible."

The two women eyed each other in open curiosity.

"Sirvak!"

"Master?"

"Your wounds. Are they—"

"I will take care of them, Dru," Xiri volunteered. She looked at Sharissa. "With your help, if that is all right."

"Of course."

Dru gave Xiri a nod of approval. She was already working to make her relationship with his daughter a pleasant one. "Good. When you are healed, Sirvak, I have a task for you." He reached into a hidden pocket and removed something. "Here!"

The familiar sat back on its hind legs and caught the object with its remaining forepaw. It peered at the tiny figurine.

"What is it?" Sharissa leaned closer. Her face screwed up into a look of absolute disgust. "It looks like Cabal! Too much, in fact!"

Xiri had also studied it. Her eyes flickered to Dru, who saw that the elf observed more than surface details. "A work of art. It almost looks alive."

"Part of my chess set. The piece that was missing. I want Sirvak to gather the pieces together. I intend on taking it with me."

"But you never play with it!" Sharissa protested.

"It has memories I want to keep," he commented, already turning back to Gerrod. "Now, Tezerenee. We have to speak about your brother."

Their eyes on Dru's retreating figure, neither Sharissa nor the elf noted the pleased look in Sirvak's inhuman visage as the familiar dropped the tiny chess piece to the floor and watched it bounce until it lay among the rest.

XXI

The sun rose above Lord Barakas Tezerenee's Dragonrealm and the patriarch could only look at the burning sphere with bitter hatred.

The clan had barely survived. Nearly half were dead or dying, and another third were injured. Night, even with the aid of the two moons, had not been able to reveal the true cost to the Tezerenee.

Tezerenee tactics, he pondered as the light of the sun glittered off the armored corpses of his people. *They knew Tezerenee tactics*.

Rendel. It could only be Rendel. Among the missing, only he would have been so willing to part with the knowledge. Gerrod was, of course, lost in Nimth; he could not have been the source, regardless. Ephraim and his band, who had been the cause of the cross-over disaster, had come to mind, but this smelled too much of Rendel. Besides, Gerrod's description of the mad state of Ephraim was enough to convince Barakas that this world had claimed its first Tezerenee blood long before this battle. That left only Rendel among the living, but not if the patriarch was ever able to lay his hands upon him. The execution would be a slow, deliberate one.

"Father!" Lochivan, still garbed for battle (though the bird creatures had apparently abandoned the war with the coming of light), knelt by the patriarch's feet.

"How many, Lochivan?"

"Forty-two. Three more will die."

Not quite as terrible as he had thought, Barakas decided in sour humor. They still numbered over sixty. Not much for a conquering army, especially since he could not field all of those

265

still functioning. It would do. They had survived the night of death from above and come out of it with the knowledge that for all their numbers, the avians had suffered worse casualties. More than twice their own number had perished. It was unfortunate that the Vraad were so outnumbered. Attrition was the one factor he could not compensate for.

If only our magic had worked.... The avians had used their talismans to good effect, mostly because the clan of the dragon had lacked reliable countermagic. Only when they summoned their strongest emotions were the Tezerenee able to trust that their spells would function as they should. Last night had been no exception. This world allowed the sorcery of Nimth to work, but only after a struggle.

We survived. We will prevail. The words, for the first time, sounded hollow even to the patriarch. *Would* they survive another assault in the night? How could they live if their days and nights were spent in constant struggle? He had no doubt that the clan had but a day to rest and repair. Had he been master of the bird people, Barakas would have divided his forces, created for himself two armies—one of the night and one of the day. Harass the foe so that they were never able to recover. Cut the weakest from the ranks until there was no one left to cut.

The Lord Tezerenee knew that the thing to do was abandon this place and find safety until he had the strength to return, but there was no place to go. The avians controlled this land, save for remnants of some other monstrous civilization. The elves survived because they respected the birds and caused no trouble. Under no stretch of the imagination could Barakas see the clan bowing to horrors like those who ruled here. He knew that the avians thought the same way. Permitting the Vraad race to establish itself would mean the end of their reign.

So this is how the Vraad race ends, he concluded, staring in the direction of the mountains where his enemies regrouped. *A last stand that will still leave its mark on those feathered misfits. They will not forget the dragon banner. It will haunt them for generations to come.*

The thought gave him morbid satisfaction, as if now the deaths would be worth it. Still, he could not help thinking that if their sorcery was more reliable or their numbers greater...

His eyes closed as something teased his senses. It was only a ripple, but there had been a disturbance in the nature of the Dragonrealm, as if it was no longer whole. A familiar feel, perhaps taste, had been his to savor in that brief moment. He recognized it as Nimth.

"Lochivan." His son, still kneeling, rose at the sound of his name. Reegan might be the heir apparent, but it was Lochivan to whom Barakas entrusted most of the tasks that he wanted completed. "Lochivan. Did you sense something to the east? Something of Nimth?"

"Sire, I felt some presence and it may have been as you say, but I could not swear to it."

"Spoken well. Could you find it?"

"I think it might be possible. What is it, Father?"

Barakas stroked his beard. He gazed thoughtfully at things only existing in his mind. "From bitter Nimth, it could be either our salvation or our death."

Recalling those left behind, Lochivan said nothing.

"Find out, but be wary. It may be that the avians' threat has become secondary. Go now!" The Lord Tezerenee chuckled to himself as his son departed to comply with his commands. The irony of what might be out there was not lost on the patriarch. It was possible that he had achieved what he had always dreamed of, uniting the Vraad race, making it one vast force with a common goal.

"How unfortunate," he finally muttered.

Nimth raged, shrieking its disapproval with thunder and accenting its fury with lightning. Whirlwinds spawned and died. The land shifted and shaped itself. A haze was slowly spreading, one that did not bode well. A few adventurous spellcasters had gone out to study it, the Vraad's belief in their individual immortality still dominant at the time. That belief, like so much else on Nimth, began to erode when it became evident that the explorers would not be returning.

Dru's domain gave the thousands some protection, but the storm was all around them, spreading the poisoned magic everywhere. The castle no longer obeyed commands without hesitation. One sorceress had already been lost, crushed between two walls that had closed on her with surprising speed. After that, no one *else* demanded the right to create for themselves private chambers. The Vraad had become, against their preferences, a socializing people. It was now the only way they felt secure while they waited their opportunity to cross to their new home.

From the top of the tallest tower, the lord of the domain and a figure nearly buried within a massive cloak watched over the proceedings. Just beyond the edges of the Zeree domain, the shrouded realm already intruded. It was a bit of a shock to both men. Their calculations had said the way would open again and it had. What they had not predicted was that it would spread to encompass a region twice as great as the castle of pearl. Dru wondered if the founders had had a hand in the stunning development.

"Dragon's blood!" the half-seen Gerrod muttered as he watched the latest band vanish. "This is unnerving!"

Dru agreed. His experience with the ghost lands had been from the inside. Seeing the change from without made him appreciate Sharissa's shock all the more. The group of Vraad riding through the phantom field had started out much the way he had, a living being surrounded by specters of another world. Solid flesh mingling with translucent unreality.

That was the way it began. The deeper and deeper they rode, the less distinct was the difference. Midway to the forest, the riders grew faded around the edges, as if the vision of those observing was failing them. Yet, it was not their vision, but those they watched who were lacking. By the time half the remaining distance was covered, the ruined landscape of Nimth was visible through the backs of the riders as nearly as much as it was through the forest and the field.

When the refugees entered the forest, they were already part of the other world.

"They're across," Gerrod said. He mentioned it every time, possibly because he still worried that the cross-over would fail before he had departed Nimth. The hooded Tezerenee had shocked Dru with his knowledge of the shrouded realm and its intrusion upon Nimth, not to mention the horrors racking the Vraad birthplace. Gerrod had not only looked over many of his brother's notes, but he had discussed Dru's work with Sharissa over their long trek to the Zeree domain. That, coupled with his own research, made him as capable as Dru in many things.

The Tezerenee was still nervous around his father's former ally. He had explained his fears, had explained why Sharissa had not received Dru's summoning, and, despite the assurances he had received in turn, still expected the elder Zeree to turn on him.

With the danger of misdirected sorcery, which they had experienced in the lands of Melenea, they had chosen to use it as little as possible. Food had been the one necessary use. The duo had walked most of the way, limiting teleportation and flight to those areas most stable.

Exhausted by their ordeal, they had finally dared to rest for a time. Sharissa had suffered most since her life had been more sheltered than his. Gerrod allowed her to sleep while he merely rested. It was during that time that Dru had reached out to the Vraad, telling them of Rendel.

"It was that which frightened me, Master Zeree," the young Tezerenee had said, his face buried deep in the folds of his hood. "I had aided your daughter, but being a Vraad, would you have seen that as sufficient cause to spare me if you, like the rest, were hunting the dragon lord's children?"

In the end, Gerrod had known he would have to face Dru, if only because the other sorcerer was the only one who knew some path out. Alone, he could never begin anew the re-creation of the Tezerenee method. He had not been all that certain he wanted to, either. It had always left him feeling disturbed, as if the final fusion of Vraad mind with draconian-forged host bodies would be some monstrous hybrid.

"How many are across, now?" Gerrod asked, returning Dru to the present. "How much longer?"

"A third are through, maybe a little more." The immigrating Vraad were crossing in groups of about one hundred, an unmentioned but symbolic reference to the founders that he had decided on. The bands, bringing only what their animals and themselves could carry, were entering the border region as soon as those before them had vanished into the woods. It kept the pace consistent enough to prevent a mad rush by those still waiting. "A good thing we have never numbered more than several thousand. This would have never worked otherwise."

"Will it be the same over there?"

"I doubt it." Gerrod seemed to want more of an answer, but Dru had none. There were too many question marks.

"What *did* happen to Melenea?"

He had tried to put that behind him, but the younger Vraad would not let him. This was the third time he had skirted around the fate of the enchantress, possibly because he could not believe she was gone. Dru could understand that; even now, he sometimes felt as if her eyes were on him. "Are you afraid you might join her?"

His companion swallowed. Dru had meant it as a joke, but Gerrod was still nervous about his own fate. "No! No," the other replied quickly. "It's just that . . . that . . ." He looked directly at Dru, who tried his best to perceive eyes somewhere within the hood. "It's just that I still feel as if she's left some last treat for us. The way she left the one that killed Rendel."

Gerrod had taken his brother's death with little remorse. It was disconcerting, however, to note that the Tezerenee had felt the same as he had. What was there about Melenea that she could still haunt them after Dru had meted out justice to her?

Below, a commotion attracted their attention. A rider was approaching, one who had *returned* from the other realm and raced to the citadel as if a horde were closing in behind him.

"Tiel Bokalee," Gerrod said. "He is one of Silesti's new dogs." Silesti wanted to make an example of the young Tezerenee now that Rendel was beyond him. He had only grudgingly allowed that the hooded Vraad was nothing like his clan and had been as summarily abandoned by the patriarch as the rest.

The newcomer, an unremarkable example of Vraad perfection, was dismounting when the two of them arrived in the courtyard. His hand twitched as if something had bitten him. The latest of the storm's minor assaults; everyone in the courtyard had been struck with pains of varying degree that came and went without warning. It was perhaps not so minor an assault. One Vraad was comatose; the searing pain in his head having ravaged his brain. No one assumed he would recover, but Dru intended on bringing him anyway.

"Dru Zeree." Tiel Bokalee acknowledged him with a bow. Gerrod received a dark glance, but nothing more. "We have a visitor. One of the dragon clan."

Gerrod turned away even though it would have been impossible to read his emotions if he had not.

Dru considered the rampant possibilities before responding. This was not the time to begin a war with the Tezerenee. "And what has Silesti done?"

"He insists this is your task to perform. Your decision will be his decision." The choice did not sit well with the messenger.

"That means you need to cross-over." Gerrod's voice wavered. "They're my cursed kin. I'll go with you, make certain they haven't something else in mind."

The unspoken reason was that he, like Rendel, did not care for the idea of separating from the one person who preserved his existence. A Tezerenee was a Tezerenee to the other Vraad.

"There will be no one to watch this end."

"Sharissa can do it. The familiar will guide her and that—your elfin friend—will be here to aid her, also." Gerrod indicated the next group of Vraad, who were already departing. "It works on its own now that they understand cooperation. She won't have much to do. The bulk of the storm is still beyond us," he added, jerking in sharp, sudden pain. *"Thankfully. We should be back before it reaches your land. We should be finished here before it grows too wild."*

Dru's hands stung. "Then let's be done with it. Give me but a moment to contact my daughter."

"I'll retrieve a pair of mounts."

He nodded absently, his mind already reaching out. *Sharissa? Father?*

Gerrod and I must be gone to the other side. The Tezerenee had arrived. I want you to watch things while I am gone. Xiri and Sirvak will aid you. I'm certain.

Her fear was evident, but she held it in check. *I understand. It won't be anything terrible?*

I don't think either side can afford a battle. If the Tezerenee have sent someone, it means they want to talk. Barakas would not talk if he held the advantage.

Good luck, then.

I leave it to you to tell Xiri and Sirvak. Watch the storm. What we've experienced is no more than a prelude. The worst is still coming. If it looks as if it will roll over the area before everyone is through . . . He held back for a breath, wondering *what* she would do if it depended on her. Even he would have been hard-pressed to come up with a solution. At last, he simply finished, *Send them all through, but not in a rout. A rush will kill more than the storm will.*

You'll be back before that, won't you?

I should be. He broke contact, hoping his own emotions had not influenced her. It was not possible to maintain complete confidence in the face of the storm and no contact whatsoever with the guardians, whom he had expected to see long before this. Were they waiting to see if the Vraad had enough sense to complete the task themselves? There was so much that made so little sense where the guardians and their enigmatic masters were concerned.

"Get down, damn you!"

Tiel Bokalee's steed, a black animal that reminded Dru of the missing Darkhorse—would the creature from the Void ever find his way back?—in both form and temperament, reared and kicked at the ground. Bokalee managed to bring the horse under control, cursing because he had to risk himself physically rather than simply use his sorcery. Any excess use strengthened the growing assaults of the storm, something no one wanted.

A tiny figure scurried over Dru's feet. He started to look down, but agony ripped his knees and he ended up half sprawled on the courtyard floor. Rats or magical imps became secondary to merely surviving the pain.

It turned out to be a mercifully short attack with no aftereffects save an uncontrollable fear that standing would bring about a relapse. Gerrod had just been returning with a pair of mounts, but he let them wander loose as he rushed to Dru's side.

"Are you all right? What happened? I heard a horse shrieking. . . ."

"He was spooked. Something tiny, but probably spawned by the storm, like my pain." Dru recalled the chaos of Melenea's citadel and realized that there must be less time than he had calculated earlier. "Forget it. Let's move on."

With Bokalee leading them, they departed the citadel ground and, before long, entered the shadowy ghost lands.

I will not fear this, Dru repeated to himself over and over again. He could not forget his first encounter and the chaos that had precipitated. They had no idea if the path through would remain open indefinitely. He had been told that the intrusion had been instigated by the mind of the land, the thing that had once been the individuals of the founding race, but not once had the guardian really said that they still controlled it. The one had even admitted that they did not understand the faceless incarnations of their lords. If it was the whim of the masters to further test their potential successors, then Dru would not put it past them to seal off Nimth at any moment and see if those trapped within were intelligent enough to find another solution. He had a nagging suspicion that the founders had not been *that* different from the Vraad.

The sun gleamed bright, nearly blinding him with its abrupt appearance. Dru blinked and looked around. They had already crossed. He had been so entangled in his fears that he had missed the entire trek. It was a loss he could live with, the sorcerer decided.

Vraad were everywhere. It was the first thing Dru noticed. It was the first thing *anyone* would have noticed. The woods and the fields were filled with men and women who stood or sat or walked about. The one thing they shared in common was an aura of disbelief, disbelief that the sky was blue and the wind was only a gentle whisper. No one thought to build themselves vast fortresses—unless they had tried and failed already—and it seemed as if no one had even broken away and departed to find their own destiny. If anything, the Vraad were even more interested in the company of one another than they had back in Dru's domicile. There, it had been forced; here, it was done out of an increasing insecurity. So used to being the masters of all they surveyed, the spellcaster's people were having trouble coming to terms with a new and very defiant land.

The lone Tezerenee stood away from the rest, visibly nervous. He wore one of the face-concealing helms, but Gerrod had evidently recognized him, for he raised a hand and shouted out the other's name. "Lochivan!"

"Gerrod?" The armored figure relaxed a bit, likely thinking that if one of his own could ride among the outsiders, then *his* life was not in danger.

Silesti stood nearby, close enough so that the Tezerenee knew he was there because of him and far enough away so that the dragon warrior knew better than to try to deal with him. The somber Vraad greeted Dru but said nothing more, emphasizing with his silence that he would listen but not take part. The hour belonged to Dru.

Dismounting, the master mage and Gerrod met with Lochivan.

"How is dear father?" the faceless warlock asked his brother, the sarcasm in his tone deep and biting.

Within the narrow slits of his helm, Lochivan's eyes closed in weariness. "Insane with anger, or perhaps just insane. We were betrayed, Gerrod, betrayed by Rendel to a race of bird creatures!"

"How appropriate! Familial betrayals seem the norm with the clan of the dragon!"

Dru silenced his companion with a curt wave of one hand. "You said 'bird creatures'? Manlike?"

"Very. They used Tezerenee tactics and Father believed it must be Rendel..."

"Well, you needn't worry about punishing him for his crimes," Gerrod broke in. "Rendel is very, very dead."

Lochivan would have asked for details, but Dru did not have the patience. "We don't have the time for this! Why did Barakas send you?"

The other Tezerenee looked uncomfortable again, but for different reasons now. "He did not... not exactly. He... he sent me to find out what was happening here and whether we faced annihilation from our own kind as well as the birds. I... when I saw what was happening, I dared to make myself known." He gave Silesti a surreptitious glance. "*He* met with me and said that if I valued my existence, word would be sent to the true benefactor of the Vraad, meaning *you*, I suppose, who would decide my fate."

Dru turned and met Silesti's gaze. The other grimaced, already reading his decision. Dru avoided Gerrod altogether and studied Lochivan, trying to find the man, not the Tezerenee.

"What did you come here for?"

Lochivan revealed a brief smile. There had still been a few doubts. Not now. He knew this outsider would listen. The clan might still survive. "Help us. Help us to push back the avians and claim the land. You *have* to do it. This is your home, too. You need our skills; we need your numbers."

"Is this your offer or your father's?"

"Mine, of course."

Gerrod snorted, but did not otherwise interrupt.

"Your offer," Dru mused, taken by the Tezerenee persistence. "Your offer and any your father might have are rejected. We won't save this world for you."

Silesti was smiling now. Both Tezerenee were confused. Dru indicated the masses idle around them. "Do you think that even I could make them fight for the Tezerenee? Do you think they want to fight at all? Does it look as if they do?"

"We will *all* perish if we remain divided!"

"This is a new... no... this is the *true* world. It has laws of its own. Have you cast spells? Has your sorcery worked true? I can see by your eyes that it hasn't."

"Our numbers—"

"Will be insufficient. Most of this continent is controlled by the Seekers." Dru's use of the name raised eyebrows, but no one cut him off. "You've fought only one group. Even combined, we don't yet have the power to face them down. Our day will come, though, if it's meant to."

"We have to survive until then!" Lochivan protested, looking to his brother for support.

Gerrod shrugged, but tried. "I think he would be open to suggestions, Master Zeree. Anything to save the clan."

"If I knew what to do, I would suggest it. I'm still concerned about those I've helped to cross. If our survival can include the Tezerenee, I have no objections." *Too many ifs,* Dru thought. *If* the guardians would help them this one time, it would be all he could ask.

For you, it will be permitted, a familiar voice within his head suddenly replied. *For you and your efforts, not for such as those.*

Dru looked around. The other Vraad stood motionless, all of them watching him. They had also heard the voice, but knew that it had been directed at only one of them.

Why now? Why after I've had to do so much have you returned?

A sensation of worry and lack of direction touched him. The guardian was no longer certain of its place in the world. *Those who have returned speak less and less with us. Their purpose is much like that which we were created to serve, but they move in ways that we do not understand and, at times, have not cared for. They are our masters and something else. We do not know whether to obey them or not. At least one among us has broken away and others have suggested withdrawing from this plane and waiting to see what it is the faceless ones have planned.*

Did your . . . did the faceless ones send you here?

This is my doing. It breaks the old laws set upon us and when I have aided you I will depart with the rest. You, I felt, were owed something. You are the potential they must see in your race. That much still remains the same from those first days when the founders sought to raise their successors. Therefore, ultimately, I perform my duties.

What will you do? Dru had difficulty believing anything would turn the patriarch from his dreams of conquest.

I have seen in your mind this Lord Barakas of the Tezerenee. He might protest your decision, but he will not protest that of his god.

Is that what you are now? came the second voice from nowhere. *Is this how you perform your duties for them? Godhood does sound much more our forte.*

The Vraad around Dru stood petrified, listening to a potential argument between entities they could not see or sense, only hear in their minds. As for the master mage, his own imagination allowed him to form images where there were none. He could see the dragon facing off against the wolf, one that, unfortunately, looked too much like Cabal.

This is my doing, the mock dragon informed its counterpart.

I am only here to support you, the wolf said slyly. *This is the very thing I desired . . . to be master, not servant.*

I still serve in my way! This is for the completion of the original task set upon us when we still had masters we knew!

My desire, also. Their desire, too, if you will permit.

Though Dru could not sense them, he knew that the other guardians had joined the first two.

All of you are agreed, then? the dragon asked in tentative tones. *What was suggested once will be done?*

"Dru, what is happening?" Silesti shouted. Everywhere, Vraad were standing and staring into the sky as if that would allow them to see the creatures deciding their fate. They had thought they had come to their new homeland, only to wonder now if they had merely postponed their destruction.

"Be quiet, fool!" Gerrod returned, yet he, too, looked to his companion for answers.

While the Vraad had been talking, the other guardians gathered here had given their assent to whatever plan had been put forth. Dru could understand no other part of what was going on save that there had been a full revolt against the creatures who had once been the unquestioning masters.

Not a revolt, manling, though some would like to believe it so, said the guardian who favored Dru.

The darker one stirred, but it did not respond to its opposite.

The mock dragon continued. *Your people must make one last journey to a place where they can grow in strength and mind. Once you have been placed there, we will leave you be. It is not right that we interfere.*

Except when necessary, the wolf whispered in Dru's mind. *Only when necessary.* It sounded too much like Melenea in tone and personality. He wondered whether it was touching upon his own memories, forming for itself a personality. Only those guardians who had actually spoken with him seemed to radiate any image of self. The rest were like ants, identical in feeling and response despite earlier claims of individuality.

The guardians had made their decision. He would have to return to Nimth immediately and inform those still there, but if—

They know, his guardian interrupted. *All Vraad save the Tezerenee now know. Such was how it was decided.*

"What do you even need us for?" he shot back, unable to keep the helplessness and the bitterness from his voice. Why had he struggled so hard just for this?

Because if you had not, we would have chosen not to interfere and the Vraad race would have died out, a failure for the second and final time.

Founder law, the wolf chuckled.

"You'll need me for the Tezerenee," Dru suggested out loud, so that all could hear. "Barakas will trust me more than anyone else here, even his kin. He'll know that the Tezerenee can rejoin the Vraad race without fear of reprisal." *Hopefully,* he added to himself.

It may be that the guardians had caught the last, for the mock dragon's tone lightened a bit. *It could not be done without you . . . and this one as well.*

Gerrod stirred and what little of his face was visible was pale with fright. "Me?"

You, came the very final reply.

With that, the world blinked, sending Dru, who had almost expected this, and Gerrod, who had not, to a place of carnage . . . where they found themselves standing before the startled yet fearsome gaze of the Lord Barakas Tezerenee.

XXII

"Dru Zeree. Gerrod. I hardly thought to see either of you again."

"Yes, it's a pity, isn't it, Father?" the patriarch's son retorted.

"You'd do better than to speak that way to me."

Dru ignored the exchange, surveying the carnage that the surviving clan members had still not succeeded in clearing. Bodies dotted the area, both Vraad and Seeker. Not surprising, the Tezerenee had taken their toll on the attackers. They would not survive a second major assault, however, not as reduced in numbers as they were.

"Lochivan came to you, didn't he, Zeree?" the Lord Tezerenee asked, his eyes burning as he noted Dru's interest in his losses. "He has lost his nerve."

"He's regained his sanity, O conqueror father!"

"Gerrod, be quiet." Dru wondered why the guardian had chosen to include the hooded Vraad in the confrontation. For that matter, there was no sign of the guardian itself. He could sense its presence, but it had not yet made itself known to Barakas. Why?

The younger Tezerenee quieted. His father glared at the two, as if actually wondering why they had come. Having silenced, for the time being, the argument, the robed sorcerer chose to press on. "We've crossed, Barakas."

"Obviously." Several armored figures, now aware of the newcomers, had been drifting toward the trio. More than one pointed at Gerrod. Dru began to understand why the shrouded Vraad was with him. Gerrod was one of them, but had been abandoned back in Nimth. Now, he stood in their midst, facing his father. He served as a beacon, something they recognized from a distance that they knew should not be here.

"Not like you," Dru continued. "We found a true path, one that allowed us to cross physically. More are coming. The entire Vraad race will soon be across."

The patriarch's face was as pale as bone. "You have my congratulations and my growing impatience. Why don't you tell me why you're truly here? Terms for surrender? Is that what you want? Do you think we will turn our lives over to those who would love nothing less than our living hides stretched across racks where they could inflict us with whatever tortures suited their desires?"

As horrifying as the image might be, Dru could not deny that there were those who would have gladly done exactly as the patriarch had said. Yet he also knew that the Vraad were capable of other things.

"Let the past fade with Nimth, Tezerenee! The time has come for the Vraad race to meld itself into a people, not a vast collection of spoiled and sadistic individuals."

Dragon warriors, female and male, now surrounded them completely. Barakas glared at them, but did not order them back to their grisly tasks. "We need nothing. The clan will survive!"

"Is *this* survival?" another voice challenged. Heads turned in simultaneous fashion as the Lady Alcia strode into the center of the circle. She was still the warrior woman, beautiful, elegant, and deadly, but there were signs of exhaustion evident in her visage. "How many of the children you purport to love must die? Anrek and Hyria are among the bodies!" Her cool facade began to crumble away before their eyes.

Dru could not place the names and neither, it appeared,

could the patriarch. He brushed them aside by turning back to the fate the Tezerenee would supposedly receive at the hands of their cousins. "We might live longer by returning to the fold, outsider, but what is life when pain is all that you offer?"

"I can't promise you that the clan will be accepted without conflict. If I did, I would not blame you for turning away and walking off. I'd do the same."

"Things have changed, Father," Gerrod offered. "Most of the people have changed, though I doubt forgetting will be possible."

"That was *Rendel's* doing! If I could . . ." Barakas clamped his mouth shut, the Lady Alcia's expression warning him of the potential for personal disaster if he carried his anger at his son further.

Dru glanced at Gerrod, who turned his way and shrugged, his shadow features an emotional mystery. Neither of them felt it was the time to discuss Rendel's demise.

"All this talk is nonsense!" Barakas straightened to his full height. His presence was nearly overwhelming. Everyone stepped back or froze save Dru. He had faced the bearlike Vraad before and would do it again. "Nonsense! We will all perish unless we combine! This is a land we must struggle to tame, a land we must take by force from the monstrosities that abound here! There is no other place for us to go!"

Do not tell him of me yet! the guardian's voice suddenly warned Dru, speaking only to him. *Tell him only that there is another place and it can be reached. The time is not yet right! Let him hear all before . . .*

Before what? Running a hand through the silver band of hair he had given himself what seemed a millennium ago, Dru told Barakas, "There is a land beyond the seas in the east. We have a way of reaching there and a way of ensuring that the Seekers—the avians—do not disturb us. There will be land we can tame and time for us to renew our strength. Relearn our sorcerous skills as well. This is a world where different paths must be taken than those that turned Nimth to the rotting shell it now is."

Hopeful gazes and encouraging whispers spread through the Tezerenee and the handful of outsiders who had come with them and survived the attack. Barakas seemed to weigh his words.

His answer will be the same, said the guardian to Dru. *He has set his own path and can find no way to turn from it without his pride and mastery suffering.* There was some hint of surprise in the guardian's tone. *He would rather they all die here, futilely battling to the end. It is a thing I have watched all too often. It is one of the reasons so many hopes failed over the endless aeons.*

What can we do?

Stall a few moments more, that is all. He will have his excuse to accept your terms.

What does that mean? the sorcerer asked. Dru received only silence as an answer. A chill ran through him. The guardian was planning a show of strength, so to speak, something more than his eruptive appearance from the earth. *That* should have been enough by itself. Certainly, it had impressed Dru. Yet he recalled that once he had known the wolf would not attack, he had lost much of his fear and wonder. This guardian planned a lesson of some kind, then... but what?

"You have betrayed your position, Zeree," the patriarch said, suddenly drawing strength from somewhere. The mood of his people sank as his own rose. They were so used to being controlled that no one even spoke out, even though it was their own future, their own lives, that were at risk. "The Vraad have always subsisted on their magic. All Vraad save the *Tezerenee!*" Barakas looked triumphant. "Even in a land without danger of foe, you would be unable to survive. None of you know how to exist long without the aid of sorcery! Sickness, hunger, accidents, weather... all factors that you do *not* understand! If anything, *you* need us! You need our knowledge, our skills at survival! It might be better asked that instead of we joining you, you join us!"

"Astounding!" Gerrod muttered. "Lochivan had the same arrogant offer! In the face of so much death, you can still be so damned demanding!"

Be ready! came the alert from the guardian. It would say nothing more of what it planned.

The air was filled with the now much too familiar sounds of great wings beating.

"They're back!" one of the Tezerenee shouted. His voice did not sound eager or determined, but rather almost terrified. For all their battles in Nimth, they had never faced a true foe in so great numbers.

"Barakas—" Dru started.

"This is the time to fight, not flap your mouth, Zeree! You'll find escape by teleportation impossible; they have some way of countering it with their blasted medallions!"

The Tezerenee were already doing their best to organize for battle. Two flying drakes were brought up. Weapons of every sort materialized in hands. Archers were already positioning themselves. A few confident souls were doing their best to work themselves into a will strong enough to cast competent spells.

Lady Alcia remained behind as her husband ran off to direct his people. "Master Zeree, if you have anything that will aid us, as you seem to indicate, this is the time! If not, you will surely die with us!"

Gerrod whirled on Dru. "What has that blasted bit of living magic put us into? Would it not have been sufficient to merely drop us from a great height and see if we can cast a spell before we splatter on the ground?"

"Just wait." It was easy to tell them to do that, but believing that they had not been abandoned was almost even impossible for Dru to believe now.

Such a pessimistic lot, the welcome voice said. *The time has come for my appearance.*

"What was that?" the Lady Tezerenee asked in shock, turning in a vain effort to see something that was not visible. "What is that I sense?"

The Seekers dove from the sky in numbers that boggled even the most hardy of the Vraad. Barakas himself hesitated, visibly overwhelmed. Death had surely come to the Tezerenee. Not even at their best could they hope to fight so many. Aeries from miles had likely added their numbers to the ranks. Seeker tactics did not apparently match those of the humans. The avians intended to destroy the invaders once and for all, not whittle away at their ranks.

The earth erupted. Only Dru knew what was coming. For everyone else, it was as if the world had chosen this particular moment to wipe from its surface the annoying little creatures that sought to wreak such havoc on it. Even Gerrod, who should have had an inkling, looked to his feet, as if the ground beneath him would be the next to open.

Molten earth and rock from the bowels of Barakas's Dragonrealm—Dru found that even he had fallen prey to the use of the term since there was no other—rose in so furious a geyser that, in its initial explosion, it seemed likely to shower every avian and Vraad in sight.

In the midst of so much chaos, with humans scurrying for cover and Seekers frantically trying to keep themselves high enough above the danger, Dru found himself wondering what the land itself thought of this. It was strangely silent for being so abused. The mind of the land certainly had to know what occurred and how one of its former servants was breaking the rules that it had once imposed when it had been the individual minds of the founding race.

Perhaps it *did* know. Perhaps the actions of the guardians were not so revolutionary as they *thought*. From what he had seen, the ancients had been master manipulators.

It was slowly becoming evident to the rest that there was something unique and unnerving about this searing geyser. None of them had been burned; they were just realizing that the storm of death had never taken place. Instead, the vague shape that Dru already recognized was beginning to draw their attention. Both sides were spellbound by the sight and each knew that the other was not responsible for this.

A rainbow of colors danced about the nearly complete outline of the great beast the guardian favored. It nearly made the form of the dragon itself look mottled, as if it had sprouted from the rainbow.

There will *be no more war.*

It was said with only the barest inflection, as if the speaker were such a power that this clash was only the least of annoyances. Dru allowed himself a brief, hidden smile. The guardian had a sense of theatrics, a sense of the greatest moment when it could best deliver its message. He understood why it had waited; it had known the Seekers would soon strike, perhaps even timed the encounter with Dru and the others so that they would arrive just a few minutes before. This drama was not merely being played for the Vraad. The guardian was assuring that the avians would have no desire to cross the seas again in a second quest for the secrets of the founders.

As if the last idea had already been transmitted to the Seekers, the avians tried to retreat, hoping, evidently, to hide in their aeries until the danger was over.

The fiery head of the dragon turned its burning gaze in the direction of a tall male avian who had to be the leader of the assault. *You know the power I am. I will be heard or even the aeries will afford no comfort.*

As one, the Seekers froze in the air, hovering as best they could and trying to seem as harmless as doves. More familiar with the potential of what towered before them, the guardian and the artifacts of the cavern smelling of the same sorcery, they knew better than to disobey so direct a command.

It would almost be best if the lands were cleansed of all of you! The peace would be restored. The balance would be maintained.

Vraad and Seekers became allies in fear. There were shouts and squawks, none of which made any sense from where Dru stood.

The mock dragon looked down upon the insignificant humans. *There is little that redeems you, but a bargain has been made to preserve your existences, a bargain made by one who came among you.*

The eyes of several dozen Vraad turned to view Dru with new wonder. Even Barakas studied his former ally with uncertainty... and why not? Had he not made the dragon the totem of the clan and emphasized its might so much that over the centuries he had come to believe in his own words?

It is not yet your time here. Perhaps in the future, when you have adapted to the land ... or it has made *you adapt. You will be taken to that place with the rest of your kind.*

Several Tezerenee nodded in vigorous fashion, taking the words of the guardian as god-given law. Beside Dru, Gerrod snorted.

"Serves them right to think that thing's their true lord," he whispered with malevolent pleasure.

As to you, the draconian head once more focused on the Seekers. *The future will decide your fate. Return to your aeries and work to make that fate one you will survive. These creatures are not for you, nor are the ways of the ancients. Do with this land. This will be the only warning you receive.*

Knowing that they had been dismissed, the avians fluttered off in a panicked rout. Dru doubted the creatures would learn. They would probably avoid the continent to the east, but changing their ways otherwise was likely too much for even a deity, albeit a false one, to demand.

Let the one marked by silver lead you to your people and your home, the mock dragon uttered, its words taking on an even more imperious tone, *and remember that there are those that watch over this land. You would do well to respect that.*

Barakas, despite his fears, was not set to abandon everything just yet. He dared to stalk toward the blazing form and look up into what passed for its eyes. "Blood has been lost here! Blood of the Tezerenee! It cannot go unavenged! This land is meant to be ours! You said as much! Why wait until later?"

There is a time for everything. Your time is not now. The blood you speak of should tell you that. There is no honor in a wasted death. The guardian then spoke words that were intended for Dru alone. *I fear you will have to watch this one after I and my kind have departed from your lives. Despite my efforts, I think he will not let the years pass in peace.*

I could have told you that, Dru replied.

The Lord Tezerenee had quieted down, brooding over the mock dragon's words. It was clear that the imposing presence before him was having its own effect, words or not. At last he nodded. "Yes. I bow to your wisdom." The huge figure took on an air of humility and knelt. "Praise be to the Dragon of the Depths, who will guide us to our destiny!"

Around him, Dru watched in stunned amazement as the Tezerenee slowly followed the patriarch's lead. The only two figures left standing were the sorcerer himself and Gerrod, who shook his head at his kin's actions.

Dru Zeree, you must bring the two groups together. Can you do so?

I can only try.

The draconian head acknowledged his response by dipping low. *Then, we move on.*

And they did.

One moment, they had been gathered in the site of the Tezerenee's near-last stand. In the next blink of an eye, Dru found himself standing amid the wooded area near the ghostly region leading to and from Nimth. On this side, the jagged landscape of Nimth penetrated the fields and forest, a spectral sore that the master mage hoped to soon never see again.

There were few other Vraad. Silesti and a handful of those he had designated his subordinates stood waiting. Lochivan was with them, looking quite harried. It was clear that they had been awaiting the return of Dru and Gerrod.

Gerrod had materialized a little behind Dru and behind the hooded Tezerenee were his assembled kin. Though they had been kneeling when the sudden transfer had taken place, the clan of the dragon now stood, save those injured too badly, of course. The instant he recognized his situation, Barakas stepped forward to stand beside his former ally.

Silesti noticed them and bristled at the sight of the patriarch. The other Vraad grouped around him. Lochivan stood as motionless as he could, not wanting something unpleasant to develop while he remained so near to the enemy.

It was up to Dru. He cut off both the patriarch and Silesti as each attempted to talk. "No more of this! Vengeance has never done us one bit of good! Silesti, we respect one another, but both of us have been responsible for things as terrible as what the Tezerenee have done! In their position, you might have acted as they did! True?"

He knew he had been correct when Silesti could not answer. Still, it was too soon to congratulate himself. They might yet be at one another's throat. "This is a new world, both of you! This is not Nimth. This world will not let you destroy it without it trying to destroy you beforehand." Dru played his final card, the one that would strike the two warring Vraad at the heart of what they believed in. "Look at the power of the guardians. They move us as easily as we might carry a handful of dirt. The peace is *their* one demand. Which of you is willing to disappoint them . . . and to explain yourself when they come to find out the reason why?"

Silesti's swallow was audible. He had watched time and again as Vraad after Vraad were taken away to the guardians' chosen destination. There was no denying the power of something that swept up groups of the sorcerous race without effort.

Across from him, Barakas, too, was having his second thoughts. As the one sentinel had said, the patriarch was one who would bear watching in the future. Now, however, he looked from Silesti to Dru and then back to where his people lay dead. He had seen how easily the dragon being had dealt with the avians and how simple it had been to take the surviving Tezerenee and displace them. Yet, the dream of conquest was not completely forgotten, not even now.

"I will not offer my friendship," the patriarch finally replied. "But I will offer my cooperation. Silesti, it was never my intention to leave the rest of the Vraad race behind. However, it was the fault of my own blood, so I must take ultimate responsibility."

It was as close to an apology as one might ever hear from the lips of the lord of the dragon clan. Silesti knew that. "I offer my cooperation, too . . . provided Dru Zeree is the final arbiter."

Though he had expected that something such as this would eventually develop, Dru wanted desperately to decline. He had performed more than his share in the name of the Vraad race. All he wanted now was to rest. Yet he knew that an uneasy triumvirate, which was what had apparently formed here, had more chance for stability than a simple alliance between two rivals left unchecked. It would be up to Dru to keep the peace, as he had so many times already.

Barakas was nodding, his eyes having flashed to Dru in time to note the sorcerer's reaction at being chosen for the unwanted position. "Agreed, if Master Dru also agrees."

He had no choice. "I agree."

No one even suggested they shake hands.

Dru exhaled slowly, relieved that this, at least, was over for the moment. There were other matters demanding his attention, matters that had twisted his gut throughout the Tezerenee recovery. "Silesti! My daughter and my . . . my bride. Did they cross safely?"

Silesti shifted his stance, looking more like a child caught at some mischief than a master sorcerer. "No one has emerged since the group that arrived immediately after you. I sent

Bokalee back in to see what was the matter.'' The Vraad looked embarrassed. ''He still has not come back.''

''*Not returned? And you left me unsuspecting?*'' Dru searched for the first available mount. A winged drake belonging to one of Silesti's new followers was the nearest. Without a word to the others, he raced off toward the animal.

''Master Dru!'' Gerrod called. ''Wait!''

''Zeree!'' bellowed the patriarch.

They were nothing to him at the moment. His success in bringing the Vraad race to the true world and of binding, if not actually healing, the wounds between the Tezerenee and the rest would mean little if Sharissa and Xiri failed to cross before Nimth was sealed off by the guardians.

''Give me that!'' he ordered. The stunned rider handed the reins over to him. Dru leaped onto the drake's back and urged the creature upward. It fought for a moment, uncertain as to what this stranger was doing riding it, but Dru's raging will overwhelmed it. Spreading its massive wings, the drake rose swifly into the heavens.

The trip across was a blur, even more so than the last. Dru stared at the transposed landscapes without seeing them. Visions of Sharissa and Xiri, even of loyal Sirvak, were all he saw. The drake, which had begun to renew its struggles when i had first realized its new rider intended on reentering the ghost lands, flew as swiftly as it could, as much out of fear of the sorcerer as of the unsettling region around them.

Nimth welcomed Dru back with a storm that made his own rage a minuscule thing in comparison.

He had underestimated both the speed and the danger Whirlwinds were everywhere. Lightning dotted the ground with craters. Dru made out what might have been the scorched remains of one or more Vraad, but he was too high up and the weather too fearsome to take the time to look closer. He only prayed that those he searched for were not among the dead.

The haze that represented the worst of the magical storm had not quite reached the castle, but it was closing fast. If what he had seen so far was only the precursor, Dru knew that no one would survive the maelstrom before it died.

Droplets splattered both rider and drake and the mage's first thought was that it was, against all odds, actually raining. That thought died as his mount roared in agony and Dru discovered that the liquid was burning holes in his clothing.

As he steered the injured animal down to the courtyard, he made out several Vraad trying their best to organize one final cross-over. There had to be several hundred. More than a few would die before the rest made it. He was gratified to see, however, that the remnants were working in as orderly a fashion as possible. They had evidently already suffered the effects of the acidic rain, for most of them resembled nothing more than walking piles of cloth and armor.

How could his estimates have been so off, he wondered. What could have pushed the storm to greater intensity?

Several Vraad spread out as he landed. He handed the shrieking beast to one of those who dared to wait despite the danger. "How long before you leave?"

"A few minutes! No longer!" said the muffled figure.

"My daughter?"

"No one has seen your whelp!"

Dru abandoned both his mount and the helpful Vraad and stumbled inside to the safety of the castle.

"Sharissa! Xiri! Sirvak!"

There was no response. He tried to reach them with his mind. Whether Xiri would respond was questionable since they had never tried to link, but he hoped that one of the others . . .

Masterrr?

Sirvak! Where are you?

In your work chamber. The mistressessss seek to hold back the worst of the storm! Something has upset the balance, Mistressss Sharisssss says!

Let them know I'm coming! he commanded, already moving toward that direction.

They know.

Dru broke the link, the better to think over the situation. What his daughter and Xiri tried to do was a losing cause, but if they could buy everyone a little more time, that would be sufficient. A few minutes for those outside to depart and a few more for the three—four counting Sirvak—to follow.

He was up a short flight of stairs before he realized the stairs should not have been there. The breathless spellcaster looked about. He was heading away from where he had intended on going. The castle's ability to shape itself to the whims of its master had gone beyond the boundaries he had set on it. It was now shifting nearly randomly. There was a chance that he might never reach the chamber where they worked.

Sirvak?

No answer. Something kept the link from forming. Something blocked his mind.

A *huge* something blocked his path. Dru had a momentary vision of teeth, blue-green fur, and eyes that reminded him too much of a lost enchantress before a massive paw struck him on the left side and sent him hurtling against a wall that seemed to form just for the purpose of stopping his flight. The Vraad slid to the floor, his bones vibrating from the shock and his head threatening to split in two. His eyes would not obey his needs and he could barely even make out the closing form of his attacker.

"Where is my *lady*, sweet one?" Cabal asked in a snarling parody of its mistress. "She must see what Cabal has done to please her!"

The massive wolf limped as it moved, one paw having suffered great damage from a bite that seemed just the size of Sirvak's beak.

"Cabal could play with you for long or short time, little one! Tell what you have done with lady and it will be short!"

Dru tried to stall, hoping his mind would clear enough for him to defend himself. "How did you get . . . get in here? Where have you been? We never saw you!"

As the spellcaster had suspected, Melenea's vanity was Cabal's as well. "Lady carried Cabal in her pouch! Let Cabal loose when she entered here and then ordered that havoc must be created!" The endless array of sharp teeth filled Dru's eyes. "Cabal has used own magic to encourage the storm! It obeys Cabal as Cabal obeys Lady Melenea!" That reminded the beast of what it had wanted from the figure sprawled at its feet. "Where *is* the lady?"

Now! Dru thought. *I have to strike now while its mind has turned to her!* He tried to concentrate, but Cabal instantly reached out and batted him with its injured paw. The familiar whined, but had it tried to use its other forepaw, it would have likely fallen forward. Unlike Dru, Melenea had not been concerned with healing her creature. Why bother? She could always summon another.

"*Mistake*, betrayer of lady. You do not answer, you must play with Cabal." The wolf opened its maw wide, intending to take the struggling Vraad by the legs and worry him.

Masterrr! Move!

A winged form darted toward the eyes of the unsuspecting monster. The rejuvenated Sirvak tore at Cabal with its long talons. The larger familiar howled in distress and pain as blood flowed over the top of its muzzle.

"Pain! Eyes!"

Cabal reacted wildly, but Sirvak, intent on giving Dru as much hope as possible, waited a moment too long. The wolf's good paw shot up like a fleet arrow, catching the smaller creature. Cabal brought the paw down with Sirvak beneath it.

Dru had dragged himself to the stairs, but when he saw what was happening, he tried to act. Even now, though, the pain that made his head throb refused to let him concentrate enough to do anything else but shout in vain.

"Sirvak!"

The black and gold familiar had only enough time to squawk once before Cabal crushed it.

"Sirvak, no!" came Sharissa's horrified voice. She stood behind the huge wolf, her face stretched in terror at the death of the one thing she had been able to call a friend during her childhood years.

Trying to turn and seize her, Melenea's legacy slipped. Cabal had tried to stand too long on its injured limb alone, and combined with the imbalance caused by Sirvak's mangled form, the blue-green monster's front half had little sure footing. It slid midway down the staircase, nearly taking Dru with it.

"Where are you?" Cabal cried out as it tried to right itself. "Come and play with Cabal!"

It was blind. Sirvak had done that much. Though it could still scent them, Cabal had no eyes whatsoever.

Sharissa did not care whether it could see or not. Dru looked up and saw both his daughter and Xiri moving to the stairway. Sharissa's visage was cold and deadly. For the first time, she looked like a true Vraad.

To the horror of both her father and the elf, she called to the killer stumbling to its feet on the steps. "I stand above you, Cabal! I am up here! Play with *me*!"

"Sharissa! Get away!" Dru shouted madly. He hoped that at the very least he would turn the wolf's attention to him. His head was nearly clear enough. If Cabal would just stumble around for a moment or two . . .

"Speak to me, *Shari darling*!" Cabal cried, again mimicking its mistress.

"I'll do more than speak!" Rage fueled her words and her will.

"Come—" That was as far as Cabal got before flames engulfed the familiar's entire body. The monster roared, both pain and accusation in its cry. Nothing else burned but the horrible creature. Even Dru, who lay nearly within arm's reach of the magical killer, felt no heat.

Cabal tried one pitiful spell in an attempt to save itself. The attempt failed and with it the wolf. Howling mournfully, the blazing beast collapsed. The fire did not go out until there was nothing left of Melenea's last ploy. Dru recognized the source of his earlier misgivings, the sense that Melenea still waited. He suspected that the tiny creature that had run over his foot might even have been the familiar. In its tiny size, it could move from place to place, wreaking the havoc its mistress had desired.

That was ended now.

Sharissa fell back, both exhausted and disgusted, but Xiri was there to catch her. The two Vraad looked at one another. Dru nodded and smiled, though he knew neither of them felt any happiness.

Outside, thunder announced the storm's intention to continue on with or without the helpful influence of Cabal. The harsh noise brought them all back to the reality and the peril of their present situation.

"We have to leave as soon as possible," Dru commanded, rising slowly and unsteadily from the floor. "Gather what you need and come with me!"

Sharissa could not speak, but she looked at Xiri. The elf was uncommonly solemn. "Sirvak . . . took care of all of that. The last of your horses wait for us below. We knew we could not stay much longer. When we tried to contact you to tell you to stay where you were, that we would be joining *you*, we could not find you." She indicated the few traces of ash that marked Cabal's fiery demise. "I suppose it was that one that blocked the link. Sirvak offered to fly ahead and find you. It already feared the worse."

Not desiring to sound cold, Dru replied, "Then there's no reason to remain. You two go to the horses."

"What will you do, Father?" Sharissa asked, finally able to stand on her own. Her eyes were wide and gave her a hollow appearance.

"Find something appropriate for a shroud," he said quietly, testing his own ability to stand unaided. He stared pointedly at the remains of his most loyal of servants. "Even if Sirvak died in Nimth, this place will not claim the body. I won't let it."

Sharissa smiled gratefully, then let Xiri lead her down the stairs and away from the tragic scene. Dru waited until he was alone. He knelt by the battered form and picked it up. As he carried it off, searching in his mind for something that would give the familiar's crushed body a proper sense of dignity and honor, Dru whispered to the limp form of the only one who had ever really known the pain in his mind and heart, because that one had been a part of him from its creation. "Time to go home, Sirvak. Time to rest . . . at last."

XXIII

The fifth day of their new life found the Vraad still alive and whole. The Tezerenee, while unwelcome by most, had proved themselves most useful. Their well-honed talent for things unmagical made them teachers for the rest. They were, in turn, granted a grudging sort of respect that Dru hoped would blossom into greater acceptance. He had no plans of fasting until that time, however.

They lived in the remains of the ruined city of the ancients. It had already been agreed that instead of building a new home, they would repair the one left for them. Few spoke of journeying out to create their own domain, though the Tezerenee did tend to live on the opposite side of the city. There was more than enough room. The city ran deep as well as tall. Many of the buildings were connected by underground chambers and tunnels that would take months, perhaps years to explore. They seemed harmless places, though Dru was leery about descending into them. He shrugged it off as a Vraad trait. After so many centuries of having so great an expanse of land to himself, it was difficult to completely accept the new arrangements. He was not the only one who felt that way, but neither Dru nor the others would have traded their present situation for the past.

Silesti continued to organize the bulk of the Vraad race. The triumvirate still worked. Dru continued to wonder how long that would last. Sharissa had told him he was just being a pessimist.

She was popular among the immigrants. Sharissa now walked confident among the others and her understanding ways helped greatly during a time when most were trying to cope with the changes. Sorcery was still a touch and go thing. Dru was the most competent, having learned from his new wife.

He and his elfin bride now stood near the place where they had uncovered the final lair of the founders. Dru had come here every day, expecting to find the rift leading to that place. He was curious what future the faceless beings had planned for the Vraad or whether they just might leave the refugees alone. Unfortunately, his efforts had, until now, come to naught. There had been no trace of the rift. He had walked the region carefully. It had been sealed.

Today, however, was different. When he had woken that morning, a familiar voice crawling through his mind had quietly said, *Come to the place where we first met, manling. I will be there to greet you.*

Sharissa was mapping the city for the benefit of all and was already out. She had taken to this new place better than any other Vraad had and was already undisputed leader whenever talk of an expedition to some sector was mentioned. Dru was pleased that his daughter had found a place for herself after the shameless way he had kept her trapped all these years for what he had thought was her own good.

Gerrod was the only person other than his own bride to whom Dru might have talked. The hooded Vraad, however, lived far from the rest of his kind. Not completely trusted by those the Tezerenee had abandoned, he was no more welcome among his own kind, not while Barakas still commanded. Gerrod had become too independent for his father's tastes. The patriarch did not want his example to taint the clan. Dru had offered the young, shadowy Vraad a position as his second, but Gerrod had opted for his solitude. He also worked to redevelop the proper use of his abilities, but in ways that likely did not match those of the elves. Again, Dru knew that it, like so much else, was a problem not yet settled.

Only Xiri stood with him now, in the middle of the ruined square, but she was Xiri no longer. Her name was Ariela and the reason she had never told him her birth name was that in her clan tradition declared that the name be kept a secret, one which would be revealed first to the man she took as a mate. In a moment of truth after they had bound themselves to one another, the former Xiri had told Dru that she had let loose with the comment about her secret because she had been attracted to him from the first moment, despite his being a hated Vraad.

Dru sensed the presence of the guardian before it spoke to him.

The custom of mating was known to us through the ways of the founders. We congratulate you. We also give our sympathy, as best we understand the emotion, for the death of your trusted servant.

"Thank you." In the emptiness of this place, Dru felt more comfortable speaking out loud, even if it was to a being that had no form. He wished the guardian had not mentioned Sirvak; after five days, the pain had not grown any less. Dru could push it aside, but it was still there.

Your efforts with your people are also to be commended, manling.

This was leading up to something. Dru could feel that. He held on to Xiri—*Ariela*—as if he might be torn from her at any moment.

We are departing this plane now, Dru Zeree, but we will

continue to observe. The question of how to deal with those who are and are no longer our masters remains unsettled and may never even be settled, something you might understand. This, however, we have decided. No one will interfere with them or attempt to harm them in any way. It is very likely that they will take the action themselves, but if that is beyond them now, we will act instead. All of your people will wake tomorrow with this knowledge in their heads.

"Then why summon me, if you plan to inform everyone?"

I come to that in a moment. The guardian hesitated, then pushed on more quickly. *Nimth is sealed off. It could not be destroyed without affecting this world. It, for all your sakes, should never be sought. Only trouble will come from the chaos that is now Nimth.*

That was easy enough to obey. Dru wondered why anyone would *want* to open a new path to the mad world.

Now we come to the answer to your question. It was not my idea to summon you here. I act only on their behalf and it may be that I have understood them wrong.

"Them?" Ariela asked, her tone indicating that she knew who it was the guardian spoke of.

The Gate materialized before them, tall and frightening. The dark, reptilian forms raced along its edges as usual, but their eyes were always focused on the two figures standing nearby.

From the Gate's maw emerged two of the faceless beings. There was still no telling them apart and Dru decided it was not worth the effort. The two blank-visaged figures stood across from the couple and waited.

It was the guardian who broke the silence. *They want to teach you. They want you to care for this land. Most of all, I believe they want your help in keeping the future alive.*

Dru could sense that it was true. Whether it was an attempt by the creatures before him to communicate their desires or simply something he read into their stance, Dru could not say. The sorcerer only knew that he understood them, to a point. He and others like him would be guardians of sorts, just like the mock dragon and its kind.

No, much more, added the entity. *You will still be a part of the future; you are too essential to be denied that. The others are not yet ready to be left to their own devices. In some ways,*

I will envy you. You have an ending, a destiny. You and yours will change and grow where we no longer can.

The sorcerer turned to his wife. Dru knew what his decision would have been if he had never met her. This was a partnership, however. "One last journey?"

She smiled at him, as ready as he to take on this challenge providing they were together. "One last journey, *wicked Vraad*."

The featureless figures stepped aside for them. Dru looked into the sky at the last moment, as if by doing so he would see the guardian. "What about Darkhorse? He's the one thing I still feel bad about. You had no right to send him back to that place, even if it was somewhere out there he came from."

If the dweller from the Void, as you have called that place, returns, we will not exile him again . . . and I think the one you call Darkhorse will most definitely return. It might even be that from where you go you will be able to aid him in his efforts.

"One more thing, then. Do you think our race will succeed? Do you truly hold any hope for us?"

I do now. The guardian's voice was fading. Its task was done. *More important, so do they.*

Dru gave the departing entity a grateful smile. When he could no longer sense its presence, the sorcerer turned to his wife, who indicated her readiness by squeezing his hand.

They walked through the portal and stepped into the room of worlds.

The chamber was filled with more of the faceless, cowled figures. To Dru's surprise, they bowed to the newcomers. One of them, possibly the closest they had for a leader, walked up to Dru and extended a partially formed hand in an unmistakable gesture.

Dru clasped it and nodded, for some reason at last truly feeling at home.